For Martina
my inspiration and my rock!

My debut book is also available on Amazon!

Out of Office

A Vespa Midlife Crisis

Markus André Mayer

Most of this actually happened, but I've taken the liberty of turning it into a bloody good story.

First Edition: January 2026 (Original Edition)

www.la-vida-vespa.com Facebook: La Vida Vespa - 80 Days around the World by Markus Mayer

Legal Disclaimer

Notes on Content: This work is an autobiographical novel. The plot is based on the author's personal travel experiences. To protect the privacy and personal rights of third parties, names, identities, physical characteristics, and biographical details of the individuals involved have been changed, obscured, or incorporated into fictional characters.

Furthermore, locations, timelines, and specific events have been fictionalised for the purposes of dramatic structure and narrative compression. Any resemblance to persons living or dead, or to actual companies or organisations, is purely coincidental and unintended, insofar as it exceeds general inspiration from real events.

PROLOGUE (Disco Inferno)

I crouched in the cramped, filthy cubicle of a communal shower at the Paraiso hostel in Gandia – Paraiso presumably being the Spanish word for "place where dreams and personal hygiene go to die". Every touch of the water jet felt like someone was slowly scraping the top layer of my burning skin off my flesh with a blunt knife. I had just stepped out from under the jet. The water hadn't even been hot, but on my forearms it had felt like liquid lead. Now I watched as the last dark, oily broth ran from my elbows into the drain – the compacted dirt and two-stroke fumes from 180 kilometres of Spanish country roads, mixed with the black sludge from Lola's engine. I stared at my feet on the bare concrete and pressed my lips together. I was sure my toes were already itching in time with the athlete's foot spores that had probably established their own proud civilisation here since the era of Generalissimo Franco – complete with little flags and a strict border policy.

My skin was no longer my skin. It was a burning, deep red territory that the sun of La Mancha had marked as its own. My neck, my forearms, my knees – all on fire. The rest of my body? White as the whitewashed walls of the windmills I rolled past today. I looked like a botched warning sign: danger above, cheese below.

With trembling fingers, I reached for the tube of aloe vera I had bought earlier at a pharmacy in the harbour. The pharmacist had looked at me and chosen the extra-large tube. She examined me as if I were a traffic accident where you don't know whether an ambulance or a mercy shot would be appropriate. I slapped the ice-cold, green, slimy gel onto my burning skin. 'Aaah… oh God… yes…' I moaned. It sounded less like relief and more like an extremely disturbing casting call for a low-budget erotic film from the eighties.

At that very moment, another mouldy shower curtain was pulled aside. A gaunt Brit wearing a sun hat and Union Jack swimming shorts stared at me. He was holding a toothbrush and looked at me with a mixture of disgust and English politeness. 'Everything alright there, mate? Sounded like you were having… a moment,' he said dryly. I froze, my hands full of green goo, half-naked and red as a lobster. 'Aloe vera,' I croaked. 'Sunburn.' 'Right! Lovely,' he muttered and disappeared towards the sink, shaking his head.

To drown out the shame, I rammed my AirPods into my ears. I needed a distraction. The shuffle algorithm, that emotionless digital arsehole, had its big moment right then and there.

[Now Playing] The Trammps – Disco Inferno ('Burn, baby, burn …')

'Very funny, God,' I muttered. 'Very funny!' As I tried to press away the song with slippery fingers, my mobile phone vibrated on the greasy edge of the sink.

Miguel would have laughed. He always said, 'God has a sense of humour, amigo. Black humour. Like a Spaniard.' Miguel was dead. Three months. And I was standing here in a shower that smelled of his nightmares.

> **[Notification]** LinkedIn: 'Stefan is celebrating his 10th anniversary as Area Sales Manager today. Congratulate him on this milestone!'

I stared at the display. Stefan. Stefan was probably wearing a light blue business shirt that was as wrinkle-free as his CV, accepting congratulations for a decade of controlled boredom. He had milestones. I had first-degree burns and an old tin box called Lola, which was sitting in the back garden and probably rusting away quietly. He was probably toasting with Prosecco in the office, while I was here in a shower that smelled of chlorine and despair, fighting fungal infections and the mockery of my own mobile phone. And as if that weren't enough, the next message popped up:

> **[Notification]** Amazon: 'Your subscription delivery: "Premium descaler for fully automatic coffee machines (3-pack)" has been delivered to your neighbour.'

My descaler had arrived in Kempten. So my old life was waiting to be descaled, while my new life here was just trying not to fall off my burnt bones. I had let myself go physically over the last few months, and the result was now staring back at me in the fogged-up mirror: a red lobster in the body of an insurance specialist and a small soft belly leaning uninvited over the waistband of my shorts.

'What the hell am I doing here?'

A quiet rumbling in my stomach told me that the fantastic kebab I'd had earlier wasn't so fantastic after all.

This whole bizarre situation began a few weeks ago in that small, smoky bar in Kempten. With a drawer that I probably should never have opened, and a man named Miguel.

To understand why I was here in Spain, celebrating a minor midlife crisis in a hellish hostel and battling the sunburn of my life, while outside, an old Vespa waited for me between the rubbish bins, we have to go back. Back to the bar. Back to the beginning. Living the dream!

Chapter 1 – The Drawer of Truth

[Soundtrack Shuffle: Tears for Fears – Mad World]

I had firmly resolved not to cry today. Or laugh. Or get emotional. In general: no feelings. I should have known. Really. I knew as soon as I walked into the bar that it was a bloody awful idea.

We stood in front of the bar. 'El Corazón Rojo' – The Red Heart. The sign hung crookedly, as if it had also been mourning for three months.

I should have known that nothing good could happen on a Monday morning in Kempten when you voluntarily go into a Spanish bar that has been closed for months and that, even when Miguel was still alive, smelled like a mixture of old red wine, forgotten olives, a hint of garlic and old, slightly mouldy wood. It wasn't one of those premonitions that people have on television before a chandelier falls on their heads, but rather a mixture of melancholy and fear before smelling a milk carton that you forgot about for three weeks during your summer holiday.

But when you've just broken up and have been working, eating, sleeping and occasionally pretending to exercise for months, even the prospect of scraping dusty Iberico ham posters off a wall seems like a form of social activity.

'Just a few boxes,' Miguel's widow had said. 'Just a little help.' I had been easily manipulated since the break-up. If someone had told me I needed a new hair colour, I would have come out of the hairdresser's with a purple mohawk. Or a perm. Or a tattoo with the words 'Carpe Diem' in Mandarin. From a tattoo artist named Kevin.

'Thank you for coming, hijo.' Isabel hugged me so tightly that my back gave way briefly and cracked like old wood. She was one of those small but dangerous women – petite and sweet like a primary school teacher, but with the hugging power of a Romanian dancing bear. Her grey hair was tied back in a severe bun, as if she had no time for nonsense. And she didn't.

'Sure.' I tried to smile. It turned out to be more of a forced optimistic grin, the kind you have when you claim you're 'totally fine' – while still holding the box with your ex's stuff in your hands.

Isabel unlocked the door and we went inside. But when I entered the bar, I faltered. It was like a wall. A smell that was definitely not a three-month smell. More like a three-decade smell. A kind of olfactory punch in the gut. It smelled like someone had crossed a forgotten Serrano ham with a wet dog – with a hint of 'something definitely died here'. Added to this was the sweet-sour scent of old olives that had been drowned in oil when Franco was still alive, and the omnipresent smell of garlic that had eaten its way into every pore of the wood, every curtain, every tabletop over decades. Hovering over it all – like a ghostly mist – was the cigarette smoke from the past, when smoking was still allowed here and Miguel had personally ensured that no wall was ever properly ventilated.

'Bad, isn't it?' Isabel stood behind me, small, stern, her grey hair tied back in a bun. 'I haven't been in here for two months.' 'It smells… Mediterranean,' I managed to say. 'Mediterranean? It smells like a fridge after a bachelor party.' She laughed. I didn't. I remembered that evening all too well. And the fridge.

The bar itself looked like a museum still life of Spanish pub romance – or like the prop warehouse of a film about 1970s Spain. Yellowed bullfighting posters hung on the walls, depicting muscular toreros with serious expressions swinging gold-embroidered capes. Next to the door leaned a worn poster from the Feria de Sevilla, showing dancing women in flamenco dresses – the colours long since faded to a nostalgic sepia. The tables – or rather, the upright wine barrels repurposed as tables – were made of dark, grimy wood that looked as if it had survived several generations of spilled Rioja and crushed tapas. An old beer mat was still stuck to one of them, burned into the wood like a fossil imprint from a bygone era. The actual bar – a massive, dark-lacquered wooden monstrosity – ran along the left wall and looked as if it could tell stories if only you gave it enough red wine. The counter was sticky, as if it still remembered the hands of the guests from back then. Behind it stood empty wine racks, and above it all sat a dusty collection of vermouth bottles whose labels had yellowed so much that it was almost impossible to read what was inside. The chairs were stacked on the tables – as in any bar after closing time, except that this closing time had now lasted three months.

And above it all lay the faint shadow of his voice. Miguel.

'I'm sorry you have to do this,' said Isabel next to me. Her voice was quieter than it used to be. You could hear the loss in it, unclean and untidy like a half-closed window in the wind. 'I'm happy to help,' I said. And I meant it. It probably helped me as much as it helped her.

Miguel wasn't just any mate. He was the guy who taught me that you can drink vermouth in the morning 'if the day demands it.' And pretty much every day demands it. The man who held wildly gesticulating conversations with every pub wall as if it were a long-lost cousin. He was more than a bartender. He was my buddy, life coach and semi-legal taxi after a few vermouths. He was my best friend. There was no therapist, no self-help book that was anywhere near as helpful as his kitchen, a glass of red wine and his absolute conviction that every problem becomes smaller if you use enough garlic.

'It's time we tidied up,' said Isabel. 'Luisa is coming this afternoon and wants to see the rooms.' Luisa was a potential new tenant. A woman with the expression of a tax audit and the warmth of a tax office form. The kind of person who probably says 'excuse me' when she sneezes, but sounds like she's reading a warning letter. For her, this bar was just square metres, rent, business potential. She would throw out everything that smelled of Spain and probably turn it into a nail salon or another mobile phone shop.

Isabel sniffed. I hoped it was dust and not grief. I could deal with grieving people like others deal with tarantula bites: not at all. 'The old cash register has to go. And the photos. Can you do that, please?' she said and disappeared into the back room.

So I started opening drawers. The first one contained beer mats. The second one had a few corks. The third one – which I had jammed my hand between the handle and the wood with a hearty pull – contained what could probably be called a real treasure chest: old photos, yellowed documents, bills, postcards, something wrapped in aluminium foil that I preferred not to touch. A Spanish fan. A dried chilli pepper. A ticket to a bullfighting festival from 1978. A pack of condoms (expired in 2004 – brave man). And a lighter with the inscription 'Mallorca 1987 – Was awesome'. Grammatically questionable, but honest.

And at the very bottom, under a pile of forgotten stories, there it was: the photo.

Miguel, perhaps in his mid-twenties, grinning like a man who has just sent all the worries of the world on holiday. And next to him: a Motovespa GS150. Snow white. Slightly dented. Perfectly imperfect. In the background: the endless, dusty expanse of the Castilian plateau – La Mancha. Barren olive groves on the horizon, a few wind-bent trees, and that typical ochre-yellow earth where you could imagine Don Quixote fighting windmills. The heat was practically preserved in the photo – you could literally feel it, that shimmering, merciless August heat that fried your brain.

I felt a telltale tingling in my stomach. Maybe because Miguel looked happier than I had felt in months. On the back, in his scrawled handwriting, he had written: 'Mi libertad empieza aquí' – My freedom begins here.

I slumped down on one of the bar stools, which smelled of stale beer and old leather, and stared at these words as if they could explain to me where my own life had taken a wrong turn. As I sat there, I realised that, at least since my separation, I had been stuck in a state between 'functioning' and 'internally dead'. Work. Sleep. Work. Eating from Tupperware containers at the office because I didn't even have the energy to make myself a decent sandwich. I sighed over my coffee machine in the morning. Not metaphorically. Literally. Over a machine.

And now this photo. This gleaming Vespa. This sentence. 'It was his first great love,' said Isabel. 'Well… after me.' She winked. Just like he would have done. 'He always said,' Isabel continued, 'that this Vespa gave him freedom. His first adventure. The road, the wind, Spain!' She raised her arms like an opera singer at the finale.

I smiled. Just a little, but genuinely. 'Did he tell you the story? From Albacete to Barcelona? He was so proud. He annoyed everyone with it.' She laughed.

He had often told me about it – how he had bought the Vespa in 1973 in Albacete, a town in the middle of La Mancha, best known for being hotter than hell in summer and colder than a refrigerator in winter. How he had ridden it to Barcelona – a tour of over 600 kilometres through Castilian heat and Catalan coastal dreams. And how he had later sold it there to afford a ticket to Germany, where the streets were supposedly paved with work and prosperity. And how he had always regretted it later.

'A man should never sell his Vespa,' he had once said. 'Not even if he wants to start a new life.' 'Why not?' 'Because the new life will pass. The Vespa won't.'

I swallowed. Not because of the Vespa. Three months. He had only been gone for three months, and yet it felt like a lifetime.

'He wanted to go back to Barcelona,' said Isabel. 'To find the Vespa. To ride it again. Someday, he said.' 'Someday' is an arsehole.

I looked at the photo. Then at my own reflection in the window next to the bar. My tired face. The dark circles under my eyes. The grey hairs that had secretly invited themselves in without asking if they could stay. It hit me. Not suddenly, but like a realisation that slowly but surely pushes its way into your consciousness.

I had no adventure. Not even a mediocre one. I had a car loan. I had an unused gym membership. Which cost me €39.90 a month – that's about 13 cents per guilty conscience. I had Moppi, my vacuum-mopping robot. Who, incidentally, was more intelligent than me. At least he knew his limits and didn't drive into walls. Most of the time, anyway. And a boss who treated me as if having a real personality was an annoying software bug. Maybe that's why I suddenly felt this tingling sensation. A spark. A long-forgotten longing.

Then the thought came. The dangerous one. The idiotic one. The magnificent one. What if I look for that Vespa? Or at least one? Or… do something that isn't pure reflexive reason?

'You're thinking,' said Isabel. 'No,' I lied. 'Yes. I know that look. That's how he looked just before he did something stupid.' 'I don't do stupid things.' 'You lived with a woman for three years who forbade you from having garlic in the house.' Touché.

I looked at her. She looked tired. Dejected. And yet strong enough to pretend to the world that she was fine. 'What would he say now?' she asked, tapping the back of the photo with her finger.

I knew exactly what he would say. 'Come on. Get your bum moving. Life doesn't wait, amigo!'

I looked back at the Vespa. At its simple, elegant lines. At Miguel. At the smile. At La Mancha in the background. And suddenly… it felt as if this photo hadn't been in that drawer by chance. More like a final nudge from a friend who tapped me on the shoulder from the afterlife and said, 'Come on. Give it a try.' A final well-intentioned kick in the bum!

'Keep the photo as a souvenir!' Isabel said with a gentle smile. She winked with a twinkle in her eye.

> **[Notification]** WhatsApp Sabine: 'Did you accidentally take my winter slippers when you moved out? The fluffy ones from Birkenstock?'

I pushed it away. Of course I had her damn slippers. They had been standing in my hallway for three months like a textile memorial to failed relationships. But she didn't need to know that. Not yet.

'Thanks, Isabel. But I'm more of a controlled risk kind of guy. This…' I tapped the snow-white Vespa, '…that was his thing. I have a lease on a mid-range car with eight airbags. I don't need freedom, I need a new gasket for my coffee machine.'

I lied. And we both knew it.

Later, back in my flat – surrounded by cardboard boxes, half-unpacked moving boxes (for months), mountains of laundry and a plant that was officially dead but still had one leaf out of politeness – probably out of the same German sense of duty that kept me going to work – I sat down on my sofa. I placed the photo on the kitchen table, right next to a reminder from my home insurance company and a bowl of sad organic apples. And I stared at it. For a long time.

Forget it, Kai, I thought. You're forty-three. You're not going to Spain to look for a pile of scrap metal. You're going to buy a new houseplant and read a book about mindfulness.

I sat down on the sofa. My mobile phone vibrated in my trouser pocket. A haptic blow from reality.

> **[Notification]** Classified ads: 'Message regarding your ad "Ergonomic office chair (lumbar support defective)": What is last price? Will also exchange for 3 bags of potting soil or slightly defective robotic lawn mower.'

I stared at the display. This was my life. A universe of lumbar supports, robotic lawnmowers and people who considered potting soil to be currency. At that moment, I knew: if life is a barter system, I had drawn the short straw.

I looked at the photo again. The note screamed at me: MI LIBERTAD EMPIEZA AQUÍ!

I waited for reason to shout 'Stop it' in my face. But it remained silent. It had probably quit. Or was on holiday. In any case, it seemed to have decided that from now on I would have to manage on my own.

And so – without really understanding why – I started googling: 'Motovespa GS150', 'Rare model Spain', 'Albacete Vespa old models', 'Can you just escape your life at 43?' and – a little later – 'Where is the nearest flight to Spain?'.

I didn't know it at the time. But it was the beginning of everything. Of Miguel's story. Of mine. Of an adventure that I could have avoided my whole life – and now finally needed. My adventure began here. With a drawer. A photo. And the realisation that maybe I wasn't cut out to be sensible after all.

That was crazy. It's irresponsible. You can't just run away. Maybe I can!

I started to smile. A small, tentative smile that felt like the first sunny day after a winter that had lasted far too long. Maybe I needed a change. Maybe I needed a fresh start. Maybe I needed a Vespa. Or maybe – just maybe – I simply needed a really crazy story that I could tell myself.

Chapter 2 – Excalibur in 13 millimetres

[Soundtrack Shuffle: Rolling Stones – Start Me Up]

I don't know exactly when 'That's a nice idea' turned into 'I can't think about anything else 24/7', but sometime between Monday morning and Wednesday evening, I was completely lost.

Lost in forums. Lost in YouTube videos with titles like 'Motovespa – The Queen of Spanish Roads' (12,000 views, posted in 2009, comments exclusively from men over 60). I lost myself in forums where men discussed the consistency of gear oil with the fervour of sommeliers. It was a digital parallel world where a wrongly chosen spark plug was considered a social death sentence. Lost in Google image searches that drew me deeper into the world of slightly rusty beauties than I ever thought possible.

In the morning at breakfast – toast with butter, because I had forgotten to buy jam – I scrolled through Spanish classifieds sites. Wallapop. Milanuncios. Vibbo. Sites I didn't even know existed a week ago, and now they were my favourite browser tabs. I sat in the office, in a meeting about 'second quarter sales figures,' and secretly Googled 'Vespa spare parts Barcelona.' In the evening, sitting on the sofa while some series I wasn't following was playing on Netflix, I read forum posts from 2007 about the right spark plugs.

'The GS has character,' wrote a user named VespaManiac73. 'It's not just a scooter. It's a way of life.'

I should have laughed out loud. But I nodded. Like an idiot. Alone. In front of my laptop. On thc sofa. In my boxer shorts.

The problem was: I suddenly understood what this VespaManiac73 meant. It wasn't about a vehicle. It was about something I had been missing for years without knowing it. A project. A goal. A mission!

Something that had nothing to do with sales figures or deadlines. Something real.

> **[Email]** HR: 'Mandatory "GDPR" training has been postponed until next Tuesday.'

I had also found the German Scooter Forum – GSF for short – a digital breeding ground for German Vespa enthusiasts who cared for their scooters with a devotion bordering on religious fanaticism. But after opening a single, modest thread with the question 'How can I recognise a genuine Motovespa GS150?', I quickly realised that this was not a place for stupid questions. The answers came within minutes. And they were… let's call them educational.

'Read through the forum first before asking such beginner questions!!!' 'Use the search function! Why doesn't anyone do that???' 'Another noob who thinks he can just go out and buy a fancy Vespa without having a clue. Have fun burning through your money.'

I closed the tab. Quietly. Carefully. It was now clear to me that stupid questions came at a price here, and in the GSF, the currency was social humiliation. As if someone could see right through the screen.

From then on, I only researched quietly in the GSF. Like a digital ghost. I read. I learned. But I didn't ask any more questions. The internet pillory for ice cream parlour riders with beige Vespas, brown seats and whitewall tyres was real, and I didn't want to end up there.

The problem with obsessions is that they creep up on you. You don't notice it until you suddenly find yourself in the hardware store wondering what tools you would need to repair a Vespa.

I stood in the hardware store holding a 13 mm ring spanner aloft like Excalibur for the poor. When the sales assistant asked me about my project, I almost replied: 'Escaping an existence that consists solely of Netflix series marathons and lactose-free yoghurt.'

'Do you have a specific project in mind?' asked the friendly sales assistant. She was wearing an orange smock and had that professional look that sales assistants have when they suspect that the customer has no idea what they want.

'Er… theoretically,' I said, holding up the key as if it were the Holy Grail. The chrome gleamed so unused that it almost hurt. It looked like a technical illustration from a DIN standard for tools that would never see real oil.

'Theoretically?' 'I… am planning something. With an old scooter. Maybe.'

She smiled, confused. 'Maybe?' 'Probably.' 'Okay. Do you need anything else?' 'A purpose in life?'

It just slipped out. Just like that. She blinked. I laughed awkwardly.

'Just kidding. Just the wrench.'

I ended up buying a whole set. Just in case. At home, I put it on my kitchen table and stared at it. As if it could tell me what the hell I was doing.

Miguel used to tell me about his Vespa. Whenever we sat in his bar late at night, when the last guests had long since left and it was just the two of us – me with a vermouth, him with a Rioja.

'You know, amigo,' he had said, gesturing with his wine glass as if tracing an invisible road. 'When I was riding that Vespa back then, I was free. Really free. No bills. No appointments. No woman telling me to finally take out the rubbish.'

'You used to be single?' 'I was happy.'

We had laughed.

Then he had poured another glass – more for himself than for me – and slipped into that dreamy mood he always got when he thought about the past.

'The ride from Albacete to Barcelona,' he said, his gaze softening, 'that was… insane. Midsummer. August. 42 degrees in the shade. And me? I'm driving across the plateau like a madman.'

He told me how he ran out of petrol.

'And so there I am,' he spread his arms, 'in the scorching heat. No petrol station in sight…'

As he spoke, the air in the bar shimmered, as if the mere memory of the Castilian summer could make the heating costs in Kempten obsolete. He told the anecdote of the farmer who gave him petrol without asking for money when he had run out of fuel.

'You know, that was the moment I understood what freedom really means. It's not that you never have problems. But that you learn to deal with them. That you know: somehow, things always work out.'

He looked at me, and for the first time that evening, he seemed serious.

'Life is like this journey, amigo. Sometimes you run out of fuel, but as long as you don't stop the journey in your mind, some farmer will always come along with a canister.'

At the time, I nodded without really understanding what he meant. But now, months later, as I sat on my sofa at night and replayed the story in my head, I understood. Miguel had never given up inside. Even when he ran out of fuel. Even when it seemed hopeless. And somehow – always – there had been someone there to help. Maybe that was the secret: don't give up. Continue the journey in your head.

He wasn't just any mate. He was the one who called me during the worst weeks after my break-up with Sabine and said, 'Come over. I'll cook. You cry. Then we'll have a drink.'

'She wasn't right for you anyway,' he had said while cutting onions. 'How do you know that?' 'Because she left you, amigo. And not because you cheated on her. But because you weren't there for her enough and were too much in your own head.'

I remembered Sabine's wish: Mallorca, but only with drinking, beach and shopping at Ballermann as the only true idea of Spain.

'But I wanted the real Spain,' I muttered. 'I wanted to go to Barcelona, see Gaudí, those little alleys, experience the culture. But we never did.'

'That's exactly the problem!' Miguel had put down the knife and looked at me. 'You wanted culture! You compared the prices of Gaudí tickets! But did you BUY the ticket? No! You calculated the jump height and then turned around. She wanted Ballermann because at least that promised a little excitement. And you? You couldn't even offer her the little adventure that takes place in here.' He tapped his chest. 'You have to live, amigo. Not just function.'

Then he concluded his speech with his usual line:

'And do you know why I know that, amigo?' He leaned forward so that I could smell the red wine and onions. 'Because you lived with a woman for three years who forbade you to have garlic in the house, amigo. A woman who doesn't like garlic is not a woman who loves life. Garlic is life. Garlic is passion. Garlic is…' He raised his hand triumphantly. 'Garlic?' 'YES, exactly!!! And she forbade that. What else did she forbid? Laughter? Emotions? Exactly! The real adventure is the smell of garlic in your life that you don't have to hide.'

I laughed. For the first time in weeks. Now, months later, I realised how serious he had been. Miguel had always been someone who lived life to the full. He smelled of garlic and cigarettes, he laughed too loudly, he hugged too tightly. And me? I was someone who functioned. Since the break-up, my life had been an endless loop of efficiency and emptiness. No highlights. Just… mediocrity. Grey.

And then suddenly there was this photo. This Vespa. This sentence. It was as if someone had opened a door in my head that hadn't seen light for years.

'You look tired,' said Stefanie from accounting a few days later. We were standing in the coffee kitchen. She was holding a cup of herbal tea that smelled of disappointment. I was holding a cup of black coffee that tasted of the will to survive.

'I am,' I replied. 'Are you not getting enough sleep?' 'No. I'm up until three in the morning googling old motor scooters.'

She blinked. 'That was a joke, right?' 'Of course! Absolutely!' I lied.

But it wasn't a joke. I had learned more about two-stroke engines in the last few days than about my own tax return. I now knew how to change a spark plug (theoretically), how to clean a carburettor (YouTube), and that this 1967 Vespa was a damn rare piece. A model that was only produced for one year. Only in Spain. In a small factory near Madrid. A Spanish interpretation of the Vespa that never made it to Italy and was therefore as rare today as a reasonable political debate. Rarer than reasonable decisions in my life.

I had searched the internet for weeks. Scoured Spanish classified ads. Contacted clubs. Written to workshops in Barcelona. I wanted to start where Miguel's journey had ended. Most Spaniards didn't even reply. Others told me that the vehicle had already been sold. What I did find was often so rotten that even VespaManiac73 would have advised against it. Or unaffordable. Or both.

I was almost at the point of giving up on the whole thing. Then I found it. Just one for sale. In Barcelona. For €4,200. With the vague description: 'Original condition, runs perfectly, chassis number available.'

I stared at the ad as if it were a revelation. €4,200. That was… a lot of money. But then again, it wasn't. I had a savings account that I had set up 'for emergencies'. I had never touched it before. Because – hand on heart – what was an emergency? A broken washing machine? A new laptop? Or maybe… a full-blown midlife crisis that urgently needed a Vespa? I quickly closed the tab before my inner insurance agent could print out a list of reasons why this was economic suicide.

I clicked on 'Contact'. My hand trembled slightly. Not from fear. From excitement.

The seller replied within two hours. His name was Carlos. He wrote in English, concisely and matter-of-factly: 'The Vespa is in good condition. Original parts. A few scratches, but runs perfectly. If you are seriously interested, I can send more photos. The price is fixed.'

I was serious. Damn serious. I wrote back: 'Yes, I'm interested. Can you send me more pictures?'

Then I leaned back and exhaled deeply.

What the hell was I doing? I knew nothing about scooters. I had never ridden a Vespa before. Wait. Stop. That wasn't entirely true. I had ridden a two-wheeler before. When I was 16, I had a moped. A blue Puch Maxi, which I bought with the first money I ever earned myself – delivering newspapers, getting up at 5 a.m. every morning for two years. That thing had been my pride and joy. Freedom on two wheels, even if it was only 25 km/h and the engine sounded like an angry lawnmower. I still remembered the feeling: the wind in my face, the road beneath me, the feeling that the world belonged to me – at least the world between my parents' house and the next village.

But at 18 – the year you were finally allowed to drive a car – I sold it. For a small car. A used Ford Fiesta, silver-grey, with a cassette deck that only half worked and a smell I could never quite identify (somewhere between 'wet dog', 'forgotten trainers' and 'smoking corner at school'). At the time, I thought, 'Being an adult means driving a car.' Today I know that being an adult means regretting what you thought was sensible at 18.

Years later, I got my motorcycle licence. Why? I have no idea. Maybe it was a gut feeling. Maybe it was because my father had one. Maybe it was because a friend persuaded me. Maybe it was because I thought, 'You never know.' But I never bought a motorbike afterwards. Never even thought about it. Instead, I bought a sensible car. Took a sensible job. Lived a sensible life. Until now.

In the evening, I was sitting on my sofa again. In front of me on the coffee table: the photo of Miguel, my laptop, a half-empty bottle of beer and a notebook in which I had scribbled confused thoughts. Things like:

Can I really do this? What if the Vespa is a piece of junk? Should I buy a helmet already? How much does a flight to Barcelona cost? Is 43 too old for this kind of thing? Do I need insurance? What do I tell my boss?

Finally, at the bottom, in slightly shaky handwriting: What would Miguel say?

I knew the answer. Life doesn't wait! He would pat me on the shoulder, pour me a glass of wine and laugh at me for even thinking about it instead of just doing it.

I took a sip of beer. Then I opened a new tab. 'Flights to Barcelona.' There was one for next week. Wednesday. 89 euros. I stared at it. My mouse hovered over the 'Book' button. 89 euros. That was less than I had spent on takeaway food last month.

And then – without thinking twice – I clicked. Confirmation. Payment. Booked.

I leaned back and felt my pulse quicken. Holy shit. I was flying to Barcelona. To buy a Vespa. From a guy named Carlos, whom I didn't know. For €4,200.

My rational mind screamed, 'Are you completely insane?' But the other part – the part that had been buried under a blanket of routine and resignation for months – whispered back softly, 'Finally.'

Monday morning, nine thirty. I was sitting in a meeting when Schneider called me over.

'Mr Ritter. The quarterly figures.'

I got up, went to the projector, clicked through my slides. Everything was correct. Everything was prepared.

'Stop,' said Schneider.

I stopped.

'Slide seven. The bar for the southern region.'

'Yes?'

'It's blue.'

'Yes. Corporate design.'

'I said green for growth.'

'That wasn't in the email.'

'It was in my head.' He smiled. That smile that looked like a disease. 'And that should be enough for you.'

Eleven colleagues stared at their laptops. No one looked at me. No one objected.

I stood there, in front of the wrong blue, and understood: it wasn't about colours. It was about control. He wanted to see if I would buckle.

I buckled.

'I'll change it by tomorrow.'

'By tonight,' he said. 'Six o'clock. I want to see it on the server.'

I nodded. Sat down. My hands were shaking slightly.

Stefanie from accounting next to me scribbled something on her notepad. I glanced over. She had scribbled 'Kill me now' and drawn a sad smiley face. I had to grin.

I wrote back: 'Wait. Me first.'

'Do you have any questions?' my boss asked, looking directly at me. 'Yes,' I said. 'I'd like four weeks' holiday.'

The silence in the room was so thick you could cut it with a knife. My boss stared at me as if I'd just suggested setting the office on fire.

'Four… weeks?' 'I have 320 hours of overtime,' I said calmly. 'That's the equivalent of eight weeks. I'm only taking four.' 'That's… that's not possible. Not now. We're in the middle of a project!' 'We're always in the middle of a project.' 'That's unprofessional!'

I looked at him. Really looked at him. For the first time in months. He looked tired. Grey. Like someone who had spent his life creating pie charts and forgotten to actually live.

'You know what?' I said quietly. 'You're right. It's unprofessional. But you know what else is unprofessional? Working 320 hours of overtime because you're afraid to say no.' 'If you leave now, you'll jeopardise –' 'My job. I know.' 'Then don't do it!' 'Just for the record,' I replied, 'the job has been jeopardising me for years.'

I stood up, left the room and felt a smile creep onto my face. A smile that felt dangerously like a small rebellion.

Stefanie caught up with me in the hallway. 'That was… wow.' 'Thanks?' 'No, honestly. That was great. I wish I had the courage.' 'You do,' I said. 'You just don't use it.'

She smiled sadly. 'Maybe.' 'One day.' 'Maybe.'

When I got home, I sat down at my laptop and wrote an email to Carlos.

'Hola Carlos, I'll be in Barcelona next week. On Wednesday. Can we meet up? I'd like to see the Vespa in person before I buy it.'

I pressed 'Send'.

Then I opened my calendar and marked the next four weeks. FREE. The word looked strange. Foreign. As if it didn't belong in my calendar. But at the same time… right.

I leaned back, looked out the window and thought of Miguel. Of his bar. Of his laugh. Of the sentence on the back of the photo. 'My freedom begins here.'

Maybe this was the moment. Maybe my new life was starting here too. With a plane ticket. A Vespa. And the realisation that maybe I wasn't cut out to base my life on quarterly forecasts after all.

I looked at the photo of Miguel. 'Maybe,' I murmured to the picture, 'it's time I did something unreasonable.'

Miguel would have grinned back.

I opened a new Google search.

'How do you pack for a midlife crisis trip?' 'What do you need for Spain in autumn?' 'Can you take a Vespa on a plane?' (Spoiler: No.) 'Best tapas in Barcelona.'

I grinned. It really had happened. I was flying to Barcelona. To buy a Vespa. And maybe – just maybe – to find out who I was without PowerPoint presentations.

Chapter 3 – Ghettoblaster and Gin and Tonic

[Soundtrack Shuffle: Alcazar – Crying at the Discoteque]

The flight to Barcelona was one of those cheap flights where you have to pay extra for every breath you take. Seat? 12 euros. Hand luggage? 20 euros. Wake up! Want a lottery ticket? 10 euros. The illusion that you're being treated like a human being and not cargo? Priceless.

But there I sat, wedged between a woman who was aggressively using her nail file (I mean really aggressively – as if the nail had personally insulted her family and now chips were flying), and a man who apparently believed that elbow room was a fundamental right – his, not mine. And yet, I grinned. Like an idiot. Because I was on my way. For the first time since… I didn't even know when. And somewhere, a baby was screaming!

The airport had been the warm-up phase. Limbo with air conditioning. But then came the L1 towards Fondo. Let me put it this way: if you come from a town where the biggest traffic obstruction is a broken-down tractor on a Tuesday morning, nothing can prepare you for the Barcelona metro. Nothing.

The doors hissed shut, and suddenly I found myself in a sardine-can-like reality that smelled like a mixture of cheap suntan oil, cold sweat and hopelessness. It was hot. Not the 'oh, we could use some ventilation' kind of hot, but the 'I am now part of a human soup' kind of hot. All around me, people were waving their arms in fan-like movements so manic that you could have powered a small wind turbine with them. A man next to me was holding his houseplant in his arms as if it were his girlfriend. Even men in suits were fanning themselves as if their survival depended on it. And probably it did.

Just when I thought it couldn't get any worse, it happened. Two guys with baseball caps and a boombox bigger than my hand luggage entered the compartment. Latino rap. Volume: jet engine. They rapped their hearts out, complete with aggressive hand movements that would probably have triggered a SWAT team intervention in my hometown. And the people? Nothing. Absolutely nothing. The passengers stared at their smartphones as if they contained the formula for eternal youth, while the bass rearranged my internal organs.

Right behind them came a guy with a plastic bag. 'Chupa Chup? One euro! Lollipop? One euro!' He held a sticky-looking lollipop right under my nose. I shook my head, which was a mistake because my sweat splattered directly onto the T-shirt of an English woman who was part of a six-person hen party delegation.

'Wooooooo! Barcelona, baby!' she screeched, waving around an inflatable pink thing that would probably have led to excommunication in the Catholic Church. She smelled of gin and tonic and miserable decisions. I stood there, squeezed between a singing rapper and a bridesmaid on the verge of circulatory collapse, clinging to my backpack as if it were my last anchor in a world that had lost its mind.

Plaza España.

When the metro finally spat me out at Plaza España, I staggered into the open air. I thought of fresh air. A fatal mistake.

Bam. The wall hit me with full force. A mixture of scorching asphalt heat, the acrid smell of ancient urine in the corners of the walls, the exhaust fumes of eight thousand scooters and the sweet, putrid breath of overflowing rubbish bins. It was as if the city had decided to give me a good slap in the face, just to see if I would get back up.

Right at my feet, a homeless man lay on a cardboard box, his eyes closed, a picture of misery in the midst of splendour. Above me towered the majestic towers and the National Palace – so incredibly beautiful that it hurt. This city was like a beautiful woman who first kisses you passionately and then steals your wallet and kicks you in the shin.

I stood there, drenched in sweat, completely overstimulated and with a pulse that my GP in Germany would have immediately responded to with a referral to cardiology. My head screamed, 'Call home!'

But then I saw a Vespa rattling past me. Blue. Old. Loud. And I remembered why I was here. Even though I felt like an extra in a film whose script I hadn't read.

Since the break-up, I had done exactly three things: work, exist and pretend that everything was fine. Now I was standing in Barcelona to buy a Vespa that I wasn't even sure was real. This was either the beginning of something great or proof that I had completely lost my mind. Both were possible.

Carlos had replied to my email. Short, concise, efficient: 'Thursday, 3 o'clock. Carrer de Pacific 7. Bring cash.' No 'Looking forward to seeing you' or 'Have a nice flight.' Oh well. I wasn't buying friendship. I was buying a Vespa. A damn rare, beautiful scooter that might – just might – change my life. Or at least provide an exciting topic of conversation at parties I never went to anyway.

Barcelona welcomed me with sunshine, noise and heat that felt like someone was holding a hairdryer to my forehead. I had forgotten how loud cities can be when you've spent months in a grey German town where the most exciting sound is the beeping of the supermarket checkout. Here? The noise of engines, a babble of voices, the screeching of seagulls who apparently thought they were the bosses of the city. The hum of electric scooters squeezing through narrow alleys. Tourists arguing loudly in languages I didn't understand. Street musicians attempting to cover Leonard Cohen with varying degrees of success. It was chaotic. It was loud. It was alive. And for the first time in months, I felt alive too.

My rudimentary school Spanish – which consisted mainly of 'Hola', 'Gracias' and '¿Una Cerveza, por favor?' – was immediately put to the test. On the first day, I had fought my way to a small guesthouse, whereby 'fought my way' was a perfectly adequate description. The city was glowing in the late summer heat, and I hadn't expected Barcelona to still be so hot in September. I darted from shadow to shadow as if there were snipers on the rooftops.

Tourists everywhere. Jackhammers everywhere. Taxis everywhere. And me in the middle of it all, with my little rucksack and the vague hope that I wasn't about to make the biggest mistake of my life.

> **[Notification]** Bosch Smarthome: '40° white wash programme finished 18 hours ago! Remove laundry! Otherwise mould may form! 🧺⚫'

The guesthouse was tiny but clean. The owner – an elderly Catalan man with a moustache that looked like it deserved its own postcode – looked at me and asked, 'Turismo?' in Spanish.

'Sí,' I replied. Then, thinking it would make me more likeable, I added, 'Vespa.'

His eyes lit up. 'Ah! Motovespa?'

We talked about Vespas for five minutes – he in Spanish, me with my hands and feet – and in the end he handed me a map of

Barcelona and said, 'Buena suerte, amigo.' Good luck. I would need it.

Today was Thursday. 2 p.m. Time to meet Carlos. I got off the metro – line 1, towards Fondo – and got my bearings. Carrer de Pacific. I checked my mobile phone. Google Maps showed me a route through narrow streets, past cafés, small shops and graffiti that looked like someone very talented had been very angry.

My pulse quickened. I was about to see it. The Vespa. Miguel's Vespa. Or at least one that looked like it.

I still had time. An hour. So I sat down in a small café on the corner, ordered a cortado and tried to calm my nerves. It didn't work. I was as nervous as a teenager before their first date. What if the Vespa was perfect? What if it wasn't? What if Carlos was a con artist? What if I spent €4,200 on a piece of junk?

To be on the safe side, I sent one last email to the Vespa Club Barcelona, saying that I was looking for a GS150 and asking if they knew anyone who wanted to sell one or would at least meet me for a beer.

'First time here?' the waitress asked in English. 'Er, yes.'

She smiled. 'You look nervous.' 'I'm buying a Vespa.' 'Ah.' She nodded understandingly, as if it were the most normal explanation in the world. 'Good luck.' 'Thanks. I think I'll need it.'

Carrer de Pacific 7. I found the address after ten minutes of wandering around. A narrow side street, far from the sea. The kind of street that smelled of fermented beer during the day and questionable decisions at night, lined with orange trees. And there it was: 'Art Garage'.

A shop window that looked like the result of an artistic crisis. Or several. Christmas decorations next to Halloween masks. In September. In Barcelona. At 28 degrees. A stuffed fox stared at me through the window as if to say, 'Turn back while you still can.' Behind it: abstract paintings that were probably meant to be profound but looked more like paint accidents. Vintage furniture in various stages of decay. A stack of records leaning so crookedly that you had to fear it would tip over at any moment. The pictures showed the Vespa in the shop window. I didn't see it.

I tried to make out details through the window, but the light was unfavourable and the decorations were in the way. I searched in vain for the familiar metal of a Vespa. Next to the shop window: a fake bunker door from a cheap apocalyptic film. No doorbell. Just a sign: 'Art Garage – Art, Vintage, Curiosities'. I took a deep breath. Knocked.

The door opened with a squeak – the sound of an amateur horror film. Behind it: a room that looked like a mixture of a student bar, art gallery and hobby craft studio. An old pinball machine in the corner (probably not working). A worn-out 1970s sofa in orange (definitely no longer working). It smelled of alcohol and dust. On the walls: more abstract paintings, concert posters from the 80s, a few metal sculptures that were probably 'meant to say something'. And there, behind a counter made from an old wooden door, leaned Carlos. Cigarette in hand. Sunglasses on. Indoors. In dim light.

He looked like someone who had sold many things in his life – and not all of them legally. Mid-30s, I guessed. Dark hair that looked like it hadn't been washed in three days. Neatly slicked back – except for one strand. A T-shirt with a faded band logo. Sweatpants that were a little baggy in the crotch and a sling bag. A really cheap knock-off of some luxury brand.

He looked at me and nodded. 'You're the German?' he asked in English. 'Yes. Exactly.'

He nodded again. No handshake. No small talk. Just, 'Come with me.'

We made our way through the cabinet of curiosities – past a collection of broken watches, a pile of old suitcases and a mannequin wearing a gas mask (for whatever reason) – and stepped through the back door into a small backyard. The set of a mafia film. Only without the mafia. Three broken bicycles. A rusty barbecue. A few half-dead potted plants. A pile of car tyres that looked like someone had left them there 10 years ago. And a tabby cat lying on one of the tyres, eyeing me with a look that made it clear she found me guilty – even if she didn't know exactly what of. Then we stopped.

And there it was. The Vespa.

At first glance, it looked okay. White. Dented. Old. Just like in the photos. My heart was pounding. This was it. Miguel's dream. My dream. But on closer inspection… Something wasn't right. The paintwork was uneven. As if it had been freshly sprayed with a spray can – amateurish, hasty, unprofessional. The chrome parts were too new. And the shape… the shape was just wrong. The proportions were off. The leg shield was too wide. No glove compartment. This was not a GS150. Not even close.

'You can start it up,' Carlos said in English. 'Can I?' 'Sure.'

I walked up to the Vespa, looked for the kick starter, found it. Kicked. Once. Twice. Nothing. The Vespa did nothing. Silence. Awkward silence. I tried again. Still nothing. Carlos took a drag on his cigarette.

'It's just the battery.'

I stared at him. There's no battery in a Vespa. At least not in one from the 1960s. I'd learned that from the YouTube videos. These things had magneto ignitions. No battery.

I knelt down and checked the chassis number. The number he had sent me by email. It didn't match. Not even close. This was a fake. Some other type, poorly sprayed with white paint to make it look great. A cheap bluff for naive tourists like me. Like fast food in a Michelin-starred restaurant.

I stood up. 'I… I need to think about it,' I said.

Carlos shrugged. 'The price is fixed.' 'Yes. I know. I just need… some time.' 'Sure. Good luck!'

He leaned back against the wall and continued smoking as if he had all the time in the world.

Frustrated, I fled the backyard. In the first bar I found, a few old men were chatting in Catalan. I ordered a vermouth, sat down in a corner and stared into my glass.

Was this all a stupid idea? Had I really believed I could trade a life of Netflix series and lactose-free yoghurt for an adventure?

4,200 euros. For junk. I almost signed. At least I hadn't bought the Vespa. Thank goodness. But what now?

> **[Notification]** Health App: 'We have detected an unusually high heart rate – would you like to do a quick breathing exercise?'

Self-doubt gnawed at me like a cat on a piece of furniture. Maybe my colleagues were right. Maybe it was all a crazy idea. Maybe I should just fly home. Back to Kempten. Back to my grey life. I felt shame. And anger. At myself.

I sat there for a while, staring at the photo, ordered another vermouth. And another. The bartender said nothing. He just poured and nodded understandingly.

At some point – after the third vermouth – I checked my emails. One message. From Ricardo. Vespa Club Barcelona. Subject: 'RE: Looking for Motovespa GS150'. My heart leapt. I opened it hopefully. It was in English.

'Hello Kai, thank you for your message. I understand that you are looking for a Vespa. Unfortunately, Vespa Club Barcelona is not a tourist information service, and we do not normally assist with commercial purchases for people who are just visiting. Our club is for enthusiasts who live here, restore their own Vespas and are part of the local scene. We are not dealers or advisors for collectors from abroad. I hope you understand. Best regards and God bless! Ricardo'

I read the email twice. Polite. But firm. No invitation. No help. Nothing. I put my mobile phone away. Stared at Miguel's photo again. That was it, then. I had failed. After only two days. Carlos was a fraud. Ricardo didn't want to help. The Vespa didn't exist. Or at least I would never find it.

I thought of my boss and his relentless world of process optimisation. He looked like someone who had traded his dreams years ago for an ergonomic footrest and supplementary insurance. And that's exactly how I felt now: like someone who should crawl back to the footrest because he wasn't cut out for the real world. Maybe I should just fly home. Tomorrow. The day after tomorrow. Sometime. Back to Kempten. Back to my grey life.

I paid, left the bar and walked through the streets of Barcelona – through El Born, past the cathedral, through the Gothic Quarter. The city around me pulsated. I kept walking. People sat outside, drinking beer and wine, eating tapas, laughing. The smell of fried fish, aioli and garlic hung in the air. The sun was low, bathing the old buildings in golden light. I shuffled through the alleys like a zombie.

Back at the guesthouse, I sat on my bed, stared at the ceiling and wondered what the hell I was doing here. My mobile phone lay next to me. Ricardo's rejection was still on the display. I looked at Miguel's photo again.

Miguel grinned at me from the yellowed photo as if he knew exactly that I was about to back down. His gaze no longer seemed like an invitation, but like a judgement of my own cowardice. His quote like a command! Was my little escape from the prison of a dreary life ending here? After only two days?

No! Damn it, no! I hadn't spent weeks trawling through forums and googling myself to sleep, racking up overtime and telling my boss that the job was putting me at risk, just to give up after two days. Miguel had stood there in the heat, without fuel, in the middle of nowhere. And he hadn't given up. He had waited. Until the farmer came with his tractor. 'Sometimes you run out of fuel. But if you wait and don't give up, some farmer will always come along with a canister.'

I sat up, grabbed my mobile phone and wrote a reply. In Spanish, as best I could.

'Hello Ricardo, I understand that. I'm not a collector or a dealer. I'm just someone trying to honour a deceased friend. He always talked about his scooter, which he rode from Albacete to Barcelona in the 70s. He sold it here to start a new life in Germany, and he regretted it his whole life. I know you're not a tourist service. I'm not asking you to find me a Vespa. I'm just asking if you could point me in the right direction. Maybe someone you know who could help. Maybe just some advice. I'll be here for a few more days. If you change your mind, let me know. Thank you for reading this. Kai'

I pressed 'Send'. Then I put my mobile phone away.

I would stay one more day. Walk around the city. Explore the old town. Think. And if nothing happened by then, I would fly home. But tonight I would not give up. Not without at least trying.

The next day came. Friday. No reply from Ricardo. I wandered through Barcelona like a lost tourist. El Born. Raval. The narrow streets of the Gothic Quarter. History, architecture, restaurants everywhere. Medieval façades with crumbling plaster and ornate balconies. Small squares with fountains and orange trees. Churches whose bells echoed through the narrow streets. I sat in cafés, drank cortados and watched people. But my mind was elsewhere.

Had I made a huge mistake? Was this all just a crazy idea of a man at that critical age? Should I just fly home?

In the evening, I sat in the guesthouse again, scrolling aimlessly through the internet, and stumbled upon the website of the Vespa Club Barcelona. There was a notice. A club evening. Tomorrow. Saturday. 8 p.m. In a small bar in Horta. An address. Just a vague description.

I stared at the screen. Should I go? Uninvited? Unwanted? Ricardo had turned me down. He had made it clear that they didn't want tourists. But… what did I have to lose? I was already here. I had already failed. If they threw me out, it wouldn't be any worse than it was now.

I thought of Miguel. Of the photo. Of the sentence. 'Come on. Get your butt moving.' I would go. Tomorrow. To the Vespa Club. Uninvited. And I would tell them the story. Miguel's story. My story. And if they still kicked me out… Then at least I would have tried. Because if there was one thing I had learned from Miguel, it was this: you don't give up. You keep going.

Chapter 4 – The Vespa Brothers

[Soundtrack Shuffle: Apollo 440 – Stop the Rock]

Saturday evening. 7:45 p.m. I stood in front of Bodega La Massana on Carrer d'Horta 1. The open door stood like a bright slit in the warm stone of the building's façade. For almost a hundred years, this establishment had breathed with the street, since the days when Horta was still a village on the outskirts of Barcelona and farmers bought their wine here straight from the barrel. The door was simply open. Always.

On the small forecourt – more of a widening of the alley than a real square – they stood: Vespas. Five, six, maybe seven. All old. All loved. Some polished to a shine, others with patina and scratches that told stories. A black PX 200. A blue Sprint with chrome mirrors that sparkled in the light of the street lamps. A yellow Primavera that looked like it had just rolled out of the 70s. I moved closer. Like a small child standing in front of a toy shop. The smell hit me: engine oil, petrol, old leather. The scent of machines that had been loved and cared for. Around the Vespas: men with beer in their hands, parkas over their arms despite the warmth. Laughter. Voices in Catalan and Spanish. It was loud. It was lively. They seemed like a close-knit community whose access code consisted not of passwords but of oil stains on their fingers.

I went inside.

I had spent the afternoon aimlessly on the beach, staring at the sea. Then I went for a walk. Past the Basilica of Santa Maria del Mar, through the Gothic Quarter, where laundry hung like colourful flags between the balconies and every corner seemed to tell a story. I had strolled through Carrer Montcada and lost myself in Plaça del Pi. People were sitting outside, drinking wine from bulbous glasses, eating tapas from small plates, laughing. The smell of fried fish –

boquerones, fried anchovies – hung in the air. Accompanied by aioli, so thick and garlicky that you could still remember it three days later. Everywhere, that typical city smell of exhaust fumes, old stone, sea and life.

For the first time in months, I felt: I wasn't just here. I was HERE. Present. Alive. No longer that grey, functional Kai from Kempten. But someone who dared to do something. Who had the courage. Who took action.

But what if they threw me out right away? Would I be disappointed again? Ridiculed? What if they thought I was a fool? A German tourist who had no idea and just wanted to spend money? What if Ricardo recognised me and threw me right back out the door? I thought of Miguel. Of the photo. Of the sentence. 'Come on. Get your butt moving.' I took a deep breath and stepped inside.

The atmosphere hit me as soon as I entered. Old wooden barrels lined the walls. Mixed with the warm, sweet breath of vermouth, which had been tapped here since the 1930s. A hint of grilled sausage wafted over from the patio. The evening light fell amber and sluggish over the dark wooden bar. The floor was made of worn tiles, cracked in some places, smooth in others from decades of feet. On the walls: dozens of barrels, stacked from floor to ceiling. Shelves full of dusty bottles. On one wall hung a yellowed poster of a bullring, on another an old black-and-white photo of men standing in front of this very bar in the 1930s. The air was thick. Warm. Full of smells that overlapped like layers of an old, complicated history: wine, wood, garlic, ham hanging from the ceiling. It smelled almost like Miguel's bar. I breathed in the air deeply. It smelled of history. Of life. Of a place that was a vessel full of time – La Massana, the heart of Horta. It felt as if, if you closed your eyes, you could hear the ghosts of the old winegrowers who had drowned their sorrows in cask wine here a hundred years ago.

The bar was long and made of dark wood, worn and stained. Behind it stood an elderly man in an apron, pouring wine – straight from a barrel. A man who seemed to have been occupying the same stool for decades barely lifted his head and said, 'Bona nit.' It sounded less like a greeting than a confirmation that anyone who crossed the threshold was welcome here.

Everywhere: people. At the bar, at small wooden tables, standing, leaning. Regulars. Workers after work. No tourists strayed here. And there, in the back corner, in the patio, at a larger table: men between 50 and 70. Parkas hung over the backs of chairs. Fred Perry polo shirts. Harrington jackets. Old-school scooter boys. On the table, leaning against the wooden top: a hand-painted chalk sign. 'Reservat / Vespa Club Barcelona'.

They turned around. Looked at me. About ten, twelve men. The background noise of the bar seemed to die down for a moment. Then one of them stood up. Ricardo. I recognised him immediately. Mid-50s, powerfully built, broad chin. Short hair. Fred Perry polo shirt. Adidas trainers, immaculately white. He seemed like the undisputed capo of this little mechanical brotherhood. He crossed his arms.

'You're the German?' he asked. His voice was loud and broke the silence; he spoke Spanish. Distant.

I nodded. 'Yes. Kai.'

He looked at me for a while. Scrutinised me from head to toe. Then, without a smile: 'A butifarrero, right?'

'A… what?'

An older man laughed. 'Ice cream Vespa rider. Tourist.'

Ice cream parlour driver. Tourist.

I sensed that this was a test.

'I… no.' I took the photo out of my bag. Held it up. 'This is my friend Miguel. He died three months ago.'

Ricardo took the photo. Looked at it for a long time. Silence in the patio. Only the hum of the refrigerator behind the counter.

'He bought this Vespa in Albacete in the 70s,' I said. 'He rode it to Barcelona. Worked here for six months and sold it here to buy a ticket to Germany. And he regretted it his whole life. He always wanted to come back. Find the Vespa. Take another tour. Like in the old days.'

Ricardo looked at me. For a long time.

'But he never did,' I said more quietly. 'And now… I'm doing it for him.'

At that moment, the photo in Ricardo's hand no longer felt like a piece of paper, but like a sacred relic that legitimised my presence here.

Ricardo passed the photo to the older man next to him. He looked at it and nodded slowly. Another man said, 'He probably just wants to get another bargain and run off!'

'Oh, shut up and listen to him first, Ramon!' said another.

Then Ricardo said, 'Sit down.'

He called out something in Catalan. The bartender brought a beer. He placed it in front of me. Ricardo sat down opposite me.

'You know about Vespas?' 'No.' 'You have one?' 'No.' 'Have you ever ridden one?' 'When I was a teenager. A moped.'

A few men laughed.

Ricardo didn't.

'Why do you specifically want a GS150?'

'Because Miguel had one. Because he always talked about it. Because…' I paused. 'Because I've just been functioning for months. And this… this is the first thing in a long time that feels right and important.'

Ricardo looked at me. For a long time. Then he nodded slowly.

'Pedro!' he called.

An old man came out of a corner. 80, maybe older. Wild white hair. Oil-stained work trousers. Hands that looked like they had dismantled more engines than I had birthdays.

'This is Pedro,' said Ricardo. 'The oldest mechanic in Barcelona.'

Pedro took the photo. Looked at it for a long time. Whistled softly. 'Motovespa.' He looked at me. 'Your friend had first-class taste.'

'Thank you.'

'You saw one today?' Pedro asked.

I nodded. 'At least, I thought I did,' I sighed. 'At a man named Carlos. Carrer de Pacific.'

Pedro laughed. Loudly. So did the others.

'Carlos?' Pedro repeated, shaking his head. 'That's not a GS! It's some junk made from different Vespas!'

The others laughed even louder.

'You were lucky you didn't buy it, amigo,' said Ricardo, patting me on the shoulder. 'Complete junk.'

I didn't feel stupid. I felt saved.

'That's what we do here,' said Ricardo. 'We protect real Vespas. And real people.' He held out his hand to me. 'Welcome to the Barcelona Vespa Club.'

I shook it. For the first time in days, I no longer felt alone.

Pedro sat down next to me. 'Listen. I have a friend. In Albacete.'

My heart leapt. I listened intently.

'His name is Nacho. Old man. Crazy. But good heart.'

'He collects Vespas,' added Ricardo. 'Has two of the model you're looking for. Spanish. Real. Original.'

'Can I… can I buy one?'

Pedro laughed. 'Not so easy. Nacho hates guiris.'

'Guiris?'

'Foreigners. Germans, Italians, French. They come with money and steal our treasures.'

My heart sank. I could already see myself standing in the coffee kitchen in Kempten again, while the adventure failed due to national sensitivities.

'But,' Pedro raised a finger, 'I can call him. Maybe he'll at least let you come by. When he hears your story… maybe he'll change his mind.'

'Really?'

Pedro took out his mobile phone. He dialled. He spoke quickly in Spanish. I only understood a few words: 'Motovespa', 'Albacete', 'Miguel', 'Alemania', 'muerto' – dead. Long pause. Pedro listened. His face became serious. He argued. Talked. Got a little loud. Tried to convince him. Then he hung up.

'He says no.'

My heart sank.

'But,' Pedro smiled, 'he says you can visit him. Tuesday. In three days. No promises. He wants to hear your story. In person. If he likes you… maybe he'll change his mind. If not…' He shrugged.

'Three days?'

'Three days,' Ricardo confirmed and grinned. 'Enough time to show you Barcelona. And to learn how to recognise a real Vespa.'

Ricardo opened a beer bottle. Loudly. With a jerk, as if he were tearing off its head.

'To Miguel!'

'To Miguel!' everyone shouted.

He patted me on the shoulder – so hard that I almost fell off my chair. 'You've got guts, amigo. Just walking in here. Without an invitation.'

'I… had no choice.'

He laughed. Loudly. '¡Excelente! Con dos cojones! Anyone who has a choice doesn't do anything crazy!'

The others laughed along with him. Ricardo was different now. No longer so distant. Instead, he was loud, warm and funny. It was as if someone had flipped a switch.

We drank. They asked me about Germany, my journey, my life. I told them the truth – without shame. About the break-up, the job, the emptiness. About how I had been working for months and not living. They nodded. They understood. A man in his early 60s said, 'The Vespa saved my life too.' He told me about his divorce ten years ago. How he stood in his garage every evening and restored an old PX. How it had saved him. It was fascinating: these tough guys talked about mechanics as if it were a form of therapy.

Ricardo talked about his time as a mod in the 70s. Loud, gesticulating. He laughed at every anecdote, banging on the table. 'The Vespa was everything. Not just a scooter. A way of life. When you ride, you're free. Really free.'

'That's what Miguel said too,' I murmured.

Pedro put a hand on my shoulder. 'Your friend Miguel… is right! He'd be proud of you.'

My eyes welled up. I couldn't speak. Just nodded.

Ricardo leaned back. 'Three days to Albacete,' he said and grinned. 'Time to show you Barcelona. The real Barcelona. Not the tourist stuff.'

'Seriously?'

'I'll pick you up on Monday. Ten o'clock. Bring your good mood.' He winked. 'And an empty stomach. In this city, you either die of heatstroke or too many tapas. We'll take care of the latter.'

The night dragged on. Beer, stories, laughter. Around midnight, I left the bar. Walked through the illuminated alleys. The city was alive. And I was alive. I walked slowly. Wanted to capture the moment. Thought of Ricardo's shining eyes. Of Pedro's oil-smeared hands. Of the man who said the Vespa had saved his life. Maybe it was more than just a crazy idea after all. Maybe it was a real way forward.

Back at the guesthouse, I lay down in bed. Looked at Miguel's photo. 'I think I'm on the right track, amigo,' I whispered. 'Thank you for sending me here.' Three days to get ready.

> **[SMS]** Mum: 'I left a lasagne outside your door so you can have something warm to eat for once. At your age, you have to watch your vitamins!'

Perfect! Just perfect!

Chapter 5 – Magnum, P.I. does laundry

[Soundtrack Shuffle: Joe Cocker – You Can Leave Your Hat On]

I stood in front of my rucksack and stared at its contents. Three T-shirts. Two pairs of trousers. Three pairs of underpants. Three pairs of socks. All dirty.

'Shit.'

I had packed optimistically. Very optimistically. My motto was: 'I'll buy the Vespa, be back in Germany in two days, hardly need any clothes.' That was almost a week ago. Now I was sitting here. In Barcelona. Without a Vespa. With dirty laundry. And the realisation that optimism is sometimes just another word for lack of planning. I had to do laundry. The laundromat was two streets away. I had seen it yesterday while out walking. 'Lavandería Rápida' was written above the door. Quick laundry. From the outside, it looked like something out of an American film. Large shop windows. Rows of white washing machines. Neon signs. A few plastic chairs. A vending machine for washing powder. It was exactly how I had always imagined America as a child. As a teenager, I always thought I would fall in love either in a bookshop or, very romantically, when mixing up socks in a laundrette like this. Then reality happened!

But now it was time to do the washing. First, though, I needed something to wear. The souvenir shop was just around the corner. 'Barcelona Souvenirs' was written in kitschy letters above the door. Inside: the full range. Postcards. Magnets. Mugs with the Sagrada Família. Key rings in the shape of Gaudí's lizard. And T-shirts. Lots of T-shirts. I grabbed a white one with 'I ❤ Barcelona' written on the chest.

'Really?' said an inner voice. 'I know,' I replied. 'But all my clothes are dirty.' 'You could wash them and then buy new ones.' 'Too complicated.'

I took the T-shirt. 8 euros. Then I saw the shorts. Cheap cargo shorts in khaki. 10 euros. 'Perfect.'

Finally – in the corner, next to a shelf with plastic flamenco dancers: the Hawaiian shirt. Light blue. With pink flamingos. And palm trees. And surfboards. 5 euros. I stared at it. I had always wanted a Hawaiian shirt. Ever since I saw 'Magnum' on TV as a child. Tom Selleck. Red Ferrari. Moustache. Hawaiian shirt. But it had never been fashionable. Never the right time. It was awful. Sabine would have hated it! I reached for it. Held it up. Six months ago, I wouldn't have dreamed of it.

'If not now, when?'

The saleswoman – a bored woman with chewing gum in her mouth – looked at me. 'I'm sure it suits you.'

I couldn't help but notice the irony. 'I'll take it.'

Then: the Chino Bazar. Those legendary junk shops that were everywhere in Spain. Crammed with everything the world didn't need but bought anyway. Plastic bowls. Cheap towels. Kitchen appliances that gave up the ghost after three uses. And shoes. I needed open shoes. My trainers were soaked with sweat. My feet smelled like a cheese shop in midsummer. Then I saw them. Crocs. Or rather, Croc copies. 'Cloqs' was written on the box. Bright green. With holes. Rubber. 10 euros.

'Those are the ugliest shoes in the world,' said Sabine's voice. 'I know. I'm buying them anyway.'

I tried them on. They fit. Perfectly. How could it be otherwise with rubber slippers? I bought them.

Back at the guesthouse, I got changed. The 'I ♥ Barcelona' T-shirt. The cargo shorts. The green Cloqs. The Hawaiian shirt over everything. I looked in the mirror. And froze.

'Oh God.'

I looked like walking proof of bad taste. But at the same time… I looked a little like Magnum. Okay, not really. Magnum had a Ferrari and a moustache and looked like Tom Selleck. I had green rubber Crocs, chalk-white legs and looked like a middle-aged German man in a fashion crisis. But the feeling was there.

'Magnum, P.I.,' I whispered. I grinned.

The laundromat was empty. Except for an elderly man dozing in the corner and a young woman staring at her mobile phone. I put my dirty laundry in a machine. Threw in some coins. Pressed 'Start'. The machine began to rumble. I sat down on one of the plastic chairs and pretended to read El País, which someone had left there. Right under a fan that moved more air than it cooled. It smelled of artificial lilac and hot metal – the smell of a new beginning. My clothes and the water spun faster and faster behind the glass. Upside down, just like my life right now.

The phone rang and I took out my mobile. Isabel. Miguel's widow.

'Hola, Kai,' she said. Her voice sounded surprised. 'Hola, Isabel.' 'I… I just wanted to ask how you were. If everything was okay.' 'Yes, everything's fine. Why?' 'Well. You were so… different last week. When we cleared out the bar. So pensive.'

I swallowed. 'Yes. That was… an emotional day.'

'I'm worried about you, hijo. You've been so… lost since the break-up.' 'I know.'

Pause.

'Where are you right now?' she asked. 'In… Barcelona.'

Silence. Long silence.

'Barcelona? In Spain?' 'Yes.' 'What are you doing in Barcelona?' 'I'm sitting in a laundromat right now. And I'm wearing a Hawaiian shirt.'

Pause. Longer pause.

'Kai?' 'Yes?' 'Have you… gone mad?' 'Maybe?' 'What are you doing there? Why are you in Barcelona?'

I sighed. 'Do you remember the photo? Of Miguel and the Vespa?'

'Yes…' 'I… I decided to look for one. One like Miguel's.'

Silence.

'You're looking for a scooter?' 'Yes. I flew to Barcelona. Tried to buy one. The first seller was a con artist. But then I found a Vespa club. And they helped me. And now I'm going to Albacete the day after tomorrow.' 'To Albacete?' 'There's a Vespa there. A real one. One like Miguel's.' 'And then?' 'Then I'll buy it. Hopefully.'

Silence. I heard her breathing.

'Kai,' she finally said. Her voice was soft. 'That's… that sounds crazy.' 'I know.' 'But…' Pause. 'Do you know what that reminds me of?' 'What?' 'Miguel. When he was young. Before we came to Germany. He always did spontaneous things like that. Crazy things.' 'Really?' 'Yes. Once he just drove to Seville on his scooter. In the middle of the night. Because he wanted to see the feria. Without a plan. Without money. Just like that.'

I smiled. 'That sounds like him.'

'I was angry at the time. But he said, "If not now, when?"' 'Exactly.'

She sighed. 'Kai, I don't know if this is a good idea. But…' Her voice softened. 'I think Miguel would be proud. That you're doing this for him.'

'Thanks, Isabel.' 'But please. Please call me when you find the Vespa. I'm worried.' 'I will.' 'And Kai?' 'Yes?' 'Take off that Hawaiian shirt. You're not a tourist.'

I laughed. 'But I look like one right now.'

'That's what worries me.'

We both laughed.

'Take care of yourself, hijo.' 'I will. I promise.'

We hung up.

I sat there. For the first time in weeks, I felt relaxed. The washing machine hummed away. I had 20 minutes left. There was a small bar across the street. 'Bar Carmen' was written above the door. I needed coffee. I got up. Went over. The Cloqs squeaked with every step.

The bar was small. Dark. Cool. A few tables. A counter. Behind the counter: a young woman. Early thirties. Short dark hair. Tattoos on her arms. Pretty in that casual Spanish way that always looked like she had just stopped trying because she didn't need to. She looked at me. At the same moment, she scanned my outfit. Her eyebrows rose. Slowly. Incredulously.

'Wow,' she said in Spanish. Then in English: 'That's… a look.' 'Thank you?' I said uncertainly.

She grinned. 'Magnum?' 'Where did you—' 'The shirt. The shorts. The sunglasses.' She pointed to my sunglasses, which I had forgotten to take off. 'You look like a German tourist who thinks he's in Hawaii.' 'I… yes. That pretty much sums it up.'

She laughed. 'What can I get you?' 'Café con leche, please.'

She sniffed. Wrinkled her nose. 'You smell like alcohol.' 'I had… a long night yesterday.' 'Hangover?' 'A little.'

She nodded sympathetically. 'Would you prefer a carajillo?' 'A what?' 'Carajillo. Espresso with rum. Or brandy. Helps with hangovers.'

I hesitated. 'Alcohol to combat alcohol?' 'Spanish medicine.' 'Okay. Why not? It must be happy hour somewhere!'

She made the coffee. Poured in a generous shot of brandy. Placed it in front of me. I drank. It burned. Tasted of coffee and recklessness. But it helped.

'Thanks.' 'No problem, Magnum.'

I laughed. 'My name is Kai.' 'My name is Laura.' She leaned against the counter. 'So. What's a German doing in a Hawaiian shirt on a morning in Barcelona?' 'Laundry.' 'Laundry?' 'All my clothes were dirty. So I had to buy new ones.' 'And you decided on… that?' 'I've always wanted a Hawaiian shirt. Because I loved Magnum as a child.'

She nodded. 'And now you think: if not now, when?' 'Exactly.'

She grinned. 'Brave. Or crazy. Or both.' 'Probably both.' 'In this city, the line between genius and madness is just a matter of lighting anyway,' she added with a wink.

I drank the carajillo. Slowly. Laura did her job – wiping the bar, arranging glasses, chatting with a regular. And I sat there. In a Hawaiian shirt. With green Cloqs. In a bar in Barcelona. And suddenly I asked myself, 'What the hell am I doing here?' I was 43. Not 27. I was sitting here, wearing a tourist outfit that even an eighteen-year-old would find embarrassing, and I had just drunk alcohol for breakfast. Was this a midlife crisis? Had I gone mad? Was Isabel right?

Before – before the break-up, before Miguel, before everything – I had thought I would fall in love in a bookshop. Or in a laundrette like this one. Romantic. Quiet. Unexciting. But now I was sitting here. Alone. With a hangover. And a Hawaiian shirt. Was I naive?

The door opened. A group of teenagers came in. Maybe sixteen, seventeen. They ordered Coca-Cola. Laughed. Loudly. One looked over at me. Nudged his friend. Whispered. Laughed. I looked down at myself. 'Yes,' I thought. 'I look ridiculous.' But then… Then I looked out the window. Outside: a palm tree. The sun. The blue sky. I was sitting here. In Barcelona. In a Hawaiian shirt. Not in the office. Not in my empty flat in Kempten, where I talked to a dead houseplant because I had no one else. Not in my old life. I was here. I was living an adventure. And if that meant a few teenagers were laughing at me? Fuck it. It was still better than what I had before. 'I traded 320 hours of overtime for this Hawaiian shirt,' I thought grimly. 'And damn it, the exchange rate was brilliant.'

I drank the last sip of carajillo. Put down the glass. Laura came over.

'Another one?' 'No. I have to get back to the laundry.' 'Sure. Nice to meet you, Magnum.' 'You too, Laura.'

I paid. Went outside. The teenagers were still giggling. I turned around. Grinned like a winner! Waved. They stopped laughing. Looked confused.

I sat down on the terrace of Bar Carmen. Right next to the door. My rucksack with the laundry was next to me. The sun was shining. It was warm. Traffic rushed by. People hurried to work, to shop, to whatever. I sat there. In a Hawaiian shirt. With green Cloqs. And I didn't care.

Laura came out. 'You're staying?' 'I've got twenty minutes until the laundry is dry.' 'Would you like something to eat?' 'Patatas bravas?' 'Perfect. Coming right up.'

She disappeared back inside. I leaned back. Watched the people.

> **[Notification]** Calendar reminder: 'Follow-up appointment: Mr Schulze (Riester pension optimisation) – in 15 minutes.'

When I looked up from my phone, I saw him. An old man. Maybe seventy. Maybe older. Thin as a beanpole. He was wearing a red wig. Not a pretty one. One of those cheap Halloween wigs that look like they're made of plastic threads. It sat crooked on his head. To go with it: black fishnet stockings. On thin, bony legs. And over it: a fur coat. Fake fur. Pink. Fluffy. Much too big. He walked past. Slowly. Dignified. As if it were the most normal outfit in the world. No one looked. People just walked past him. As if he were invisible. Or as if that were completely normal in Barcelona. Maybe it was. I stared after him. Fascinated.

Laura came out with the patatas bravas. Placed them in front of me. Saw the man. Then me. Grinned.

'You know what?' she said, nodding her head towards the man. 'You don't look that bad.' She winked. Ironically. Friendly.

I laughed. Loudly. 'Thanks. That… that actually helps.' 'You're welcome, Magnum.'

She went back inside.

I ate the patatas bravas. Hot. Spicy. Perfect. I watched the old man, who was now turning the corner and disappearing. And I thought, 'Yes. Barcelona. Here, you can be whoever you want to be.' Here, you could wear a Hawaiian shirt. Here, you could do laundry at 43 and feel like a hero. Here, anything was possible. Life wasn't a PowerPoint presentation, it was a wildly assorted rummage box in the Chino Bazar, and I had just pulled the grand prize.

I went back to the laundrette. The Cloqs squeaked. The Hawaiian shirt fluttered in the wind like a flag. And me? I felt like a bloody hero.

The laundry was done. I packed it into my rucksack. Still warm. Fresh. Went back to the guesthouse. Folded the shirt. Put it on top of the rucksack. Tomorrow Ricardo would come. The day after tomorrow Albacete. But today I had done laundry. In a Hawaiian shirt. And it was perfect.

Chapter 6 – Bye Bye Gaudi

[Soundtrack Shuffle: Celia Cruz – La Vida es un Carnaval]

Monday morning. 9:45 a.m.

The café was located in one of those side streets in Gràcia where the walls of the houses still retained the coolness of the night and the espresso came from machines that were older than most of the tourists. I already had my second cortado in front of me, even though my stomach was protesting. Nervousness tasted like coffee and stomach acid. It was an unpalatable mixture of caffeine jitters and the dull knowledge that there was no turning back now. My fingers drummed an impatient rhythm on the tabletop.

Ricardo had said: ten o'clock. Bring good spirits. Empty stomach. The stomach thing had taken care of itself. Fear is a damn efficient appetite suppressant.

At ten o'clock sharp, a VW Beetle turned the corner. Painted black and white like an oversized football shirt, but in a condition that would have brought tears of joy to the eyes of any German TÜV inspector. The bodywork gleamed as if freshly polished. Only the engine sounded like someone had taught an old dog to sing – a deep, gurgling rumble full of character.

Ricardo leaned out of the window, his sunglasses sitting perfectly. He looked like someone who had a monopoly on coolness, while I tried not to choke on my cortado. 'Get in, German!'

The passenger door opened with a soft squeak – the only concession to the car's age. Inside: white leather interior. Seats, door panels, everything white and so well maintained, as if someone cleaned it daily with a toothbrush. It smelled of old leather, Ducados cigarettes and that sweet smell of petrol that only classic cars with a real soul have. Ricardo wore brown leather driving gloves, his fingers worn bare from years of shifting gears. In the compartment under the glove box was a half-empty pack of Ducados. The radio – a Blaupunkt model that looked as if it had lived through the Spanish Civil War – was playing the Rolling Stones. Paint It Black.

And the gear knob: a billiard ball. The black and white eight.

'Nice car,' I said, touching the gear knob. Cool and smooth under my fingers. 'And nice gear knob.'

'Thanks. Bought it in 1987. One of my passions.' Ricardo patted the steering wheel as if it were the head of a beloved dog. 'I really wanted one made in Germany and without rust. Very difficult, because you use so much salt in Germany.' He grinned. 'Runs like new.'

'I don't doubt that for a second,' I muttered and fastened my seatbelt. The belt looked as if it had been retrofitted sometime in the nineties – out of a sense of obligation to comply with an EU regulation, not out of genuine conviction.

'Today I'm going to show you Barcelona,' said Ricardo and put the car in first gear. The billiard ball slid through his gloved hand. The Beetle jerked forward like a stubborn mule that fundamentally refuses to take the first step. 'The real Barcelona. Not the tourist stuff.'

'Sounds great.'

'First we'll go to Montjuïc. Then Tibidabo. Then vermouth. Lots of vermouth.'

'Even better.'

The Beetle plunged into Catalan traffic. Through the narrow streets of Gràcia, past balconies where laundry hung like colourful flags over a medieval fortress. Old women leaned out of windows, arms propped on cushions, watching the street with that Catalan vigilance that registers every movement and later recounts it over dinner. The smell of fresh bread wafted from a bakery with its door open – yeast dough and flour mixed with the aroma of roasted coffee from the bar across the street.

'You've never been to Barcelona?' asked Ricardo.

'No. I've only been to Spain once. Mallorca. A few years ago. With my ex.'

'Ah. And? Was it nice?'

'She wanted beaches, Ballermann and boutiques. I wanted… more.'

'More?'

I looked out of the window and watched an old woman opening her shutters. 'I've always wanted to marvel at Gaudí's work. The Sagrada Família, Park Güell, Casa Batlló… everything.' My fingers closed around the door handle. 'But she wasn't interested. So we stayed on the beach.'

'And that's why she's your ex?'

'Among other things.' I swallowed the memory of the endless boredom of that holiday.

The Beetle fought its way through the morning traffic – honking taxis, their drivers steering with one hand and gesticulating with the other as if conducting an invisible orchestra. Buses that squealed like tortured animals when they braked. Mopeds squeezing through gaps that seemed mathematically impossible. And everywhere:

electric scooters. Cooltra, YEGO, Bolt – ridden by tourists in flip-flops who looked as if they were about to collide with a street lamp at any moment. Hundreds of them. Plus large, soulless plastic scooters that sounded like vacuum cleaners on speed.

Ricardo drove relaxed, as if he had all the time in the world. One hand on the wheel, the other hanging casually out the window, resting on the door.

'You know,' he said after a while, 'I love this city. Every stone. Every tree. But sometimes…' He shook his head, a cigarette between his lips. 'Sometimes it's a cross between a zoo and a theme park.'

'Too many tourists?'

'Far too many. They come, take photos, eat frozen tapas, and leave again.' He sighed, the smoke drifting out of the window. 'But what can you do? This is Barcelona. Beautiful and annoying at the same time.'

'Do you have a family?'

'Yes. My wife. My daughter. She's 17.' He grinned, but it was a grin tinged with melancholy. 'She thinks my Vespas are embarrassing.'

'She thinks I should drive a "normal" car. Like other fathers.' He shrugged. 'But what's normal? I have a few Vespas, a few Lambrettas, a few old cars. That's my passion. My life.'

'And your wife?'

'She understands. Not always. But she lets me.' He laughed – a warm, deep laugh. 'That's love, isn't it?'

'Definitely!'

We turned onto a wide road that wound its way up the mountain. Montjuïc. Barcelona's local mountain, a volcanic hump that rises above the city like a watchful giant. Green everywhere – pine trees whose needles glistened in the morning sun, palm trees with fan-shaped fronds, cypresses that towered into the sky like dark exclamation marks. The smell of resin and warm stone wafted through the open windows. Villas lined the road on both sides – some perfectly restored with white façades and wrought-iron balconies, others half-ruined, their gardens overgrown, as if time and money had given up simultaneously.

'Up here,' said Ricardo, pointing to the right, where a monumental structure of light-coloured stone towered above the trees, 'is the Olympic Stadium. 1992. Do you remember?'

'Sure. I was nine.' Images from television broadcasts appeared before my inner eye. Torch, fireworks, Freddie Mercury on tape.

'I was 28. I watched the opening ceremony here. With friends. Beer. Barbecue. All night long.' His voice softened, coated with the sweetness of nostalgia. 'It was as if Barcelona had finally woken up. After Franco. After all those years.'

The Beetle groaned on the bends, but it didn't give up. The road narrowed, becoming serpentine. Then, after one last bend, the view opened up like a theatre curtain. Barcelona.

The whole city lay spread out like a map of stone and life. A sea of roofs in all shades of ochre, church towers piercing the sky like needles, skyscrapers from the seventies standing between historic buildings like uninvited guests at a wedding. The Sagrada Família stood out – Gaudí's unfinished dream, which looked as if someone had crossed a Gothic cathedral with stalactites and then decided never to stop. Its towers reached for the sky, but not higher than the mountain we were standing on.

'The Sagrada Família,' said Ricardo, pointing to the church. 'Gaudí designed it so that it wouldn't tower over Tibidabo. "No man should surpass God," he said.'

'Is it finished now?'

'Almost. After more than a hundred years. And you know what? Gaudí was almost right. Almost.' He smiled. 'Gaudí was a genius. Or crazy. Or both. Here in Catalonia, those things are often closely related.'

Further back, the Mediterranean Sea sparkled – azure blue, endless, calm as liquid glass. Boats drew white lines through the water like careful cuts in silk. On the horizon, the sky and sea blurred into a single bright blue, as if someone had forgotten to draw a dividing line.

Ricardo stopped at a viewpoint. We got out. The wind blew warm and salty, carrying the smell of the sea and pine resin. Down below, the city honked its daily concert, but up here there was only wind and silence and the distant screech of seagulls.

'Wow,' I said.

That was all I could think of. That was all that was needed. No metaphor in the world could have captured this moment better.

Ricardo laughed. 'Yeah. Wow. So much beauty, and you didn't even polish your shoes.'

I looked down at myself. My trainers were dusty. My jeans had a stain – coffee, probably from breakfast. But I didn't care today. Today, this city belonged to me, even if I had only borrowed it.

'This is my city,' Ricardo said quietly, and for the first time he sounded truly reverent. 'I love it. Every day. Every damn day.'

'But?'

'But sometimes… I have to get away. Out. On the Vespa. Just ride.'

'Why?'

'Because otherwise I suffocate. Too many people. Too much noise. Too much… everything.' He looked at me, sunglasses in hand, so I could see his eyes. Brown, tired, but alive. 'Do you understand?'

I nodded. I did understand. It was the longing for a silence that can only be found under a helmet.

'The Vespa,' he said, lighting a cigarette, the lighter clicking in the wind, 'gives you freedom. Not the grand, romantic idea from books and films. But the small one. The possibility to say: Today I'm going there. Or there. Or nowhere. Just ride. I always had a dream of going to Brighton for Mod Weekender – on a scooter. Never did it. Family, work and a little cowardice. I envy you, amigo. You're doing everything right!'

We stood there for a while. Ricardo smoked. I marvelled. Looked at the city. Said nothing. Didn't need to say anything. Sometimes silence is the most honest form of conversation.

Ping!

> **[Notification]** BankApp: 'Your monthly savings rate of €25.00 for "Bausparen Klassik" has been successfully executed.'

Then we drove on. Across the city, past the Sagrada Família, where I stared like a tourist and Ricardo grinned. Through Eixample with its perfectly square street blocks – a rationalist grid that Ildefons Cerdà had laid over the medieval chaos in the mid-19th century like a grid over a painting. 'Cerdà wanted light and air for the workers,'

Ricardo explained. 'The bourgeoisie wanted wide streets for their carriages. In the end, both got what they wanted.'

Then uphill again. Tibidabo this time. 512 metres above sea level.

The road became steeper. The Beetle struggled, the engine howling in a tone that sounded like overload. I clung to the door handle, half expecting us to roll backwards. Ricardo whistled along as if it were the most normal thing in the world.

At the top: an amusement park from the 1920s. Old carousels with faded paint, a wooden roller coaster that looked like it was built from matchsticks and hope. And behind it, like a crown above everything else: a church. Whitewashed, neo-Gothic and pompous, with a golden statue of Christ on top, spreading his arms as if to embrace or bless the whole city, or both.

'Templo del Sagrado Corazón,' said Ricardo. 'Sacred Heart. Tourists love it.'

'And you?'

'I'm Catalan. We don't love anything that comes from Madrid. But…' He shrugged. 'The view is spectacular.'

And how.

From up here, you could see not only Barcelona, but half of Catalonia. The Pyrenees to the north, blue and distant like a mirage. The sea to the east, endless. The city spread out below like a carpet of stone and life and ten thousand stories.

'Sometimes,' said Ricardo, 'I come here. When I need to think.'

'About what?'

'About everything. Life. Death. Why my daughter finds me embarrassing.' The corner of his mouth twitched. 'Why my Vespa makes strange noises.'

I laughed.

We drove down again. This time to the old town. Through narrow alleys, past clotheslines hanging like banners between the balconies. Then Ricardo suddenly stopped.

'Here,' he said, pointing to a square in front of us. 'Plaça Masadas.' He pronounced the name in Catalan.

The square was beautiful. A former market, redesigned into a classic village square in the middle of the big city. In the centre: a fountain whose water splashed lazily. All around: colonnades with small pubs and cafés. Tables and chairs in the shade. Old men reading newspapers and drinking coffee as if they had all the time in the world. Children playing tag, shouting and laughing.

'We'll have our first beer here,' said Ricardo. We sat down at a table under the columns.

Ricardo looked around, scrutinising the bar with the critical eye of a man who had eaten too many bad tapas.

'Very good,' he said. 'Everything here is still original.'

'What do you mean?'

'Look at the waiter. Catalan. Look in the kitchen. Catalan too.' He lit a cigarette. 'That's important.'

'Important?'

'Eighty per cent of the bars in Barcelona,' said Ricardo, letting the information hang in the room like cigarette smoke, 'are now run by Chinese people.'

I waited for the punchline. It didn't come.

'And?'

'And nothing. Good people. Very hard-working. Make fantastic fried rice.' He took a drag. 'But the tapas…'

'What about the tapas?'

'Frozen food. All of it.' He said it without judgement. Simply as a fact. 'You order patatas bravas. They come out of the microwave. You order croquetas. Deep freezer. Pimientos de Padrón? Used to be green, then white with ice, now green again.'

'And… that bothers you?'

'Me?' He shrugged. 'I eat fried rice there. Excellent. But tapas…' He shook his head. 'It's like going to a pizzeria in Germany and ordering bratwurst. You can do it. But why?'

I didn't quite understand what the problem was, but I nodded anyway.

'Here,' Ricardo tapped on the table, 'everything here is still authentic. The owner is Catalan. His father was Catalan. So was his grandfather. The patatas bravas are homemade. The olives come from the family. Everything is authentic.'

The waiter came – in his mid-forties, wearing an apron, looking tired – and brought two Estrella Damm. Ice cold. The glass immediately fogged up in the warmth, condensation dripping down like tears of relief.

'Salud,' said Ricardo, raising his glass.

'Salud.'

We drank. The beer tasted like salvation after the heat. Cold, bitter, perfect.

Ricardo lit a cigarette. 'Do you know when I rode a Vespa for the first time?'

'When?'

'When I was seventeen. My father had an old Primavera. Blue. Dented. But it ran.' He smiled, his eyes half closed, as if he were watching a film that only he could see. 'I took it secretly. Drove to a mod concert. In Mataró.'

'Mod concert?'

'Yes. The Jam. Paul Weller. 1982.' He closed his eyes. 'I rode there on the Vespa. Alone. Along the coast. The wind. The sun. The rattling of the engine. It was… perfect.'

'And? Did your father notice?'

'Of course. The Vespa had a scratch.' Ricardo grinned. 'He was angry. Very angry. But then he said, "If you're going to steal my Vespa, at least learn how to ride it properly." And the next day he taught me how to ride it.'

'Good father.'

'The best.'

We finished our beer. Ricardo got up and threw a few coins on the table.

'Now I'll show you real vermouth. Come on.'

We parked the Beetle in Ricardo's garage and took the metro – then walked the rest of the way. Through the narrow streets of El Born, the old commercial district where merchants once sold their wares and today there are boutiques selling things that no one needs but everyone wants. Small shops everywhere – antiques, vintage clothing, bookshops with yellowed covers in the window. The smell of roasted coffee and fresh bread hung in the air like an invisible net that wouldn't let you go.

The bar was small, dark, cramped. Old photos of footballers and bullfighters hung on the walls – black-and-white shots, their faces washed out by time. The counter was made of dark wood, worn and stained, polished by a thousand elbows. Behind it stood an old man in an apron who looked as if he had been working here since before the Civil War. Perhaps he had.

'Dos vermuts,' said Ricardo in Catalan.

The man nodded, took two glasses – thick-walled, heavy, honest – and poured vermouth directly from a barrel. Dark red, almost black, like coagulated blood. He placed a bowl of olives on the bar. Green, plump, glistening with oil that pooled in small puddles on the porcelain.

'Salud,' said Ricardo, raising his glass.

'Salud.'

We drank. The vermouth was sweet, but not too sweet. Spicy. A little bitter. Herbs I couldn't name. Perfect.

'Good, isn't it?' asked Ricardo.

'Very good.'

'That's real vermouth. Not the stuff tourists drink.'

We stood at the bar, eating olives and drinking vermouth. Ricardo told me about Barcelona. About his childhood here, when the city was still grey and poor. About the changes after Franco's death. About the tourists who flooded the city like a tide that never receded.

'It's not the same anymore,' he said quietly. 'But it's still my city.'

The second bar was in Gràcia. Even smaller. Even darker. On the walls: wine barrels, stacked up to the ceiling like a giant's building blocks. The smell of wood and wine was so strong that you felt drunk before you had even taken a sip.

There were no olives here. Instead: anchovies. Small, salty, preserved in oil, shiny like little treasures. Accompanied by bread. White bread, lightly toasted, still warm, the crust crispy.

'Try it,' said Ricardo.

I took an anchovy, put it on the bread and bit into it. The flavour exploded. Salt. Oil. Fish. Sea. It tasted like Spain. Like summer. Like life that was lived and not just existed.

'Do you like it?'

'Incredible.'

'See? That's why I could never leave here. The food. The wine. The people.' He looked at me, seriously this time. 'In Germany, you have good beer. But do you have this?' He pointed with a casual hand gesture at the plates in front of us.

'No.' We have efficiency, but less of this taste of the soul.

'Exactly.'

We stayed a while longer. Drinking, eating, talking. About everything. About Vespas, of course. But also about women, jobs, dreams, disappointments, small victories.

'You know,' Ricardo said at some point, his third vermouth in his hand, 'I have it good. My family. My friends. My Vespas. My city. But sometimes… sometimes I have to get out. Just ride and feel!'

'I understand that.'

'That's what they give us. An escape. An empty head that makes room for new possibilities.' He looked at me seriously. 'That's what you're looking for too, isn't it?'

'Yes. I think so.'

> **[Notification]** HelloFresh: 'Your Mediterranean Specialities Fresh Box has been delivered and is waiting at your door. Bon appétit!'

In the evening, we met the rest of the club in a small bar. In a small alley in Gracia. The pub was smaller, fuller, louder. The Vespas were parked outside, neatly lined up like soldiers in front of the barracks. Inside: beer, wine, laughter, the clinking of glasses.

A DJ was playing. Not exactly David Guetta. An older man with grey hair, reading glasses on his nose, hands full of scars. A checked shirt and a slipover over it. He was playing Northern Soul. The others were bobbing to the beat with a cold beer in their hands.

I sat there, drank my beer, smiled. Didn't understand a word because it was loud. But it didn't matter. Some things you don't understand with your head, but with something else.

Somewhere between squealing brakes and dusty alleys in Barcelona, I thought, I understand: it's not just about the Vespa. It's about finding your courage again. Courage to live. Courage to feel. To be brave!

Ricardo looked over at me and raised his glass. I raised mine. We drank.

Not a word. Just a smile.

Sometimes you don't need words.

Tuesday morning. Estació de Sants.

Barcelona's main railway station. Large, modern, full of people who had to go somewhere or were coming from somewhere. I stood on the platform, rucksack over my shoulder, ticket in my hand. The display board above me clicked mechanically through the departure times.

Ricardo stood next to me, hands in his pockets. 'You've got everything?'

'Yes.' 'Money?' 'Yes.' 'Courage?'

I hesitated. 'A little.'

He laughed. Patted me on the shoulder, his hand heavy and warm. 'That's enough. Nacho's a good guy. Just a little… strict.'

'Thanks. For everything.'

'No problem, amigo. And listen: if he says no, you come back. We'll find another Vespa.'

'And if he says yes?'

Ricardo grinned. 'Then you're one of us. A scooterist. Forever.'

Chapter 7 – Where the shadow has resigned

[Soundtrack Shuffle: Iggy Pop – The Passenger]

The train pulled in. A modern Renfe, silver and red, fast like a promise that might be kept. Or like a tradesman's promise to come by next week. I got on and found my seat by the window. Ricardo waved from the platform, one hand raised, the other holding a cigarette. I waved back, but didn't know if he could still see me. It was that strange moment of transition when you trade the security of a friend for the uncertainty of distance. Like switching from Netflix to a new streaming subscription. You know it will work out somehow. At least, you hope so.

The train started moving. Slowly at first, as if it had to convince itself that it was a good idea. Then faster. Barcelona glided by. Skyscrapers from the seventies, their balconies studded with satellite dishes like pin cushions. Or like the face of a teenager who has discovered chocolate for the first time. Factories with broken windows. Graffiti-sprayed wastelands where nothing grew but grass and hopelessness. Sometimes both at the same time, which is botanically remarkable. Then: fields. Hills. Vastness.

The Castilian plateau.

I leaned back, my head against the cool glass, and looked out of the window. The landscape passed by like a film running in slow motion, even though the train was racing along. Endless. Dry. Beautiful in a barren, honest way that made no compromises. Like my grandmother when you asked her for her potato salad recipe.

The Meseta Central. Spain's geographical heart, high and empty like a burnt-out volcano. A landscape that either swallows people up or sets them free – it knows no middle ground. This is where the Moorish armies marched north, swords flashing in the sunlight. This is where the Reconquista wrote its bloodiest chapter, century after century. This is where Don Quixote fought windmills because loneliness had driven him mad. Or wise. Depending on who you asked. Perhaps the difference between madness and wisdom out here is just a question of the right angle of light. Or the alcohol level. I'm not judging.

The train window framed the panorama like a canvas: olive groves whose silvery leaves trembled in the wind like nervous fingers. Or like me at the dentist. Vineyards laid out with mathematical precision – vines standing in rows like Prussian soldiers on the parade ground, each vine precisely measured. German tourists would weep with happiness here. Small white villages with churches whose bell towers rose against the sky as if they wanted to shout something to God himself. Probably a complaint about the heat. Individual farmsteads, lost in the vastness, like stranded ships on a sea of earth. Flocks of sheep, guarded by dogs that looked as if they had done nothing else for generations and would never do anything else. Civil servant dogs, so to speak.

And everywhere this ochre-coloured soil. Dusty. Cracked. Baked by the sun like old pottery in a kiln that never goes out. Those who lived here lived hard. Those who survived here survived everything. It was a land that gave you nothing, but in exchange for sweat offered a deep, archaic tranquillity. Like a gym, only without the guys taking photos of themselves between sets.

I leaned my forehead against the glass. Outside, the heat shimmered over the fields like invisible ghosts dancing across the earth. Windmills in the distance turned their blades lazily, as if they too had realised that there was no point in rushing here. Miguel had driven through this landscape. On his Vespa, the engine singing papapap, helmet in the wind. Through this heat. Through this loneliness. And somewhere here – perhaps between two of these villages, perhaps under one of these windmills – he had understood that freedom does not mean arriving nowhere, but being able to arrive everywhere.

My fingers relaxed on my rucksack. My shoulders slumped. For the first time in days, my breathing didn't feel like work. The vastness outside seemed to break open the tight space in my chest bit by bit.

The train stopped briefly in Cuenca. A few people got off, immediately swallowed up by the heat like ice cubes in hot coffee. Some got on, lugging bags and looking tired. The universal face of people who use trains. Then onward. The landscape became even more barren, even drier. But also calming. No distractions. Just sky and earth and the line between them, sharp as a razor. Minimalism before it became a lifestyle.

> **[SMS]** Cousin Dieter: 'Hey, can you recommend a good rate for supplementary dental insurance? LG Dieter'

After three and a half hours: Albacete.

I got off. The heat hit me like a sledgehammer. With a running start. From behind. It was early September, but here it felt as if someone had forgotten to tell summer that it was allowed to leave. Thirty degrees, maybe more. The air was dry and dusty and smelled of hot stone and burnt grass. My body reacted as it does to every crisis: with mild panic and an urgent desire for a cool drink. I squinted against the brightness, looking for shade, but found none. Shade had apparently resigned. Understandable. The station was small. Modern, but small. A few taxis were waiting outside, the drivers leaning against their cars, smoking, talking quietly to each other in a subdued tone that you only use when it's too hot for volume. Or when you're talking about someone who's just getting off the train and looks like the air conditioning has personally offended them. I took the first one.

'¿Adónde?' asked the driver. Where to? He was in his mid-fifties, with a moustache and a shirt with sweat stains under the armpits. The moustache looked like the 70s wanted it back.

I gave him the note with Nacho's address. He read it, smiled, shook his head. I didn't like that order.

'¿Vas a ver a Nacho?' You want to go to Nacho's?

'Sí.'

He laughed – a warm, deep laugh that came from the belly. 'Ah, el loco de las Vespas.' The madman with the Vespas. He started the car and lit a cigarette. 'Everyone knows him. Three years ago, he wanted to park a Vespa on the roof of his house. Like a monument, you know? The fire brigade had to come. They helped him in the end.' He shook his head, laughing, smoke billowing from his mouth. 'Nacho. Completamente loco. But good. Muy bueno.'

I nodded. Of course. I drove across Spain to buy a Vespa from a man who put scooters on roofs. That was the plan. That had always been the plan. Anything else would be boring.

We set off. Albacete was bigger than I had imagined. Not a sleepy little town, but a real city – wide streets, roundabouts with fountains in the middle, modern shopping centres made of glass and steel, glistening in the sun like the dreams of an architect who had read too many IKEA catalogues. But there were also old neighbourhoods. Narrow cobbled streets. Balconies with laundry hanging from them. Dilapidated houses with peeling plaster, next to which suddenly stood ultra-modern apartment blocks, as if someone had jumbled up different centuries and forgotten to sort them out. Like a history book bound by an intern.

After ten minutes, we turned onto a road on the outskirts of the city. Industrial area. Warehouses with faded company signs. Car repair shops. A scrap yard where gutted cars rusted away in the sun with the dignity of old warriors who had seen better days. And then, between two abandoned buildings that looked as if they were still standing only out of habit: an old house. And on the roof, a Vespa.

One storey. Whitewashed, but the plaster was flaking off in large flakes like skin after a sunburn. Small windows with closed wooden shutters. A heavy door made of dark wood that looked like it could withstand any storm. Or any tax office. A sign, hand-painted, half faded: 'Taller Nacho – Motos y Vespas'.

So this was the place. It looked like a cross between a car repair shop and the hideout of a Bond villain on a very limited budget.

'Aquí,' said the driver. Here. I paid and got out. He drove away, leaving behind a cloud of dust that slowly dissolved in the heat like a ghost. Or like my certainty that this was a sensible idea. I stood there. Alone. My heart was pounding – not fast, but hard, as if it were hammering against my ribs and asking: Are you sure? I wasn't sure. But I was here. That had to be enough.

I walked to the door. Knocked. The wood felt warm under my knuckles, almost hot. No answer. Knocked again, louder this time. Still nothing. Either no one was home, or Nacho had decided to ignore the knocking. Both were possible. Both were unsettling. I pressed the handle – the door swung open. Unlocked.

In Germany, I would have called the police. In Spain, I entered.

And stood still. My mouth opened slightly. My hand found the doorframe and clung to it.

The room was much larger than the façade suggested – someone had added an extension at the back, knocked through the walls and created space. And it was full. Not chaotically full, but curated full.

Museum full. Full like the basement of a collector who has stopped questioning his collection.

Full of Vespas.

About twenty of them, maybe more. Each one different. A mint green Primavera from the sixties that looked like a sweet. A black T5 with chrome mirrors that caught the light like little moons. A light blue 150 with the typical thick side panels that you saw in old Italian films – Fellini, Pasolini, the Dolce Vita years. A fire-red PX 200, polished to perfection, every screw gleaming.

And at the very back, lined up side by side like two queens on their thrones: two GS150s. One snow-white. One jet-black.

My heart skipped a beat. It wasn't a stumble of shock, but the recognition of a goal that I had only known from stories until then.

On the walls: tools, neatly hung – spanners sorted by size, screwdrivers in rows like soldiers. Shelves full of spare parts in labelled boxes. Posters of old Vespa advertisements – 'Vespa, la Dolce Vita', women in summer dresses, men with sunglasses, the world young and full of possibilities. A yellowed calendar from 1985. Framed photos of rallies: Vespas in the rain, in the snow, on mountain passes, going further and further.

The smell: engine oil, petrol, old leather, metal dust. The smell of passion. Of obsession. Of a life that revolves around one thing and is proud of it.

A temple for two-stroke gods.

'Are you the German?' I spun around in alarm.

A man was standing in the doorway to the back room. Small, wiry, in his late sixties. Grey hair, cut short in military style. Moustache, carefully trimmed. Blue dungarees, smeared with oil, faded at the knees. Arms crossed. Eyes that scrutinised me like a customs officer examining a suspicious suitcase.

'Yes,' I said. My voice sounded thinner than I intended. 'My name is Kai. Kai Ritter.'

He nodded. Said nothing. Long silence. His eyes wandered over me – shoes, jeans, shirt, face. Scrutinising. Suspicious. As if he were looking for a mistake or a reason to say no. I suddenly felt like a machine being put through its paces before being approved.

Then: 'Pedro told me your story.'

'Yes.'

'Tell me again.'

I took the photo out of my bag. It was warm from my body, the corners slightly creased. I held it out to him. He took it, held it up to the light coming through a dirty window. Looked at it for a long time. Turned it over, read the back with his fingers.

And I told him. Everything. With a lump in my throat.

'I'm not here to steal anything,' I said at the end. 'I'm here to honour my friend. To finish what he wanted to do. To feel what he felt. Just once.'

Nacho looked at me. For a long time. His face betrayed nothing – neither approval nor disapproval, just a kind of neutral alertness. He gave me back the photo.

'Wait here,' he said and disappeared into the back room.

I stood there. Alone among the Vespas. Fifteen minutes passed. Maybe twenty. Time felt different in here – slower, thicker, as if it were mixed with oil and flowing viscously through the air.

I walked around. I touched the Vespas carefully, as if they were sleeping animals that I didn't want to wake up. Each one told a story. One had a dent in the side panel – deeply jagged, as if it had negotiated with a wall and lost. Another had a worn seat, the leather cracked like old skin that had seen too much sun. A third was so immaculately restored that it looked as if it had never seen dust, let alone roads.

I stopped in front of the two elegant scooters.

The white one was a poem. Perfectly restored. The paintwork gleamed like freshly fallen snow in the sunlight. Not a scratch. Not a blemish. Every screw was in place as if God himself had tightened it. The chrome parts reflected my face, distorted and small.

The black one next to it was different.

Original condition. Patina on the paintwork – not dirty, but lived-in. Small rust spots on the chrome that looked like freckles. The seat had a small tear, revealing the light-coloured foam interior. A scratch ran across the leg shield, deep and honest, a scar with a history.

But that was exactly what made it beautiful. Real. Lived. It looked like someone who had seen a lot and was proud of it. The white one was for admiration, the black one was for survival.

Nacho came back. In his hands: two small glasses and a bottle with a handwritten label. 'Orujo' was written on it – Castilian firewater, the stuff Spanish grandfathers are made of.

'Sit down,' he said, pointing to two old folding chairs next to a workbench. The seats were worn, the metal rusted, but they held.

I sat down. He poured. Handed me a glass.

'Salud.'

'Salud.'

We drank. The orujo burned through my throat like liquid fire that someone had diluted with petrol. I coughed, my eyes watered. Nacho smiled – for the first time. A small smile, but genuine.

'Strong, isn't it?'

'Very.' My voice sounded hoarse, broken. 'I think my oesophagus has just been resealed.'

He leaned back, the chair squeaking. Looked at me. 'See those two over there?' He pointed to the scooters. 'The white one. That's my baby. My first love.'

'It's beautiful.'

'I bought it in 1973. In Valencia. From an old man who couldn't ride it anymore. His hands shook too much.' He took a sip, staring at the white Vespa as if he were looking at an old friend. 'It was broken. Rusty. The tank had a hole in it. Nobody wanted it. But I… I saw potential.'

'You restored it.'

'Yes. Every evening. After work. For two years.' His fingers drummed lightly on the glass. 'Every screw. Every part. I made it perfect again. More perfect than new.'

'And the black one?'

'I found that one five years ago. In a barn near Cuenca. Under tarpaulins. Covered in dust like a blanket.' He smiled, a melancholic smile. 'Original condition. Never restored. Some people said I should make it perfect too. Like the white one. But no.' He shook his head. 'It tells a story. The scratches. The rust. The broken mirror. That's its beauty. That's its truth.'

I nodded. 'I understand.'

'Do you?' His eyes narrowed. 'Many people say they understand. But they don't. They see a scooter. Metal and rubber. Transport. But I see…' He paused, searching for words in the air. 'I see memories. Life. The elegance of the real.'

'That's what Miguel saw too. Stories. First freedom. Adventure.'

'Exactly.' Nacho nodded slowly, several times. 'Your friend was quite wise.'

Nacho poured us another round. The second orujo burned less. Or maybe I had already become resistant, my throat numb. 'I started collecting when I was twenty,' he said quietly. 'My father had a Vespa. An old one. From the fifties. He died when I was eighteen. The Vespa was all I had left of him.'

'I'm sorry.'

'Don't be. He lived a good life. He died quickly. Heart attack. In his garden. Under his favourite tree.' Nacho smiled sadly, the corners of his mouth turned down. 'I kept the Vespa. Repaired it. Rode it every day. At some point… I wanted more. More Vespas. More stories.'

'How many do you have now?'

'Twenty-three.' He gestured across the room, his arms spread wide. 'Most of them are here. Some are at my house. Some I lend to friends.'

'You lend them out?'

'Yes. What's the point of having them if no one rides them?' He looked at me seriously, his eyes fixed on mine. 'A Vespa isn't a museum piece. It's a vehicle. It has to be ridden. Breathe. Live.'

I looked at the black Vespa. 'And that one? Do you ride it?'

'Sometimes. When I need to remember.' 'Remember what?'

'That life is short. That we should do what makes us happy. Not what others expect.' He emptied his glass and set it down hard on the workbench. 'I could have been a lawyer. My mother wanted that. Good money. Good life. But I wanted Vespas. So I opened this.' He gestured around him, to his empire. 'Forty years now. No regrets.'

We sat in silence for a while. The orujo warmed me from the inside, spreading like a little sun in my stomach. Outside, something metallic clattered in the wind.

'The white one,' Nacho said suddenly, 'I'll never sell that one. Never.'

My heart sank for a moment, fell like a stone. But then I looked at the black one. With the patina. The scratches. The history.

'But the black one…' He looked at me. For a long time. 'The black one… I might be able to sell that one.'

'Really?'

'Maybe. If you earn it.' 'How do I earn it?'

He got up, walked over to the black Vespa, ran his hand over the seat, lovingly, like you would stroke a dog's fur. 'See that?' He pointed to a deep scratch. 'That's from 1976. The original owner drove into a wall. Drunk. Idiota.' He laughed softly. 'But he survived. The Vespa survived. The scratch remained.'

I got up and walked over to him. I touched the scratch. The paint was rough under my fingers, like old tree bark.

'And that.' He pointed to a rust spot on the chrome. 'Fifty years of sun. Rain. Wind. Salt from the coast. That's life, you understand?'

'Yes. I understand.'

'Your friend Miguel. His Vespa. Was it perfect?'

'Far from it. It had dents. Scratches. But that's why he loved it.'

'Exactly.' Nacho nodded several times, as if confirming it to himself. 'This one is like his. Not perfect. But real. Honest.'

'It's beautiful.'

'Yes. It is.' He looked at me, straight into my eyes. 'I think I'll sell it to you.'

The world stood still for a moment. Even the wind outside seemed to stop. In the silence of the workshop, I could only hear a cricket through the window.

'Are you serious?'

'Yes.' He paused. 'Two thousand five hundred euros.'

I stared at him. 'That… that's… fair.'

'For this rare model in original condition? Very fair.' He tapped the tank, the metal sounding dull. 'It works. The engine is fine. The gearbox shifts. But…' He shrugged. 'It will need some love soon. Some maintenance. New cables, perhaps. An oil change. The usual.'

'But it works?'

'Yes. It runs. I rode it last month. No major problems.' He grinned properly for the first time. 'Well, minor problems, but nothing you'd die from.'

'That reassures me immensely.'

'I'm trying.' He winked. Then he became serious, the grin disappearing like the sun behind clouds. 'But there's one condition.'

'What condition?'

He took a sip of orujo. Slowly. As if he were arranging the words, forming them in his mouth before he spoke them.

'You have to drive it home. To Germany. Not in a lorry. Not on a trailer. Drive. All the way.'

I stared at him. My mouth opened, but no sound came out. I thought I had misheard him, but Nacho's gaze was as unyielding as the steel of the Vespa.

'You heard me.'

'But… I… I haven't ridden a moped or motorbike in twenty years!'

'I know. Pedro told me.'

'And… that's over 2,000 kilometres!'

'Two thousand six hundred, more or less,' he grinned.

'You looked it up?'

'Of course. Albacete to Kempten. Google Maps.' He grinned. 'You think I'm old and crazy, but I do my homework.'

'I've never ridden a Vespa with a manual gearbox before!'

'You'll learn.'

'Learn? Just like that?'

'Why not? Your friend Miguel learned. Somewhere on these roads. On his good old Vespa.' He tapped the seat, the leather crackling. 'If he could do it, so can you.'

I rubbed my face, feeling the sweat on my forehead. 'That's… that's crazy.'

'Maybe. But that's the deal.' He crossed his arms, the muscles under his dungarees tense. 'It needs to be ridden. Heard. Felt. Not transported like furniture. If you can't ride it, you don't deserve it. Are you a transportista or a vespista?'

'But what if I… I don't know… fall off? Or have an accident?'

'Then you fall. Crash. Learn.' He shrugged as if it were the most natural thing in the world. 'Life is dangerous. Riding a Vespa is dangerous. But staying at home in your safe little life and not living? That's more dangerous.'

I looked at my black dream. It stood there, waiting. It almost seemed to be looking at me, challenging me. A silent duel between my reason and this piece of metal.

'I… I need to think about it.'

'Okay. Think about it. Sleep on it.' Nacho smiled, but it wasn't a friendly smile. It was a smile that said, I know what you're going to decide. 'Come back tomorrow. Ten o'clock. If you say no…' He shrugged. 'Then it stays here. With me. Where it's safe.'

'And if I say yes?'

'Then I'll teach you. A day or two. What can break. How to drive it. How to shift gears. How not to die.' He grinned. 'More or less.'

'More or less?'

'I'm no magician either, amigo.'

I laughed. Nervously. Half hysterically. The laughter sounded strange to my ears. 'This is completely crazy.'

'Yes. But the best things in life are, aren't they?' He held out his hand to me. 'Sleep well, Alemán.'

I shook his hand. It was warm. Rough. Honest. Full of calluses.

'See you tomorrow.' 'Hasta mañana.'

I walked to the door. Turned around once more. Nacho was standing next to the black Vespa, his hand on the seat. Almost lovingly, like a father caressing his child.

'Nacho?'

'Yes?'

'Why are you doing this?'

He looked at me. For a long time. His eyes half-closed against the light coming through the dirty window.

‘Because your friend Miguel… he would have done the same. For you.’ He smiled. ‘And because I’m old. And bored. And I want to see if you have the cojones to do it.’

I laughed. ‘Thanks. No pressure.’

‘You’re welcome.’

I stepped outside. The door closed behind me.

Chapter 8 – Maria's Legacy and the Death Sentence on Two Wheels

[Soundtrack Shuffle: Queen – Don't Stop Me Now]

The heat hit me like a wall of fire. The sun was already low, casting long shadows, but it was still thirty degrees. Dust lay over everything like a blanket that couldn't be pulled away. I stood there. Breathed. I tried to sort out my thoughts, but they swirled around like leaves in the wind.

Two thousand six hundred kilometres. On an old Vespa. A Vespa with manual transmission. A Vespa I had never ridden before. My phone beeped. A message from Ricardo.

'Well, how did it go?'

I typed back, my fingers trembling slightly: 'He wants me to drive it home. 2,600 km. I think I'm going to die.' The reply came immediately: 'Perfect! When are you leaving? '

'You think that's funny?'

'Very funny. But also very Nacho. He did the same thing to me once. I had to drive a Lambretta from Madrid to Barcelona. In the pouring rain.'

'And you survived?'

'Obviously. I'm writing to you, aren't I?'

I put my phone away. Called a taxi. Drove to the Pensión La Mancha. Checked in. My room. A simple room. The narrow bed. The fan on the ceiling, which only circulated the hot air instead of cooling it, spinning pointlessly. I lay down. Stared at the ceiling, where shadows moved.

'Drive her home! All the way.'

It wasn't just a long journey. It was an impossible journey for me. Through Spain. Through France. Over the Alps, through valleys and over passes with names I couldn't pronounce. On a Vespa that was older than me.

'What if I can't do it?' 'What if the engine breaks down?' 'What if I have an accident?' 'What if...'

My phone beeped again. This time it was Pedro.

'Ricardo told me. Congratulations! You're officially a little crazy. I like that.'

I wrote back: 'I haven't said yes yet.'

'But you will. I know you will. Because you're not stupid enough to fly home empty-handed.'

'Maybe I am that stupid.'

'No. You're the other kind of stupid. The better kind. The kind that does crazy things because the alternative is worse.'

I put the phone away. 'The alternative is worse.' Back to Germany. Without a Vespa. Without adventure. Back to my job, my empty flat, my life that was no life, just existence. I sat up. Took the photo of Miguel out of my bag. He was standing there, grinning as if he had just heard the best joke in the world. 'What would you do, amigo?' I whispered into the empty room.

I knew the answer. Of course I knew it. Miguel would laugh. He would say, 'Are you stupid? Of course you're going! What's the worst that can happen? You die? So what? At least you'll die on a Vespa on an adventure and not at a desk!'

I laughed. Loudly. Alone in my room. The laughter echoed off the white walls. It was a liberating laugh that swept away the last remnants of my hesitation. 'You're right. You were always right.' I got up. Went to the window. Down in the square: a party. Music drifted up. Guitar, accordion, singing. Laughter. Life.

The Pensión La Mancha was located right on the village square in Albacete's old town. I had hardly noticed it earlier – too tired, too nervous, too caught up in my thoughts. But now I saw it: lights between the trees, hung like glowing fruit. Tables and chairs that someone had set up. People. Families with children. Old men with wine. A small band on a makeshift stage – guitar, accordion, singing that sounded like something between flamenco and folk. My stomach growled because I hadn't eaten all day.

I put on my shoes and went downstairs. The square was full of life. Voices, laughter and music mingled with the smell of grilled meat. Chorizo sizzling on the grill. Morcilla, the black blood sausage that I had never liked until I tried it in Spain. Cordero – lamb slowly roasted over coals, the fat dripping and sizzling. I found a free table at the edge and sat down. A waiter came over – young, maybe twenty, with an apron around his waist.

'¿Qué quieres?' he asked. What would you like? 'Vino tinto, por favor.' Red wine. '¿Y de comer?' And to eat?

I remembered Miguel. A conversation we had had years ago when he told me about his trip. He had told me about a speciality from La Mancha, a dish his grandmother used to make. Pisto Manchego. Braised vegetables with egg.

'¿Tienes Pisto Manchego?'

His face lit up as if I had said a password. '¡Sí! ¡El mejor!' The best! He disappeared. Came back with a glass of wine. Dark red, almost black, the glass fogged up. I drank. It tasted heavy and velvety, with the warmth of the south and a tart depth. Like Spain – like this country that I was just beginning to get to know.

The food arrived. A plate full of colours. Tomatoes, peppers, courgettes, aubergines – all stewed, soft, glistening in olive oil. On top: a fried egg, the yolk still runny. Next to it: bread, thickly sliced, the crust crispy. I ate. Slowly. Enjoyed every bite. It tasted of sun, of earth, of life that had been lived and not just endured.

Three old men were sitting at the next table. They drank wine, smoked, talked with the intensity that only old men who have seen everything and no longer have anything to prove can muster. One of them looked over at me.

'¿Eres turista?' he asked. Tourist? 'Sí. Alemán.' German.

'¡Ah!' All three of them laughed, a warm laugh. They drew me into conversation. About Germany – beer, cars, Merkel. About Spain – sun, siesta, Franco (in hushed tones). About football (of course), about life (inevitably). They told jokes that I didn't quite understand, the punchlines lost somewhere in a dialect I didn't know. My Spanish wasn't good enough. But I laughed anyway. The way they told them – with their hands, with their whole bodies, with faces that showed every emotion – was funny enough.

One asked, '¿Por qué estás aquí?' Why are you here? 'Vespa,' I said. 'Motovespa.' Their eyes lit up as if I had performed a magic trick. '¡Ah! ¡Nacho!' 'Yes. Nacho.'

They laughed. '¡El loco!' The madman! But it was meant affectionately. They told me about Nacho. How he had repaired Vespas as a young man, how he had competed in rallies, once even to London. Muy buena gente. How he had never sold a Vespa –

except to people who deserved it, who understood it, who knew that a Vespa was more than just metal and rubber.

The night dragged on. The band played. People danced – old couples spinning slowly, locked in an embrace as if they were the only two people in the world. Young couples dancing faster, laughing, stumbling. Children ran between the tables, chasing each other, squealing with delight, falling down, getting up again. I sat there, drank my wine, smiled. A genuine smile, from within.

Maybe it wasn't just about the Vespa. Maybe it was about living again. Feeling. Laughing. Being. Being here, in this moment, in this place, among these people I didn't know and who didn't know me, but who nevertheless welcomed me like an old friend. The Vespa was just the key, but the engine that drove me again was this community.

I lay on the bed and caught myself smiling. Not the press-optimistic grin of someone who claims everything is okay. But a genuine smile. From within. One that remained, even when no one was looking.

> **[WhatsApp]** House group: 'Who put the organic waste in the yellow bin? The refuse collectors left a yellow sticker!'

Around midnight, I went back to the guesthouse. The music was still echoing through the alleys, quieter now, but still there. I lay down in bed and listened through the open window: Guitar, singing, laughter, slowly fading like an echo. And I slept. Deeply and dreamlessly. For the second time that week.

The next day. 9:45 a.m. I stood in front of Nacho's workshop. Again. The sun was already burning as if someone had forgotten to adjust the thermostat. The sky was cloudless, a harsh, merciless blue. The air shimmered above the dusty ground. In my bag: the photo of Miguel. My passport. My credit card. And a feeling in my stomach that was somewhere between nausea and excitement, churning like laundry in a washing machine.

Today would be the day. Not whether I would get a Vespa. But whether I had the courage to ride it home. Whether I had the courage to live. I held my breath and knocked on the door. The door opened. Nacho stood there. Looked at me. Waited.

'Well?'

I took a breath. My fingers closed tighter around the passport in my bag, feeling its rough surface. 'Yes.'

'Yes?'

'Yes. I'll drive it home. The whole 2,600 kilometres.'

A grin spread across his face. Wide. Genuine. It made him look twenty years younger, transformed him. It was the grin of an accomplice. 'Excellent. Then we have a deal.' He held out his hand. I shook it. Firmly. And at that moment, I knew: my life would never be the same again.

'Come on,' said Nacho, pulling me into the workshop. 'We've got work to do. Today you learn. Tomorrow you start dying.' He laughed, a deep belly laugh. 'Just kidding. Maybe.'

'That's not funny.' 'Ahh – a little funny.'

He walked over to the black Motovespa and pulled the tarpaulin off with a theatrical gesture. It stood there. Waiting. Waiting for me. I felt the atmosphere change. Nacho's hand remained on the seat. Too long. Too still. I knew that moment. The moment before a serious announcement. The same moment my father always made before saying, 'We need to talk.' The moment when you know:

things are about to get emotional. And I've never been good at emotional.

'You know…' Nacho began.

Oh God. A 'you know.' That was never promising. 'You know' was the introduction to things like 'You know, your mother and I are getting divorced' or 'You know, the dog is dead.' I tried to put on a sympathetic face.

'You know,' he said quietly, 'that Vespa… it wasn't meant for you. Not for some German who shows up here dreaming of adventure.'

I was silent. Waited.

'It was for Maria.' His voice broke a little at the name. 'My wife. Married for thirty-four years. She died last winter. Cancer. Quickly. Too quickly.'

The workshop fell silent. Only the ticking of an old clock on the wall. 'I'm sorry,' I said quietly. He took a crumpled photo from the breast pocket of his dungarees. Showed it to me. A small woman with dark eyes, smiling at the camera. Next to her, a young Nacho. They were standing in front of a bar in Seville. Behind her: a fountain, orange trees.

'When I found this Vespa… at that moment I thought: This is Maria's Vespa. We'll ride it to Seville. Like we used to.' He laughed bitterly. 'But Maria? She thought Vespas were noisy. Uncomfortable. "Nacho," she said, "that's your thing. Not mine. I prefer to drive in a car. With air conditioning."'

I nodded. Said nothing. Sometimes silence was better.

'But in my head…' He tapped the tank. 'In my head, this was always Maria's Vespa. The Vespa we could have ridden. If she had wanted to. If we'd had time. She died in February. This Vespa stood here, under the tarpaulin. I couldn't look at it. It was for Maria. Even though Maria never sat on it. When Ricardo called and told me about you… about your friend who died… about this crazy idea of riding a Vespa to Germany… I thought: Maybe this is a sign. Maybe this Vespa is meant to go on a journey after all.'

He looked at me. Directly. His eyes moist, but steady. 'That's why I have one condition. You're going to ride it home. All the way. No shortcuts. No lorries. Maria couldn't live anymore. But this Vespa… it should live. For her. Do you understand?'

I nodded. Slowly. I understood now. 'I promise,' I said. 'I'll drive it. Every kilometre.'

'Good.' Nacho wiped his face. Put the photo back. 'Sorry. I'm getting old. Emotional.' 'It's okay.'

He took a deep breath. Tapped the Vespa. 'Right. Enough crying. We've got work to do.' I nodded. Tried to process the mood. My brain was racing: a Vespa for a woman who hated Vespas. A deal with a man who cried. Two thousand six hundred kilometres of rolling mourning. Life had a strange sense of sales contracts.

'Then we have a deal, Alemán.' 'Yes,' I said. 'A very special deal.'

'The best deals are always special.' He grinned. Almost the old Nacho again. 'Okay. Now I'll show you how to ride this Maria Memorial Vespa without crashing it into a wall. That would be embarrassing.'

'Very embarrassing.'

'Maria would be looking down from above and thinking: Typical. That's exactly why I didn't like Vespas.'

I laughed. Briefly. So did he. 'It's yours now. But first…' He took a helmet from a shelf. Old. Black. With scratches that looked like battle scars. 'You need this. You can't die without a helmet. That would just be stupid.'

I took the helmet. It smelled of old leather and adventure, of a thousand rides and a thousand stories. 'And now,' said Nacho, swinging himself onto another Vespa – a blue Primavera, dented but loved – 'let's go out. And I'll show you how not to kill yourself.'

'Fantastic.'

'Don't worry, Alemán.' He grinned, putting on his own helmet. 'It's easy. Throttle. Brake. Gear shift. Try not to crash. What could go wrong?'

'Everything. Everything could go wrong.' 'Well, that's the fun part!'

He started the Primavera. The engine roared – a high-pitched, singing two-stroke sound that sounded like a little threat to me. I looked at the black Vespa… my scooter. 'Okay, Miguel,' I whispered. 'If I survive this, I'll buy you a beer. In heaven. Or wherever you are.'

I put on my helmet and swung myself onto the Vespa. My hands were shaking slightly, but I smiled. Because strangely enough – completely unexpectedly, completely crazy – it felt right.

'Ready?' asked Nacho. 'Not at all.'

'Nobody is.' He grinned. 'That's why we're learning today. So,' said Nacho, 'today: theory. And practice. Lots of practice.'

'How much?' 'Until you don't fall over anymore.' 'That could take a while.'

'We have two days.' He tapped the Vespa, the metal sounding dull. 'That'll have to do.'

Chapter 9 – Flying Lessons for Storks

[Soundtrack Shuffle: Bee Gees – Stayin Alive]

The following day, ten o'clock, and I was standing in Nacho's workshop, which was more than just a workshop – it was a museum, a sanctuary, a place where old machines weren't just repaired, but treated with a devotion normally reserved for religious relics. Next to me stood the scooter, which at that moment looked less like a means of transport and more like a personal challenge from the universe to my physical and mental integrity – a two-stroke judgement on my hubris. In my hand I held a helmet that smelled of old leather and adventures I would definitely not survive.

'Come on,' said Nacho, pulling the Vespa out of the workshop and into the dusty courtyard with an ease that only people who have spent their lives working with machines possess. The courtyard stretched out behind the building like a small arena of failure, about the size of a tennis court, with dusty ground that looked as if no one had even thought of watering it for years. An old workbench against the wall, a few rusty barrels that had probably once contained oil, petrol or other liquids that were better left unidentified, and lots and lots of space to die.

'Okay,' said Nacho, patting the seat of the Vespa with the paternal affection of a man who had spent his entire life with these machines. 'Now you try it.'

'Now?' My voice sounded higher than intended, which, for a forty-three-year-old man who considered himself an adult, did not necessarily exude the confidence that the situation might have required. It was more like the squeak of a teenager about to take a surprise maths test.

'Do you want to wait until you're eighty?'

'I thought you'd show me the theory first,' I said, sounding like a schoolboy hoping that the maths exam might be postponed after all.

'Theory is for Germans who think too much.' He grinned, and it was the grin of a man who had seen a lot. 'You learn by doing. Or by falling. Both are good.'

'Both are good?'

'Falling teaches you faster.'

I realised at that moment that this was not a particularly reassuring educational philosophy, but I hadn't really expected Nacho to suddenly start showing me PowerPoint presentations on driving dynamics. So I just nodded and tried to look like I was ready for whatever was coming, even though my brain was already running through all kinds of scenarios, most of which ended with my untimely demise.

I put on the helmet, and it was too tight – much too tight – and my ears were pushed forward like a basset hound that had just learned there were no more treats. At least my head would remain intact in a fall, and considering the alternatives, that was some small consolation, even if my ears might never return to their original shape. I probably looked like an overripe olive on a toothpick.

'So,' said Nacho, beginning an introduction that was both detailed and alarmingly incomplete, 'this is the throttle,' he pointed to the right handle on the handlebars, 'you turn it, it goes.'

'Okay.' That sounded easy. Almost too easy.

'This is the front brake.' He pressed the lever on the right handlebar, and I heard a soft squeak that didn't sound particularly confidence-inspiring. 'Front. But important: only gently! Very gently!'

'Why?'

'Because the Vespa is light at the front. Heavy at the back. Engine at the back.' He pointed to the rear of the Vespa, where the engine sat like a small, vibrating metal heart. 'If you brake too hard at the front…' He made a movement with his hands that looked like someone doing an elegant somersault over the handlebars, except that in reality it would probably look much less elegant and much more painful. 'Somersault.'

'Got it. Gently at the front.' I tried to memorise this, but my brain was already busy imagining myself flying through the air. A flying German over Albacete – not an image for a tourism advert.

'Exactly. You brake eighty per cent at the back.' He pointed to a lever on the right side of the footboard that looked like something you would find in a World War II aeroplane. 'Foot brake. Right. That's your main brake. Rear. Strong. Front only for support. Very light.'

'Eighty percent rear, twenty percent front,' I repeated like a mantra that might save me from death.

'Exacto. And more importantly…' He raised a finger and his expression became serious, more serious than anything I had seen from him before. 'Left hand. ALWAYS on the clutch. Always!'

'Always?'

'Always. When riding. All the time. Finger on the clutch lever.' He demonstrated the position: left hand on the handlebars, index and middle fingers loosely on the lever, as if it were the most natural position in the world. 'If the engine seizes, you have to pull the clutch immediately. Immediately! Otherwise – disaster. Engine damage. Broken.'

I stared at him, and the realisation slowly began to dawn on me that I had gotten myself into something that was much more complicated than I had thought. 'The engine can just… seize?'

'Old Vespa. Two-stroke. Happens sometimes. Engine runs hot, piston seizes.' He patted the engine like the back of an old friend who occasionally falls over drunk. 'When that happens and you don't pull the clutch immediately – bang. Engine broken.'

'That's very reassuring.' My voice was flat, but I don't think Nacho heard the sarcasm, or he didn't care.

'That's why: always keep your hand on the clutch. Not just for changing gears. All the time.'

'That's a lot,' I said, and that was an understatement of the kind you make when you actually want to scream but social conventions prevent you from doing so.

'That's riding a Vespa.' He grinned again, and this time it was the grin of a man who knew he had just drawn someone into something from which there was no turning back. 'Welcome to the sixties, amigo.'

'Very funny.'

'I'm trying.' He pointed to the left handle. 'Manual transmission. You turn the handle: backwards for first gear, forwards for the rest.'

I raised my eyebrows. 'Clutch and shift with the same hand?'

'Sí. That's the tricky part,' Nacho grinned. 'Pull the clutch with your fingers while turning the handle with your wrist. It's an unfamiliar movement.'

I tested the resistance. 'It'll take some getting used to. My left foot is going to get pretty bored.'

He laughed. 'It'll be kicking into thin air every time. There are four gears. You know how to use a manual gearbox?'

'Sure. But the classic way, with my foot.' I pulled the lever and turned my wrist – it felt awkward, but the logic was simple. 'It's like the old Zündapp machines, isn't it?'

'Exactly.' He watched my hand. 'At first it feels impossible. Then it becomes automatic. Or you get used to driving through the whole of Spain in first gear.'

'It'll be fine,' I said, feeling my old mechanical instincts slowly returning. 'It's like riding a bike. You never forget, you just look a bit silly at first.'

'I forgot how to ride a bike once. I crashed into a tree last year.'

I looked at him, unsure if he was joking. 'How do you ride into a tree?'

'Long story. Involves a wasp, a phone and panic.'

I realised that this wasn't necessarily a story that strengthened my confidence in Nacho's driving skills, but I had come to understand that confidence was a relative category in this situation anyway.

'Okay,' Nacho said, laughing at his own story. 'No wasps today. Just a Vespa. Close enough, right?'

'Very funny.'

'I'm trying.' He patted me on the shoulder with a camaraderie that suggested we were both in this adventure now, whether I liked it or not. 'Now. You.'

I got on the Vespa, and the seat was narrow – much narrower than I had expected – and harder, and my legs dangled down on either side like those of a large, clumsy bird, and I felt like a stork on a scooter, inelegant and completely out of place. A stork with a helmet that was much too tight and a looming existential crisis.

'Feet on the ground,' Nacho said, as if he had to explain it to a child. 'OK. Now. Kick starter.'

'What?'

'The pedal. Right. You step on it. Engine starts.' He pointed to a heavy metal pedal that looked like it would kick back and break my shin if I even looked at it the wrong way.

'Just… step on it?'

'Yes. Firmly, but with feeling.'

Firmly and with feeling. It was an instruction that was both precise and completely useless, but I nodded anyway and put my right foot on the pedal, gathered momentum and stepped down with what I thought was appropriate force. And as if it sensed that the foot belonged to a complete beginner, it fought back. The kick starter kicked back and scraped against my shin with a bang. I realised immediately. Skin gave way. Blood appeared. It burned like hell. There'll probably be a scar. But the Vespa didn't make a sound.

'Harder! But not while sitting. Stand next to the Vespa and then control it nicely!'

I kicked again, harder this time, and the pedal gave way, the engine stuttered, made a noise that sounded like a dying animal, and then died.

'Again! A little gas!' My shin hurt.

'How do I accelerate when starting?' It was a reasonable question, I thought.

'Turn the throttle WHILE you're kicking. Feel the engine!' He said it as if 'feeling the engine' was a skill that everyone should intuitively possess.

I turned the throttle, kicked the starter again, and this time the engine started with a high-pitched, singing two-stroke sound that was both mechanical and strangely alive, and smoke came out of the exhaust – blue, thick smoke that smelled of burnt oil and nostalgia and definitely pollution, and the Vespa vibrated beneath me like a living creature, the whole thing shaking as if it had Parkinson's, the handlebars trembling in my hands, and it felt like I was sitting on an angry, vibrating insect that could decide to throw me off at any moment. My whole body was set into a frequency that made my teeth chatter.

'Good!' Nacho grinned broadly, his eyes shining with the enthusiasm of a man who saw his plan slowly taking shape. 'She's alive!'

'Okay,' Nacho said, now more serious, more focused. 'Now. Clutch. Pull.'

I pulled the left lever, and it felt heavier than I had expected, as if I had to work against something that didn't want to move.

'Good. Now. Left handle. Turn it back. First gear.'

I tried – really tried – pulling the clutch with my left hand and fingers, and at the same time I had to turn the handle backwards with my wrist, and my brain protested loudly against this unnatural movement, my hand did something that felt like I was trying to break my own arm, but then – a click, hard and metallic – first gear.

'Perfect! Now. Slowly… release the clutch. A little gas.'

I released the clutch, slowly, very slowly, as he had said, and the Vespa jerked once, spluttered, and the engine died with a sad little cough. Silence. The engine was off. The Vespa stood there like a silent indictment of my lack of skill.

'Shit,' I said quietly.

'No problem. Again.' Nacho didn't even sound disappointed, more like he had expected exactly that. His patience seemed to be made of the same sturdy steel as the Vespa.

I started the Vespa again – kick starter, swing, throttle – and the engine started, and I repeated the process: pull the clutch, turn the left handle back, first gear, and this time, because I had learned from my first mistake or because my survival instinct kicked in, I gave it more throttle, significantly more throttle, and the Vespa shot forward like a small black rocket that had suddenly come to life.

'WHOAAA!'

I clung to the handlebars with a desperation normally reserved for people falling out of aeroplanes, my fingers cramping around the grips, and then – because panic has a wonderful way of doing exactly the wrong thing – I accelerated even more, by accident, out of pure instinct, out of a survival reflex that was so fundamentally wrong that it was impressive. The Vespa continued to accelerate, the engine screeching in a tone that sounded like it was protesting – suddenly, unexpectedly, against all logic and physics that I thought I understood – the front wheel lifted off the ground. Too much throttle. Way too much!

A wheelie. A bloody wheelie. On a Vespa.

I hadn't been on a two-wheeler for twenty-five years, and now I was doing a wheelie on a fifty-seven-year-old Vespa in a dusty courtyard in Spain, and my brain was having trouble processing this information because it was simultaneously preoccupied with pure fear of death.

'NAAAACHOOOOOO!'

The front wheel was maybe thirty centimetres in the air – not much, objectively speaking, but it felt like three metres. I saw the sky, I saw the blue stretching above me like a friendly abyss, I saw my life flash before my eyes in a rapid succession of images – my childhood, my ex, my failed career, Miguel laughing somewhere in the afterlife – and I saw the accident report in the newspaper: 'German tourist dies in Vespa wheelie. Experts puzzle over how this was even possible.'

Panic. Pure, unadulterated panic. I reached for the front brake – the handbrake on the right, the one Nacho had told me to use gently – and pulled, hard, much too hard, with all the strength my cramped hand could muster. Mistake. Big mistake. Fundamental, potentially life-threatening mistake. Wheels don't brake in the air.

I let go of the throttle – finally, much too late, but at least I did – and the front wheel slammed down onto the ground with an impact that vibrated through the entire Vespa, hard, brutal, and the Vespa bucked like a stubborn horse that had just decided it didn't like me, and I slid forward on the seat, my knee crashing into the leg shield with a pain that was sharp and immediate.

'FOOT! FOOT BRAKE!' Nacho yelled, his voice cutting through my panic like a knife.

I stepped on the foot brake – on the right, the pedal on the footboard – the Vespa drifted to the right and I desperately tried to stabilise it. My hands on the handlebars, my left foot in the air, it skidded forward uncontrollably. Somehow, by some miracle or pure luck, I managed to catch myself, with the Vespa almost lying on its side. The Vespa was standing. I was standing. The engine had stalled. My knuckles ached from the impact.

> **[Notification]** Amazon: 'Your subscription delivery of Deluxe Extra Soft 4-Ply Toilet Paper has been delivered.'

The scooter seemed unimpressed by my near-death experience. I was breathing heavily, gasping for air, my heart racing as if I had just run a marathon, my hands shaking on the handlebars, and sweat running down my forehead under the helmet that was too tight and was pressing on my ears.

'That was…' I gasped, trying to find words for what had just happened, but my brain wasn't working properly. 'That was…'

'Interesting!' Nacho exclaimed, clapping his hands like an enthusiastic spectator at a circus. 'Very interesting!'

'Interesting? I ALMOST DIED!' My voice was higher than normal, almost hysterical.

'But you're not! That's something!' He grinned, and it was the grin of a man who was having the best entertainment of his day.

'I did a WHEELIE! On a VESPA!' I almost shouted, and I didn't know if I was angry or proud or just shocked.

'Yes! Very impressive for the first time!' He came closer, still grinning. 'Most people just fall. You fly!'

'I used the wrong brake!' I tried to understand what had just happened.

'That too. Front brake on a wheelie. Very creative. Very suicidal.' He laughed, and it was a genuine laugh, without malice, but also without much sympathy. 'But you caught yourself! That's what matters!'

'What matters?' I repeated incredulously. 'The important thing is that I'm not dead!'

'Exactly! That's what I'm saying!' He patted me on the shoulder, and I almost fell off the Vespa. 'Again. This time, less throttle. Much less.'

'Again?'

'Of course again. You think you're done learning?' He laughed again. 'That was just the beginning, amigo.'

Chapter 10 – Two Hours of Failure

[Soundtrack Shuffle: Survivor – Eye of the Tiger]

And so I spent the next two hours learning how to ride a Vespa without dying – although 'learning' was perhaps the wrong word; it was more a process of repeated failure with occasional moments of non-disaster – I stalled the engine (seven times), I slipped off the footrests when starting off (five times), I drove into an oil drum (once, but it was slow), I managed to shift into second gear (three times), I managed to drive in a straight line (twice for about twenty metres each time), and in the end, when the sun was already low and my arms were shaking and my brain felt like mush, I managed to drive the Vespa once around the entire courtyard – slowly, shakily, but without a wheelie, without a fall, without drama.

'Good!' said Nacho, and this time he actually sounded satisfied. 'You're learning. Very slowly. But you're learning.' He grinned.

'I'm completely exhausted,' I gasped and got off the Vespa, my legs feeling like jelly.

'That's normal. The first lesson is always hard.' He took off my helmet, and I felt the air rush to my compressed ears. 'Tomorrow again. Eight o'clock.'

'Tomorrow?' I looked at him as if he had suggested we climb Mount Everest tomorrow.

'Yes. Tomorrow. And the day after tomorrow. You need practice. Lots of practice.' He walked to the workshop and turned around. 'You're leaving in three days. To Barcelona. That's hundreds of kilometres. Open country roads. Traffic.'

'I know,' I said, and the reality of what I was planning hit me like a cold shower. Hundreds of kilometres suddenly sounded like an expedition to Mars.

'You have to be ready. The Vespa is old. You are inexperienced. A very bad combination.' He looked at me seriously. 'But I think you can do it.'

'Really?'

'Well, maybe. Fifty percent.' He grinned again. 'But that's better than nothing.'

'Very encouraging.'

'I'm a realist, not an optimist.' He went inside and called back over his shoulder: 'Tomorrow. Eight o'clock. Be on time!'

I stood there in the courtyard, looking at the Vespa, which was now standing still, its engine off, and I thought: What have I done? I had agreed to ride two thousand six hundred kilometres on a machine I couldn't control, through countries I hardly knew, to a destination that only existed because a friend had died and left me his crazy inheritance, and I had just proven that I couldn't even ride a hundred metres without nearly dying.

'This is madness,' I muttered. But then I thought about the option of simply flying back to Germany, without the Vespa, without the adventure, back to my job, my empty flat, my life that was no life at all, just a slow wait for something that would never come. 'No,' I whispered, looking at the Vespa, at its black metal gleaming in the evening sun. 'I'd rather die on a Vespa in Spain than go on living like this.'

It sounded dramatic, exaggerated, maybe even a little ridiculous, but at that moment, with my hands shaking and my heart racing, it felt right. I walked back to the guesthouse, my legs feeling like rubber, as if someone had taken out the bones and replaced them with soft material not meant to support a human body, and my head was full of images – the front wheel lifting, the sky opening up in front of me, Nacho's laughter – and I muttered to myself: 'I did a wheelie on a Vespa, how is that even possible?'

> **[Email]** Gym: 'We haven't seen you in a long time! Come by and work out your back muscles. Tomorrow only: a protein shake on the house.'

I googled it later, lying in bed, with my mobile phone, which glowed faintly in the darkness, and found out that it is apparently possible to do a wheelie on a Vespa and that there are even people who set strange world records for it. If the inventors had wanted to, they could have left out the front wheel.

Great – so I was a suicidal idiot with a natural talent for surviving wheelies without a clue. But I didn't feel the urge to set a record.

At the guesthouse, I went straight to my room, lay down on the bed, stared at the ceiling, which was white and had cracks that looked like a map of places I would never visit, and I thought: What have I done? I had agreed to ride two thousand six hundred kilometres on a Vespa I couldn't control, through Spain, through France, through Italy, maybe over the Alps, alone, clueless, inexperienced, with nothing but the vague hope that Miguel was laughing somewhere up there and watching over me.

'This is crazy,' I whispered again. But then I thought of the alternative – back to Germany, without the Vespa, without the adventure, back to my empty flat, to my job that had no meaning, to a life that felt like waiting for death, only slower and more comfortable.

My phone beeped – a message, bright and intrusive in the darkness – and I looked at the screen: Ricardo.

'Pedro told me you did a wheelie. A WHEELIE! You Germans always have to exaggerate, huh?! ●●●'

I wrote back, my fingers tapping wearily on the display: 'It was an accident.' The reply came immediately: 'The best accidents are the ones you survive. Congratulations! You are now officially a Vespa wheelie rider.' 'I almost died.' 'That's how you know you're alive, amigo.'

I put the phone away, smiled despite everything – despite the exhaustion, despite the fear, despite the fact that I had to get back on that damn Vespa tomorrow – and I thought: Maybe he's right, maybe that's what it's all about, feeling alive, being afraid, trembling, sweating, but still carrying on.

I took the photo of Miguel out of my bag. 'Miguel,' I said quietly to the photo, as if he could hear me, 'if you're up there – and I'm pretty sure you are up there and you're laughing your head off – then protect me, okay? I need all the help I can get.' Or at least a little less gravity when starting off. The photo didn't answer, of course, but it still felt better to have said it.

I got up, went to the window, looked down at the small square in front of the guesthouse, where children were playing football in the last light of day, where a woman was hanging laundry on a balcony, where an old man was sitting on a bench, smoking and watching the world with the patience of someone who understood that there was no reason to hurry. Normal life, I thought. Quiet life. Safe life.

'But not my life,' I whispered. My life – at least for the next few days, maybe for the next few weeks – would be loud, dangerous, crazy, and that was exactly what I needed, exactly what I wanted, even though part of me still wanted to scream: What the hell are you doing?

It was evening, and I was sitting alone in a small restaurant in the old town – a place with whitewashed walls that glowed warmly in the light of the few light bulbs, with low ceilings lined with wooden beams, darkened by age, with a few tables that looked as if they had seen generations of guests – and on the wall hung a faded poster of a bullfight next to a crucifix, Spain summed up in two images: violence and faith, death and redemption.

I ordered wine – red wine from the region, as the waitress said, and she spoke so fast that I only understood half of what she said, but I nodded anyway – and food, something with lamb, which sounded good, and when it arrived – lamb chops, grilled, with rosemary and garlic, the meat pink and tender, served with fried potatoes and a salad consisting mainly of tomatoes and olive oil – it smelled so incredible that I forgot everything else for a moment. It was the taste of surrendering to one's own reason.

I ate slowly, savouring every bite, letting the meat melt on my tongue, drinking the wine, which was heavy and fruity and tasted of summer, and thought: Tomorrow training starts again, maybe again the day after tomorrow – then I'll set off for Barcelona, hundreds of kilometres on foreign roads, on a Vespa I can barely control, and the fear was there, big and loud and unyielding, but behind it, very quietly, almost too quietly to hear, there was something else: anticipation.

My phone rang – Isabel, the name lit up on the display – I answered.

'Hola, Kai.' 'Isabel! Hi!' I was happy to hear her voice, warm and familiar. 'Hi! You've got the Vespa?' 'Yes. I've got it. It's in Nacho's workshop.' 'How are you going to get it home?' She sounded half concerned, half amused. 'I have to ride it all the way home. That is, if I don't die first.'

She laughed, and it was a warm laugh that reminded me of Miguel. 'Miguel would be proud of you.' 'Miguel would laugh himself to death over my wheelie today.' 'A wheelie? Oh dear – yes, he would like that! Don't kill yourself!' I heard her smile. 'But he would be proud. You're doing what he couldn't do. You're bringing the Vespa home.' 'Unfortunately, he had to sell his. In Barcelona.' 'Sí. But his heart remained with her. Always.' She paused, and I heard her breathing. 'Take care of yourself, hijo. And when you're back… come by. We'll have a drink. To Miguel.' 'I will. I promise.' 'Vaya con Dios, Kai.' Go with God. 'Thank you, Isabel.'

I hung up, finished my wine, ordered another, and when it arrived, I raised the glass to the empty air of the restaurant, to no one and to everyone, and whispered, 'To you, Miguel, this is for you, everything.'

Back at the guesthouse, I lay in bed, again, as I had every night since my arrival, and above me the fan turned slowly, almost sluggishly, the ceiling was white with cracks, the window was open, and outside there was silence, only now and then a car passing by, a dog barking, life going on, no matter what happened. I couldn't sleep – my head was too full of thoughts, images, fears and hopes and the strange mixture of both – and I whispered into the darkness: 'Two thousand six hundred kilometres. What do I need?'

> **[Notification]** Payback: 'Get 10 times the points on your next purchase of "pretzel rolls and organic apples"!'

I made a mental list, like a man trying to control something that had long since spiralled out of control:

Clothes (I have some, not much, but enough) Rain gear (I don't have any, should buy some) Tools (I don't have any either, no idea what I need) Spare parts (even less idea) A map (or Google Maps, if the internet cooperates, which it probably won't) Courage (definitely not enough, maybe stubbornness will suffice) Luck (a lot, more than a person normally has)

'I'm so screwed,' I whispered, and that wasn't even an exaggeration, it was just the truth, naked and terrifying. But then I thought of Nacho, Ricardo, Pedro, the Vespa Club, all these people I hardly knew, but who helped me, who believed in me for reasons I didn't understand.

'They're helping me. They promised.' And they would help, I knew that, because that's what Vespa people do, they help, they share, they understand that it's not about the machine, but about something else, something bigger, something to do with community and feeling alive. I closed my eyes, tried to sleep, and whispered: 'Tomorrow, tomorrow I'll learn to ride, to ride properly, without wheelies, without near-falls, just… riding.'

It sounded easier than it was, and I knew that, but I would manage it somehow, I had to manage it, because the alternative – flying home and knowing for the rest of my life that I hadn't even tried – wasn't a real option.

'Mi libertad empieza aquí,' I whispered into the darkness of the room, into the silence of the night, and the words sounded strange in my mouth, but also right. My freedom begins here. And this time – for the first time in a long time – I meant it. No matter how many wheelies might still come.

Chapter 11 – The Sorcerer's Apprentice

[Soundtrack Shuffle: Beastie Boys – Fight for Your Right]

Nacho led me into the workshop. The Vespa stood under a lamp like a patient on an operating table, ready for a diagnosis that would change my life. The cold light of the fluorescent tubes reflected off the paintwork, lending the scene a surgical feel.

'This,' said Nacho, pointing to the Vespa, 'is a 1967 Motovespa GS150. Spanish production. Original engine. 150 cubic centimetres.' 'Okay.' 'Manual transmission. Four gears. No electric starter. Just the kick starter.'

He removed the right side cover as if lifting a curtain. 'Here. The engine.'

I looked inside. What I saw was something I only knew from YouTube videos, where everything had seemed so much simpler: a tangle of fan blades, cables, metal and the carburettor. It looked like a mechanical puzzle for which I lacked the instruction manual.

'Here,' he pulled out a cable, 'the spark plug. You have to check it. Clean it. Maybe replace it.' 'How often?' 'When it stops firing.' He grinned, an expression somewhere between wisdom and schadenfreude. 'You'll notice when the engine won't start.' 'Very helpful. Should I also check if the tyre is flat when I'm riding on the rim?'

'Here: clutch cable, throttle cable.' He pointed to two thin steel cables at the top and bottom of the engine. 'If they break… you're stuck.' 'And then?' 'Then you repair it. Or you push.' 'How far is the nearest Vespa shop from… let's say… the middle of nowhere?' 'Far.'

Fantastic. My inner optimist was already packing his bags and looking for the nearest emergency exit. Nacho took an old, small tool roll off the shelf. Black, worn, with patches sewn on from Vespa rallies that told of better weather and more experienced riders.

'This is for you. On-board tools.' He opened it with a ceremonious gesture. Inside: spanners, screwdrivers, a spare spark plug in a plastic box, two spare cable pulls, wire, cable ties and a roll of adhesive tape. The survival kit for the modern Don Quixote on two wheels.

'For emergencies,' said Nacho. 'How many emergencies do you expect?' 'Over 2,600 kilometres?' He thought about it, staring at the ceiling. 'Three. Maybe four.' 'That's reassuring.' 'Could be worse. Could be ten.'

I stared at the tools. No idea how to change a spark plug. Or a cable. 'I understand half of it,' I said quietly. Nacho put a hand on my shoulder. 'You'll learn quickly on the road.' 'Really?' 'Yes. Because you have to.' He winked. 'The best motivation.'

Fear of death and time pressure – the classic pedagogical miracle weapons. The yard behind the workshop. The scooter. Me. Nacho with his arms crossed.

'Now we're going,' said Nacho. 'Right.' 'I rode yesterday.' 'That wasn't riding. That was flying. And almost dying.' He grinned. 'Today: riding. Carefully. Controlled. Not like yesterday.' 'Thanks for reminding me.' 'You're welcome.'

I got on. Put on my helmet. Started the Vespa – this time on the first try. A small, mechanical triumph that felt like a knighthood.

'Good,' said Nacho. 'Now: clutch, first gear, gently accelerate, start driving. Slowly.'

I did everything in slow motion. Clutch. Reach back – first gear. Throttle. Release the clutch. The engine jerked briefly, spluttered and died. 'More throttle when starting,' said Nacho. 'It needs more.'

I started again. This time with more momentum. The Vespa shot forward like a frightened animal. 'Less! Not so much!' I let go of the handle. The machine rolled. Slowly. I kept my balance and drove a first cautious lap around the yard.

'Perfect! Now second gear! Shift!' I tried. Pull the clutch – with my fingers. Turn the handle forward – with my wrist. It stuck. At the same time. KRRRRCH. An ugly, metallic sound like a circular saw chopping up cutlery for dinner. My heart contracted painfully at this scream from the gearbox.

Nacho grimaced. 'Clutch! Pull it all the way!' 'I am pulling it!' 'All the way!' I pulled harder until the metal of the lever hit the handle. I tried to shift gears again. This time: a soft click.

'Better! Now accelerate! Release the clutch!' Second gear. The Vespa picked up speed. I drove the next lap. Then the next. 'Third gear!' Clutch, shift, accelerate. This time it worked smoothly. 'Yes! Good! Keep going!'

I drove. Lap after lap. Shifted up, shifted down. Braked – with the foot brake, as I had learned. I was slowly becoming more familiar with the machine. The vibration, the noise, the way it reacted to every nuance of my uncertainty. It was a conversation between me and the old piece of metal, and gradually we understood each other.

After two hours, I got off. Sweat was running down my back. My hands were shaking from gripping so tightly. My legs felt like jelly, my neck was completely tense. But: 'I did it. I rode.'

Nacho nodded. 'Better. Much better.' 'Yes?' 'You didn't fall over. You shifted gears. You braked.' He patted me on the shoulder. 'Tomorrow we'll ride on the road.'

I stared at him. 'The road?' 'Yes. Real traffic. Real test.' 'I've only been riding for two hours!' 'Exactly. That's why we'll practise more tomorrow. Much more.' He grinned. 'Today at lunchtime: break. Lunch. Then we'll continue.'

[Facebook]: 'Reminder: Eight years ago, you were at Oktoberfest with Sabine Meier. Want to share memories?'

Lunch break.

Nacho invited me to lunch. A small restaurant in the old town: 'Casa Pepe' – hand-painted sign, checkered tablecloths, tiles from the seventies. Nacho ordered the menú del día. When the waitress came, I remembered Miguel's words.

'Nacho, I'd like Criadillas de Toro,' I said firmly. 'Miguel always told me, "Kai, if you ever visit the real, authentic Spain, you have to try Criadillas. Otherwise, you haven't really been there." He always grinned knowingly when he said that.'

Nacho paused briefly, a fork in the air. A strange sparkle came into his eyes. 'Ah, Criadillas… Miguel, that old rascal. He knew what was good. A speciality for real men, amigo.' He ordered them for me with a curt nod to the waitress, who also suppressed a suspicious twitch around the corners of her mouth.

The starter was gazpacho – cold tomato soup, refreshing after the morning's exertions. Then the waitress served a plate of golden brown, sliced pieces. They looked like small schnitzels and smelled seductively of garlic.

'Not bad at all,' I remarked after the first few bites. The consistency was tender, almost like fine veal. 'That was really tasty. Miguel was right.' I chewed with relish and took a sip of the heavy red wine. 'But tell me, Nacho… what exactly is this part of the bull? Loin?'

Nacho leaned back slowly and looked at me with a mixture of pity and mischievous delight. 'Well, Kai… a bull has many muscles, but it also has things that make it… very masculine.'

I stopped chewing. 'Things that make it masculine?' 'The testicles, Kai. You're eating the balls of a fighting bull.'

Time seemed to stand still. The piece of meat in my mouth suddenly felt huge. Nacho let out a throaty laugh that shook the entire restaurant. 'Your face! Holy Mother of God, your face! I wish Miguel could see this!'

I swallowed hard and stared at my plate. The thought was horrifying, but then I saw Miguel's face in my mind's eye – that mischievous grin. I knew that if I stopped now, he would have won. So I speared the next piece. 'That bloody… he tricked me from beyond the grave,' I forced out. I chewed, fought against the psychological resistance and swallowed. Piece by piece. I ate the whole plate while Nacho almost fell off his chair laughing.

'A classic Miguel joke,' Nacho gasped, wiping a tear from the corner of his eye. 'Respect, Kai. You ate them all. Welcome to Spain. Now you have courage in your stomach – or at least what used to be responsible for it in the bull.'

We both laughed until we were breathless. Then Nacho calmed down again. 'Tell me about your first Vespa,' I finally said, enjoying the lamb – a sure reward – and the patatas panaderas.

Nacho leaned back and took a sip of wine. 'I was seventeen. My father had just died.' He paused. 'I had saved money. From work.

And I bought an old Vespa. A 125. Green. Rusty.' 'Did it work?' 'Barely.' He laughed. 'But I repaired it. Every evening. Sometimes all night. And then… I drove off.' 'Where to?' 'Everywhere. To the sea. To the mountains. To girls.' He grinned. 'The Vespa changed my life. It set me free.'

I nodded. 'That's what Miguel said too.' 'Your friend… he understood.' Nacho looked at me seriously. 'Not everyone understands. Some people just see a scooter. But we…' He pointed between us. 'We see more.' A smile connected us – a secret alliance of those who found a soul in metal.

9 o'clock. 'Today,' said Nacho, 'we're going to the next village.' 'How far?' 'Twenty kilometres. There and back.' My stomach tightened. 'Real traffic. Real roads.' 'Yes.' 'What if I have an accident?' 'You won't. I'll be with you.' He swung himself onto his own Vespa – a blue PX 200 with chrome mirrors and a sticker that read: 'Vespa Club Albacete'. 'Follow me. Not too fast. Not too slow.' 'How fast is right?' 'You'll know.'

Very helpful. Typical Nacho pedagogy. I started the Vespa. First gear. Off we went. Nacho rode ahead, I followed behind. We left Albacete behind us. The city receded into the distance. Ahead of us lay the Castilian plateau. Endless. Flat. Yellow. The sky was huge. Not a cloud in sight. Just blue and more blue. To the left and right: fields, olive groves in the distance, isolated farmhouses. The road stretched straight ahead as if someone had drawn a line through the landscape with a ruler.

I was tense at first. My hands gripped the handlebars tightly, my shoulders hunched. Fear sweat everywhere. Every car that rushed past made me flinch. But after five kilometres… I relaxed. Slowly. My shoulders dropped, my hands loosened. I felt the wind, warm and dry. It tugged at my shirt, at my helmet. I felt the sun, hot on my back. I felt the Vespa beneath me: the vibration, the hum of the engine, the way it glided along the road. 'Maybe I can do this after all,' I thought. A tentative spark of hope flared up inside me.

A lorry overtook us. Big. Loud. It rushed past me, just a metre away. The draught pulled at me, the Vespa wobbled. I held on tight and stayed in my lane. The lorry was gone. I relaxed. Nacho turned around: thumbs up. I grinned under my helmet. I was no longer a tourist; I was a road user.

The village was small. Maybe a hundred houses, a church, a square with trees, a bar. We parked the Vespas, got off and went into the bar. 'Two coffees,' said Nacho. 'Café con leche.' We sat down at a table outside. I plopped down on the chair like a boxer between rounds. The coffee arrived: hot, milky, sweet. 'How are you feeling?' Nacho asked. I thought about it. 'Alive,' I finally said. Nacho smiled. 'Good. That's the point.'

The return journey was easier. I drove more confidently, changed gears more smoothly. I even enjoyed the landscape – the vastness, the light, the silence. 'I'm in the process of achieving something I never thought possible,' I thought. The fear was still there, but now it was just sitting in the back seat instead of driving.

Back at the workshop. Nacho quickly checked the scooter: oil, brakes, spark plug, tyres. Everything was fine. 'You're ready,' he said. 'Really?' 'No.' He laughed. 'But you're ready enough.' 'That's not very convincing.' 'You'll learn the rest along the way. Trust the Vespa. Trust yourself.'

He went into the workshop and came back with a folded piece of paper: addresses of Vespa repair shops in Spain and France. 'If you have any problems, call them. Say you're a friend of Nacho's.' 'Thanks.' 'And here.' He gave me a spare spark plug and a cable. 'You'll need them. Trust me.' 'So much trust.' 'I'm a realist.'

He took a handwritten document out of a drawer. In Spanish: sales contract. I signed it, and so did he. I took out my cash, counted out 2,500 euros and gave it to him. The notes felt heavy, like a ticket to another life.

'It's yours now.' He handed me the papers: chassis number, bill of sale, old Spanish registration. 'Take care of it.' 'I will. I promise.' He let me drive the Vespa to Germany on his papers and his insurance. An incredible amount of trust that left me almost speechless.

Nacho hugged me tightly. Almost too tightly. 'Your friend Miguel,' he said quietly, 'he would be proud.' 'Thank you. For everything. For your trust.' 'I trust the Vespa. It will take you home.' He looked me in the eyes. 'Listen to her. She will tell you what she needs.' 'I will.' 'One more thing.' Nacho smiled. 'Will you give her a name?'

I thought about it. About Miguel. About his family. About his daughter. 'Lola,' I said. 'After Miguel's daughter.' Nacho nodded. 'Beautiful name. She'll protect you.' A part of Miguel would be travelling with me.

My last night in Albacete. I sat on my bed in the guesthouse. The window was open. Tomorrow the journey would begin. 2,600 kilometres. Alone. The fear was there – big and loud. But so was the anticipation. 'I can do this. I want this.'

I picked up my phone and dialled Isabel's number. She answered after two rings. 'Hello?' 'Isabel? It's me, Kai.' '¡Hijo! Where are you?' 'In Albacete. I bought the Vespa.' Silence. Then crying. 'Miguel would be so happy.' 'I know. I'm riding it home. To honour him.' 'Be careful, Kai. Please.' 'I will. I promise.' I paused. 'I named her Lola. After your daughter.' More tears on the other end. 'Thank you. Thank you.' It was a promise to the living and the dead alike. What could go wrong, right?!

We talked for a while about Miguel, the journey and life. When I hung up, I felt calmer. I lay down. Through the open window, I heard the crickets, the wind and the voices in the village square. 'Tomorrow. Tomorrow it begins.' 'Tomorrow my journey begins.' I closed my eyes, smiled and fell asleep. For the first time in many months, the morning didn't feel like a threat. Okay, maybe a little.

Chapter 12 – One Hundred and Twenty Millilitres for a Hallelujah

[Soundtrack Shuffle: Ennio Morricone – The Good, The Bad and The Ugly (Main Theme)]

The next morning, shortly after eight o'clock. The sun was already high enough to bathe the road in front of Nacho's workshop in a harsh, dusty light. The air smelled of dry grass, hot asphalt and two-stroke oil – a mixture that would work its way deeper into my clothes over the coming weeks than any detergent advert had ever promised.

I stood in front of the workshop with my rucksack on my back. Passport, wallet, phone in my pockets. Lola stood in front of me, black and shiny in the morning sun. She was ready. I wasn't. The workshop door creaked. Nacho came out, a thermos flask in one hand, a small green bottle in the other. He held it up like a priest holding a communion wafer.

'This,' he said, his voice taking on that patient tone teachers have just before they explain something that could save your life, 'is two-stroke oil. For the mixture.' 'Mixture?' The word sounded harmless. Almost cute. '1:50.' He tapped the measuring scale on the bottle. 'That means 50 parts petrol to 1 part oil. For three litres of petrol, you need 60 millilitres of oil. Understood?'

I nodded. My fingers closed around the bottle. It was warm from his hand, and for a moment I felt the responsibility that lay in this little green thing – as if I were holding not just oil, but the fate of an engine.

'And don't forget,' he added, his voice dropping a notch. 'No oil in the petrol, no engine. After ten, twenty kilometres – piston seizure.

Game over.' He made a motion with his fist like an upward swing and made a sound I will probably never forget: 'Kkkkkrrrrhhhhh!'

The word piston seizure sounded like a Spanish death sentence. Death by friction. It wasn't romantic. He handed me the helmet. I took it. It was heavier than I had expected, and the leather inside was worn smooth, polished by decades of other heads having been inside it. Maybe they had crazy or stupid ideas like me. Who knows! I gave it a quick sniff. Four decades of other people's sweat, preserved in leather. Wonderful.

'It got me through forty years,' said Nacho. 'Now it's yours.' What do you say to something like that? 'Thanks for four decades of other people's sweat' seemed inappropriate. I nodded my thanks.

He patted Lola's seat twice – as if patting a faithful horse goodbye. '180 kilometres today. To Gandia. That's nothing. You can do it.' 180 kilometres. The number felt like a mountain viewed from below – large, steep, possible and impossible at the same time. He hugged me. Briefly, firmly, in that Spanish way that is both brutal and tender. 'Take care of her,' he said. A pause. 'And yourself.'

I put on my helmet. The world narrowed to the field of vision of the visor. I started Lola – the kick starter resisted briefly, then gave way, and the engine roared to life with a deep, throaty rattle. 'Thank you,' I said. For everything. 'Good luck, amigo.'

I opened the throttle. The vibration travelled through my hands, my arms, my whole body. The first few metres felt less like 'freedom' and more like a terribly slow fall into the unknown. The road lay ahead of me – wide, empty, flooded with morning sun. Albacete glided past me: low houses with peeling facades, closed shops, a stray dog watching me with the disinterested gaze of a creature that has seen many tourists come and go.

I was alone. With a Vespa that was older than most of my colleagues. And more than two thousand kilometres between me and – what exactly? Kempten? Safety? Or just the next excuse for a real life? The first thirty kilometres ate away at me like a creeping poison. Not because anything happened. But because anything could happen.

I was driving at 40 km/h. Maximum 45. Lola could go faster – much faster. Nacho had explained to me that in good conditions she could reach up to 90 km/h, a figure that seemed as unrealistic to me at that moment as a trip to the moon. My hands clenched the handlebars with such force that my knuckles turned white. My shoulders hunched as if trying to pull my head back into my body like a turtle into its shell.

The landscape around me was vast and empty – endless fields, low stone walls, scattered olive trees shimmering in the heat. The sky was so blue it almost hurt, a kind of blue I didn't know from Germany. Every sound was a disaster waiting to happen. A crack somewhere beneath me? The engine dies. Immediately. Irrevocably. A squeak from the brakes? Failure. Guaranteed. I could already see myself in a side note: 'German tourist crashes into stone wall at 45 km/h – experts puzzle over his plans.'

Behind me: a car. I first saw it in the rear-view mirror – a silver Seat Leon. It was getting closer. Closer and closer. So close that I could see the wrinkles on the driver's forehead, deep, angry furrows. Then: the horn. Not short. Not polite. But a long, aggressive blast of noise that said, 'You idiot, get off my road.'

He overtook. The driver – in his mid-forties, sunglasses, moustache like a memorial to the 70s – turned his head. Said something. I didn't hear it, but I saw his lips, the movement, the gesture of his right hand, which was clearly not friendly. Probably detailed instructions on where I could stick Lola. Then he was gone, and I drove on, and the Castilian plateau shimmered around me like a dream someone had forgotten to write down. Welcome to Spain. Welcome to the 'adventure'.

After thirty kilometres, I stopped. A petrol station. Small, lonely, two pumps that looked like they had seen better decades. An old man sat in the shade on a plastic chair and watched me get off as if I were a rather uninteresting television programme. I filled up. Three litres. The petrol smelled sharp, chemical, like departure and adventure. Then I stood there, the bottle of two-stroke oil in my hand, the sun burning on my neck, trying to remember Nacho's instructions. 60 millilitres for three litres.

I measured it out. Looked at the scale. Poured the oil into the tank. It glistened green in the sun, as if it were a magical ingredient that would make Lola immortal. I went into the shop. Bought some water. The cashier asked where I was from and where I was going. Friendly small talk. I stayed for fifteen minutes. Also to hide from the heat. As I was leaving, this thought suddenly occurred to me: 'Did I put oil in?'

Panic. 'Game over,' Nacho had warned. 'Kkkkkrrrrhhhhh'. To be on the safe side, I took the bottle out again. Measured out 60 millilitres. Poured it in. Better safe than sorry, right?

Ten kilometres later, I saw it first in the rear-view mirror: a thick, blue cloud of smoke rising behind me like a failed chemistry experiment or a heavy metal band's stage show. It wasn't subtle. It was present, persistent, unmistakable – a blue trail of smoke following me like a loyal but embarrassing dog. I was now officially a mobile environmental disaster. In my mind's eye, I could see Greta Thunberg's reproachful gaze.

Cars swerved out of the way. A white delivery van veered sharply to the left. A motorcyclist honked his horn and shook his head with the universal gesture for 'you have no idea what you're doing'. A child in a passing car – a little girl with long, dark hair – pointed out of the window, her mouth wide open. I stopped. Got off. Lola was smoking. Almost dramatic, almost cinematic. Almost as if she were calmly smoking a cigarette and reflecting on life. But it was too much. Far too much.

A car stopped next to me – an old white Renault with paint flaking off in large flakes. An elderly man stuck his head out of the window. He was wearing a white shirt and a straw hat, and his skin was brown and leathery. '¡Demasiado aceite!' he shouted. He laughed – loudly, heartily, the way you laugh at a tourist trying to eat paella with chopsticks. It wasn't a malicious laugh. More like a laugh that said, 'We've all been there, lad.' Then he waved and drove on.

I stood there alone. The street was empty. The wind carried the blue smoke westward. Too much oil. Of course. Fearing that Lola might die like a forgotten Tamagotchi, I had refilled twice. The result: a mobile disco driving through the Spanish countryside, trailing blue clouds behind it. For a moment, I thought of 'Smoke on the Water' and laughed. Somewhat hysterically. Then I had a catchy tune in my head!

And as if the blue fog wasn't warning enough, Lola started to sputter a few kilometres later. A metallic pop-pop-pop mixed with the engine noise, as if someone were hitting the cylinder with a spoon. I pulled over to the hard shoulder again. I took off the side cover and looked at the engine as if I actually knew what I was doing. Sure!

I remembered Nacho's warning finger: 'Always tighten the spark plug, Kai. Not too tight, but tight.' I pulled out the spark plug connector and promptly burned my fingers on the hot cylinder head cover. Of course. I checked the fit with the spark plug wrench from the tool kit. Sure enough, it was loose. Only half a turn, but enough to let the compression escape. I tightened it by hand, put the connector back on and prayed. It started.

One problem solved, two dozen more probably waiting around the next bend. I drove on. The road was quieter now, the landscape more expansive. Kilometre 80. The blue smoke had cleared – Lola was breathing more evenly now, as if she understood that panic wasn't helping either of us. The sun was high, but not yet brutal. My arms began to tingle – the first sign of what was to come later – but at that moment it felt almost pleasant. Warm. Alive.

I was driving at 60 km/h. Not out of fear. Out of enjoyment. The vibration of the engine travelled through my body like a gentle pulse. The wind tugged at my helmet, but not uncomfortably. The landscape glided by – ochre-yellow fields, low stone walls, scattered olive trees whose silver-green leaves shimmered in the light. For a brief moment – perhaps twenty or thirty kilometres – everything was relaxed. I had survived two breakdowns. Two repairs. I was riding. Alone. On a Vespa from the sixties. Through Spain.

In front of me, at the side of the road: a ruin. An old finca. The walls were still standing – made of rough, weathered stone that must once have been whitewashed, but had now taken on the colour of the earth. The roof was gone. Beams jutted into the sky like the ribs of a dead animal. A window without a frame. A door that was missing. Weeds grew rampant from the cracks. I stopped. Parked Lola. Got off. It was quiet. Only the wind whistling through the empty windows – a soft, high-pitched whistle that sounded like a memory of better times.

I walked closer. The walls were thick – half a metre, maybe more. Built to last for centuries. And yet: dilapidated. Abandoned. Forgotten. I stood there and looked through the empty window. Behind it: nothing. Only sky. Blue. Endless. A metaphor, I thought. It was a bloody metaphor.

This finca had once been something. Someone had built it. With sweat. With hope. Perhaps a family had lived here. Children who had run through this door. Food on a table. Laughter. And then?

At some point, someone had left. Or died. And no one had come to carry on. Just like my life, I thought. I was this finca. Solidly built. Once promising. But then: abandoned. Empty. A roof that was no longer there. Windows without frames. Only walls that defied the wind, but no longer protected anyone.

I stood there for a while. The sun was beating down. Lola stood behind me, engine off, waiting patiently. 'But,' I said aloud to no one but myself, 'I'm not completely ruined yet.' I looked at the walls. Thick. Strong. Still there. 'And you can put a roof back on it.' I nodded. To myself. To the finca. To Lola.

It was a strange moment. The moment when you realise that you may be a ruin, but you're a damn sturdy ruin. And that ruins are sometimes more interesting buildings than perfectly plastered new constructions. I went back to Lola. I stroked her seat briefly – a gesture that was foreign to me, but somehow right.

> **[NOTIFICATION]:** Dating app: 'There are hot singles near you. Say hello!'

Sure!

'Let's go,' I said. I started her up. The engine rattled. Reliable. Alive. I drove off. And for the next twenty kilometres, I actually felt free.

After ninety kilometres, my skin began to speak. Softly at first – a pulling sensation, a slight burning. Then louder. Then it screamed. I was wearing a T-shirt – a simple, grey T-shirt – and shorts. No jacket, no protection, no idea. 'It's just a Vespa ride,' I had thought. The Spanish sun thought otherwise.

My forearms glowed a deep, aggressive red – not the red of a tomato, more the red of a prawn that had been forgotten on a barbecue grill. My thighs were scarlet, a red that was almost artistic in its intensity. My neck felt as if someone had pointed a blowtorch at it and forgotten to turn it off. I couldn't turn my head without my skin protesting. Every touch of the handlebars was a minor torture. But I kept riding. Because I was an idiot. Or because I didn't want to be an idiot anymore. The difference between these two things was very, very small that day.

Second petrol station – this time it went better. Much better. Kilometre 170. The air had changed. It was no longer dry and dusty, but humid, salty, almost tangible. I smelled the sea before I saw it – a deep, salty smell mixed with diesel, sunscreen and fried fish. Gandia lay ahead of me. Buildings. Traffic. People on pavements. Civilisation. An intersection. A traffic light. Red. I braked. Stopped. Pulled the clutch. The engine idled – a reassuring, steady 'papapap'.

The traffic light turned green. I wanted to shift into first gear. A simple movement. I pulled the clutch. The lever went all the way down. Without resistance. Without that familiar, firm point. It just went all the way down, as if I were reaching into pudding. What the hell?

I tried to shift gears. The gear lever didn't move. The clutch didn't engage. Behind me: a horn. Short, impatient. I looked in the rear-view mirror. A red Fiat Punto. The driver was gesticulating. 'Come on, move.' I tried again. Pulled the clutch lever. Nothing. Just that awful emptiness. Behind me: a second horn. Then a third. A chorus that swelled.

'¡VAMOS!' someone shouted. Panic crept up my throat. I was sitting in the middle of the intersection. The engine was running. But I couldn't shift gears, couldn't drive away, couldn't back up. 'Adventure!' I thought grimly, feeling the angry breath of the queue on the back of my neck. If this was freedom, then it was damn loud and smelled of exhaust fumes.

I frantically pushed Lola to the side of the road and onto the kerb. I pressed the kill switch. The sun was beating down. My burnt arms throbbed in time with my heartbeat. People walked past. Cars drove past. No one stopped. No one paid any attention to the shrimp in a helmet. I was just another tourist with problems, an everyday sight in a coastal town in summer.

Then I saw it. The clutch cable – the thin steel cable that ran from the lever on the handlebars to the engine. Torn. The end hung down like a severed nerve, frayed, useless, dead. 'Shit,' I said. Loudly. To no one. For a moment – a long, heavy moment – I seriously considered whether this was the end. Whether I should call a taxi, leave Lola somewhere. 'Sorry, Nacho, it was worth a try.'

Then: Nacho's voice. Not loud. Not dramatic. Just there. In my head. Three days earlier. Nacho's workshop. Tuesday afternoon. He had pulled the clutch, pointed to the cable. His hands moved quickly, confidently, with the precision of a surgeon. 'See that cable? If it breaks, you won't be able to change gears.' 'And then?' 'Then you change it.' He had smiled. 'It's not difficult. Like changing shoelaces.' 'Shoelaces,' I had repeated. 'Sure.'

He had given me a new cable. 'That goes in the tool roll. In the glove compartment.' Then he showed me: loosen the screw on the lever. Pull out the old cable. Thread in the new one. Adjust the tension. 'You can do it.'

Now I understood. I opened the glove compartment and found the tool roll. Sweat ran into my eyes, burning like acid. I unwrapped the oil-soaked cloth. A new clutch cable and a screw nipple! Shiny, perfect, untouched. 'Thanks, Nacho,' I said quietly.

The repair began. The screw on the lever was stuck – too tight. I pushed, pulled, my fingers slipped on the hot metal. Finally: a click. It gave way. Pull out the old cable. It was stuck. Of course it was stuck. I tugged at it. Finally, it came out. Thread in the new cable.

First into the lever on the handlebars, then into the cable housing. Through the guide on the engine casing – a narrow, narrow opening, barely visible because of grease and dirt.

I tried. The cable slipped past. I tried again. The sun was beating down. Sweat dripped onto the asphalt, evaporating immediately with a soft hiss. Ten minutes. Fifteen. Twenty. I fumbled with black fingers, and my mouth slowly felt like the Gobi Desert. People walked by. I saw them out of the corner of my eye – tourists with beach bags, locals with shopping bags, a couple laughing. No one stopped.

'You can do it,' I heard Nacho say. 'You can do it.' I threaded the cable through. Screw nipple on. Really tight! Unscrew the adjusting screw a little. Adjust the tension. I pulled the lever. Felt resistance. Good. That was good. Started Lola. She rattled – that familiar, deep sound. I pulled the clutch. Shifted into first gear.

Clunk. The sound was like music. Like a promise kept. Better than any philharmonic orchestra. I put everything in the glove compartment and stepped on the gas. I drove off. And for a moment – a brief, precious moment – I didn't feel like a clueless tourist. I felt like someone who could do something. Who had learned something. Like the guy who can assemble his Ikea cabinet without instructions.

Chapter 13 – Paraiso (and Other Lies)

[Soundtrack Shuffle: Guns N' Roses – Paradise City]

6 p.m. The light was golden – that warm, soft light that transforms seaside towns into something magical. I drove into town. Palm trees lined the streets. The smell of the sea mingled with grilled fish, diesel and sunscreen. It was tranquil. Probably beautiful. I was too exhausted to really notice.

But I had a hunger. A monumental, all-consuming hunger that made everything else unimportant. I stopped at a kebab stand by the roadside. 'Döner Kebab Istanbul,' said the sign. Next to it: a glowing meat skewer, slowly rotating like a hypnotic tower of browned protein. The man behind the counter – moustache, white undershirt, beads of sweat on his forehead – looked at me.

'Döner?' 'Yes. Grande. With everything. And a cold Coke.'

He nodded. Began to cut. The knife slid through the meat with the precision of a surgeon. Tomato, onions, lettuce, sauce – one white, one red, both generous. He wrapped everything in aluminium foil. Handed it to me.

'Siete euros.'

I paid. Took the kebab. It was warm in my hands. Heavy. Perfect. I stood at the edge of the pavement. Next to Lola. Unwrapped the kebab. The first bite. Heavenly. The meat: spicy, juicy, slightly charred. The sauce: creamy, with a hint of garlic and heat. The onions: crunchy. The cola ice cold!

I ate. Quickly. Greedily. With both hands. Sauce dripped onto my T-shirt. I didn't care. After 180 kilometres on a Vespa, after blue smoke and broken clutch cables and sunburn that felt like a second skin of fire, this kebab was the best thing that had ever happened to me. Better than sex. Better than a holiday. Better than anything.

Afterwards: a pharmacy. 'Farmacia' was written on the green cross above the door. I went inside. The air conditioning hit me like a blessing. A woman behind the counter. Middle-aged. Glasses. Friendly.

'Hola. ¿Qué necesitas?' I pointed to my arms. Red. Bright red. 'Sunburn. Muy mal.'

She nodded. Understanding. Went to a shelf. Came back with two things: a large tube of aloe vera gel and a pack of calcium tablets. 'Aloe vera. For the skin. Cools.' She made a motion as if she were rubbing it in. 'And calcium. For inside. Helps with burns.'

'Perfect. Thank you. Gracias.' 'De nada.' She smiled. 'Drink lots of water. And stay out of the sun.'

I paid. 12 euros. Went outside. A sign: 'Hostel Paraiso'. The paint was peeling. The name was ironic. 18 euros a night. Perfect. The guy at the reception desk – dreadlocks, surfer shirt with a faded Bob Marley print, about twenty years old – looked at my passport as if it were the most boring thing he had seen today.

'Germany. Cool.' He handed me a plastic key. 'Room 3. Six-bed room. Upstairs.' 'Six beds?' 'It's a hostel, man. You know?' He said it as if it were the most natural thing in the world. 'You've really burned yourself, man!' 'No shit?'

He understood and said nothing. I took the key. Went upstairs. Hostel Paraiso Room 3 was… a challenge. Six bunk beds, paradise had no window, a bare light bulb hanging from the ceiling on a cable, flickering like a tired lighthouse. The room smelled of damp towels, sweaty T-shirts and the slightly sweet smell of abandoned dreams. And a hint of cheese feet so thick you could cut it with a knife. Perhaps a pilgrim had once hidden his socks behind the locker after walking a few hundred kilometres to share his experience with posterity. Quite possible. It was hot – I looked around but couldn't find any air conditioning. Of course not.

Four of the six beds were occupied. Two young guys – in their early twenties, both on their mobile phones – were lying on their beds scrolling. A third – thick beard, Birkenstocks, cargo shorts, the epitome of the German backpacker – was already snoring. Loudly. Very loudly. It sounded like someone was trying to cut down a tree with a blunt saw. I put my rucksack on my bed – bed 5, at the top, next to the door, the place where probably no one else wanted to sleep.

One of the mobile phone guys looked up. 'Hey, mate. Are you German too?' 'Er… yes?' 'Wow.' He grinned – the grin of someone who had long since given up fighting certain things. 'That's Klaus from Wanne-Eickel.' He pointed to the snoring man. 'He's been snoring for three hours. Non-stop. Like clockwork. I'm Nico!' 'Great,' I said. 'And Wayne is coming later. He's from Liverpool. He snores too. But differently.' 'Of course.'

But before I could lie down, I had to do something about my skin. It was burning. Really burning! I took the aloe vera tube and a towel. I went to the communal shower at the end of the corridor. The shower: tiles. Neon light. Four cubicles. No door on cubicle 3. Of course. I chose cubicle 2. Stepped inside. Took off my T-shirt. Then my shorts. First, I showered for 20 minutes with almost cold water. God, it was wonderful!

Later, in my underpants. I stood there in front of a small, milky mirror hanging on the wall. And saw myself. Red. I was red. Arms: bright red. Thighs: scarlet. Neck: deep red with a hint of purple. In between: chalk white. Pale. German. I looked like the Austrian flag. Red-white-red. Pretty. Lanky. Pot belly. Not an athletic figure. More like: office body with Vespa ambitions.

'Great,' I muttered. I opened the tube. Squeezed a large amount of aloe vera gel into my hand. It was green. Cool. Smelled of mint and hope. I began to rub it on my arms. The relief came immediately. The gel was cold, almost icy on the hot skin. I groaned. Quietly. Then louder. I continued rubbing it in. Forearms. Upper arms. Shoulders. Like a Greek wrestler before a fight, rubbing himself with oil.

Except I wasn't a Greek wrestler. I was a red-and-white, lanky German with a pot belly in a hostel communal shower in Gandia. I rubbed the gel on my thighs. On my neck. As far as I could reach. The tube was now half empty. I stood there. Shiny. Glowing green in the neon light. Dripping.

The door opened. Wayne came in. The guy from Liverpool. He looked at me. I stood there. In my underpants. Covered in green gel. Shiny like a fish. Sighing.

'Mate,' he said slowly. 'You alright?' 'Sunburn,' I said. 'Very bad.' He nodded. 'Ah. Right. Aloe vera. Good call.'

Then he went into his cabin. I waited until the gel had been absorbed a little. Got dressed. Not the T-shirt. That was ruined. Kebab sauce. Sweat. Oil. I put on my Hawaiian shirt. The one with the palm trees and flamingos. That way, I wouldn't stand out so much at my age in 'Paraiso,' I thought. And the shorts. I looked like a tourist on his way to the beach bar. Or like someone who had given up. Both were true in a strange way.

9 p.m. I lay in my bed, the blanket pulled up to my chin, even though it was much too warm. The ceiling was about 20 cm in front of my nose. Slightly claustrophobic. The Hawaiian shirt stuck to my skin. The aloe vera had soothed the burning, but not stopped it. Klaus was snoring. No, Klaus was sawing wood. Industrial style. With an amplifier.

RRRRROOOAAARRRRR … FFFHHHHH …
RRRRROOOAAARRRRR …

A pause. Short. Hopeful. Then: Wayne. Wayne had come back – tall, muscular, tattooed, he looked like someone who would be a bouncer in another reality. He was snoring too. But differently. Deeper. More rhythmic. Like a diesel truck idling.

BRUUUMMMM … BRUUUMMMM … BRUUUMMMM …

They were competing to see who could snore the loudest. Klaus: RRROOOAAAR. Wayne: BRUUUMMM. It was a symphony from hell that would have moved Tchaikovsky to tears – but not out of admiration.

10:30 p.m. I lay there, staring into the darkness. My arms were burning. My neck was burning. Every inch of my skin felt like it had been fried in a pan. And above me, around me: acoustic Armageddon. I stared into the darkness. This is hell, I thought.

I got up. Grabbed my blanket and pillow. Left the room as quietly as I could, although at that noise level I could probably have brought a whole brass band with me. The roof terrace. I had seen the sign when I checked in – 'Rooftop Chill Zone', hand-painted, probably by someone who was very relaxed or very high. Or both.

I went up. The terrace was small – a few plastic chairs, their white colour already bleached by the sun, an old two-seater wicker sofa that looked like it had seen better days. Fairy lights, half of which weren't working. Silence. Glorious, wonderful, almost sacred silence. The sound of the sea in the distance – quiet, rhythmic, soothing. The wind, which was warm and salty. I lay down on the wicker sofa. It was uncomfortable – too short for someone of my size, too narrow. The wicker pressed against my sunburnt back like a thousand tiny needles. But here was peace. No Klaus. No Wayne. Just me, the stars and the distant sound of the sea. I closed my eyes.

3 a.m. I woke up because my back hurt and my legs had fallen asleep. I was curled up like a failed origami project, my spine bent into a shape that was probably not intended by nature. The wicker sofa had left marks on my skin – a pattern of lines and dots. Above me: stars. Millions of stars. More stars than I had ever seen in Germany. The Milky Way stretched across the sky like a wide, white ribbon, and I could make out individual constellations – the Big Dipper, Cassiopeia, Orion.

Backpacker hostels, I thought, are not made for men who want to regain control of their lives. I was too old for dormitories. Too old for snoring roommates who sounded like a mixture of construction site noise and terrible experimental music. Too old for wicker sofas on roof terraces that felt like medieval stretching racks.

But here I lay. Under millions of stars. With burnt skin and oily hands and a black Vespa down on the street that had carried me 180 kilometres. And tomorrow I would ride on. Because now I could. Because I had learned that sometimes you can do things you thought you couldn't.

'Okay, Miguel,' I whispered into the night as I looked at my glowing forearms. 'You were right. Life isn't a pony farm. But it feels damn real.'

I smiled. And just before I fell asleep. Ping.

> **[Notification]** Weather app: 'Severe weather warning for Memmingen: Hailstorm possible. Have you parked your vehicle safely?'

Chapter 14 – A slightly above-average Friday

[Soundtrack Shuffle: The Clash – Should I Stay or Should I Go]

Friday morning, shortly after eight, I woke up on the wicker sofa on the roof terrace. My back cracked like old wood, and the seagulls screeched as if they had decided to scream every guest awake personally. I sat up. My arms burned, my thighs felt sandpapered, my neck was stiff.

Downstairs in the breakfast room – a converted storage closet – I drank coffee from a thermos that had been sitting there since yesterday, lukewarm and bitter, and ate toast with jam from plastic portions, vintage 2015. Through the window, I watched a man walking a dog that didn't want to walk. The man pulled, the dog remained seated. Maybe he had to sleep on a wicker sofa tonight, too.

The snoring still came from Room 3 – Klaus from Wanne-Eickel and Wayne from Liverpool, the symphony of hell. I shook my head.

> **[Notification]:** LinkedIn: 'Stefan updated his status: "Proud of our team! Q3 targets exceeded by 12%! #Leadership #Success"'

I stared at the message. Stefan exceeded targets. Yesterday, I repaired a clutch and, as an "adult," survived a hostel from hell. Who was more successful here? The question was more complicated than it should have been.

Outside, Lola stood between two rubbish bins. I patted the seat – warm from the morning sun – said, "Good morning, girl," and kicked the kickstarter. On the third try, she started – blue smoke, less than yesterday. A small victory! Then I rolled off. It was one of those days that start innocently, so you can't blame anyone later.

The N-332 was one of those roads that didn't promise much and delivered exactly that: two lanes, dead straight, the sea on the right – flat, grey, sluggish in the morning sun – orange groves on the left in perfect rows, as if planted by a pedantic gardener who considered disorder a personal insult. I drove at sixty to seventy kilometres per hour, no faster, no slower, and Lola purred evenly, almost meditatively, a steady contentment-clatter that dug into my bones.

The air smelled of salt, warm asphalt and a hint of citrus fruits ripening somewhere in the distance. I took a deep breath, filling my lungs with this mixture that didn't exist in Kempten. My hands rested loosely on the handlebars, no longer cramped as they had been yesterday when I had clung to the grips, and my thoughts wandered not to PowerPoint presentations or quarterly reports, but to what lay ahead: the road, the wind, the rattling. One day survived. A few hundred kilometres still lay ahead of me to Barcelona.

After about an hour, I reached the outskirts of Valencia – the road became wider, louder, lorries overtook me so close that I could feel the draught – and I followed the signs to the Ciudad de las Artes y las Ciencias. And when I saw them, these white skeletons rising from the ground, I was breathless for a moment.

I parked Lola, got off, pulled my helmet from my head – my hair was stuck to my forehead, wet with sweat – and walked closer, along the road, until I stood in front of a shallow pool of water that stretched out like an artificial lake, reflecting the buildings. The Hemisfèric lay half submerged in this basin – a giant eye made of glass and steel, its lid made of white concrete ribs that opened like eyelashes, and the eye stared at the sky, not blinking, just waiting.

And I stood there and stared back, and for a moment I had the feeling that the eye was looking at me, that it was looking at everyone who came here and wondering what these little people wanted here in this city of concrete and glass.

Next to it, a few hundred metres away, stood the Palau de les Arts Reina Sofía, an opera house that looked like a stranded sailing ship from the future – white, elegant, organic, with curved lines that knew no straight lines, only curves and arcs, as if the architect had decided that corners were out and everything had to flow. And behind it, the Museu de les Ciències, a skeleton of ribs, steel and glass, organic and technical at the same time, like a dinosaur that had decided that extinction wasn't its thing after all and that it would rather go into the future.

The structures seemed alive, as if they were breathing – these curved lines that rose and fell like the ribs of a sleeping giant. The water not only reflected the buildings, it doubled them, creating a parallel world beneath the surface where everything was more perfect, clearer, purer. I stood at the edge and looked down into this mirrored world and thought: maybe this is the real version, and we only live in the shadows.

Calatrava had created something here that refused to fit into categories – not architecture, not sculpture, but something in between, something third. It reminded me of his train station in Liège, that cathedral of steel and glass I had once seen in a photo – there, too, those organic forms, that refusal to submit to gravity. Except that here in Valencia, the water changed everything, softened everything, almost like a dream.

There was water everywhere – shallow pools in which the buildings were reflected, perfectly, symmetrically – and children ran barefoot through them, tourists took photos, someone had an ice cream that melted faster than he could eat it, and the sun beat down on the white skeleton, which reflected it back like a mirror.

"Calatrava," said a voice next to me, and I turned to an older man with grey hair and a camera around his neck. "Santiago Calatrava. The architect. From Valencia. He built this in the nineties. Some love it, some hate it. Too expensive, too futuristic, too much." "And you?" I asked. He laughed dryly. "I'm an architect. I'm jealous."

I looked back at the buildings, at the eye reflected in the water like a second eye beneath the surface, and thought: If someone can build something like this – something that everyone thinks is crazy, but that remains nonetheless – then maybe I can ride a few hundred kilometres on an old Vespa. And if not, at least I would have seen something beautiful before I failed.

[Notification]: Calendar: 'REMINDER: 2026 annual planning with board – TODAY 2:00 p.m.'

I looked at my watch. 12:47 p.m. In an hour and thirteen minutes, Stefan was now sitting in a conference room, drinking lukewarm coffee from paper cups and nodding at pie charts about efficiency gains. I stood in front of a giant glass eye staring at me and thought about gravity. Who had made the better decision here? I wasn't sure yet.

Lunchtime arrived with the clarity of a law of nature. Hunger, loud and unrelenting. I drove back towards the old town, through alleys that grew narrower, lined with four-storey houses with wrought-iron balconies, their facades plastered in ochre yellow and pale pink, cracks in the plaster, faded by the sun. Laundry hung on lines between the balconies – bed sheets, T-shirts, underpants, fluttering in the wind like flags of everyday life. Down on the street, old men sat on plastic chairs in front of cafés, drinking coffee from tiny cups and not talking, just staring.

I found a restaurant, small and inconspicuous, with "La Pepica" written above the door in faded red letters bleached by the sun. Through the window, I saw people sitting, plates clattering, someone laughing loudly, and the smell of saffron and roasted garlic wafting through the open door. This is the place, I thought.

Inside, it was packed – tourists, locals, a mix of languages flowing together like water in a river. A waitress in her mid-forties, her black hair tied back in a tight ponytail, came up to me, saw my red arms, my dusty boots, my jacket that smelled of petrol and two-stroke oil, and smiled as if she had seen a hundred like me before. She pointed to a table outside under a parasol that had seen better days but at least provided shade.

"Paella Valenciana," I said without looking at the menu, because I knew what I wanted. She nodded, said "Quince minutos," fifteen minutes, and disappeared into the kitchen.

I waited, watching the people. At the next table sat a couple in their early thirties, discussing the menu in English with a Nordic accent – she wanted the seafood paella, he insisted on the Valenciana, authentic, traditional.

A few tables away sat a man alone, in his mid-fifties, wearing a suit despite the heat, staring at his mobile phone with the expression of someone who had just read an email from his boss. I knew that look. I had seen it in the mirror for years. Now I was the guy with oil-smeared hands and sunburn who ordered paella without looking at the prices. That was an upgrade. Definitely.

Then my paella arrived, carried by the waitress with both hands, a black cast-iron pan, about forty centimetres in diameter, heavy, steaming, and she set it down in front of me with the care one would treat sacred relics, and perhaps it was. Yellow rice, infused with the aroma of saffron, which rose in the heat like incense in a church. Chicken and rabbit, the skin crispy, the meat tender, almost falling off the bone. Green beans and white beans, rosemary, the leaves still fresh. No seafood, no chorizo, nothing touristy, just the ingredients that had been grown, harvested and cooked for centuries in the Albufera, the rice-growing region south of Valencia. She warned me about the hot pan and wished me a good appetite.

I took a forkful, and the rice was perfect – not mushy, not too dry, each grain separate, slightly burnt on the bottom of the pan, the socarrat, the best part, crispy, bitter and sweet at the same time, a thin layer of toasted rice that was the secret of every original paella. The saffron, the herbs, the meat, everything tender and spicy, and I ate slowly, savouring every bite, letting the flavours melt on my tongue, and thinking: this is culture, not just the buildings, not just Calatrava's art, but the food, the way people sit together, laugh, eat, live, without haste, without stress.

When I was finished – the pan empty except for a few burnt grains of rice on the edge, which I scraped off with my fork – the waitress returned. "Postre?" Dessert? I nodded. "What do you recommend?" "Flan de la casa." She made a gesture as if describing something heavenly. "Homemade. My grandmother's recipe." "Perfect."

The flan came in a small ceramic bowl, the top caramelised to a golden brown, glistening with sugar glaze that lay in small puddles around the flan like liquid amber. I took a spoon, cut into it – it was firm but not too firm, creamy but not too soft. The first bite: sweet, but not cloying, with a slight hint of bitterness from the caramel, which melted on my tongue like butter. Vanilla, eggs, milk, sugar – simple ingredients, but together they felt like a hug from someone who means well.

I ate slowly, scraped the caramel residue from the plate, licked the spoon like a child with no manners, and I didn't care. No one was watching. And even if they were, what would they think? That a German with sunburn appreciates good food? That was no crime. I paid and went back to Lola.

On the way, I noticed that my arms were not only red, but also hurt when the wind blew over them, a stinging sensation like salt in wounds. I needed protection. Two streets away, I saw a sign: "Motos Valencia". I went inside. It smelled of leather, rubber and new textiles. The man behind the counter looked at my sunburnt arms and laughed quietly. "Primer día en moto?" "No. Fourth. But the first without common sense."

He grinned and fetched a black textile jacket with protectors on the shoulders and elbows. It fit – tight enough that the protectors stayed in place, but loose enough to breathe. Then a pair of dark blue Kevlar jeans, stiff, heavy, with protectors in the pockets. Finally, he picked out a pair of lightweight leather gloves with protectors. He tapped on a calculator. "Chaqueta, ciento cincuenta. Pantalones, ciento treinta. Guantes, veintinueve."

Three hundred and nine euros. Steep. But my arms were burning, and I didn't want to look like a boiled crab. Besides, if I had already spent money on pointless things – building society savings plans that earned me 0.4% interest, a gym membership that I had used three times – then I could also spend three hundred and nine euros on something that would protect me from skin cancer diagnoses. I paid and went outside. The sun was still beating down, but now it was on the fabric rather than my skin, and that was a huge difference.

[Notification]: BankApp: 'Your credit card statement is available. Current balance: -1,847.23 €'

I stared at the message. Minus one thousand eight hundred and forty-seven euros. Probably three hundred of that for motorcycle gear, one hundred and fifty for hostels, two hundred for food, and the rest for… what, actually? Petrol? Aloe vera? A kebab that had saved my life?

Money well spent, I thought. All money well spent.

Chapter 15 – Casa Carmen and the Rubber from the 80s

[Soundtrack Shuffle: Rocky Horror Picture Show – Time Warp]

Back at Lola, I patted the seat and said, 'Well done, girl, now let's get going,' swung myself on – strapped my rucksack to the luggage rack, zipped up my new jacket and put on my gloves – and kicked the starter. A scene like something from Bond. If only he'd had such a beautiful Vespa and played a burnt-out insurance salesman. We were ready!

She woke up with a bright, cheeky rattle. I put her in first gear, released the clutch, wanted to drive off – and felt it immediately: the rear wheel felt soft, spongy, as if I were riding on a half-inflated balloon.

I got off, walked to the back, looked at the tyre, and my heart, which had been beating steadily just a moment ago, took a little leap downwards. The tyre was flat. Not completely, but definitely not enough air, maybe twenty per cent, maybe less.

'Of course,' I said aloud to no one. 'Why should even one day go normally?'

I knelt down, inspected it, my hands on the warm rubber, and searched for the spot. Finally, I found it: a nail, small, rusty, stuck deep in the tread like a little metallic middle finger from the universe. I stood up, took out the tool kit – a simple set, pliers, wrench, all old, all rusty – knelt down again, placed the pliers on the head of the nail and pulled. The nail didn't budge. I pulled harder, sweat already running into my eyes, and then it slowly came out, millimetre by millimetre, squeaking as if in protest. No hissing, just silence. The air had been escaping for hours, perhaps since this morning. I was probably lucky that it was so short and that the air hadn't escaped suddenly while I was driving.

I bent down lower, inspected the tread, looked for more holes, and at that very moment I noticed it: under the left side cover, through a narrow gap, the spare wheel. Black, old, dusty. I opened the side cover, flipped it up, and there it was, the spare wheel, secured with two nuts and a bolt. Thanks to the genius of their developers, the old Vespas were the only two-wheelers that came with a spare wheel as standard. Perfect.

I took the socket wrench – short, maybe ten centimetres long, with little leverage – placed it on the first screw and turned. It didn't budge. I pressed harder, sweat running down my forehead, and the screw gave way, squeaked and turned. The nuts were even more stubborn, but they too came loose as I cursed away in the heat.

I pulled out the spare wheel, carefully, and then, as I held it in my hand, I saw it immediately: It had quite a lot in common with me. It was over forty, slightly battered and porous in places, and the air was pretty much gone! I pressed my thumb on it and it gave way, much too soft. The rim was covered with surface rust. I turned the tyre, looked for the date, and there it was, small, barely legible: 1980.

The spare wheel of a hopeless optimist.

'Over forty years old,' I said aloud, and then I laughed, a dry, humourless laugh. 'Of course the spare wheel is older than me. Of course.'

For a moment, I considered just staying there. Sitting down on the ground next to Lola and waiting for someone to come. Someone would come. The fire brigade. A helicopter. God himself, to explain to me why he thought it was funny. But God didn't come. Only a taxi was parked twenty metres down the road, the driver leaning outside, smoking. I walked over, the old wheel in my hand, my hands already black.

'Do you know where there's a tyre repair shop?' He looked at the wheel, nodded, gave me an address. I got in.

The industrial estate was far out, on the edge of town, flat and grey and full of warehouses and workshops and a DIY store with a car park bigger than some German villages. The first garage was large, modern, with three lifts and cars everywhere – BMWs, Audis, a Mercedes – but no motorbikes. A man came out, in his mid-fifties, wearing overalls, oil stains everywhere, on his chest, on his arms, as if he had just taken apart an engine.

'Solo coches.' Cars only. He looked at the wheel in my hand, shook his head, turned around and went inside.

But of course, I thought. That would have been too easy. I stood there with the wheel, the sun beating down – thirty-two degrees, maybe more – and looked around. A few hundred metres further on, I saw another workshop on Google, and I thought, 'Fuck it!' and set off.

After two hundred metres, I had sweat on my forehead; after four hundred metres, sweat everywhere – under my jacket, on my back, in my hair. The rubber was heavy and hot, my hands slipped, already black with dirt. A car drove by slowly, the driver looked at me, grinned, and I didn't grin back. A German man in his early forties carrying a Vespa wheel through a Spanish industrial estate in thirty-two degrees. This wasn't the freedom Miguel had talked about. This was a midlife crisis with sunstroke.

The second workshop had motorcycles in the yard – two old Hondas, a Yamaha without a tank. A man sat on a plastic chair, smoking, tattooed arms.

'Hola,' I said, out of breath. He looked at the tyre and slowly stood up. 'Vespa?' 'Sí. 1967.'

He whistled softly, admiringly, went into the workshop, came back with a tyre – used, but still almost new, tread still there, no cracks. 'Veinte euros por el neumático, diez por montaje.' Thirty euros. I nodded. 'Perfecto.'

> **[NOTIFICATION]:** Health App: 'Congratulations! You've reached your goal of 10,000 steps today!'

The mechanic went to the machine, an old, rusty machine that looked like it came from the same sixties as Lola, and I watched as he pulled off the old tyre – the tyre was so old and hard that it almost broke, and he muttered, 'Madre de Dios,' Mother of God, and shook his head. The rim was practically rusted to the tyre. He cleaned it with a drill with a steel brush and coarse sandpaper. He also had a new inner tube and put everything together. He pumped it up, and fifteen minutes later it was done. It would probably have taken me two hours to do it myself on the road. I paid, took the tyre, said, 'Gracias,' and he said, 'De nada, buena suerte' – you're welcome, good luck.

A taxi took me back to Lola, with the new tyre on my lap. Now came the difficult part. I took out the socket wrench – short, little leverage – and said aloud, 'Okay, first off the back wheel, then on with the new one.'

The next thirty minutes were hell. Five nuts held the rear wheel to the brake drum, and they were tight, rock solid, as if they had decided they wanted to stay there until the end of time. I knelt down, placed the short socket wrench on the first nut, pulled, pushed. Little leverage, little force. The nut moved, one millimetre, two, three. Sweat ran into my eyes, stinging, and I wiped it away with my forearm, continuing to pull. Finally, it came loose, then the second, the third.

The fourth nut was the worst – I pulled with all my strength, my hands were shaking, sweat dripped from my chin onto the floor, the wrench slipped, I banged my fist on the floor, took a deep breath, cursed in three languages, tried again. Finally, it gave way. The fifth one too. The rear wheel came off, heavy, heavier than I thought, and I put it aside, exhaled, thought: Done.

And at that very moment – without the weight of the rear wheel, without the balance she needed – Lola tilted to the right, slowly, almost elegantly, as if in slow motion, and fell onto the lawn with a thud.

'NO!' I shouted, jumping up, trying to catch her, too late. She lay there, on her right side, the engine ticking quietly, as if offended. I stood there, staring, my hands shaking, clenching into fists, opening again. That was the moment when other people cried. Or screamed. Or gave up. I did none of those things. I just stood there and thought: Thank you, universe! Fuck!

'Okay,' I said aloud, to myself, to Lola, to the universe. 'Okay, it's not that bad.'

I took a deep breath, knelt down next to Lola, inspected her with trembling, dirty fingers: the mirror had a scratch, deep, ugly. The side panel had a scratch. But nothing was broken, the engine was fine, the lights were fine, just scratches, just surface damage. My ego was somewhere between grass and self-respect, but I could now mount the new wheel more easily. Silver lining, damn silver lining.

I lifted the new wheel, put the nuts on, one by one. While attaching the old wheel as a spare, a nut fell out of my hand and rolled under a car. 'You've got to be kidding me.' I crawled under, felt around in the dirt, found it. I lifted Lola up, heavy, my arms trembling. I got on, kicked the kickstarter. Nothing. Again. Nothing.

The taxi driver came over, new cigarette. 'Petrol, too much. Engine flooded. Take out spark plug, dry, five minutes.' He unscrewed it – wet, dripping – and put it in the sun. 'I also had a Vespa when I was a student, a PX 125. Best time of my life.'

We waited. After five minutes, he screwed it back in. On the third kick, it started – blue smoke.

'Thanks!' 'You're welcome. Drive carefully.'

4:30 p.m. Three and a half hours for a tyre change. Like a pro.

I opened the email. 'Kai, did you forget the expense report for Q3? Stefan is freaking out. Please get in touch ASAP!!!'

I read the email twice. Expense report. Q3. Stefan is freaking out. I had carried a tyre from 1980 through a Spanish industrial estate. I was sweating like a pig (even though pigs can't sweat). My hands were black, my back hurt, and my soul was hanging by a thread. Stefan could kiss my arse.

I wrote back: 'I'm on holiday. Best regards from Spain.' Then I deleted the email and drove off.

On to Castellón, another hundred kilometres. The sun sank faster than I thought – orange, then red, then grey – and I drove faster, eighty, eighty-five, Lola vibrated, but she held on, and I clung to the handlebars. Shortly before sunset, I reached Castellón de la Plana, a big city with traffic and noise. My mobile phone vibrated: 'Your reservation at Casa Carmen in Moncofa.'

Shit. Moncofa was twenty kilometres south of Castellón. I had driven past it, missed the exit. I turned around, drove back, and the sun sank behind the hills, and it got darker, quickly, too quickly. Then it started to drizzle lightly, just a few drops, but enough that the road began to glisten, that my visor collected drops that I had to wipe away.

And then – just at that moment, as if the universe had decided that a flat tyre wasn't enough – my headlight flickered, once, twice, then went out, completely dark.

'NO!' I shouted, pulled over to the side of the road, pressed the switch, once, twice, nothing. The headlight was dead, and the road ahead of me was black, and it was getting darker, the sun was gone. Fuck it, I thought. I drove off in the dark, without lights, at twenty kilometres per hour, maybe less, following the tail lights in front of me like a blind man following a voice. My heart was pounding loudly, fast, every bend a risk, every intersection a danger, and the rain continued to drizzle, not heavily, but enough.

Then I saw the sign, barely legible in the light of a street lamp: 'Moncofa – 2 km'. Almost there. I drove quickly into the town so I wouldn't be showered any longer. The streets were dark, narrow, I was looking for Calle de la Mar, and suddenly – FLASH! Bright, glaring, once, right in front of me, and I flinched, braking instinctively. I had been flashed. Sixty-five in a fifty zone, without lights, in the rain. What else.

'Perfect,' I said aloud to no one. 'Just perfect.' The universe had a sense of humour. Black, dry, malicious humour. But humour nonetheless. A kilometre further on, I found number 17.

A small house, yellow plaster, white shutters and a pent roof, in front of it a front garden with artificial turf and terracotta flower pots with geraniums. A Hollywood swing squeaked in the wind under a lemon tree, and between the pots stood garden gnomes –

at least five, all wearing red caps. The front door opened. A woman came out, in her late sixties, grey hair in a loose bun, wearing a cardigan over a floral dress.

'Kai?' 'Yes.' 'Carmen! Welcome!' She smiled warmly. 'You look like you've had a long day.' 'You could say that.' She looked at my black hands. 'Breakdown?' I nodded. 'Two. But who's counting?' 'Come in, I'll show you your room.'

I pushed Lola into the front garden, between the flower pots. Carmen closed the gate with an old padlock. The inside of the house was cramped, crammed with memories and things that no one needed anymore – a sofa from the seventies, orange and worn out, its fabric threadbare in places, the television blaring with a telenovela. The shelves were full of photos in silver frames, faces I didn't recognise, all in black and white, yellowed, from a time long past. Religious kitsch covered the walls: Jesus on the cross in a gold frame, bleeding, suffering, his eyes turned towards heaven, Mary with child, a statue of Saint Anthony on a shelf, rosaries hanging on hooks like forgotten jewellery. It smelled of lavender, old wood and something sweet that I couldn't identify.

Carmen led me up a narrow staircase that creaked with every step, as if the wood were complaining, and opened a door at the end of the hallway. 'This is your room.'

I stepped inside. The left wall was painted pastel pink, faded, with small patches where posters had probably hung. The curtains had pink ruffles and small bows, and on the bed lay a pink blanket with embroidered flowers. Above the bed hung a large crucifix, Jesus in gold, bleeding, suffering, the thorns in his head sharply and intricately crafted. On the bedside table stood three porcelain dolls with blue glass eyes and frilly dresses, staring at me with that empty, glassy gaze that was both innocent and creepy. Two more dolls sat on a chair in the corner, all in frilly dresses, and one had a crack in its face that looked like a tear.

So that was what happened when you booked spontaneously: you ended up in a pink nightmare with surveillance dolls and a bleeding Jesus. If I had known when I booked that 'charming guest room' actually meant 'doll museum with religious superstructure,' I might have preferred to stay in a real hotel after all.

'That was my niece's room,' Carmen explained with a nostalgic smile. 'She's thirty-five now, lives in Madrid, has three children. But I left it as it was, for memories, you know.' 'It's very… cosy,' I said – a lie, but a polite one. She beamed. 'Wonderful! The bathroom is at the end of the hall.'

She left. The door remained open – no lock, no bolt, just a handle. In Spain, many doors in residential buildings had no locks. No one had told me that. A cultural difference. I found that moderately strange. I stood there, alone with the dolls. Six doll's eyes stared at me. Eight, if you counted Jesus, but he looked more like he was suffering than watching over me. I sat down on the bed, which creaked loudly, plaintively, as if protesting. Above me hung a bare light bulb with a crocheted lampshade in pink, sixty watts, glaring. I looked for the light switch, found it next to the door, but left the light on. Jesus hung above the bed, the thorns sharp. One of the dolls on the bedside table had a crack in its face.

I can't stay here, I thought. Not here, not in this room, not with these dolls and this bleeding Jesus. I waited five minutes, then went downstairs. Carmen was standing in the kitchen.

'Carmen, I'm tired. I'm going out for a bit, some fresh air, maybe something to eat.' She nodded. 'Okay. But don't be late, I close at eleven.' 'Thanks.'

Outside, I took a deep breath. The air smelled of salt and evening and was cool after the confines of Carmen's house. I walked down the street, past closed shops, a few lanterns casting faint light on the asphalt, and after about five hundred metres I found a pizzeria

– 'Pizzeria Da Marco' – small, inconspicuous, but through the window I saw people sitting, normal-looking people without religious kitsch.

I went inside. Inside, it smelled of basil, tomatoes and baked dough, a mixture that was immediately comforting. A young man behind the counter nodded to me, and I ordered a Margherita and sat down at a table in the corner. The beer was cold, the pizza hot, the cheese still bubbling, and I ate slowly, enjoying the normality, the absence of pink and porcelain. This is better, I thought, much better. There were no dolls here. Just pizza. Pizza was good. Pizza didn't judge.

Around half past ten, I went back. Carmen was sitting in the living room, knitting something pink – a scarf, perhaps – and looked up when I came in.

'Ah, there you are. Did you eat well?' 'Yes, thank you. Excellent.' 'Good. I'm glad.' She smiled. 'Sleep well.' 'Thank you, you too.'

I went to the bathroom at the end of the hallway. The door squeaked as I opened it. Everything inside was pink – the carpet, fluffy and old, the towels, all in different shades of pink, even the shower curtain, with pink flamingos dancing on it. I took a quick shower, the water was warm and fragrant, and I washed away the day, the sweat, the oil, the miles.

Back in the room, I lay down on the bed. I turned off the light. It was better in the dark, but not much. Something squeaked somewhere, maybe the swing outside in the wind. Jesus hung above me, invisible now, but I knew he was there. And then – I swear I'm not imagining this – one of the dolls on the chair moved, just a little bit, barely noticeable, as if it had turned around.

I was too tired to get upset. Too exhausted from the day, from changing the tyres, from the miles. The unease was there, quiet, but

I accepted it. Tomorrow I would drive on. Tomorrow I would be gone. If the dolls killed me before then, at least it would make for an interesting obituary: 'German dies in Spanish doll's room – police baffled.'

Sometime, while the swing set creaked outside and the dolls kept their silent watch, I fell asleep.

Chapter 16 – The Lost Wallet

[Soundtrack Shuffle: Edith Piaf – La Vie en Rose]

Six o'clock.

I woke up in a pink room, in a pink bed, with pink curtains that coloured the first sunlight pink. It was as if someone had pureed a My Little Pony in a blender and wallpapered the walls with it. Even the dream I'd just had was probably pink. If dreams could have colours.

I crept quietly down the stairs. Hopefully Carmen was still asleep. I wanted to change the headlight bulbs before I had to leave. I quietly opened the front door and went out into the front garden.

Lola was standing where I had parked her last night. Next to the rose bed.

I took out my mobile phone. YouTube. 'Vespa headlight replacement tutorial'. A video in broken English, recorded by an Italian who spoke more with his hands than with words.

I knelt in front of Lola. Screwed. Turned. Carefully pulled out the old bulb.

'Buenos días!'

I jumped. Turned around.

Carmen was standing in front of the house. Pale pink bathrobe. Plush slippers with cat ears. Big curlers in her hair. Like the Golden Girls from a cheesy telenovela.

She beamed at me.

'I made breakfast,' she said. 'Thought you might want to get an early start.'

I stood up. 'That… that's really nice. Thank you.'

'First fix the headlights. Then eat.'

Ten minutes later, I was sitting in her kitchen. The headlights were working. My ego had grown to the size of a Spanish compact car.

Carmen slid a tostada con tomate across the counter to me. She still had her curlers in.

'Did you sleep well?'

'Like a baby,' I said. And I meant it. The pink bed had been more comfortable than any hotel bed I'd ever had.

'Good. You have a long day ahead of you.'

I nodded and bit into the tostada. The olive oil dripped, the tomato tasted like summer, the toasted bread was perfectly crisp. Carmen didn't make breakfast. She composed it.

'How far is it to Barcelona?' she asked.

'About three hundred and fifty kilometres.'

She whistled softly. 'On the Vespa?'

'On the Vespa.'

'That's… how many hours?'

I thought about it. 'Six? Seven, maybe?'

'And when do you want to arrive?'

'In the afternoon. Around two or three. The Vespa Club meets at four.'

She nodded. 'Then you should leave soon.'

I looked at my watch. Six twenty. 'Yes. Soon.'

But I didn't want to. This breakfast. This moment. Carmen with her curlers, pouring coffee. The morning light streaming through the window. It was too beautiful to end.

But the road was waiting. Barcelona was waiting. Pedro and Ricardo were waiting.

I finished my coffee. Ate the last tostada. Got up.

'Thank you,' I said. 'For everything.'

'My husband always wanted to go to Germany,' she said quietly. 'Munich. He always dreamed of it.' She stroked the doorframe. 'He died four years ago. Never made it.'

I swallowed. 'I'm sorry.'

'You don't have to be.' She smiled, but her eyes were moist. 'Drive for him, won't you? A little way.'

She hugged me. Tightly. Like a mother.

'Drive carefully. And come back when you're passing through again.'

'I will.'

I went outside. Lola was waiting. I strapped on my rucksack. Started her up. She rattled. Satisfied. Ready.

I waved to Carmen, who was standing in the doorway. She waved back.

Then I drove off. North. To Barcelona.

The N-340 was almost empty that Sunday morning. A few lorries. A few cars. But otherwise: no one. The world belonged to me. And Lola. And the road. The sun was low, painting the landscape in warm gold. It was one of those moments when you think you've understood the meaning of life, just before you realise that you're actually just hungry. To my right: the Mediterranean Sea, blue and sparkling, as if someone had thrown diamonds on it. To my left: orange groves, the trees heavy with fruit. The air smelled of salt and citrus.

I drove relaxed. 70 kilometres per hour. Not fast, but steady. Lola purred beneath me like a contented cat. Everything was perfect.

Around half past nine, I stopped at a petrol station in Vinaròs. A small town, right on the coast. The petrol station was one of those older stations – not modern, but clean. An elderly man behind the cash register who looked like he had been working there for thirty years. Not because I needed to refuel – the tank was still half full – but because I needed coffee. And maybe a croissant. Or two. The toast at Carmen's had been good, but my stomach had other plans. Croissants that contained so many preservatives that they could probably have survived a nuclear war.

I parked Lola next to the petrol pump and went inside. The man nodded to me in a friendly manner. I took a coffee from the machine – it tasted surprisingly civilised, like real coffee – and two packaged croissants. I put everything on the counter next to the coffee machine while I rummaged in my jacket pocket for my wallet.

'Cuatro euros veinte,' said the man.

I put my wallet on the counter. Next to the coffee machine. Took out the money. Four euros twenty. 'Gracias.' – 'De nada. Buen viaje.' I took the coffee and croissants, went outside, drank the coffee in three big gulps, ate a croissant standing up. Threw the packaging in the bin. Got on Lola. Started her up. Drove off.

An hour and a half later – shortly before half past eleven – Lola began to stutter. The engine coughed. Once. Twice. Then it ran smoothly again. Petrol. Of course. The tank was empty. I felt panic rising inside me. Panic is a horrible passenger, but it loves to grab the handlebars.

I reached between my legs to the fuel tap on the leg shield and turned it from 'Normal' to 'Reserve'. Lola ran smoothly again immediately. Nacho had shown me how to do it: 'Five litres in the main tank. When it's empty, she stutters. Then you reach down and turn on the reserve. Two more litres. That's enough for forty kilometres. You can even do it while driving. But then you have to refuel. Otherwise you'll be stuck.'

The reserve would last until the next petrol station. Hopefully.

Ten minutes later: 'Platja de Miami' petrol station. Large. Modern. Full. The petrol station was one of those modern, clean, impersonal stations. Glass. Chrome. Neon lights. The complete opposite of the small petrol station in Vinaròs. I stood at the pump, turned the fuel tap back to 'Normal' and filled the tank. Seven litres. Ten euros. I went to the cash register to pay.

I reached into my jacket pocket. Nothing. Strange. I reached into the other pocket. Nothing. In my trouser pocket. Nothing. I felt my heart beating faster. My wallet. Where was my wallet? My brain was going haywire. It was that kind of 'I'm doomed' feeling you usually only get when you're sitting in an aeroplane and the pilot announces, 'Does anyone have an instruction manual?'

I searched all my pockets. Jacket. Trousers. Even the pockets on my cargo shorts, where I usually only kept tissues and loose change. Nothing.

'Señor?' The cashier – a woman in her mid-thirties with a severe hairstyle and a sceptical look – looked at me. 'Everything all right?' 'My… my wallet,' I said. In German. Because my brain was busy panicking. 'It's gone.' '¿Qué?' 'Mi cartera.' My wallet. I pointed to my empty hands. 'No está.'

Her gaze grew colder. 'You don't have a wallet?' 'I… I had one. I don't know where it is.' She crossed her arms. 'You filled up. Twelve euros.' 'Yes. I know. But I… I can't find my wallet.'

A queue formed behind me. Three people. Then four. I could feel their stares. Impatient. Annoyed.

'Just a moment,' I said. 'Maybe it's with the Vespa. In my rucksack.' I ran outside. Opened the rucksack. Rummaged through it. Clothes. Toothbrush. Miguel's photo. Spare parts. But no wallet. 'Damn it. Damn it. DAMN IT.' I swore so intensely that a flower nearby probably wilted.

> **[SMS]** Sabine: 'The remaining boxes in the basement have to be gone by the end of the month. Otherwise, I'll put them out for bulk waste collection.'

I went back inside. The cashier was waiting. The queue was now six people long. 'I… I don't have it,' I said. My voice trembled slightly. Not from fear. From despair. While the woman looked at me as if I were a particularly dim-witted petty criminal, I took out my mobile phone. I frantically googled the station in Vinaròs, found the number and pressed call. My heart pounded against my ribs like a caged bird. A man answered. I explained the situation to him in a wild mixture of Spanish, English and desperate hand-gesture acoustics. '¿Cartera? ¿Café?' He said yes. He had it. Next to the coffee machine.

I hung up. A weight the size of Gran Canaria lifted from my heart. 'It's there,' I said to the cashier. 'Next to the coffee machine.'

'Sí. But you have to come and get it.'

I offered her my rucksack as collateral. 'It's… it's valuable. My clothes. Spare parts for the Vespa. A photo of my friend. Who died.' It was a cheap trick. Emotional. Manipulative. But damn it, I was desperate. She looked at me. Then at the rucksack. Then she sighed. 'Okay. But if you don't come back…' 'I'll come back. I promise.' She nodded. 'Leave it here.'

I put the rucksack behind the cash register. 'Thank you. Really. Thank you very much.' She shrugged. 'Go. Before I change my mind.'

As I walked out, the realisation hit me like a wet sledgehammer: that was eighty kilometres. Back. And then eighty again to get here. A hundred and sixty kilometres detour. Three hours. At least. What a bloody mess.

I drove at full throttle. Well. Lola's version of full throttle. Eighty kilometres per hour. Maybe eighty-five, downhill, with a tailwind. A speed at which even ambitious hikers overtake you with a pitying look. The road flew by. Or crawled. Hard to say. Time had lost its meaning. I stared at the road, kept the throttle open, ignored the pain in my bum, which was screaming that an hour and a half on a hard seat was not a smart idea. I did the maths. Doing maths under stress is like playing indoor halma in a hurricane – it leads nowhere.

I looked at my watch. It was just after twelve. I had breakfast there at half past nine. Two and a half hours had passed since then. That meant… if I was lucky, I'd be there around half past eleven. Then get my wallet. Then back. Around half past one. Then on to Barcelona. If all went well, I'd arrive around half past seven. Not at four. But at half past seven. I had missed the Vespa Club. Damn.

But at least I would have my wallet. And my money. And my credit card. Without it, I was… nobody. A person without identity. A traveller without means. I drove on. Southwards. Against time.

Vinaròs. I parked Lola in front of the petrol station and ran inside. The older man was still standing there. He saw me and smiled. 'Ah! You're back!'

'Hola,' I gasped. 'My wallet. I left it here this morning… next to the coffee machine…'

'Sí, sí!' He smiled even more broadly. He reached behind him and picked up my wallet. 'This one?' I could have cried. Almost. 'Yes! That's the one!' He gave it to me. I opened it. Everything was there. Money. Credit card. ID. Even the receipt from Carmen's Pensión. I looked at the greasy leather like it was a relic. My ID stared at me as if to say, 'Glad you're here too, you complete idiot.'

'Gracias,' I said. 'Muchas gracias. You saved my life.' He waved it off. 'De nada. It happens every day.' 'I still owe you something. From this morning.' He shook his head. 'No, no. You paid. But you left your wallet behind.' I laughed. Relieved. 'Thank you. Really.'

I ran back to Lola. Started her up. But before I drove off, I took out my mobile phone. If I left now and everything went well, I would arrive in Barcelona at half past seven at the earliest. The Vespa Club meeting started at four. I would miss it. Completely.

I opened WhatsApp. Wrote to Ricardo: 'Emergency. Lost my wallet. Had to make an 80 km detour. Won't be there until around 7:30 p.m. Sorry! Can't make the meeting.' I stared at the message. Then I pressed 'Send'.

The reply came after thirty seconds: 'No problem, amigo! Even better. There are more people there in the evening. After work. We'll wait for you. You have to tell the story! ●'

I smiled. Put my mobile phone away. Turned around. Headed north. Again.

Platja de Miami petrol station. I parked. Went inside. The same cashier. There were three people behind me in the queue. She saw me. Smiled slightly. 'You're back.' 'I promised my rucksack.' She handed it to me. 'Here. Everything's still in it.' I opened it, checked briefly. Everything was there. 'Thank you,' I said. 'Really.' 'You could have just driven on.' 'No. I… I keep my promises.'

She nodded. 'Good. More people should do that.' I paid the twelve euros for petrol and a cold Coke. She took the money and gave me the receipt. 'Where are you going?' 'Barcelona.' 'Long journey.' 'Yes. Very long.' 'Drive carefully.' 'I will.'

I went out. Got on Lola. And drove off. For the third time today. Towards Barcelona.

The afternoon sun was slanting across the sea as I reached Sitges. The town lay there like a white jewel on the coast, the houses glistening in the golden light, and for a moment I forgot the stress, the detour, the lost hours. It was beautiful here. Just beautiful.

I drove on. The N-340 now wound its way along the coast, and then it began: the Costa de Garraf. The cliffs. The road became a serpentine. Curve after curve. To my right, the land dropped steeply to the sea, the rocks rugged and wild, the water turquoise blue and endless. To my left: bare mountain slopes, barren and sun-scorched, with scattered cacti and low bushes that looked as if they were clinging to the rock.

I shifted into second gear. Then into third. Back into second. The bends came quickly, tight but not dangerous. Lola took them perfectly, as if she had been waiting for this moment. I felt the weight shift, felt the road beneath me, the wind coming from the left, smelling of salt. This was it. This was motorcycling. Not the desperate driving straight ahead on the motorway. But this: curves, sea, wind and the feeling that Lola and I were one. A feeling of freedom so great that it barely fit under my helmet.

I smiled under my helmet. Broadly. Genuinely.

The winding road took me higher, then down again, then up again. Sometimes I could already see Barcelona – far ahead, a hint of a city on the horizon. Then it disappeared behind a hill, reappeared, bigger, closer. The last few kilometres before Barcelona. They belonged to me. I didn't slow down. I didn't speed up. I just rode. In the moment. In the curve. On this road that looked like it had been built just for Vespas.

7:30 p.m. I arrived in Barcelona. Not at 4 p.m. as planned. But at 7:30 p.m. But that was okay. Ricardo had written that even more people would be there. After work. I had driven five hundred and ten kilometres. One hundred and sixty more than planned. My bum was numb. My arms ached. My back felt like a board. But I had my wallet. And the crew was waiting for me.

I drove straight to Pedro's workshop. The gate was open. The lights were on inside. I parked Lola. Got off. Went inside.

Pedro was standing at a workbench, working on a Vespa. He looked up when I came in.

'Kai! You're late!'

'I know. There were… complications.'

'What kind of complications?'

I told him the story. Forgot my wallet. Detour. An extra hundred and sixty kilometres.

He stared at me. Then he started laughing. Loudly. Heartily. He laughed so deeply that you could have measured it on his diaphragm as a magnitude 4 earthquake.

'You drove five hundred and ten kilometres in one day? On that Vespa?'

'Yes.'

'I read it on WhatsApp. But I thought you were exaggerating!'

'No. Every kilometre was real.'

He patted me on the shoulder. Then he went outside to Lola. I followed him.

He walked around her. Slowly. Professionally. Kneeled down by the rear wheel. Turned it. Listened.

'It's grinding.'

He stood up. Looked at the engine. Ran his finger over the casing. Oil. He rubbed it between his fingers.

'Engine is losing oil.'

Then he reached for the clutch lever. Pulled it. Checked the play. Let it go again.

He shook his head.

Then he kicked it. Once. Twice. On the third try, it started. He listened. Head tilted slightly to the side. Eyes closed.

After thirty seconds, he turned it off.

He looked at me.

'Kai. Listen. What you've done – from Albacete to here on this Vespa – is brave. It's commendable. You're inexperienced, spontaneous, and you still managed it. Respect.'

Pause.

'But you were lucky. Very lucky.'

I nodded. I knew that.

'The rear wheel is grinding. The engine is losing oil. The clutch has too much play. You got here because the Vespa is strong. But for the rest of the way home…' He whistled softly. 'How much is that?'

'Seventeen hundred. Approximately.'

'Seventeen hundred.' He shook his head. 'You won't make it. Not like this.'

I swallowed. 'What do you suggest?'

'You leave it here. In my workshop. Over the next few days, we'll overhaul it completely. Together. I'll help you. Rear wheel, engine, clutch, everything. Then you'll make it home. No problem.'

I hesitated. 'I don't want to give you any work.'

'Work?' He laughed. 'It's not work. It's an honour. You came all the way from Albacete on this Vespa. That deserves respect. So: it stays here. We'll fix it up properly. Yes?'

I nodded. 'Yes. Thank you.'

'Good.' He patted me on the shoulder. 'But now: the others are waiting for you in the bar. Ricardo has told everyone. You're already a legend.'

I smiled. Tired. Exhausted. But happy.

'Okay.'

We went out together. To a bar two streets away. Inside: Ricardo, Henry, Pau. The whole crew. They saw me. Called out. Hugged me.

'Kai! You did it!'

I told the story again. The lost wallet. The detour. The five hundred and ten kilometres.

They laughed. Patted me on the back. Ordered me a beer.

And I sat there. In this bar. With these people. And I thought: That was the longest day of my trip. But also the best. Because I had learned: No matter what happens. You can always turn around. Go back. Fix it. And then move on. Keep going. Until you arrive.

Because in the end, it's not the kilometres that count, but the stories you can tell when you wash away the dust of the road with a cold beer.

Chapter 17 – Barcelona Redux

[Soundtrack Shuffle: Queen – We Are the Champions]

Eight o'clock in the morning. I stood in front of Pedro's workshop and felt like it was my first day at school. Nervous. Excited. And with the same certainty in my stomach that I was guaranteed to break something very expensive today. Probably my finger. Or Lola's entire engine. Or – even worse – Pedro's trust in the German work ethic.

Pedro opened the roller door. The squeak echoed through the alley. He was wearing his blue overalls – old, faded, with oil stains that looked like a map from decades. His hands were already dirty. As if he had been working for two hours, even though he had only just arrived.

"Buenos días, Kai," he said with a grin. "Ready to learn?"

"Ready," I said. And lied.

He led me inside. A "hole in the wall," as he called it. Tiny. Maybe four by five metres. Three Vespas just about fit inside. His own – a blue Motovespa 150 from the sixties. And two "customer vehicles," as he said. Lola was on the lifting platform. Naked. Almost. The side panels were off. The engine was exposed. The wheels had been removed. She looked like a patient on the operating table who had just had her organs removed.

The walls were covered. Tools. Tools everywhere. Wrenches. Pliers. Hammers. Ratchet wrenches in all sizes. And in between: photos. Dozens of photos. Of grateful friends. Vespa riders. People laughing. Thumbs up. Next to their restored Vespas. And in the middle: a large framed photo. Black and white. Late fifties. A young man in overalls. Proud. Beaming. Next to him: an older man in a suit and tie. Between them: a brand-new Vespa. Faro Basso. Headlights on the handlebars. Classic.

"Is that you?" I asked.

Pedro nodded. "1959. My first workshop. The man there?" He pointed to the man in the suit. "NASA engineer. Wanted a Vespa. The best one. I built it for him."

"You had your own workshop?"

"Sí. A big one. With employees. For years." He smiled. "But then came retirement. And I… I couldn't stop."

"That's why this?"

"Sí. I rented this 'hole in the wall'. Small. Cheap. But enough." He looked around. "I'm happy here. Tinkering every day. It keeps me young."

I looked at him. Over eighty. But fit. Agile. He climbed a narrow ladder up to the false ceiling. Fetched a spare part. Came back down. Without panting. Pedro pointed to a small workbench. "Sit down. I'll explain."

I sat down. He took out a book – old, worn, filled with sketches and notes in Spanish and Catalan – and opened a chapter. "This is your Lola. Built in 1967. A very special model." He showed me the engine. The cylinder. The carburettor. The ignition.

"The two-stroke engine," he said, tapping the drawing. "Simple in principle. But sensitive. Like a beautiful woman. You have to understand how she ticks. Or she'll leave you. In the middle of the Pyrenees."

"Leaves me?"

"The engine dies. You don't." He grinned. "Probably."

I swallowed. Pedro continued, explaining the mixture, the oil, the ignition, and I tried to follow, nodding in the right places – the professional nod of a man who understands absolutely nothing but doesn't want to be rude. To be honest, I only understood half of it, and the other half sounded like magic, like alchemy, like something you couldn't learn in three days, but only through years of practice, through a thousand broken engines and bloody knuckles. I didn't have the years, nor did I want the bloody knuckles. But Pedro didn't seem to notice. Or he didn't care. Probably the latter.

"Today," said Pedro, closing the book, "we're changing the wheel bearing. At the back."

"Okay."

"You've driven 870 kilometres with it. It was almost dead. Listen."

He went to the lift, turned the rear wheel. It crunched. Loudly. Like gravel under shoes. Like sandpaper on metal.

"Do you hear that?"

"Yes."

"That's the bearing. It's dying. Another hundred kilometres and it would have seized up. Then: blockage. You'd fly over the handlebars."

"Shit."

"Sí. Shit." He smiled. "But today we're going to learn how to change it. And then you'll be safe."

The next three days were a masterclass. Not only in Vespa repair – although I learned a lot about Vespa repair – but also in humility.

In the realisation that I knew nothing. That I was a beginner. That every move I had taken for granted was wrong.

Day 1 – Disassembly

Pedro explained to me that it would probably be better to do a complete overhaul. I nodded. Together, we removed the engine from Lola. First, we cleaned the entire unit with petrol and a brush. After just half an hour, I was as high as I had been at my prom – except that back then, at least I could still dance, whereas now I was standing there disoriented with a spanner in my hand, wondering whether I was hallucinating or whether Pedro really looked like my tax advisor in blue.

We clamped the engine onto the workbench as if it were a sinner on the rack. Then he showed me how to dismantle the entire inner workings into its individual parts, step by step. With each part I unscrewed, he explained its function and how to tell if it needed to be replaced. I understood maybe half of it, but nodded like a student in the front row and have never said "Sí, sí" so many times in a row in my life. The slight fog in my brain from petrol fumes didn't help much either.

He also showed me how to remove the bearings with a hot air gun. Warm up the bearing seat and wait for the clunk. Simple. He said. I immediately burned my fingers. I swore a lot!

"Swearing sounds nicer in Spanish," he said. "¡Joder! ¡Me cago en la puta!" And then, smiling: "But German has more energy. More… anger."

After four hours – four bloody hours in which I thought I would never in my life rummage through the exposed, oily innards of an engine like a paramedic for shot-up Vespas, in which I thought at least seven times, "That's it, I give up," and twice seriously considered whether Pedro might adopt me so I could stay here forever and continue to fail – everything lay before us. Every single part of the "totally simple" 150cc two-stroke engine. I stared at the pile. It looked like the 10,000-piece jigsaw puzzle from last Christmas. Which I hadn't finished either. My track record with complicated things was miserable.

"Well done, Kai." Pedro grinned.

I smiled back uncertainly. We took a break at noon. Siesta. Pedro went home – he lived three streets away, in a flat above a bakery, and I could imagine him sitting there, a glass of red wine in his hand, his feet up, reading the newspaper or just looking out the window – and I went to Khan's Kebab, that Pakistani snack bar two blocks away that looked like it was about to collapse at any moment, but which made the best chicken tikka in all of Barcelona, spicy and smoky and with rice that was interestingly both dry and juicy at the same time.

I sat outside on a wobbly plastic chair and ate slowly. The rice was perfect. The air smelled of spices and hot oil. Two pigeons fought over a chip. My mobile vibrated.

[LinkedIn] Your network: "Congratulations! You are among the top 5% of profile visitors in the insurance industry."

I dismissed it and continued eating. And for the first time in weeks – maybe months – I didn't think about my ex, my boss, Kempten, or my old life. I thought about the wheel bearing. About the hammer. About Pedro's patience. About the way he had shown me this morning how to remove a bearing without destroying it. Slowly. Concentrated. With respect.

I'm learning something, I thought. Finally. After years of stagnation, I'm learning something real. Something that didn't fit into Excel spreadsheets. Something that no one could take away from me. When I returned to the workshop, Pedro was already sitting there, with a stool next to the lifting platform, and he waved me over.

"Now we're going to replace the front brake together."

"What could possibly go wrong!" I thought to myself.

"Brakes," said Pedro, his voice serious, almost solemn, "are life. Broken brakes mean: you die."

He showed me the old brake pads, and they were worn down to the metal backing, with almost no lining left, just a wafer-thin layer between me and an accident.

"You had maybe ten per cent left," he said. "On a mountain road in the Pyrenees? That's nothing. You wouldn't have been able to stop. Do you understand?"

I understood. I understood very well. And I felt queasy at the thought of how often I had braked in the last few days, how often I had relied on Lola to stop, without knowing that she was almost unable to do so. We changed the brake pads and Pedro showed me how to adjust them, the right tension, not too tight, not too loose, and how to test whether they were working, and I pressed the brake lever and felt the brake engage immediately, firmly and securely, and it felt like a promise, like a guarantee that maybe I wouldn't die after all.

In the evening, I arrived at the guesthouse completely exhausted. My hands looked like they had been in a failed action film shoot. Cuts. A torn nail. And under the other nails, about a kilogram of black gunk had accumulated – probably a mixture of oil, petrol, dirt and what remained of my dignity. I took a hot shower. The water turned brown. Fawn brown. I scrubbed until my hands looked like hands again and not like tools. I had a slight headache from cleaning the engine and the million pieces of information Pedro had fed me raw today. I ended my day in a bar on the corner with a beer, an ibuprofen and a few croquetas.

Day 2 – Reassembly

The next morning, Pedro went through every single part in the pile on the workbench with me first thing and explained whether it could still be used. Every part that was "dead" flew with a loud bang into a metal bin in the corner. Not much was left.

"A little love," Nacho had said. I stared at the mountain of broken parts that ended up in the metal bin. That wasn't "a little love." That was intensive care. That was organ donation. That was: Lola had exactly three working parts, and two of them were the tyres. But Pedro radiated enough confidence for both of us. Probably for all of Barcelona.

He then came back with a storage box from the mezzanine. It was a bit like Christmas. Lots of shiny new parts for Lola's heart! Step by step, we put everything back together. In reverse order from yesterday. He showed me how to re-line a clutch and clean a carburettor. The second time around, I understood a little more and the fog in my brain cleared. But I still said "Sí, sí" too often when I should have said "Häääh". After five hours, we were done. Exhausted. The seals were in place. We filled it with oil. Everything was tight. The engine looked like new.

Day 3 – Wedding and Connection

We checked all the cables and wires, as far as they were visible. "They are Lola's nerve strands. And if something breaks, then she won't work anymore," Pedro explained to me with a serious expression. "We have to check everything!"

"Everything?"

"Everything. Because if a wire breaks – and they always break at the worst possible moment – then you're stranded. Somewhere. Alone."

He showed me how to change cables, and it looked easy when he did it, his hands moving quickly and precisely, like a surgeon performing an operation he's done a thousand times, but when I tried it, it was hell. The cables had to be threaded through narrow guides in the handlebars, through holes in the frame that were so small you could barely see them, and every time I thought I'd done it, the cable would get caught, twist, and I'd have to start all over again.

"Patience," said Pedro. "The cable is not your enemy. The cable is your friend."

"This friend is a bastard," I muttered.

Pedro laughed. Loudly. So loudly that the three Vespas in the workshop seemed to vibrate, that the photos on the walls shook.

"Sí," he said, wiping a tear from the corner of his eye. "Sometimes friends are bastards. But you still need them." He looked at me. Not like a teacher looks at a student. But like a father. Or an older brother. Someone who understands that sometimes you have to swear to keep going. "Keep going," he said quietly. "You can do it." And I believed him.

After four hours – four hours of swearing, sweating, wondering if I should just give up and scrap the Vespa – all the cables were in place. Clutch cable, throttle cable, both brake cables, all new, all perfectly threaded, and when I pulled the clutch lever, I felt how smoothly it ran, without resistance, without jerking, and I suddenly understood why Pedro had said that cables were the nerves of the Vespa, because without them Lola was just a piece of metal, but with them she was alive.

"Now," said Pedro, "adjust it. The tension has to be perfect. Too loose – the clutch won't disengage. Too tight – the cable will snap." He showed me how to adjust the tension, millimetre by millimetre, with feeling, not force, and when I was done, he nodded with satisfaction. "Now you can do it," he said. "If a cable snaps, you can replace it. Anywhere. Even without a workshop."

After we had everything back in place – tank, seat, fuel hose connected – we slowly lowered Lola and pulled her off the lift out in front of the small workshop.

"Kick her," said Pedro, grinning like a father watching his child's first attempt at riding a bike.

Nervously, I put my hand on the kick starter. Kicked. Nothing. Again. Silence. I looked at Pedro. He nodded. "Again." I kicked. Harder. First a stutter. Then a cough. And then – papapapapapapap.

The engine was running. Smoothly. Richly. Alive. It sounded like a bloody miracle. I had a tear in my eye. I tried to blink it away, but Pedro saw it anyway. He said nothing. He just patted me on the shoulder. Firmly. Like a promise. I stood there, next to this old Vespa that I had brought back to life with my own hands – together with an eighty-year-old Spaniard who had taught me more than any boss in ten years of office work – and for the first time in months, I didn't feel like a failure. I felt like someone who had achieved something. Something real.

Pedro patted me on the shoulder. "Well done, Kai. Lola is ready now. For the Pyrenees. For the Alps. For anything." I looked at the Vespa. She gleamed. New. Strong. "Tomorrow," said Pedro, "we're going to Freixenet. Cava tasting. You deserve it."

Day 4 – Freixenet and the Ceremony

Ten o'clock. Twelve Vespas gathered in front of Bodega La Massana. I stood next to Lola, wearing my Hawaiian shirt – turquoise, with huge palm trees – and felt like a member of a gang, a cool gang, a gang I never wanted to leave.

Ricardo came up to me. "Ready for Freixenet?"

"What's Freixenet?"

"Cava. The best cava in Spain. We're going there. Tasting. Drinking. Having fun."

"Sounds good."

"Sounds very good."

We set off. A caravan of twelve Vespas. Through Barcelona. Through the suburbs. Out into the countryside. People stared. Children waved. Old women smiled. Drivers honked their horns – some annoyed, some appreciative. We were loud. We were colourful. We were impossible to miss. And damn, it felt good.

After an hour, we reached Sant Sadurní d'Anoia. A small town. In the middle of the Penedès wine region. "Freixenet," said Ricardo, pointing to a huge sign. "The largest cava producer in Spain. We have… connections."

The winery was gigantic. Modern buildings. Old cellars. And everywhere: bottles. Millions of bottles. A man in a suit welcomed us. Miquel. A friend of Pedro's. Former Vespa rider himself. Now a manager at Freixenet.

"Welcome, amigos!" he exclaimed. "Park your Vespas. We have a tour for you." The tour was impressive. Deep cellars. Kilometres long. Bottles stored on shelves. Hundreds. Thousands. Millions.

"This cava is three years old," explained the guide. "Traditional method. Like champagne. But better."

After the tour: the tasting. We sat in a large room. Wooden tables. High ceilings. And in front of us: six glasses. Filled with cava. "From dry to sweet," explained the guide. "Try them all. Find your favourite." I tasted them. One after the other. The first: Brut. Dry. Tart. Perfect. The second: Brut Nature. Even drier. Almost sharp. The third: Semi-seco. Sweeter. Softer. Just a small sip each time. I still had to drive, and even when I was sober I didn't exactly drive like Márquez in MotoGP. Didn't want to take any chances.

Ricardo leaned over. "Do you like it?"

"I love it."

"Good. Because we bought you a case. It'll be waiting for you when you get home. That is, if you get home." He laughed dirty.

"What?"

"Six bottles. From all of us. For Germany. When you arrive, open one. And think of us."

My eyes welled up. Damn cava. "Thank you. From the bottom of my heart."

"No problem, hermano. You're family now."

We drove back to Barcelona. The sun was low. Golden. The vineyards glistened. The Vespas sang their pap-pap-pap in chorus. And I thought: This. This is it. This is real life.

The Ceremony

We met at the Bar Antilles. Not just the twelve from today. But everyone. Thirty people. The entire Vespa Club Barcelona. The bar was small. Too small for thirty people. But it didn't matter. We stood outside. On the street. Beer in our hands. Pedro tapped on a glass. Everyone fell silent.

"Amigos," he began. "We are here for something special." He pointed at me. I felt my heart beating faster. "Kai came to Barcelona three weeks ago. Lost. Broken. Looking for a Vespa." Laughter. But friendly. "He found her. Lola. And then… he rode her. 870 kilometres. Through Spain. With problems. With breakdowns. But he made it." Applause. Loud. I blushed. "And then he came here. And he learned. For three days. In my workshop. He worked. Like a real mechanic."

Pedro held up a T-shirt. The club shirt. Black. With the Vespa Club Barcelona logo on the back. "This is for you, Kai. You're now an honorary member. Forever." The crowd exploded. Applause. Whistles. Shouts. Ricardo came forward. Put the shirt over my shoulders.

"Welcome to the family, hermano."

I tried to speak. But my voice failed me. My eyes were wet. "Thank you," I finally whispered. "For everything." Pedro hugged me. Tightly. "You deserve it, hijo., You deserve it."

We drank late into the night. Beer. Cava. Stories. Ricardo told us about his first Vespa. A PK 125. "I wrecked it after three days. Into a well. The Vespa survived. My pride didn't." Javier told us about his rally through the Pyrenees. "There were seven of us on Vespas. Only four came back. But those four… we were brothers forever." And I told them about Lola. About Nacho. About Carmen. About the wallet disaster. They laughed. Patted me on the back. Refilled my glass.

"You're one of us now," Ricardo said for the third time that evening. "And we never forget our own."

Around midnight, I was standing outside. In front of the bar. A cigarette in my hand – even though I didn't smoke. But someone had given it to me, and I hadn't said no. Pedro came out. Stood next to me.

"You're leaving tomorrow."

I nodded. "Eight o'clock."

"The journey home will be tough."

"I know."

"But Lola is strong now. And you… you know her. Every part. If something breaks, you can fix it."

"I hope so."

He put a hand on my shoulder. "I know it." We stood there. Silently. Two men in front of a bar. One over eighty. The other forty. Both tired. Both happy.

"Thank you, Pedro. For everything."

"No, Kai. Thank you. For reminding an old man why he does this." He patted my heart. "For love. Not for money."

I nodded. Couldn't speak. "Now go. Sleep. Tomorrow is a big day."

I stubbed out my cigarette. Went to my hostel. I wore the shirt. Even in bed. I was now part of something. Something bigger. And tomorrow I would set off. To France, Italy, Austria… to Germany. Home. But part of me would always stay here. In Barcelona. With the Vespa brothers. Forever.

Chapter 18 – The Last Turn

[Soundtrack Shuffle: Desireless – Voyage Voyage]

The farewell came too soon. Or maybe it was just right. I didn't know. But when I stood in front of Bodega La Massana at eight o'clock in the morning, Lola beside me.

Ricardo was the first to arrive. Of course. The man moved through life like someone who had never learned that there was such a thing as a quiet entrance. He was wearing his usual Fred Perry polo shirt – today in navy blue – and his Adidas trainers were as immaculately white as if he had just taken them out of the box, even though I knew he had been wearing them for years. How he managed that was a mystery to me. Spanish magic, probably. Or he had twenty identical pairs.

"So you're really going," he said, folding his arms. It didn't sound like a question. More like a statement from someone who couldn't quite believe it was actually happening.

"Looks like it," I replied, trying to smile, but it felt shaky, like a table with one leg too short.

Pedro stepped beside him. The old man looked the same as always: oil-stained work trousers, wild white hair sticking out in all directions as if he'd just been electrocuted, and those calm, knowing eyes that looked at you as if they could see right into your soul and diagnose your engine's misfire at the same time. He put a hand on Lola's handlebars, stroking them slowly, examining them, lovingly.

"She runs well?"

"Like new," I said.

"Take care of her," said Pedro. "And yourself."

"Drive slowly – remember what I said about the running-in period. The engine is practically new now."

I nodded.

Ricardo patted me so hard on the shoulder that I stumbled forward a step. "You'll come back, amigo. Promise?"

"I promise," I said, and I meant it.

"Good. Because if you don't, we'll drive to Germany and get you." He grinned broadly. "And German motorways are boring. No curves."

The others laughed. Someone handed me a café con leche that I hadn't ordered, but I gratefully accepted it. Another handed me a bag of bocadillos – sandwiches so thickly packed that they looked like small bricks. "For the road," he said. "So you don't starve before you reach France."

We stood there, a small group of men in parkas and polo shirts, surrounded by Vespas, in a square in Barcelona that smelled of coffee. The sun was still low, casting long shadows on the cobblestones. It was one of those moments that felt like the end of something important. And the beginning of something else.

Pedro held something out to me. A small round metal badge, no bigger than a playing card, with the Vespa Club Barcelona logo on it and a kind of double-sided tape on the back. "For your Vespa," he said. "So everyone knows she belongs to us. And you too."

I took it, it felt cool in my hand, and suddenly my eyes were wet, and I had to look away because I didn't want to cry in front of these men, damn it, even though they had probably seen enough crying Germans to not be surprised anymore.

"Thank you," I murmured. That was all I could manage.

"Vuelve pronto," Ricardo said quietly. Come back soon.

"Sí," I said. "Soon."

I cleaned a spot with my sleeve and stuck the badge on the front of Lola's leg shield, directly opposite the chrome nameplate, where everyone could see it. It looked great. Then I swung myself onto the Vespa, started the engine – which started right away, of course, because Lola now ran like Swiss clockwork – and waved one last time. They waved back, all of them, a row of men who had taken in a stranger because he had told a story and because Vespas were more than just machines. They were promises. And memories. And bridges between people who probably had nothing in common except the knowledge that life was too short to spend standing still.

I drove off. Slowly. Not because Lola had to, but because I had to. Because every metre I moved away from Bodega La Massana felt like a small loss. But also like a step forward. And at some point, I couldn't see them anymore, and I was alone. Just me and Lola and the road ahead of us.

The Costa Brava unfolded like a painting that someone had painted with too much enthusiasm and too little fear of colour. On the right: the sea. Blue. Not just blue, but that aggressive, challenging Mediterranean blue that looked as if someone had taken liquid sky and poured it into the water. On the left: rocks. Red-brown, sharp, wild, with pine trees that looked as if they were growing out of sheer defiance, their roots clawing into crevices that were actually too small to sustain life. In between: me. A German insurance salesman on an old Vespa, trying not to miss the bend while at the same time trying to soak up everything – the colours, the smells, the feeling of wind and sun and freedom that was so tangible I could have filled a jar with it and taken it home with me.

I only stopped to refuel. After a few hours, I saw the sign: "Cadaqués 5 km". The small white village by the sea that Dalí had loved because it was so far away from everything that even reality struggled to reach it. But before I wanted to have lunch in Cadaqués, there was a detour I had to make. Or wanted to. Or needed to. The distinction had become blurred by now.

I turned onto the narrow road, which was even more winding than the main road – something I wouldn't have thought possible – and which led eastwards, to where the peninsula ended and only the sea remained. The sign said: "Parc Natural del Cap de Creus". The easternmost point of Spain. The end of the world. At least, that's how it felt.

The landscape changed. Became barren. Wilder. The pine trees disappeared, replaced by low, shaggy bushes that clung to the ground as if they knew that the wind here was merciless. And the wind came. Immediately. Not gentle, not friendly, but like a slap in the face that hit me as soon as I reached the coast. Lola swayed, and I had to hold both hands firmly on the handlebars, leaning my upper body forward to avoid being blown off the road.

Then it happened. A bend. Sharper than the others. To the left. A gust. Stronger than the others. Gravel under the rear wheel. The sound: like bones breaking. The crash barrier came towards me. Behind it: nothing. Rocks. Thirty metres of air. The sea.

Time stretched out. I smelled rubber. I smelled my own fear – metallic, sour, sticking to my palate. My hands clawed at the handlebars, knuckles white, finger joints aching. A wave of cold shivers from the end of my spine to the tips of my hair. That's it, I thought. That was it, for sure now. My heart stopped. Or beat so fast that it felt like it had stopped.

Then the tyre gripped again. A jolt. My weight to the left. Lola stabilised. The crash barrier was beside me. Not in front of me. I drove. I breathed. I was alive.

I stopped. Immediately. At the next viewpoint, which was more like a pile of gravel with a view of the sea. I turned off the engine. Sat there. My hands were still shaking. My pulse was pounding in my ears like a dull techno track. And my brain caught up with what had just happened, with the delay of an office finally processing the application. I had almost died. Not metaphorically. Not as a figure of speech. But actually, concretely, physically almost flown off a cliff because a gust of wind had decided that today was a good day to send a German insurance salesman into the Mediterranean.

I laughed. It wasn't a happy laugh. More like the laugh of someone who has just realised how absurd it all was. I had risked my secure job, left my secure flat, my secure life, to ride an old Vespa through Europe. I almost crashed doing a wheelie and almost had heatstroke. I slept in hotels that probably violated all hygiene regulations. And now I was almost killed by a gust of wind. Not from a heart attack in the office, surrounded by file folders and the smell of stale coffee. But here. At the easternmost point of Spain. With a view of the sea. Diagnosis: death in a Hawaiian shirt.

Miguel would have liked that. The place, I mean. Not my near death. Although, who knows. He had a strange sense of humour. I took a deep breath. Then another. My hands stopped shaking. My pulse returned to normal. Somewhere above me, a bird circled – a hawk, perhaps, or a buzzard, I'm no ornithologist – looking as if it were wondering what that idiot down there was doing. Good question, bird. Good question.

I looked at Lola. She stood there, motionless, patient, as if nothing had happened. As if she hadn't just almost had the flight of her life. 57 years old and still cooler than me.

"That was close," I said to her.

She said nothing. She was a Vespa.

"But we're still alive," I added.

Still nothing. But I swear the chrome mirror flashed briefly in the sun, as if she were winking. I got back on. Started the engine. It started, reliable as ever. And I drove on, slower now, more carefully, both hands firmly on the handlebars, the wind at my neck instead of in my face.

Life was dangerous. I had known that. In theory. But theory and practice were two different things. Like insurance policies and actual claims. You could calculate everything, insure everything, plan everything. And then a gust of wind came and wiped the whole plan off the table. But I was still alive. And that was more than some plans could claim.

The lighthouse stood where the road ended, on a rocky outcrop that looked as if someone had simply thrown it into the sea and hoped it would stick. White. Slim. Lonely. Around it: nothing but rocks, sharp and jagged, worn by the wind into strange shapes that looked like frozen waves or the thoughts of an artist who had stared at the sun for too long. And behind it: the sea. Endless. Blue. Wild. It crashed against the rocks with a fury that sounded like applause, and the spray flew so high that it reached my skin, salty water on my lips.

I parked Lola next to the only other vehicle – a dented Renault that looked like it had spent the last twenty years up here and had no regrets – folded out the side stand and got off. My legs were stiff, my back ached, but it didn't matter. I walked to the edge of the cliff, where there was a low stone wall that seemed more symbolic than protective, and leaned against it, feeling the wind tugging at my Hawaiian shirt as if it wanted to tear it off me.

[Email] Wine Club Germany: "Your monthly selection: 6 bottles of Pinot Gris from the Palatinate have been shipped."

The easternmost point of Spain. The place where the sun first rose. I stood there and looked at the sea that stretched to Italy, to Greece, to the end of the known world, and I thought of Miguel. Of the photo. Of "Mi libertad empieza aquí". But where exactly was this "here"? In Albacete, where he had bought the Vespa? In Barcelona, where I had found the Vespa brothers? Here, at the end of Spain, where there was nothing but water and sky? Or was "here" everywhere I stopped, breathed and understood that life did not take place in the office, but right at that moment, with the wind in my face and salt on my lips?

A voice snapped me out of my thoughts. "¿Quieres algo?"

I turned around. A woman was standing in the doorway of a small bar I hadn't noticed. She was maybe sixty, wearing faded jeans and a cardigan, and in her hand was a cigarette whose smoke was blown away by the wind before it left her lips.

"Una Coca-Cola," I said. "Por favor."

She disappeared inside and came back with an ice-cold bottle. I paid, drank, and the stuff was so cold it burned my throat, but it was perfect.

"Bonito lugar," I said. Nice place. My Spanish was still terrible, but it was enough for three words.

She nodded. "Tranquilo. La mayoría no llega hasta aquí." Quiet. Most people don't come here.

"¿Por qué no?"

She shrugged, took a drag on her cigarette. "Demasiado lejos. Demasiado viento. Demasiado vacío." Too far. Too windy. Too empty. She smiled. "Pero eso es bueno. La tranquilidad es buena." But that's good. The tranquillity is good.

I nodded. I didn't understand every word, but I understood enough. Too far, too windy, too empty. That sounded like a description of freedom. I finished my Coke, put the empty bottle back on the counter and nodded to the woman, who nodded back and lit another cigarette. Then I went back to Lola, swung myself onto the saddle and started the engine. The wind hadn't died down, but that didn't matter. I was ready. And more cautious. I took one last look at the lighthouse, the rocks, the sea. Then I drove off, back to the main road, towards Cadaqués.

Cadaqués was exactly what I had expected, and at the same time not. The houses were white. So white that they dazzled in the midday sun. With blue shutters that creaked in the wind and narrow alleys that wound like drunkards. Fishing boats lay in the small harbour, their colours – red, blue, yellow – shining against the white of the houses like splashes of colour in a monochrome painting. And everywhere: tourists. Of course. This was Dalí country, and Dalí attracted people like light attracts moths.

I parked Lola at the edge of the harbour, next to a row of other scooters – almost exclusively modern plastic: Yamahas, Hondas, etc. – and walked through the narrow alleys. The famous Dalí house, the Casa Salvador Dalí, was located in Port Lligat, a few kilometres away. But here in Cadaqués, too, his traces were everywhere: postcards, posters, souvenirs with melting clocks and burning giraffes. The man had been dead for decades, but his merchandising lived on. Capitalism knows no mercy. Not even for surrealists.

I decided to visit the museum another time. Or never. Some things were better as an idea than as an experience. Like ice bathing. Or sushi from the station kiosk.

There was a small restaurant right on the waterfront, with plastic chairs and wobbly tables that looked like they would fly away with the next gust of wind. But the smell coming from the kitchen was so good that I couldn't help but sit down. A waitress – young, bored, with a piercing in her nose – came over and handed me a menu that was sticky with unidentifiable substances.

"Suquet de peix," I said without looking any further. Fish stew. Catalan. It had to be good here, or the restaurant would have no reason to exist.

She nodded and disappeared. Ten minutes later, a bowl arrived, steaming like a small volcano. The suquet smelled of the sea, garlic, saffron and tomatoes, a combination that worked perfectly, and how. I dipped bread into it – thick, hard bread that crunched – and it tasted like the essence of Spain: intense, honest, uncompromising. Fish that had been swimming in the sea a few hours ago. Potatoes that tasted of earth. Olive oil as green as the hills. And with it, a glass of wine, white, fruity, cool.

I ate slowly. My gaze lost itself in the vastness of the sea, sweeping over the boats rocking in the water, over the seagulls screeching and fighting over breadcrumbs. And I thought: This is it. This is life. Not meetings, not quarterly reports, not coffee machines that sigh. But this. Food that tastes good. Places that breathe. People who laugh.

> **[Notification]** Todoist: "3 overdue tasks! 'Finish tax return' open for 127 days."

I paid – too much, but that didn't matter – ran back to Lola and drove off. North. Towards France.

The border came sooner than I expected. La Jonquera. A small town, nothing more than a collection of warehouses, outlet shops and truck parking lots. But important. Because this is where Spain ended and France began. This is where capitalism showed its truly ugly face. No matter what you needed: drugs, women, tobacco or gambling, it was just a stone's throw away. An ugly place where you wanted to check every three minutes whether the wheels were still on the vehicle and your wallet was still in your pocket. Let's get going!

There was no barrier. Just a sign. Just a road that suddenly widened and a sign saying "France / Francia". I stopped, parked Lola and got off. I stood there, one foot in Spain, the other in France. Or at least it felt that way, even though the border was nowhere to be seen. I placed Lola in front of the Spain sign and took a picture – for her – as a farewell.

Three weeks. I had been in Spain for just under three weeks. And it felt like a lifetime. Like several lifetimes. I had arrived as someone who had been empty. Numb. Functioning, but not living. And now? I didn't know exactly who I was now. But I was different. I could feel it. In the way I sat on Lola without being tense. In the way I looked ahead without fear. In the way I breathed, deeply and calmly, as if I had only just learned how to do it.

I took out my mobile phone and dialled Isabel's number. It rang three times, then she picked up.

"Kai?"

"Hola, Isabel."

"Where are you?"

"At the border. France. I'm leaving Spain."

Silence. Then: "Miguel would be proud of you, hijo."

My throat tightened. "Thank you," I said quietly.

"Take care of yourself. And come home safely."

"I will."

I hung up, put my mobile phone away, and stood there for a moment. Then I got back on Lola, started the engine, and drove off. To France. To the north. Home. Or what was left of it. But as I drove, the French countryside around me – flatter, more orderly, different from Spain – I thought: Maybe "home" is no longer the place where I come from. Maybe it's the place where I belong. And maybe I'm still looking for it.

I reached Perpignan around six in the evening. The sun was already low, painting the sky orange and pink, and the city smelled of bread and wine and something I couldn't name, but which was French, definitely French. I found a small hotel not far from the station, paid for one night, pushed Lola into the courtyard and carried my rucksack up to a room that was small and smelled of lavender. I took a long shower, letting the hot water run over my back, washing away the salt of the sea, the dust of the road, the fatigue of the last few days. Then I lay down on the bed, stared at the ceiling and thought of nothing and everything at the same time.

Outside, I heard the hum of engines, the laughter of people, the clinking of glasses. Life went on. Always. Everywhere. And me? I was right in the middle of it. I smiled.

Chapter 19 – Massacre and Dropouts

[Soundtrack Shuffle: ZAZ – Je veux]

Saturday morning, seven o'clock, and I was standing in front of the Hôtel de la Gare in Perpignan. The air was already warm on my skin, the sky cloudless and a deep blue that tells you you're in the south. The hotel behind me – simple, clean, decent. The road was waiting.

Lola was ready. Everything was fine. I put my rucksack on the luggage rack and tightened the straps. I studied the road map. Today I would leave the coast and ride inland – first to Béziers, then on to Montpellier. A hundred and ninety kilometres in total, a long day, but doable. For people with a functioning backbone.

I started Lola. She woke up reliably, like an old friend who says "good morning" without being intrusive. I smiled and drove off into the French morning. Perpignan lay somewhat sleepily before me, the streets empty except for a few rubbish trucks and a baker raising his blinds. I drove through the city, then out onto the N-9 heading north. The road led away from the coast, inland, through rolling hills and vineyards.

The landscape was like something out of a photo book – Mediterranean, warm, peaceful. Vines climbed the hills, small villages with ochre-coloured houses dozed in the morning sun. The air smelled of thyme and dry grass, and I felt relaxed. Better than good. Free. I drove leisurely, calmly and steadily. Lola purred contentedly, the wind was warm, and the road stretched through the landscape like a ribbon. If you ignored the occasional pain in parts of the body for which there are no polite terms in the German language.

After an hour and a half, I saw it for the first time: Béziers. The city lay on a hill, and the first thing you saw was the Saint-Nazaire Cathedral – enormous, imposing, towering like a fortress over the Orb River. It didn't look like a church. It looked like something Sauron would have designed in his Gothic phase. A castle cathedral. A church fortress. An architectural identity conflict from the Middle Ages.

"Impressive," I murmured, steering Lola off the main road towards the city centre. The road led downhill to the river, and then – suddenly – I was standing in front of the Pont Vieux, the old bridge. A medieval arched bridge made of solid stone, spanning the Orb like the backdrop for every other medieval fantasy film. And behind it, high up on the rocky ridge: the city, the cathedral, everything golden in the sunlight, Instagram-ready since 1209.

I stopped, parked Lola, and got off. I leaned against the bridge railing and stared. It was one of those moments when you just stand there and think, "Okay. This would have made a good cover page for my non-existent travel blog." The water of the Orb flowed sluggishly beneath me, green and calm. The cathedral sat enthroned above like a stone memorial. I did a quick Google search and learned that a massacre had taken place here in 1209 during the Albigensian Crusade – twenty thousand dead, men, women and children. "Kill them all, God will recognise his own," the papal legate had allegedly said. A medieval PR disaster of the first order. Today, that would have caused at least a shitstorm on Twitter. Probably #CancelChurch.

I looked at the cathedral, at the battlements and towers. A city that had stood here for millennia, survived wars, massacres, revolutions, probably even French finance ministers. And my biggest problem in recent years had been that my presentations weren't finished on time and that the printer in the office always had paper jams, preferably five minutes before important meetings. Perspective.

You get it for free when you get off the couch and visit a few old cities.

I got back on Lola and rode up to the old town. The alleys were narrow, steep, paved with cobblestones that looked so old that they probably knew Napoleon's horses personally. Lola rattled up the road like an asthmatic lawnmower in a mountain marathon, every bump felt in my spine and various other parts of my body that I had successfully ignored for years. To the left and right, houses made of light sandstone crowded together, some with cracked facades, others freshly renovated. Blue and green shutters, laundry hung between the houses like southern French prayer flags.

Once at the top, I drove to the cathedral. I stood in front of it, engine off, and stared up. It was enormous – towers, battlements, massive stone walls. More fortress than house of God. I took a few steps closer, stood in the shadow of the walls, and suddenly felt tiny. Which was probably the point. Medieval architecture as psychological warfare. "Look how small you are. Now donate something for the restoration."

Behind the cathedral, I found the esplanade – a wide viewpoint from which you could see the entire Orb Valley. Hills, vineyards, the first foothills of the Cévennes in the distance. I stood there, hands in my pockets, and took a deep breath. Up here, it was quiet and peaceful. Only the wind and the distant hum of the city below.

"Spectacular! Wow!"

I walked back through the alleys, pushing Lola through the narrow streets until I reached the Allées Paul Riquet – a wide promenade lined with plane trees that ran through the city like a green lifeline. Here, people sat in cafés, drinking coffee, reading newspapers, talking. Life here seemed slow, relaxed, without hustle and bustle. No one was frantically checking their smartphones. No one was rushing to a meeting. It was disturbingly beautiful.

I found a small café – "Le Chantecler" – and sat down outside under a tree. A waitress came over, young, friendly, with a smile that said, "I have time, and you should too."

"Bonjour! Vous désirez?"

I took a deep breath. Time for the international language disaster. "Hello. Do you speak English?"

She shook her head. "Non, désolée."

Of course not. Why should she? We were in France, the only country in the world where English doesn't work on principle. "Eh… café? Espresso?"

"Ah oui! Un café."

"Si. And… eh…" I pointed to the menu, to something that looked like a small pastry. "This?"

"Une tielle sétoise?"

I had no idea what that was, but it sounded like food. "Si! Perfetto! Tielle!"

She smiled amusedly, took my order, and left. My Itanol took France by storm.

I leaned back and watched the people. Old men played boules under the trees with the seriousness of UN delegates, children ran around between the benches, a woman fed pigeons with a devotion I had last seen in stamp collectors.

The coffee arrived – strong, hot, perfect. And then the pastry: a small, round pie, baked golden brown. I took a bite. Inside was spicy octopus in tomato sauce, hot, salty, incredibly good. It tasted like the south of France, like the sea and sun and honest cuisine that had never heard of molecular gastronomy.

"Perfect."

> **[Notification]** Amazon: "Your subscription order 'Printer paper, 10,000 sheets' has been delivered!"

I stared at the display. Printer paper? I was sitting in Béziers, a two-thousand-year-old city, eating octopus pie under two-hundred-year-old trees, and Amazon thought I was interested in copy paper. It was the perfect metaphor for my old life. Or perhaps for the problem of Western civilisation. Hard to say. I paid, got on Lola, and rode on.

The ride from Béziers to Montpellier was long but beautiful. The road wound through rolling hills, past vineyards and small villages. The sun was high, the heat was bearable, and Lola ran perfectly. For about two hours, I felt like I was in a French road movie – only without Juliette Binoche and with significantly more neck pain.

Around three o'clock, the weather changed. The sky turned grey, clouds rolled in, dark and heavy like my mood on an average Monday morning at the office. The wind picked up, suddenly cool, and I felt the first drops.

"Not now. Please, not now."

But the weather didn't care about my pleas. The weather was French and therefore, by definition, unimpressed by German wishes. Five minutes later, it started to rain – lightly at first, then harder, then with the determination of a man who has found his life's purpose. I pulled my jacket tighter, lowered my head and kept riding. My visor fogged up immediately. The road became wet and slippery. Lola chugged on bravely, but I could feel the tyres sometimes losing their grip on the wet asphalt, as if they were considering whether they might prefer to go on holiday.

I slowed down, sixty kilometres per hour, then fifty. The rain grew heavier, drumming on my helmet, running down my back. My hands were cold, wet, stiff. I looked like someone who had just been fished out of a swimming pool. With clothes on. And in a bad mood.

"Only twenty kilometres to go. Only twenty."

Then I heard it: a horn. I looked in the rear-view mirror – a car, right behind me. An old Renault R4, beige, rusty, with dents and scratches, as if someone had used it as a punching bag. It drove slowly, matching my speed, staying close behind me. I got nervous. Did he want to overtake? Why was he honking? Was I too slow for him? Was this the French version of road rage?

Then the R4 pulled up alongside me, and I saw two men inside – the passenger, perhaps in his late forties, grey hair and a friendly face. The driver was younger, bearded, smiling. The passenger wound down the window – yes, with a crank, mechanical, like in the old days – and called something over to me. I couldn't understand anything, the rain was too loud. He pointed to the right, to the side. I understood: stop.

I nodded, pulled over to the right and stopped at the side of the road. The R4 stopped behind me. I got out, soaked, freezing, looking like an advertisement for "Why you shouldn't ride a Vespa in the rain". The two men got out and came over to me. The older one smiled. "Bonjour! Ça va?"

"Hello. Sorry, no French. English?"

"Ah! English! Yes, a bit." He pointed to Lola. "Spanish number plate. You are Spanish?"

I shook my head, water droplets flying. "No, German. The Vespa is Spanish, but I'm German."

"German!" His face lit up. "Me too! I'm German!"

I stared at him. "Seriously?"

"Yes! Originally from Hamburg. I'm Christian. This is Philippe, my mate, he's French. But he hardly speaks any English."

Philippe nodded at me and said something in French that sounded friendly.

"Kai. From the Allgäu."

"Beautiful area." Christian looked at me, soaked, freezing, on an old Vespa in the pouring rain, probably close to hypothermia. "Do you need a dry place to stay? Do you have accommodation for tonight?"

I hesitated. "Eh… not yet. I wanted to look for something in Montpellier."

"Montpellier is expensive. And wet." He laughed. "We live nearby, ten minutes away. An old railway station, converted. Want to come with us? Dinner, wine, a dry bed?"

I stared at him. A stranger I had met thirty seconds ago was inviting me to his house. It was either the best or the stupidest idea of the day. On the other hand, I was wet to the bone, had nowhere to stay, and the man was German. Statistically speaking, Germans are less likely to murder other Germans in France than other nationalities.

Philippe said something in French, and Christian translated with a grin: "He says you look like a drowned rat on two wheels. You need to dry off."

I laughed. "Okay. Yes. Thank you. That's… very kind."

"Just follow us! Ten minutes, no more!"

I followed the R4 through the rain for fifteen minutes. The road narrowed, leading away from the main road, through fields and small woods. The R4 in front of me chugged along leisurely, as if haste had never been part of its vocabulary. Then, suddenly, it turned left onto a gravel path.

And there it stood: an old railway station. Small, made of light-coloured stone, with tall windows and a red tiled roof. But it was no longer a station – the tracks were gone, the platform overgrown. Instead, there was a garden, minimalist, with gravel and a few olive trees. The building itself looked like a modern villa – large windows, clean lines, but the old charm was still there. Somewhere between "Architectural Digest" and "We renovate ourselves because craftsmen are too expensive".

Christian parked the R4, I parked Lola next to it. We went inside. Inside, the station had been transformed. The old waiting room was now a large, open living space – high ceilings, exposed wooden beams, white walls. On one side was an open kitchen, on the other a sitting area with old leather sofas that looked like they had stories to tell. There were tools, engine parts and books about classic cars everywhere. It smelled of wood, oil and fresh coffee. It was exactly the kind of home you see in real estate magazines and think, "I want to live like this too," before you look at the price and return to reality.

"Welcome. Sit down. I'll make some coffee."

I sat down, still soaking wet. Philippe brought me a towel and I dried myself off as best I could. The towel immediately became so wet that you could probably have watered plants with it. Christian came back with three cups of coffee. "So. You're travelling on a Vespa. From Spain to Germany?"

"Yes. I started in Albacete. I'm on my way home."

"Why?"

I hesitated. "Long story. My best friend died. I… had to get away. From my life. My job. Everything."

Christian nodded slowly, as if I had just said the most obvious thing in the world. "I understand. I did the same thing. Five years ago."

"Really?"

"Really. I was a marketing manager. Big agency, good salary, nice car, nice flat in Hamburg. And I was as unhappy as a goldfish in the desert."

"What did you do?"

"I quit." He said it as if he had said, "I made myself a coffee." "Sold everything. Bought this station. Now I restore old French cars. Sell them to collectors."

I stared at him. "And… you're happy?"

"Very." He gestured around him. "Look. I have space. I have time. I have work that I love. No meetings, no PowerPoints, no bosses who want to 'just discuss something quickly' at eight in the morning, which then takes two hours. Just me, my tools and beautiful old machines."

Philippe said something in French, and Christian translated with a grin: "He says I'm crazy, but he's just jealous."

All three of us laughed. The evening passed quickly. Christian cooked – simple, but good. Pasta with tomatoes, garlic and olive oil. Accompanied by red wine, heavy and dark, from the region. The kind of wine you drink and think, "Ah, that's why French people live longer."

We sat at the large wooden table in the kitchen, drinking and talking. Christian told us about his departure – about the fear at the beginning, the uncertainty, the doubts. "The first year was tough. I had no money, no plan. I thought: Maybe it was a mistake. But then I restored my first car – a Renault 4, like the one out there. Sold it to a collector in Zurich for twelve thousand euros. And I thought: Okay. This works."

"And now?"

"Now I restore four or five cars a year. Enough money to live on. Not rich, but free." He looked at me. "That's the deal, you know? Money or freedom. You can't have both. At least not for people like us who haven't inherited millions or sold tech start-ups."

I nodded. "I'm starting to understand."

Philippe said something, Christian translated: "He's asking: Are you going to go back to your old job?"

I thought about it. "I don't know. Maybe. Maybe not. I'm still figuring it out."

Christian smiled. "That's okay. The journey is the answer, not the destination."

It sounded a bit like a calendar quote, but here, in this converted train station, with this man who had completely turned his life around, it sounded right. Besides, wine makes everything more profound.

Later, Christian showed me his workshop – a large room in the old goods shed, full of cars. A Citroën 2CV, half dismantled. A Peugeot, freshly painted and so shiny you could see your reflection in it. A Renault 16 that looked as if it had just undergone a makeover.

"Beautiful, isn't it?" Christian stroked the bonnet of the Peugeot as if it were a pet. "Forty years old, but look at it. Like new."

"How long does it take to restore a car?"

"Three months, maybe six. It depends. Some just need paint and polish. Others need everything – engine, gearbox, interior." He smiled. "But I have time. That's the luxury."

I looked at the cars, the tools, the parts everywhere. "You love this."

"Yes. Every day I wake up and think: Today I'm going to work on something beautiful. Today I'm going to make something old new again. It's… meaningful. Do you understand?"

I understood. Or at least I was beginning to understand.

Later, we sat outside under the canopy. The rain had stopped, and the air was fresh and cool. Christian had brought another bottle of wine, and we drank in silence, looking into the darkness.

"You know," Christian said after a while, "when I quit my job, everyone said I was crazy. My family, my friends, my colleagues. They all said, 'You have everything. Why are you throwing that away?'"

"What did you say?"

"I said: I don't have everything. I have money and status and a nice car. But I don't have myself." He looked at me. "Do you understand?"

I understood.

"The Vespa trip isn't about the Vespa. It's about you. Who you are. Who you want to be."

I nodded. "I think I'm starting to learn that."

"Good. Then the trip is working."

I slept in a small guest room on the first floor – simple, clean, with a bed, a chair, a window overlooking the fields. Outside, it was quiet, except for the distant sound of the wind in the trees and the occasional chirping of a cricket. I lay in bed, hands behind my head, staring at the ceiling. I thought of Christian, of his departure, his new life. Of the cars in the workshop, the peace and quiet here, the freedom.

"Could I do that?" I whispered into the darkness. "Just throw everything away? Start over?"

I didn't know the answer. Not yet. But I knew something else: I was no longer the man who had arrived in Barcelona. I had changed, a tiny bit every day. The journey taught me. The people I met taught me. Lola taught me. Even Amazon with its copy paper taught me – albeit mainly what I no longer wanted.

And maybe that was enough. Maybe I didn't need to have all the answers. Maybe I just needed to keep driving, kilometre after kilometre, and see where the road took me.

I slept deeply and dreamlessly, with the smell of rain and wet grass in my nose and the feeling that I had learned something important today. Not every encounter is planned. Not every invitation is expected. But sometimes it's precisely these moments – the random, unplanned ones – that mean the most. Maybe all it takes is a rainy afternoon, a rusty R4 and a German in exile in France to be reminded that getting out doesn't mean giving up.

It means courage.

Chapter 20 – Flamingos and Glowing Pistons

[Soundtrack Shuffle: Bananarama – Cruel Summer]

The next morning, eight o'clock, and I was standing in front of Christian's converted train station. The air was fresh after yesterday's rain, the sky bright blue. Lola still had some dew on the seat, the straps tight, ready for the next leg of the journey.

Christian came out of the kitchen with two cups of café au lait in his hands and a paper bag under his arm. "Breakfast to go," he said with a grin. "Croissants from the bakery, still warm." We sat down on the bench in front of the station, drank coffee and ate croissants.

"Where are you going today?" Christian asked.

"Along the coast. Montpellier, then on towards Toulon. Let's see how far I get."

Christian nodded. "Nice route. But be careful in the Camargue – it gets hot there. Scorching hot."

"I'll be careful." I nodded. "I will."

We finished our drinks and stood up. Christian hugged me – tightly, warmly, like an old friend. "It was nice to meet you. Good luck on your journey. And whatever you decide – whether it's back to the office or something new – do it for yourself, not for others."

"Thank you," I said. "For everything. For last night. For… the perspective." He smiled. "You're welcome. And if you're ever in the area, you know where to find me."

I got on Lola and started the engine. She started up reliably. I waved one last time, then we chugged out of the yard, down the gravel path, back to the main road. In the rear-view mirror, I saw Christian still standing there, waving. Then he disappeared behind the trees.

I drove back to the coast, then continued east. The road wound through rolling hills, past vineyards and small villages. The sun was already high, the air was warm, and with every kilometre it got hotter. Lola ran perfectly. No rattling. No stuttering. Just that steady hum that sounded like a mechanical purr. I felt invincible. That was the mistake. You should never feel invincible on an old Vespa. The universe hears that. And the universe has a dark sense of humour.

After an hour, I reached the Camargue, and the landscape changed dramatically. The hills disappeared, the vineyards ended, and everything became flat – endlessly flat. No more mountains, no relief, just sky, water and salt. The road became dead straight, as if drawn with a ruler, and I could see five kilometres ahead, maybe more. Nothing but asphalt, sky and horizon.

The salt lakes began – large, flat basins full of water on the left and right of the road, but not normal water. Pink, white, turquoise, unreal, like on another planet. The pink came from algae, I had read somewhere, and from the flamingos. Hundreds of flamingos stood in the water, pink dots in the endless expanse. Some flew up, slowly, elegantly, as if in slow motion.

And then I saw them – the white horses. They stood on the right side of the road in a flat pasture, perhaps ten or fifteen animals, white as snow against the dry grass and blue sky. The famous Camargue horses, half wild, completely at home in this strange landscape. One raised its head, looked over at me, decided that a Vespa chugging past was no threat, and lowered its head again to graze. They seemed timeless, as if they had been standing here since Napoleon was a child.

I slowed down to sixty kilometres per hour, wanting to see it, to soak it all in – this strange, beautiful, empty landscape with its pink birds in the water and white horses in the pastures. The heat grew stronger with every minute, with every kilometre. At eleven o'clock it was thirty degrees, maybe more. The air shimmered above the asphalt like in the desert, and I sweated under my jacket, under my helmet. Sweat ran down my back, down my forehead. I opened the helmet fastener a crack, letting air in – hot air. It didn't help much, but I drove on.

The road stretched out straight ahead, kilometre after kilometre. No cars, no people, no houses. Just me, Lola and the heat. And then – I don't know why – I accelerated. The straight road, the emptiness, the wind in my face. No one was there, no one could see me. I wanted to go faster, wanted to feel what Lola was capable of. Seventy kilometres per hour. Seventy-five. Eighty.

Lola ran well, the engine singing higher and more powerfully. Eighty-five kilometres per hour. I grinned under my helmet. "Yes! That's how it's done!" The wind grew stronger, tugging at my jacket. I had to hold on tight, countersteer, but it felt good – like flying. Only on an Italian lawnmower. I rode like that for twenty minutes, maybe longer. The speed, the heat, the empty horizon – I was in a trance.

Then I noticed it: a smell. Burnt. Oil? Petrol? Rubber? I didn't know. I sniffed, tried to identify it, ignored it and drove on. Maybe it was the heat, the asphalt, the air. Then, from one moment to the next, the engine changed. The bright singing turned into a hollow, metallic ringing, as if someone had thrown a handful of washers into an industrial mixer. Lola became sluggish. It was that moment when the universe tells you that the party is over, but you still briefly have a chance to put your shoes on. A "rubber band effect" – as if an invisible giant were holding me by the luggage rack.

And then it happened: a short, painful jolt. The rear wheel let out a short, agonised squeal – a black greeting on the tarmac. The piston had just decided that from now on it wanted to form a perhaps inseparable molecular unit with the cylinder bore. A kind of metallic forced marriage at eighty.

"Shit. SHIT!"

Instinctively, I slammed the clutch before my brain could even spell the word "seize". The engine acknowledged the service with an offended little pop. Silence. Well, almost silence. There was still the whistling of the wind and the sound of my own pride falling down the stairs with the grace of a wet sack of rice. I let Lola coast while I used the remaining momentum to get the dying diva off the road uncertainly. I shifted down – third, second, first – and looked to my right. There! An abandoned farm, half-ruined, stones crumbling from the walls. In front of it, an old sign: "Vente de Vin" – wine for sale. Long closed, weathered, forgotten. But: a canopy! Shade! I steered over to the car park, gravel crunching under the tyres. Rolled under the canopy. Engine off. Silence.

I got off, my legs trembling. I looked at Lola. The engine was hot, very hot – I could feel the heat half a metre away, like an inadequately insulated raclette grill on Christmas Eve. I immediately opened the fasteners and removed the right side cover. The engine was exposed – metallic grey, cylinder cover, cooling fins peeking out from underneath – and the heat poured out like from an oven in which you had just forgotten three kilos of lasagne. I put the cover aside. "Breathe. You have to breathe, girl." The engine ticked loudly, metal contracting. Tick. Tick. Tick.

> **[Notification]** Lieferando: "Your favourite pizza, 'salami, no onions', is available today with a 15% discount!"

I stared at the display. Seriously? Right now? Right now I'm the captain of the little man's Titanic and they want to sell me dough with sausage on it. I looked around. The farm was old, very old, maybe two hundred years old. Stone walls, ochre-coloured, cracked. A window on the first floor was broken, the curtain was moving in another. Someone was inside. I stared up. A face – old, male, suspicious – looked down at me, at Lola, at the removed cover. I raised my hand, tried to smile. "Bonjour!" No reaction. The man stared at me as if I were a particularly stubborn form of vermin. Then the face disappeared, the curtain fell. A classic French "piss off" moment.

The engine continued to tick, quieter now. I touched the cylinder cover carefully with one finger and immediately pulled my hand back. "DAMN!" Too hot to touch. I opened my water bottle and drank greedily. The water was warm, almost hot, tasted of plastic and despair, but it was wet. I poured a little over my head – it didn't really refresh me, but it was better than nothing. Then I sat down on the ground, my back against the stone wall, in the shade of the canopy. The wall was cool, pleasant. I closed my eyes. "That was close. So damn close."

I thought back to that moment – that thermal act of love between aluminium and grey cast iron. When the metal gives way because you've been hammering it through the countryside like a madman. If I had pulled the clutch half a second later, the piston would now be welded shut for eternity. I could have left Lola here as a monument. "To the man who gave too much gas." But I had reacted. The mechanical sensitivity of a middle-aged man who really just wanted to eat vanilla ice cream had prevailed.

"Maybe," I whispered, "I did learn something after all." I thought of Nacho's words. "Listen to Lola. She'll tell you what she needs." I hadn't listened. I had only thought of myself, of the speed, of the feeling of being a great guy. "Idiot," I muttered. "Damn idiot."

I waited. Five minutes, ten. The heat was brutal – thirty-five degrees, maybe more. Sweat ran down my back, dripped from my nose. I took off my jacket, then my jumper, sat there in my T-shirt, but it hardly helped. I looked like someone who had just run a marathon in a sauna. A car drove by slowly. The driver looked at me, thought for a moment about stopping, saw my sweaty face and sped off. Understandable. I looked like someone you wouldn't even want to stand next to in a lift.

After twenty minutes, I got up and touched the engine again. Carefully. It was still warm, but no longer boiling hot. I could leave my hand on it for three seconds, then it became uncomfortable. But the kick starter could be moved again. A good sign. The piston was free again, even if it now probably had grooves like the A7 motorway after a hard winter. Nacho had explained it to me: "If it seizes – wait and pray!" I prayed!

After 45 minutes in total, I tried again. I stood up, walked over to Lola, pulled the choke, put my foot on the kickstarter. Took a breath. One kick. Nothing. The engine just coughed weakly, like a pug in the fog. Another kick. The engine turned, stuttered, died. My heart sank to the region where you normally wear socks. "Please. Please, please, please." Third kick. The engine coughed, spluttered, started – irregularly at first, like a chain smoker after getting up who has to cough for a quarter of an hour before he can say a word. Then calmer, more even, accompanied by a new, slight rattling. The "piston tilt". The scars of the crisis.

It ran. "Thank you. Thank you, thank you, thank you." Tears welled up, out of relief, out of shame. I swallowed them down. You don't cry over a two-stroke engine. Even if it rattles so beautifully. I let the engine run for two minutes at idle speed. Listened to every sound, every tick. It sounded okay. Not perfect, but it wanted to live on. It was like me: a little battered, a little overheated, but not ready for the scrapyard yet.

"I promise you," I whispered, "this will never happen again."

I got on, carefully, as if on a wounded animal. I accelerated, gently, very gently. Lola rolled away. I shifted up – second gear, third – and kept the speed at sixty kilometres per hour. No more. Never again. The engine ran smoothly, coolly, contentedly. And me? I had learned. Once again. You can't ride a fifty-seven-year-old Vespa like a modern machine. You have to listen to it. It gives signals – smells, noises. And you have to react, immediately. It doesn't forgive arrogance.

I drove on, slowly, respectfully, humbly. The Camargue passed by – flamingos, white horses, salt lakes, hot air. The road was straight as an arrow, kilometre after kilometre. But I stayed at sixty kilometres per hour, sometimes sixty-five downhill, never more. And the engine? It ran perfectly. No stuttering, no smell, no heat. Just a steady, contented purr.

I thought: "I am no longer the nervous beginner from Albacete, the man who was afraid of every bend. But I am not invincible either. I am not the master. I am a student, and I must continue to learn, every day, every kilometre. The journey teaches me. Lola teaches me. And I must listen."

After another two hours, the landscape changed again. The Camargue gave way to rolling hills, then it became more mountainous. The road led closer to the coast, and I could see the Mediterranean Sea – blue, sparkling, endless. Around two o'clock in the afternoon, I reached Toulon – a city, large, loud, bustling after the silence of the Camargue. A port town, but not a small one – a naval base, a trading port, life everywhere. Trams, cars, people everywhere. I drove through the streets, slowly, carefully, looking for accommodation.

After twenty minutes of wandering around one-way streets, I found it: "Pension Marie-Claire", a narrow building in a side street near the harbour, three storeys high, ochre-coloured façade, shutters in faded blue. A handwritten sign in the window: "Chambres disponibles". I understood: rooms available. I parked Lola in front of the door, chained her to a lamppost and went inside.

The entrance hall was small, dark and cool. A fan on the ceiling turned sluggishly. To the left was a reception desk – an old wooden counter, behind it a woman, perhaps sixty, grey hair, friendly eyes, reading glasses on her nose. She looked up. "Bonjour, monsieur."

"Hello," I said and smiled. "Do you speak English?"

She shook her head. "Non, désolée. Français seulement." Only French. Of course. I took a deep breath. Time for my language skills. "Eh… yo… I… una habitación?" Spanish. Wrong country. I corrected myself immediately. "No, sorry. A room? Chambre?"

She nodded. "Ah! Une chambre. Oui." She pointed to a form.

"Yes! Si! Oui!" I nodded vigorously, glad that we had understood each other. She pushed the form over to me and pointed to the lines. Name, passport, signature. I filled it out. Then she pointed to a price list on the wall. Single room: 30 euros. Double room: 45 euros. "Chambre simple?" she asked.

"Si! Eh, yes. Simple. Solo. One person." I held up one finger. My Itanol – that mixture of Spanish, Italian and desperation – was making its French debut.

She smiled. "D'accord. Trente euros." I nodded, counted out the money and placed it on the counter. She gave me a key – old-fashioned, heavy, with a wooden tag. "Deuxième étage. Chambre sept." She pointed upstairs, held up two fingers, then seven.

"Second floor, room seven. Perfecto. Grazie. Merci." I took the key, nodded gratefully and headed for the stairs. Behind me, I heard her laugh softly. Understandable.

The room was small but clean. A single bed, a wardrobe, a small table by the window. The window was open, warm air was coming in, and I could see Lola down on the street – black, dusty, waiting. I brought my rucksack upstairs, put it on the bed, and went to take a shower. The shower was at the end of the corridor, shared with the other guests, but it was clean. I stood there for ten minutes, fifteen, letting the hot water run over me, washing away the dust, the sweat, the fear. When I came out, I felt renewed – clean, light, grateful.

Back in the room, I sat down by the window. Outside, the sun was slowly setting, turning the houses golden. I looked down at Lola. I almost lost her today. Almost. I thought about that moment on the road – the stuttering, the smell, the heat, the fear. "I could have killed her. With my stupidity. With my greed for speed. With my ego."

"That was the lesson," I whispered into the evening. "Respect. Always. No matter how good you feel. No matter how empty the road is. You're not alone out there. You're with her. And she needs you, just like you need her."

My stomach growled. I hadn't eaten much since Christian's croissant in the morning. Not enough. I got up, put on some fresh clothes and went downstairs. The woman was still sitting at the reception desk. She looked up and smiled. I tried: "Restaurant? Food? Eh… manger?"

She nodded eagerly. "Ah oui! Un restaurant!" She took a pen and drew a little map on a piece of paper – three streets away, left, then right. "Le Bistrot du Coin. Bon!"

"Gracias. Merci. Thank you." I took the piece of paper and nodded gratefully. She said something in French, quickly, melodically. I didn't understand a word.

"Sorry, no… comprendo… understand… capito?" The part of my brain responsible for language was now completely out of control. She laughed, shook her head, and repeated more slowly: "Bon appétit."

"Ah! Yes! Buon appetito! Gracias!" I beamed. International communication was possible after all.

I found the restaurant – small, cramped, full of people. An old-fashioned bistro with wooden tables and red curtains. I squeezed myself into a free table in the corner. A waiter came over, young, fast, stressed. "Bonsoir!"

"Hello," I said. "Do you have… a menu? In English?"

He shook his head. "Non." Then he handed me a menu – completely in French, no pictures, no translations. I stared at it. Nothing but words I didn't understand. "Blanquette de veau." "Confit de canard." "Ratatouille niçoise." I had no idea. The waiter waited, impatiently.

"Eh… I want…" I pointed to the first word I recognised. "Steak?"

"Steak?" He frowned.

"Si! Steak! Carne! Meat!" I made chewing motions.

He nodded slowly. "Ah. Entrecôte?"

"Si! Entrecôte! Perfect!" I had no idea what that was, but it sounded like meat.

"Et comme accompagnement?" I stared at him. "Sorry?"

"Accompagnement. Potatoes? Vegetables? Eh… vegetables?"

"Ah! Yes! Potatoes! Patatas! Kartoffeln!" I nodded vigorously.

"Frites ou purée?"

"Frites! Si! Frites!" I understood frites.

"Et à boire?"

"Vino. Red wine. Vin rouge."

"Un verre ou une carafe?" I understood: glass or carafe. "Eh… grande. Carafe."

He wrote it down, nodded, and left. I exhaled. That was more exhausting than the seize. The food arrived – a large steak, rare, juicy, with a mountain of chips. The wine was heavy, dark, good. I ate slowly, enjoying every bite. Around me, French conversations, fast, melodic. I didn't understand a word, but it was beautiful – foreign, but beautiful.

The waiter came by, saw my empty plate. "C'était bon?"

I nodded enthusiastically. "Very good! Muy bueno! Molto bene!" I was always better at maths than languages at school.

He laughed. "Vous parlez beaucoup de langues!" I didn't understand exactly, but he laughed kindly, so I laughed along with him. "Si! Languages! Muchas!" I held up four fingers. German, English, a little Spanish, a little Italian. Technically, that was correct. He shook his head amusedly and brought the bill.

Back at the guesthouse, I climbed the stairs slowly, full and tired. In my room, I lay down on the bed, the window open. Outside, there was street noise, voices, life.

Tomorrow I would continue along the coast, towards Italy. But slowly. Always slowly. Respectfully. Lola would thank me for it, and I would arrive. That was enough, more than enough. I slept deeply and dreamlessly, with the smell of salt and sun still in my nose and the knowledge that I had learned something today – something important, perhaps the most important thing.

Humility.

And I had learned something else, something Pedro had once said: "When you travel by Vespa, it's always up and down. Like in life. One day everything runs perfectly. The next, you're on the side of the road waiting for the engine to cool down. That's normal. That's the journey."

Today had been a down day. Tomorrow would be an up day – or maybe not. But that was okay. I was no longer the man who needed perfection, who needed control, who had to plan everything. I was someone who could wait, who had patience, who understood that life is not a straight path. It is one curve after another. Sometimes up, sometimes down. And that's okay. As long as you keep going.

Chapter 21 – Riviera for the Poor

[Soundtrack Shuffle: The Eagles – Hotel California]

The morning in Toulon began with a croissant that tasted like butter, hope and probably a whole day of sport. The coffee was so strong that I was pretty sure my heart would keep beating for the next three days, whether I wanted it to or not. I sat in a small café next to the guesthouse, looked at Lola, who glistened in the morning light like an ageing actress wanting to make one last appearance, and thought: Today is going to be a good day.

The Côte d'Azur. The French Riviera. Nice. The city of the rich, the beautiful, the people who drank champagne for breakfast and didn't even feel like something was wrong. I wasn't one of them. But for one day, I could pretend.

The drive from Toulon to Nice was… strange. Beautiful, but strange. Like a date with someone who looks too good to be true. I avoided the motorway – the A8, the Autoroute du Soleil, which sounded like a promise from an advert that was too good to be true. Instead, I took the country road, through small coastal towns and hills overlooking the sea. The road took me through places whose names I couldn't pronounce – Saint-Raphaël, Fréjus, Cannes – and through landscapes that looked like something out of a travel brochure. Provence was getting ready for winter like someone who's already taken out their jumper.

And then I saw it. The Côte d'Azur. The Mediterranean Sea, which looked different here than in Spain or Toulon. Bluer. Or maybe just more expensive. Villas that looked like small palaces sat enthroned on hills. Yachts lay in harbours so large that they probably needed their own postcode. And everywhere: cars. Not just any cars. Porsches. Ferraris. Lamborghinis. A Bentley overtook me with a sound that sounded like a quiet, arrogant snort. Lola rattled on, unimpressed, at seventy kilometres per hour, while the world of the rich rushed past me like a film I couldn't afford to watch. I felt like an ant on a red carpet, and no one saw me because everyone was looking up, where real life was happening.

At a red light – even the traffic lights looked more expensive here – a Porsche 911 pulled up next to me. Bright red. Convertible. At the wheel was a guy, maybe in his late fifties, hair too long for his age, sunglasses too big for his face, Rolex on his wrist so heavy that it would probably sink him if he went swimming. He was wearing a linen shirt that was unbuttoned to the third button because he wanted everyone to see his chest hair and gold chain. Mission accomplished. I saw them. I didn't want to, but I saw them. Spontaneously, I thought of a German reality show with a screaming old woman who always yelled "Rooobert!"

He looked at Lola. Then at me. Then back at Lola. His gaze was appraising, like an antique dealer who has discovered something interesting at a flea market.

"Hey!" he called out. American accent. Of course. "Cool Vespa! Is it for sale?"

I looked at him. Then at Lola. Then back at him. "No."

He laughed. A laugh that said: Everything is for sale, you idiot, you just don't know it yet. "Oh, come on! What do you want for it?" He pulled out his mobile phone as if he were about to make a transfer. "I collect vintage stuff. Name your price. Five thousand? Ten thousand?"

Ten thousand euros. For Lola. That was more than I had budgeted for the entire trip. More than I had in my account. More than I earned in three months, if I was honest. My brain did a quick calculation and came to the conclusion: that would be reasonable. But reason was the reason I had sat in an office for thirty years selling insurance policies. Reason was the reason I got up at 6:15 every morning to be stuck in traffic on time. Reason was the reason Miguel had called me a coward. Shortly before he died. That would have been a shameless betrayal of Nacho. No way!

"It's not for sale," I said.

"Everything's for sale." He grinned. His teeth were too white. Bleached. Probably more expensive than my car at home. "Twenty thousand."

Twenty thousand. I thought of Miguel. Of his letter. Of the route he had left me. Of all the kilometres Lola and I had already travelled together. Of the nights under the stars. Of Ricardo and his workshop. Of Nacho and his Vespa museum. Of Christian and his converted train station. Of all the people I had met because I was riding this little old scooter.

"No," I said. "You can't buy dreams."

He stared at me. For a moment, he looked as if I had spoken Chinese. Or as if I had told him that the earth was flat. Then he laughed. Loudly. The laugh of someone who was used to getting what he wanted and who thought people like me were a joke. "Dreams?" He shook his head, still laughing. "Mate, I buy dreams for breakfast. This is just a rusty scooter."

The traffic lights turned green. He accelerated. The Porsche shot off with a noise that sounded like a rocket trying to prove it cost more than my entire life. I stood there. Let him drive away. Watched him disappear between the other expensive cars, a red speck in a sea of money. Then I looked at Lola. I stroked the handlebars. The warm, worn, perfect handlebars. "Rusty scooter," I muttered. "Did he just insult you?"

Lola said nothing. She was a Vespa. But I swear the engine sounded offended as I drove on. Slowly. At my sixty kilometres per hour. The Porsche was long gone, probably already three kilometres away, probably already at the next shop, the next purchase, the next attempt to buy happiness. And me? I had little money in my account, a Hawaiian shirt that smelled of sweat, and a Vespa that was older than most marriages. But I also had something he couldn't buy: I knew where I wanted to go. And why. That was worth more than twenty thousand euros. That was worth more than his Porsche. It was – and I knew how corny that sounded, but it was true nonetheless – priceless. Besides, he had chest hair like a carpet from the seventies. So I had won anyway.

After Cannes, the traffic got heavier. Cars, motorcycles, buses – everyone was crowding the road as if there was a free concert by someone famous somewhere. The heat was oppressive – thirty-two degrees, even though it was October – and I was sweating in my Hawaiian shirt, which now smelled more like sweat than coconut. My back was sticking to the seat. My hands were slippery on the handlebars. And Lola? Lola did what she always did: she ran. Bravely. Stubbornly. Like an old dog too proud to admit that he actually wanted to go to his basket.

Nice announced itself with signs in a font that looked like, "We are elegant, and you are not." I drove along the Promenade des Anglais – that famous road by the sea. Palm trees. Sandy beach. Blue water. People in designer clothes whose biggest problem in life was probably what sunglasses to wear today. Ray-Ban or Gucci? So difficult.

I drove slowly, taking it all in. Yes, it was beautiful. But it was also strange. As if I had stumbled into a world that wasn't made for me. As if I had walked into a club where everyone knew I couldn't afford the cover charge. The hotels on the promenade had prices starting at a hundred and fifty euros per night. Per night! That was more than I had spent in a week in Spain. I scrolled through

Booking.com on my mobile phone while waiting at a red light, and with every swipe, my heart sank a little deeper. One hundred and eighty euros. Two hundred euros. Three hundred euros. For a room where I would only sleep. Crazy!

I quickly did the maths. Four hundred euros left in my account. For the rest of the trip. For food, petrol, hotels. If I spent a hundred and fifty euros here, I would probably starve in Italy or have to hitchhike. And hitchhiking on a Vespa was probably not very successful. So I scrolled further. Downwards. Further and further down. Until I found the cheap hotels. The hotels that no one talked about. The hotels that weren't on the promenade, but somewhere between motorways and industrial areas, where tourists usually only ended up if they had lost their way.

After a few loops, I found it: Formule 1. A French hotel chain. Cheap. Very cheap. Thirty-five euros per night. A third of the price of everything else. There was a photo on the website – a bed, a shower, a window. An archive photo from the nineties that looked like, "This is a hotel. Don't expect anything." Nothing special. But what more did I need? I was just going to sleep. How bad could it be? Spoiler: it could be very bad.

I booked it. Clicked "Confirm" before my brain could intervene. The address said "Zone Industrielle, Nice." Industrial area. That sounded… not good. But hey, it was cheap. And money was tight. So I set off. It took me half an hour to find the Formule 1. It wasn't in Nice. It was somewhere between Nice and hell. On Google Maps, it was a small dot surrounded by grey rectangles that could mean "warehouses" or "factories" or "places where you get disposed of if you don't pay the wrong bill".

I drove through an area that looked like the back of a postcard. The side that no one wanted to see. Concrete walls. Graffiti that wasn't even artistic. Rubbish bins. A rusty gate. A stray dog staring at me with a look that said, "What the hell are you doing here?" Good question, dog. Good question.

The hotel came into view. A flat, grey building that looked like a shoebox someone had thrown into the landscape and then forgotten. Three storeys. Windows like loopholes. A car park full of lorries. Vans. Cars that looked older than Lola and significantly less well maintained. And next to the car park: the A8 motorway. Not in the distance. No. Right next to it. So close that I could read the number plates. I parked Lola between two vans that looked like they were about to fall apart at any second and stood there, looked at the hotel and thought: Okay. This is going to be interesting. Or traumatic. Probably both.

The lobby was… well, there was no lobby. There was a machine. A screen. You entered your booking number and the machine spat out a code. No people. No reception. Just a screen that lit up at me like a cynical robot that knew I had made a mistake and was enjoying it like a sadistic quiz show host. I typed in the number. The machine hummed. Beeped. Thought. Then a number appeared: "317". Third floor. Room seventeen. And below it: "Code: 4782". I wrote it on my hand because I knew I would forget it otherwise, and went to the stairs. There was no lift. Of course not. Because this was Formule 1, not the Ritz. Or even the Ibis Budget.

The stairs smelled of disinfectant and disappointment. The walls were beige. Or maybe they had once been white and had decided over the years that beige was more depressing. Someone had sprayed graffiti on the wall: "Welcome to Hell!" Welcome to hell. I laughed. It wasn't funny, but I laughed anyway. The way you laugh at a horror film before everyone dies.

On the third floor, the smell became… more complex. A mixture of cheap women's perfume that was supposed to smell like strawberries but smelled more like a chemistry lab, cold kebabs and damp carpet. The carpet was dark brown and felt like a wet sponge under my shoes. I tried not to breathe in too deeply. Third floor. Room 317. I typed in the code. The door clicked. I pushed it open. And there it was. My room for the night. My home for the next eight hours. My personal French adventure.

It was… small. Claustrophobically small. Eight square metres, maybe. A bed that looked like it had been recycled from a prison cell. Hard. Saggy. With a blanket that had once been blue, but now was more the colour of "I've given up". Next to it: a tiny window, so small that it was more of a peephole than a window. And through that peephole: the motorway. So close that I could read individual number plates. Lorries thundered past, and the walls vibrated with each one like in a cheap action film.

I went to the shower. Or rather, to the shower cubicle. It was so cramped that I could hardly turn around. If I had taken a shower and tried to raise my arms at the same time, I would probably have knocked myself out. The tiles were white, but there were dark spots in the corners that were clearly not white. Mould. Definitely mould. Or small portals to another dimension. Hard to say. The shower head hung crookedly, as if it had given up years ago, and the water – I tested it briefly – was lukewarm. Not hot. Not cold. Lukewarm. Not even that was possible in this "hotel". I sat down on the bed. It squeaked. Of course. As if it wanted to complain that I was using it. I lay down. It was hard. So hard that I could feel my spine, every single vertebra, like an anatomy textbook. I stared at the ceiling, which had a water stain that looked like a map of the world – or like Australia, which had decided to be alone – and thought: So this is the French Riviera. Champagne and caviar. Celebrity parties and luxury yachts. Or just this.

The night was… spectacular. In the worst sense of the word. Like a performance where you don't want to applaud, but you can't leave either. The noise started at ten o'clock. No, that's wrong. The noise had always been there. The traffic never stopped. Trucks, cars, motorcycles – they drove through the night, a constant hum that penetrated the thin walls like a German pop song you can't get out of your head. A song that consisted of only one chord: BRRRMMMMM.

But at ten o'clock, new noises joined in. Next door – to my left – was someone snoring. Not normal snoring. But the kind of snoring I imagined a walrus would make if it had a cold and was trying to sing an opera aria at the same time. Loud. Rhythmic. Relentless. I knocked on the wall. Nothing. The man continued snoring as if it were his job. As if he were being paid for it.

On the other side – to my right – there was another noise. Voices. A woman. A man. They spoke French, but with an accent. He sounded like someone who spent all day on construction sites – rough voice, direct tone. She sounded professional. Very professional. They laughed. Probably negotiating. Then: silence. Then: other noises. The rhythmic squeaking of a bed that was definitely not built for that purpose. A deep, masculine groan. A female voice saying things that were probably good for business, but didn't sound particularly authentic. The creaking of wood. A dull thud against the wall – once, twice, then at regular intervals, like a rather unromantic metronome. The walls were so thin that I was practically in the same room. Or at least an unwanted participant in something that others were paying for and I was only getting the audio version of. For free. Whether I wanted to or not.

I put a pillow over my head. It didn't help. I tried listening to music. My headphones were dead. Of course. Because the universe had decided that I should suffer today. Completely.

> **[Notification]** Netflix: "New episodes available: Suits (Season 10)."

At midnight, I heard footsteps in the hallway. Heavy footsteps. A man laughed loudly, hoarsely, drunkenly – the laugh of someone who had just made a deeply questionable decision and was happy about it. A door slammed. The door next door. On the right. Then: silence. For about ten minutes. Then it started again. The squeaking. The creaking. A different voice this time – deeper, older. But the woman sounded the same. Professional. Experienced. Business was booming. The French Riviera might be expensive, but at least here at the Formule 1 there was service. Around the clock. At the same time, the traffic outside grew louder, as if the truck drivers had decided that midnight was the perfect time to thunder through the south of France at full throttle, honking their horns.

I lay awake. Stared at the ceiling. In the dark, the water stain looked like a face. A sad face that stared at me and seemed to say, "Welcome to the losers. Here's your membership card." At two in the morning, I got up. Went to the window. Looked out. The street was brightly lit. Lorries. Still. More and more. As if there was a warehouse somewhere that had to be delivered to all night long. Urgently. With… I don't know. Desperation? I opened the window a crack. Immediately, the stench came in. Exhaust fumes. Diesel. Rubber. And something else I couldn't identify, but which smelled like the opposite of hope. I closed the window again. Lay back down on the bed. The snoring concert next door had stopped. Instead, I now heard another voice. A man talking on the phone. Loudly. In Russian. Or maybe Polish. Hard to say, but the emotions were universal: "I'm tired, I'm in a shitty hotel, and someone's going to pay for this." I could relate to that. Very much so.

At six in the morning, I gave up. Surrendered. Threw in the white towel. I had tried for six hours. Six hours of walrus concert, long-distance symphony and Russian telephone tirades. Now it was over. I got up, put on my jeans, packed my rucksack. I couldn't take it anymore. Not another minute in this room, in this hotel, in this nightmare that called itself the French Riviera, but in reality was just France's revenge on tourists with small budgets.

It was still dark when I went downstairs. The stairs were quiet now. Outside, it was pitch black, only the streetlights cast their glaring light on the car park, which was so bright that you would have thought a UFO was about to land there. A few lorries stood there, their engines off, the drivers asleep in their cabs. They were probably dreaming of better times. Of hotels with windows that didn't face motorways. Lola stood among them, small and black and somehow out of place, like a vintage car in a scrapyard or like me at a yacht party.

I sat down on a bench – yes, there was a bench, for whatever reason, perhaps for people like me who had given up – and waited. For what, I didn't know. For the sunrise. For a sign. The night dragged on like chewing gum stuck to your shoe. It was cold. Maybe fifteen degrees. I pulled my jacket tighter and stared into the darkness. And I thought: This is the French Riviera. Not the Promenade des Anglais. Not the yachts. Not the champagne. But this. A car park. A bench. A hotel that looks like punishment for sins from a previous life. And a guy who's too tired to think, but too awake to sleep. Welcome to hell. Indeed. The graffiti hadn't lied.

At seven o'clock, the sun rose. Slowly. Hesitantly. As if it wasn't sure whether it really wanted to, or whether it would rather stay in bed like any sensible person. The sky turned pink, then orange, then yellow. The first light crept across the car park like something that wasn't quite sure it belonged there. The lorry drivers woke up, started their engines, drove off. The car park emptied. And I sat there, on my bench, tired, exhausted, but surprisingly relieved.

I had survived. A night at the Formule 1. The craziest night of my trip. So far. Perhaps the worst night of my life since I was seventeen and slept on a park bench in Füssen because I had missed the last train. But I had survived. I was still alive. I was still breathing. I could still think. More or less. I went to Lola, stroked her handlebars as if she were a horse meant to calm me down. Or a therapist. "Come on," I said quietly. "Let's get out of here before they send us a bill for therapy."

I started the engine. It started on the first kick. Lola, you bloody miracle. You functioning, loyal, never-let-me-down miracle. I drove off, down the car park, back onto the road, away from this place that called itself Riviera, but was really just a memory I wanted to forget as quickly as possible. With alcohol. Lots of alcohol.

But strangely enough – and this surprised even me – I smiled as I did so. Because I knew: this was all part of it. Part of this journey. Part of this life. The sleepless nights. The cheap hotels. The moments when you ask yourself what the hell you're doing here and why you didn't just stay at home and watch a series. And the answer was: I was living. Finally. Really. With all the horror hotels, walrus snorers and traffic noise.

I drove on. Towards Italy. Towards San Remo. Towards the next disaster. Or the next miracle. Hard to say. But I was ready. For both. As long as it had a better bed.

Chapter 22 – The Park Bench (or: How Stars Taste)

[Soundtrack Shuffle: Abba – Money Money Money]

The coastal road to Italy was beautiful, presumably. I only saw half of it. Everything blurred into a mush of blue and grey with occasional splashes of green. Lola sang beneath me like a loyal friend who knew that now was not the right time for conversation. Fifty kilometres to San Remo. Fifty kilometres to the Italian border. Fifty kilometres that felt like five hundred.

The border came sooner than expected. Or maybe I just wasn't paying attention. Suddenly there was a sign: "Italia". No checkpoint, no barrier, just a road winding from France to Italy as if it were the most normal crossing in the world. Which it probably was. For everyone except me.

After another twenty kilometres, I reached San Remo. Palm trees, colourful house facades, a harbour with boats bobbing in the morning light. All very picturesque. All very Italian. I was too tired to really appreciate it.

I drove through the city, slowly, searching, until I found a small café that was just opening. "Bar Centrale". An older man – in his mid-sixties, bald, white apron – placed chairs in front of the door and wiped down the tables. I parked Lola and got off. My legs felt like jelly. The cheap kind, from a packet. Not even the vanilla-flavoured kind.

"Buongiorno," I said.

He looked up and nodded. "Buongiorno."

Inside, it was warm and smelled of fresh coffee and pastries. He made me an espresso without asking. Small, black, strong. He placed it in front of me. I drank it in one gulp. The bitterness burned my tongue, but it was good. It was life. It was Italy.

"Quanto?" I asked. How much?

"Uno e cinquanta." One euro fifty.

I gave him two euros. He gave me fifty cents back. I nodded, thanked him, and went back to Lola. The coffee had helped. A little. My brain was now functioning at the level of a coffee machine that at least knew it was broken.

I checked the fuel gauge. A quarter full. Not critical, but not comfortable either. There was a petrol station two streets away, I had seen it when I drove in. I drove there.

It was one of those modern petrol stations, all glass and chrome and self-service. I parked Lola next to the pump, took my credit card out of my pocket and inserted it into the slot. The pump beeped. Thought for a moment. Beeped again. Then a message appeared on the display: "PAGAMENTO RIFIUTATO".

I stared at it. Blinked. It was Italian, but I understood it. Payment declined.

Maybe I had inserted it wrong. I pulled the card out and inserted it again. Slower this time. More deliberately. As if that would make a difference.

"PAGAMENTO RIFIUTATO".

A cold feeling spread through my chest. The feeling you get when you realise that something fundamental has gone wrong and you don't know exactly what, but you know it's not good. Rather fatal.

I went into the shop. A young woman was standing behind the till, in her early twenties, ponytail, bored look. She looked up from her mobile phone when I came in.

"Scusi," I said, holding out my card. "La mia carta… no funciona." My card doesn't work. Spanish words with an Italian accent, itañol, my personal language creation.

She took the card and swiped it through her terminal. Waited. The terminal beeped. She shook her head.

"Bloccata," she said. Blocked.

"Bloccata?" I repeated the word, as if that would make it make sense. "Por qué? Uh… perché?"

She shrugged. The universal gesture for: "No idea, and it's not my problem."

I nodded. Thanked her. Went back to Lola. Took out my mobile phone. 15 per cent battery. Of course. Because the universe had decided that today was the day when everything would go wrong. Completely. Without mercy.

I tried to call my bank. The German hotline. It rang for a long time. Then a recorded message, then finally a voice. A woman, friendly, professional.

I explained the situation. Credit card blocked. Italy. Vespa. Please help.

She checked my account. "Yes, I see the problem. Your card has been blocked for security reasons. Unusual activity in Italy."

"Yes," I said. "That's me. I'm in Italy. On a Vespa. Can you unblock the card?"

Pause. Keyboard clicking. Then: "That will take at least twenty-four hours. We have to lift the block manually, it can't be done immediately."

"Twenty-four hours?" My voice sounded higher than I intended. "I have nine euros. I need the card now."

"I'm sorry. That's the security protocol. Tomorrow morning at the earliest."

"Seriously? Okay. Thank you."

"Have a good trip," she said, without irony, and hung up.

I stood there, mobile phone in hand, feeling my last hope crumble like stale bread. Twenty-four hours. A whole day. A whole night. And I had nine euros and ten cents.

But maybe – maybe there were hotels that accepted modern payment methods. PayPal. Mobile payment. Anything.

I sat down on Lola, started the engine and drove through San Remo. Looking for hotels.

The first hotel was small, clean, right on the waterfront. "Hotel Roma". I went in and asked for a room. The woman at the reception desk – in her late forties, with a friendly smile – nodded. "Sì, abbiamo una camera. Sessanta euro." Sixty euros.

"Puedo pagar con… teléfono?" Can I pay with my mobile phone? Spanish. Itañol didn't always work.

She shook her head. "Solo contanti o carta." Cash or card only.

"Pero mi carta no… uh… non funciona. Está bloqueada. Bloccata." I mixed Spanish and supposed Italian wildly. "Otra posibilità?" Another option?

She shrugged her shoulders. Regretfully, but firmly. "Mi dispiace." I'm sorry.

I nodded. Thanked her. Went outside.

Outside, a man was leaning against the wall, smoking. He was wearing a linen suit and looked like someone on holiday. A proper holiday. With a working credit card and a hotel room and probably a breakfast buffet offering three types of scrambled eggs. He looked at my Hawaiian shirt, then at Lola, then at me. His gaze said: interesting life choices.

I nodded to him. Collegially. From tourist to tourist. He didn't nod back.

The second hotel was larger, more modern. "Hotel Riviera." Large lobby, marble floors, thoroughly elegant. The man at the reception desk wore a suit and tie and looked like someone who had never had a problem in his life that couldn't be solved with money.

"Posso pagare con… smartphone?" I tried in Itañol. "PayPal? Google Pay?"

"No. Carta o contanti." His tone made it clear: this was non-negotiable.

The third hotel was small, inexpensive, tucked away in a side street. "Albergo Roma". It smelled of cleaning products and old carpet. The old woman at the reception desk – at least seventy, grey hair tied back in a bun – looked at me over her glasses like a teacher who knew I hadn't done my homework.

"PayPal?" I tried. "Teléfono? Qualcosa?" Anything?

"Contanti o carta." She spoke the words slowly, as if I didn't understand the language. "Solo."

I gave up. Thanked her. Went back to Lola. My mobile phone vibrated in my pocket. I took it out. 10 per cent. Of course. Perfect timing.

Three hotels. Three rejections. Same answer: cash or card only. And now a nearly dead mobile phone. Welcome to modern Italy, where technology existed, but only in theory.

The harbour of San Remo was beautiful. Really beautiful. Boats bobbed in the water, palm trees swayed in the wind, the sun bathed everything in warm, golden light. All very picturesque. None of it mattered, because my brain produced only one thought, over and over again: "You're stuck here. For twenty-four hours."

I drove to the harbour. Parked Lola next to a row of other scooters. I went to a bench – not the financial kind, but the seating kind – and let myself fall down.

It was around eleven in the morning. The sun was high, warm, friendly. People strolled by, eating ice cream, laughing, living. And I sat there, on a bench, wondering what the hell I was supposed to do now.

Option 1: Call Isabel and ask for money. But that felt wrong. Like failure. Like giving up.

Option 2: Call Ricardo. Same problem. Plus, he was in Barcelona. Even if he wanted to help, how could he?

Option 3: Stay here. All day. All night. Until the card worked again tomorrow.

I could have solved options 1 or 2 with Western Union, but I was too proud. I chose option 3. Not because it was the best option, but because it was the only one that didn't require any energy and didn't mean I had to beg for help.

I sat there. Stared at the sea. The water was blue, clear, beautiful. Boats passed by. Seagulls screeched. The world kept turning as if nothing had happened. As if I wasn't stranded.

Time lost its meaning. The sun moved across the sky. People came and went. And I stayed.

Around two in the afternoon, my stomach growled. Loudly. Aggressively. I remembered that I hadn't eaten anything since my espresso that morning. My last proper meal was… when? The suquet de peix in Cadaqués? It felt like a month ago, but it was only three days.

I got up and walked along the promenade until I found a small kiosk. "Bar Gelato & Snack". A young guy – in his early twenties, baseball cap, tattoos on both arms – stood behind it, scrolling on his mobile phone.

"Ciao," I said. "Cosa posso… with six euros?" I showed him a five-euro note and a one-euro coin, hoping that gestures were more universal than my itañol.

He looked up, thought for a moment. Pointed to the display. "Panino? Tramezzino?" Then to the fridge: "Acqua?"

"Sì. A sandwich. Y agua. And water."

He made me a tramezzino – a triangular Italian sandwich with tuna, tomato and lettuce, thin but edible. The bread was soft. The tuna was from a tin. The tomato had seen better days. So had I. And a bottle of water. Half a litre.

"Sei euro." Six euros.

I gave him the money. No change. I now had three euros and ten cents left. For the rest of the day. And the night.

I went back to my bench, sat down, and ate the sandwich slowly. It tasted of tuna and a sticky mass that pretended to be bread. The water was cold. At least.

I just sat there. For hours. Looking at the sea. Thinking. About everything. About nothing.

Around four in the afternoon, a seagull came and sat down next to me on the bench. It looked at me. I looked at it. We probably had similar daily balances: it had gotten hold of a few chips. I had eaten a sandwich. It had more dignity. At least it could fly.

I could have called someone. Maybe. If my mobile phone hadn't been almost dead. Isabel. Ricardo. But even if… what could they have done? Send me money? How? Western Union took hours. A bank transfer took days. And I wasn't going to beg. Not after everything I had already achieved.

I would manage it myself. Somehow. I just had to… wait. Twenty-four hours. I could do that. I had to.

Night fell slowly. The sun sank behind the hills of San Remo, painting the sky orange and pink and purple, like an artist who didn't know when to stop. The water shimmered golden, then silver, then dark blue. People slowly disappeared, going home to their families, to their warm beds, to their lives.

And I stayed.

Around seven o'clock in the evening, I got hungry again. My stomach growled like an offended dog. I counted my money. Three euros and ten cents. Enough for… what?

I walked along the promenade until I found a small bar. "Bar Stella Marina". Inside, a few locals were sitting, drinking beer, watching football on a television hanging on the wall. I went in.

"Ciao," I said to the bartender, an older man with a grey moustache. "Una Moretti, per favore."

He nodded and put a beer in front of me. The bottle was ice cold, fogged up, perfect. Then I saw the bowl on the counter. Grissini. Those thin Italian breadsticks that are available in every restaurant in Italy. Usually free of charge. But I didn't want to risk anything.

"The… um… grissini… sono gratis?" I asked in itañol, hoping that my mixture of Spanish and Italian would be understood.

He nodded. "Sì, sì. Prendi." Take them.

I took a handful. Maybe six or seven. Thin, dry, but edible. That would be my dinner. Beer and breadsticks. The menu of the stranded adventurer.

"Recarrgar Telefono un momento, Please?"

"Si." He plugged the phone into the charger behind the bar.

"Quanto costa?" I asked, pointing to the beer.

"Tre euro." Three euros.

I gave him the three euros and ten cents I had left. Everything. He gave me ten cents back. I now had ten cents left. Ten damn cents. For the night. For the next day. For everything.

I sat down at a table by the window and drank the beer slowly. It tasted of hops, slight despair and Italy. The breadsticks were dry, crunched loudly when I bit into them and left crumbs everywhere. But they filled my stomach. Somewhat. Enough to survive the night.

I looked out of the window. The sun was almost gone now. The sky turned dark blue, then black. Stars appeared. One after the other.

I finished my beer, gathered a few crumbs from the table, and thanked the bartender with a nod. He gave me my phone and I walked back to the harbour. 25% battery. A ray of hope? But what for?

I pushed Lola right next to the bench. So close that I could touch her. In case anyone got any ideas. In case anyone thought an old Vespa would be easy prey. I put my rucksack on the bench. It would be my pillow. Hard. Uncomfortable. But better than nothing.

And just then – as I was about to sit down, a stranded tourist with a Vespa and ten cents – two Carabinieri came by. Italian police. Dark blue uniforms, caps, serious faces. They looked at me. Then they looked at Lola. Then at the rucksack. Then back at me. The younger of the two – maybe in his mid-thirties, dark hair, friendly eyes – came closer.

"Documenti?" he asked.

I sat up and took out my passport. Handed it to him. He looked at it, nodded, gave it back. Then he said something in Italian that I didn't understand. I shook my head.

"Sorry," I said. "No hablo italiano. Er… non parlo italiano. Deutsch. O inglés. English."

"Ah, English," he said, switching languages with ease. "You are okay?"

Was I okay? Good question. I thought about it. Then I said, "My credit card is blocked. My mobile phone is almost dead. I have… ten cents." I showed him the single coin in my hand as proof. "And I don't know what to do. The card will work again tomorrow. The bank said twenty-four hours."

He looked at me. Then at his colleague, who was older, had a moustache and a sceptical look. They spoke briefly in Italian. Then the younger one said, "You have a hotel?"

I shook my head.

"Where you sleep tonight?"

I pointed to the bench. To my rucksack. To Lola. "Here. Aquí. Here."

He nodded. Thought about it. Looked again at my passport, at Lola, at me. Then he said, "You can sleep here. On the bench. But no trouble, okay? No alcohol. No noise. You understand?"

I understood. "Yes," I said. "Thank you. Grazie. Thank you."

He nodded again. Then they walked on, their footsteps echoing on the pavement. And I sat there, on my bench, and realised: I would spend the night on a park bench. In San Remo. At the Italian harbour. Because I had no money. Because my mobile phone was dead. Because everything had gone wrong.

> **[Notification – Xiaomi Smarthome]**: ERROR 24
> Moppi robot vacuum cleaner blocked by object!
> Start emergency reset! 🤖

And strangely enough – very strangely enough – I had to laugh. Not loudly. Not hysterically. Just a quiet, tired laugh that sounded like, "Of course. Of course it ends like this."

I lay down. The bench was made of wood, hard, too short. My legs hung over the end. The air was cool, maybe fourteen degrees. Not cold, but not warm. Just the right temperature to keep you from falling asleep, but not freeze to death either. The temperature of discomfort.

Above me: the sky. Clear. Cloudless. And the stars. So many stars that I couldn't count them all. More stars than I had ever seen in Kempten, where the streetlights illuminated everything. Here, at the harbour, with the sea in front of me and the sky above me, they were everywhere. An entire universe that was simply there, indifferent, beautiful, endless.

I lay there and looked up. I heard the water lapping softly against the quay wall. I heard the boats rocking and creaking. I heard voices in the distance, laughter, the clinking of glasses from a bar. Life went on. Always.

And I thought: So this is it. Rock bottom. The moment when you realise you have no control. Over anything. No money. No mobile phone. No plan. Just a park bench and a sky full of stars.

And then – and this surprised me – I thought: Maybe that's okay.

Maybe it had to happen this way. Maybe I had to lose everything to understand that it was never about control. Not on this journey. Not in life. You could plan, organise, write lists, take out insurance, secure everything. But in the end, life happened anyway. It just happened. And you could either fight it or you could… let go.

I lay there on my park bench and felt something inside me give way. Like a fist that finally opened. Like a rope that finally came loose. I had nothing left to lose. And that was… liberating.

I wasn't a victim. I wasn't a failed insurance salesman who had been stupid enough to ride a Vespa across Europe. I was… an adventurer. An idiot, perhaps, yes, but an adventurer. And adventurers sometimes slept on park benches. That was part of it. That was part of the story. The part you told later and everyone laughed about.

I smiled. In the dark, alone, on a park bench in San Remo. And it felt real. Not like the smiles I had put on in the office. Not like the smiles I had given Sabine when everything was already broken. But real. From the inside out.

The water rushed. The boats creaked. The stars shone.

And I fell asleep.

I woke up around three in the morning. Not because I was well rested, but because the bench was so uncomfortable that my body had decided that three hours was enough. My back ached. My neck was stiff. My legs had fallen asleep and tingled when I tried to move.

And then I realised: I was cold. Really cold. The temperature had dropped during the night – perhaps to twelve or thirteen degrees. The wind from the sea blew directly across the promenade, finding every gap in my clothing, creeping through the thin fabric like an icy thief. I was shivering.

I sat up and rubbed my arms. That didn't help. I needed more layers. More insulation. More… everything.

I opened my rucksack and rummaged around in it. In the dim light of the street lamps, I saw: a T-shirt. My Hawaiian shirt. And two extra pairs of underpants. Fresh. Clean. Unworn.

I looked around. The harbour was empty. No people. Just the boats rocking in the water and the lanterns casting their orange glow on the pavement. Perfect. Time for a night-time striptease on the park bench.

I stood up and began to undress. Trousers down. Then I pulled the second T-shirt over the first one. Then the Hawaiian shirt over that. In the end – because I was really, really cold and because desperation knows no vanity – I pulled another pair of underpants over the ones I was already wearing. Then the second pair of underpants over the second pair. Three pairs of underpants in total. Three layers of cotton between me and the cold. Then I put my trousers back on.

I looked like the Michelin Man. Or like someone who didn't know how clothes worked. My upper body was padded with three layers, my hips looked like I was wearing nappies, and my Hawaiian shirt bulged over everything like a colourful circus tent. But damn it, I was warmer.

I lay down again. The rucksack under my head. The extra layers helped. I wasn't shivering anymore. At least not like before.

Eventually, I fell asleep again.

Sabine stood in front of me. She was wearing that white dress she always wore in cruise photos – the photos she showed me when she was still trying to persuade me. Behind her: a huge cruise ship, white and bright, with pools and balconies and people in cocktail dresses.

"Look at that," she said, spreading her arms. "We could have had that. The Caribbean. Buffet. Cabin with a sea view."

I looked down at myself. I was wearing three pairs of underpants on top of each other and a Hawaiian shirt that smelled of sweat and two-stroke fuel.

"But no," she continued, her voice becoming shrill. "You just had to ride a Vespa through Europe. Like a student. Like a bum."

"I'm not a—"

"You sleep on a park bench, Kai." She laughed. Coldly. Scornfully. "With ten cents in your pocket. In three pairs of underpants on top of each other."

I wanted to say: Technically, it's three pairs of underpants and two T-shirts. But that wouldn't have improved the situation.

"I wanted adventure, Kai. Not homelessness. There's a difference."

She pointed to the cruise ship behind her. "This is adventure. New ports every day. Exotic places. But with comfort. With style. With a bloody bed."

I wanted to say something, but my voice failed me.

"Do you know what the sad thing is?" She shook her head, almost pityingly. "You think this makes you free. But look at yourself. You're not free. You're just poor."

The ship behind her began to honk its horn. Long. Loud. Deafening.

I jumped up.

My heart was pounding. The horn – it wasn't a cruise ship. It was a fishing boat leaving the harbour, its horn sounding a morning greeting.

I sat upright on the bench, breathing heavily. The stars were gone. The sky was slowly getting lighter, from black to dark blue to grey. It was just before six.

Sabine's voice still echoed in my head. Adventurous, not homeless.

I rubbed my eyes. My body felt as if I had been run over by a lorry. Twice. My back was one big cramp. I could barely move my neck. But I was alive. And I had survived the night.

And Sabine? Sabine had been a dream. Just a dream.

An elderly Italian man walked past with his dog. The dog – a small terrier with more self-confidence than me – stopped and peed on a lamppost. Right next to my bench. The man looked at me. Then at my Hawaiian shirt. Then at the three layers of clothing that stood out under my trousers like a textile onion.

"Buongiorno," I said.

He said nothing. Pulled the dog on. The dog gave me one last look. Pitying. Being pitied by a terrier was a new low. Or high. Hard to say.

At that very moment, I felt something warm on my shoulder. Wet. Sticky. I looked down. A whitish-green blob adorned my Hawaiian shirt. A seagull circled above me, screeched once – triumphantly, I thought – and disappeared towards the sea.

Of course. Of course.

I wiped it with a handkerchief. It just smeared. Now I had a Hawaiian shirt with a seagull shit accent. Limited edition. Exclusively for park bench sleepers.

I got up. Stretched as best I could. The air was fresh, smelling of salt and sea and morning. A few fishermen were already out and about, preparing their boats, checking their nets. They didn't look at me. Or at least they pretended not to see me. I probably wasn't the first tourist to sleep on a bench here.

But I didn't get up to hide or feel ashamed.

I thought of Kempten. Of my flat, which was so clean and empty that it felt like a waiting room. Of my desk in the office, where I had spent eight years of my life. I thought about Sabine, who had said that I wasn't there anymore. And she had been right. I hadn't been there. I had been somewhere else. In a state between existing and living, where you breathed and functioned, but didn't really feel.

And now? Now I was here. On a park bench in San Remo. With ten cents, an empty mobile phone and a blocked credit card. Dressed like the Michelin Man with three pairs of underpants on top of each other. And it was the most terrible night of my trip. And that was after the thing at the Formule 1. Maybe the worst night of my life.

But I felt. Finally. I felt the cold, the discomfort, the fear. But I also felt something else. Liveliness. The here and now. Not the kind you buy or plan. But the kind that happens when you stop fighting life and just… go with the flow.

My freedom begins here, Miguel's photo had said. And I had thought "here" was Albacete. Or Barcelona. Or some perfect place where you arrive and suddenly you're free.

But maybe "here" was everywhere. Maybe "here" was this very moment. This park bench. This starry sky. This realisation that it was okay not to have everything under control. That it was okay to fail. That it was okay to just… be.

Sabine was wrong. Cruise ships weren't an adventure. Cruise ships were floating hotels with buffets. This – this park bench, this night, this moment – this was adventure. Real. Uncomfortable. Unforgettable.

I walked over to Lola. Stroked her handlebars, as if to greet her. "Good morning," I said quietly. "We survived."

She said nothing. But that was okay. I knew she understood.

I had ten cents left. Ten bloody cents. And a dead mobile phone. And a blocked card that would – hopefully – work again this morning.

Ten cents. I couldn't buy anything with that. Not even a coffee. Not even a bread roll. Not even one of those cheap chewing gums they had at the checkout. Ten cents in Italy was the equivalent of: nothing.

I looked at the coin in my hand. Small. Shiny. Worthless. And I thought – half seriously, half desperately – that if the card didn't work right away, I might have to follow the example of the woman from the Formule 1 hotel. Professional services. At the harbour. With ten cents starting capital. The market regulates it, but no one wants to see it.

I laughed. Loudly. A little hysterically, perhaps. But damn it, it was funny. In a heartbreakingly sad way.

I took out my mobile phone. Pressed the power button. Black screen. I held my breath. Then – the Apple logo. It started up. Top right: three per cent battery. Three bloody per cent. Apparently, the mobile phone had survived the night better than I had.

I had to be quick.

I called my bank. The German hotline. It rang for a long time. Then a recorded message, then finally a voice. A man, friendly, professional.

I explained the situation. Credit card blocked. Since yesterday. Italy. It should take twenty-four hours. Is it free now?

Pause. Keyboard clicks. I heard my mobile phone beep. Four per cent. The battery was melting away like ice in the sun.

Then: "Yes, Mr Ritter. Your card has been activated. You can use it again immediately."

I smiled. "Thank you," I said. "Thank you very much."

"You're welcome. And sorry for the inconvenience. Have a good trip."

Three per cent. I hung up. Two per cent. The mobile phone would die any moment, but it didn't matter anymore. The card worked. I had access again. To money. To options. The crisis was over.

But strangely enough – very strangely enough – I didn't feel relieved. Not really. I felt… different. As if something had changed. Not the situation. But me.

I had spent a night on a park bench. Without money. Without a plan. Without control. And I had survived. Not just survived. I had understood something. Something important.

That a good life didn't mean having everything under control. But exactly the opposite. Letting go. Accepting. Trusting that somehow things would work out. Always.

I swung myself onto Lola and started the engine. It rattled, as always. Reliable. Faithful.

I drove to the petrol station – the same one as yesterday. The young woman with the ponytail wasn't there. An older man was now standing behind the cash register.

I filled up. The credit card worked. No error message. Just a green tick and a beep.

Twelve euros. That was less than the hotel would have cost. Less than dinner. Less than the dignity I had left on that bench last night. But more than ten cents.

And I drove off. Towards Genoa. Towards the east. Towards home.

But I was no longer the same. I had left something behind on that park bench in San Remo. Something heavy. Something that had weighed me down for a long time.

The fear of losing control.

And I had taken something with me. Something light. Something I hadn't felt in a long time.

Peace.

Chapter 23 – People are Good in Genoa

[Soundtrack Shuffle: Zucchero – Senza una Donna]

The coastal road between San Remo and Genoa was one of those routes that would probably have been breathtaking under different circumstances. The Mediterranean Sea to the right, deep blue and sparkling in the morning sun. Small villages clinging to cliffs like stamps on an envelope. Palm trees waving in the wind. Again, very picturesque. Again, very Italian. But I only saw half of it because my body was busy telling me that I had spent the night on a park bench and that it was not happy about it. Not at all. Beautiful, the Italian coast – if you can actually see it, that is.

My back felt like a collection of shaken-together bricks. My neck was stiff as a board. My hips ached from the hard wooden bench, and my legs – they had given up complaining at some point and were just numb. On top of that – the leaden tiredness. The kind of tiredness that wasn't just physical, but felt like a heavy blanket covering everything. My thoughts. My perception. My ability to think anything meaningful that wasn't: "Bed. Now."

But there was no bed. There was only Lola and the road winding ahead of me, and Genoa, which lay somewhere up ahead. Three hours. Maybe four, at Lola's pace. I just had to hold on. Just a little longer. Then I could sleep. Really sleep. In a bed. A real bed. With a mattress. And a blanket. And maybe even a pillow that wasn't my rucksack.

The Autostrada A10 was different from the winding coastal road I knew from France. Here there were tunnels. Lots of tunnels. Long, dark tunnels that ate their way through the mountains like giant worms. I drove into one, and suddenly the sun was gone, replaced by orange sodium vapour lamps that bathed everything in a ghostly light. The rattling of Lola's engine echoed off the concrete walls, growing louder, more intrusive. Cars overtook me, their headlights blinding me in my rear-view mirrors. I clung to the handlebars, rode straight ahead, concentrating on not falling asleep, not drifting off, not crashing into the wall.

Then: light. The tunnel ended. The sun exploded back into my face like a slap. I blinked, squinted my eyes. Then darkness again. The next tunnel. Light. Dark. Light. Dark. It was like a strobe light that someone had invented to torture people sitting on a Vespa after a sleepless night.

After the fifth or sixth tunnel – I had stopped counting – came a viaduct. One of those absurdly high bridges that were simply built over valleys as if gravity were only a suggestion. I looked down. A mistake. The valley was deep. Impressively deep. Houses looked like toys. Trees like green dots. And between me and the valley: nothing. Just air. And a thin concrete bridge on which I was travelling at eighty kilometres per hour on an old Vespa that could decide at any moment that today was a good day to die.

I looked ahead again. Concentrated on the road. On the white line. On breathing.

Genoa announced itself with signs that grew larger and traffic that became denser. Lorries crowded onto the motorway, cars changed lanes without indicating, motorcycles shot between the rows like bullets. Italian traffic. Creative. Chaotic. Deadly. I kept to the right, let everyone who wanted to pass go by, and prayed silently that no one would decide that my place on the road was actually theirs.

And then I was there. Genoa. The city spread out like a giant, living organism, rolling up and down the hills until it reached the sea. Harbour cranes towered into the sky like skeletal fingers. Container ships lay in the water, so large that they looked like floating cities. And everywhere: buildings. Old buildings, new buildings, dilapidated buildings that looked as if they were only still standing because they had forgotten to fall down.

I drove off the motorway and followed the signs for "Centro". City centre. Wherever that was. The streets grew narrower. The buildings moved closer together. People sat on chairs in front of their doors, old women in black dresses, men with newspapers. They didn't look at me.

First, I needed an espresso. And I stopped.

I sat in a tiny bar in the winding caruggi of Genoa, the artificial light of a flickering neon sign above me, staring at my espresso, which seemed as black and unyielding as my future prospects in the insurance industry. I was a visual wreck: my 7-day beard scratched like a wiry pot scrubber, and my face was a two-tone disaster of deep red sunburn ("danger above") and chalk-white patches where my sunglasses had been. Beneath my light blue flamingo Hawaiian shirt, the three layers of underpants I had pulled on to protect myself from the cold of the San Remo park bench night bulged bizarrely, giving me the silhouette of a slightly deformed Michelin man on holiday.

Suddenly, I saw him through the fogged-up window: a gaunt guy in a greasy leather jacket and side-buttoned jogging pants was sneaking around Lola and fiddling with my rucksack with suspicious energy.

At that moment, the insurance specialist in me died a silent death. Adrenaline, distilled from two thousand kilometres of road dirt and lack of sleep, shot straight into my legs. I threw open the door and stormed outside. My tiredness was gone, replaced by anger!

"Get lost, you bum – you've got a screw loose!" I yelled in a voice that sounded like I had just got a handful of gravel in my carburetor. I ran across the cobblestones. I swung my 40-year-old black helmet wildly above my head like a medieval mace, the chin strap cracking through the air like a whip.

The crook froze. He was probably expecting an easy victim, a tourist who smelled of sunscreen and fear. Instead, he saw a roaring, bearded creature in a fluttering flamingo tent that looked like it came straight out of a closed institution for two-stroke enthusiasts. My appearance was apparently so disturbing that the thief took off running before my helmet had even completed its first orbit around my head. He tripped over his own feet and disappeared into the dark alleys as if the devil himself were after him. With my practically new motorcycle jacket! Shit! Well, at least not with the whole rucksack. A small victory, but a victory!

I stood there panting, my eyes fixed on Lola, the Hawaiian shirt fluttering in the wind like the victory flag of a very poorly dressed army. I stroked my wild beard, adjusted the flamingo pattern and took a deep breath. "Yeah, just get lost, you!" I yelled after him and looked around demonstratively to see if everyone had noticed.

Then I turned around and strode back to the bar. My gait was now slow, a majestic shuffle in green rubber slippers, my back as straight as if I had just saved the universe (or at least a piece of metal from 1967). A group of American tourists at the corner bar, armed with cameras and guidebooks, stared at me with a mixture of reverential horror and deep respect. One of them even took off his sunglasses as I walked past them – a bearded Marvel hero of the little man, who smelled of a night on a park bench and the pride of the street. Well, maybe they were just wondering what was wrong with the German loudmouth.

I sat back down on my bar stool, lifted the small cup and drank the now almost cold espresso with the stoic calm of a man who knows that he has his "cojones" not only in theory. The coffee tasted like victory, but I was clearly too tired for such nonsense!

I needed a hotel. Urgently. But not just any hotel. A cheap hotel. Because my budget now looked like the result of a failed diet: theoretically still there, but practically finished. I drove through the old town, slowly, searching, until I saw a sign: "Albergo Centrale". A small, hand-painted sign on the wall of a house. Above it: a balcony with flowers. Geraniums, red as blood. It looked like the setting of an Italian film. Or like the place where someone had been shot. Hard to say.

I parked Lola in front of the entrance. Folded out the side stand. Got off. My legs were shaking. Not from fear. Just because they were tired. Because they'd had enough. Because they thought that 180 kilometres after a night on a park bench should actually be illegal.

The entrance was a narrow passageway, barely wider than me, leading to a small courtyard. Tiles. Old, colourful tiles that were probably already here when Genoa was still a trading power and where Christopher Columbus began to discover the world. On the wall: a sign. "Reception 1st floor". I took the stairs. Slowly. Shuffling. Because going fast was no longer possible.

The reception was a small room with a desk, a telephone and a woman who looked as if she herself were part of the inventory. Signora Bellini. I guessed she was in her late sixties, maybe early seventies. Grey hair tied back in a bun. Glasses hanging from a chain around her neck. A blue dress with flowers on it. And eyes that looked at me and knew everything immediately.

"Ragazzo!" she said and stood up. "Madonna! Che cosa ti è successo?"

I tried to smile. It didn't work very well. "Buongiorno, Signora. Er… avete… una camera?" Do you have a room? My Italian was still a disaster, but at least I was trying.

She came around the desk, stood directly in front of me, and put a hand on my cheek. Her hand was warm, soft, smelled of soap. "Sembri uno zombie," she said, shaking her head.

"Io… dormito… eh… panchina," I tried in Itanol. "San Remo. Carta di credito… bloccata? No dinero." I pointed to my empty pockets. "Muy cansado."

She nodded. As if it were the most normal thing in the world. As if she had tourists who had slept on park benches every day. "Vieni," she said, pointing to the stairs. "Ti do una camera. Hai bisogno di riposo. E di mangiare." She pointed to her mouth and made chewing motions. "Tu – mangiare? Quando?"

"Ayer," I said, holding up one finger. "Tramezzino. Y cerveza. Con… eh…" I made a bar motion with my hands.

"Dio mio." She shook her head, went back to the desk, pulled out a book, an old-fashioned guest book with handwritten entries. "Come ti chiami?"

"Kai. Kai Ritter. Germania."

She wrote down my name. Slowly, carefully, in handwriting that looked like calligraphy. "Quaranta euro," she said, holding up four fingers. "Per una notte. Okay?"

"Okay, sì," I said, pulling out my credit card. The card that had been blocked yesterday, that had banished me to a park bench, but now worked again as if nothing had happened. She took the card and swiped it through an old card reader. It beeped. Green light. Approved.

"Camera sette," she said and gave me a key. A real key. Not a plastic card, but a heavy metal key with a tag engraved with a seven. "Secondo piano." She pointed upstairs. "Aspetta – non andare via!"

She disappeared through a door behind the desk. I heard pots clattering. Water running. Then she came back with a plate. A large, white porcelain plate piled high with pasta. Not normal pasta. Trofie. Those little twisted noodles that looked like tiny snails. And on top: pesto. Real Genoese pesto. Green like fresh grass, glistening with olive oil, with little bits of basil, pine nuts and grated cheese. It smelled like summer. Like gardens. Like life.

"Pesto Genovese," she said proudly. "Fatto in casa." She made stirring motions with her hands. "Tu – mangia! Adesso!" She pointed to a bench. "Poi dormi."

She pressed the plate into my hand, then a piece of bread – a piece of ciabatta that was crispy and had holes so big you could see through them – and a glass of wine. Red wine. Sweet and heavenly.

"Mangia!" It wasn't a suggestion. It was an order.

I sat down on a bench next to the stairs. Balanced the plate on my knees. Picked up the fork, poked at a few noodles. Put them in my mouth.

And almost – almost – I started to cry.

The pesto tasted like… like I had imagined Italy to be when I was a child and had never been here. Basil, fresh and intense, not like the dried stuff from the supermarket, but like the plant itself, freshly picked. Pine nuts, roasted, crunching between my teeth. Garlic, but not too much, just enough to say: I'm here. Cheese – Parmigiano, probably, or Pecorino – salty, sharp, perfect. And olive oil that held it all together, smooth and silky and so green it looked like liquid summer.

I ate slowly. Every bite. Every noodle. I dipped the bread into the pesto that remained on the plate, wiping everything up until the plate was clean. The wine tasted of cherries and earth and years spent maturing in some cellar. And I sat there, on that bench, in that little hotel in Genoa, and thought: people are good. There are lousy hotels. There are blocked credit cards. There are nights on park benches. But there is also Signora Bellini. And that's enough.

When I was finished, I got up and took the plate back to reception. She was sitting at her desk again, leafing through a book. She looked up and smiled.

"Meglio?" she asked.

"Mucho meglio," I said. "Grazie. Mucho grazie."

She waved it off as if it were nothing. "Vai a dormire. Domani è un altro giorno."

I nodded, took the key, and went up the stairs. Second floor. Back right. Room seven.

The room was small. Cosily small. Maybe ten square metres. But it had a bed. A real bed. With a mattress that was soft. And a pillow that smelled of lavender. And a blanket that looked like a quilt from the sixties, but was clean and warm. The window opened onto a courtyard where laundry was hanging and a cat was sitting, staring at me with the look of someone who understood the world and knew that it was meaningless, but okay.

> **[Notification]** Booking.com: "Kai, how was your stay at Formule 1 Nice – Zone Industrielle? Did the accommodation meet your expectations? Share your review now! 🏨⭐"

I took off my shoes. My trousers. My Hawaiian shirt, which now smelled more of sweat than palm trees. I lay down on the bed. Pulled the blanket over me.

And fell asleep. Immediately. Deeply. Dreamless. Like a stone.

When I woke up, it was dark. Not the darkness of night, but the darkness of late afternoon, when the sun has already disappeared behind the buildings, but the sky is not yet completely black. I looked at my watch. Five o'clock. I had slept for four hours. Four hours that felt like fourteen. My body still ached, but differently. No longer like a complaint, but like a memory. Like something that had happened but was over.

I got up, got dressed, went downstairs. Signora Bellini was still sitting at her desk. Or again. Hard to say.

"Buonasera," I said.

"Ah! Il tedesco!" She smiled. "Hai dormito bene?"

"Sì. Grazie."

"Bene, bene." She pointed to the door. "Adesso – vai! Guarda Genova. Bella città. Vecchia." She smiled. "Ma bella."

I nodded, thanked her again, and went outside.

Genoa at dusk was… strange. Beautiful, but in a way that was hard to describe. The old town – the Centro Storico – was a labyrinth of narrow alleys, known as caruggi. So narrow that you could stretch out your arms and touch both walls at the same time. Laundry hung between the houses, stretched from balcony to balcony, colourful sheets and shirts and underpants. The ground was cobbled, uneven, slippery, worn down by centuries. The houses were tall, four or five storeys high, with peeling facades, faded colours and crooked shutters. Everything looked as if it were about to collapse. As if it were only still standing because it was too stubborn to give up.

But it was also beautiful. In a raw, honest way. No tourist traps. No polished facades. Just life. Real life. People standing in doorways smoking. Children playing football in alleys barely wider than a car. Old men sitting on plastic chairs playing cards. Women calling out from windows, chatting from balcony to balcony, across the street, as if the houses were just furniture in a large living room.

I walked without a destination. Just wandering around. I turned into alleys so narrow that I thought they would end in a dead end, but then they suddenly opened up onto small squares with fountains and trees. I passed churches, small and inconspicuous from the outside, but when I looked inside, they were full of gold and frescoes and marble. I passed palazzi, old palaces from the time when Genoa was rich, when it was a maritime power that rivalled Venice. Some had been restored and gleamed like new. Others were dilapidated, their facades broken, windows bricked up, balconies threatening to fall off.

I reached the old harbour. Porto Antico. Where history had begun, when Genoa was still the gateway to the world. Now it was a tourist spot, with restaurants and bars and an aquarium that looked like a spaceship. But behind it, in the shadows, were the old warehouses, the cranes, the docks. Abandoned. Forgotten. Beautiful in their melancholy.

I sat down on a wall by the water. Looked out to sea. The sun was almost gone now, just a narrow strip of orange on the horizon. The water was dark blue, almost black. Boats rocked. Seagulls screeched.

And I thought: I can really do this.

Not the journey. The journey was almost over. Just a few hundred kilometres to go. A few more days. That wasn't the problem. The problem was: I can do this life. The life I would leave behind when

I returned to Kempten. The life that no longer worked. The life I no longer wanted.

I had slept on a park bench. With ten cents in my pocket. Without a plan. Without control. I had survived. More than that. I had learned something. Something I would never have learned in an office. In a meeting. In a PowerPoint presentation.

That you couldn't control everything. But you could keep going. Always. Even when it was hard. Even when it seemed impossible. You could keep going.

And sometimes – sometimes there was Signora Bellini. People who made pasta. Who asked, "What happened?" And who cared. For no reason. Just because.

I sat there until it was completely dark. Until the stars came out. Then I got up and went back to the hotel.

Signora Bellini was no longer there.

I went up to my room. Got undressed. Lay down in bed.

And slept. Deeply. Peacefully.

Chapter 24 – The Deceptive Calm

[Soundtrack Shuffle: George Michael – Freedom]

I stood at the port of Genoa, and the sun sparkled on the water as if someone had thrown a thousand tiny diamonds onto it, and the seagulls screeched above me like a choir of deaf singers all trying to hit the same high note at the same time, and the smell of salt and diesel hung in the air, that typical harbour smell that smelled equally of freedom and of industry, of adventure and of work.

Lola stood next to me, dusty and scratched, but ready. Always ready.

Today: heading north. To Lake Garda. The last stop before the Alps. The last breather before things got serious.

I started her up. She was ready. Confident. As if she had no idea what was ahead of us. Or as if she knew exactly and had long since come to terms with it.

"Let's go, girl," I said, patting her handlebars. "One last beautiful day."

Then: the Alps.

But that was the future. Now was: Italy. Sunshine. The road.

The road led through Liguria, the SS1 — Strada Statale —, later it would become the A7 motorway, but I avoided motorways whenever I could because Lola looked like a toy among the lorries on motorways, and I didn't feel like a driver there, but like an obstacle that other people found annoying. So instead, I took smaller roads, the SP456, through villages and valleys and hills that looked as if someone had folded Italy like a piece of paper and then decided that the folds should now be roads.

Italy changed with every kilometre, and it was fascinating how quickly that happened, how the landscape transformed, as if you were driving through different countries, even though it was just one country, just a country that couldn't decide what it wanted to be. On the coast: palm trees, lemons, Mediterranean light that bathed everything in gold. Here, inland: vineyards stretching across hills like green carpets, cypress trees towering into the sky like dark exclamation marks, medieval villages on hilltops that looked like paintings from an art book that someone had forgotten to tidy away.

I drove slowly because Lola didn't drive fast anyway, and because there was no reason to rush, and because I knew that tomorrow everything would be different, that tomorrow the mountains would come, and that I wouldn't have time to enjoy the scenery because I'd be too busy trying not to die.

I reached Parma around noon.

I didn't know the city, had never heard of it before, except in connection with two things: Parma ham and Parmesan cheese. Two things I liked. Two things that were reason enough to stop.

I parked Lola in Piazza Duomo, the large square where the cathedral stood, a Romanesque dome, enormous and old and so solid that it looked as if it had decided to stand for another thousand years, and I walked through the old town, through arcades with ochre-coloured façades that looked as if someone had carved the colour of the sunset into stone, and it was quiet here, almost no tourists, just a few locals drinking coffee and reading newspapers and pretending that life was something you could take at a leisurely pace.

I found a small trattoria, "Da Giuseppe". The entrance looked small, but inside it was larger, with wooden tables and checkered tablecloths and a smell of garlic and basil and everything that was good.

I ordered a plate of Prosciutto di Parma with melon and a glass of Lambrusco, that sparkling red wine that was light and fruity and felt like liquid summer, and when the prosciutto came, thinly sliced, pink like a sunrise, salty and sweet at the same time, it melted on my tongue, and I thought: The best thing about travelling is the food.

Not the sights. Not the photos. But the food. The way every place tasted different, the way food was a language that everyone understood, no matter where they came from.

After lunch, I checked Lola, walked around her as Pedro had shown me, and checked everything that needed to be checked.

Tyres: okay. Still enough tread, no cracks yet. All nuts tight.

Ignition: okay. No stuttering, no misfires.

Brakes: okay. Responded sharply, no spongy levers.

"You're in top shape," I said to her, patting the seat. "Ready for the Alps."

She didn't say anything because she was a Vespa and Vespas didn't talk, but I imagined that she agreed, that she was ready, that we could do this together.

I drove on, through the Po Valley, this flat land that stretched out like a sea of earth, rice fields and corn stubble and a veil of mist on the horizon, and it smelled like autumn, like the season coming to an end, like the end of something and the beginning of something else, and the air was cool, no longer summery, and I was only wearing a T-shirt and I thought: I should have brought warmer clothes. And then my jacket had been stolen.

But: too late now. Too late to go back. Too late for regrets.

Around 5 o'clock in the evening, I saw them.

The mountains.

At first they were just outlines, dark against the sky, like shadows someone had painted on the horizon, but then they became clearer, the peaks sharp and jagged, covered with snow, white against the grey, and I felt my stomach tighten, a mixture of awe and nervousness, of "This is beautiful" and "That up there? I have to cross that?"

The Alps.

On a fifty-seven-year-old Vespa.

"We can do this," I said aloud to Lola, my voice echoing in my helmet. "We've done worse."

But my voice sounded less convincing than I had hoped. It sounded more like hope than certainty.

I reached Peschiera del Garda around 6 p.m., the southern tip of Lake Garda, a small town, touristy in summer, but now in autumn quiet, almost empty, and the lake spread out before me, blue and smooth as glass, surrounded by mountains reflected in the water, and it was breathtaking, truly breathtaking, not in a postcard kind of way, but in a quiet, honest way that made you forget that you were tired, that you had been sitting on a Vespa for hours, that your bum hurt and your shoulders were stiff.

I parked Lola on the shore, got off, took a deep breath. The wind was cold, carrying the smell of water and pine trees, and I stood there, hands in my pockets, and whispered, "This is beautiful. This is really beautiful."

I found a small hotel, "Albergo Il Lago", Lake Hotel, with a sign that was illuminated and glowed in the dark like a lighthouse, and the receptionist, a man in his mid-forties with a paunch and friendly eyes, saw my Vespa outside and came around the counter.

"Una bella Vespa!" he exclaimed. "Spagnola?"

Spanish?

I nodded. "Sì. Motovespa. GS150."

My Italian was a disaster. But it was enough for Vespa conversations.

He whistled appreciatively, went to the door, looked at it, walked around it once like an art connoisseur around a painting. "Rara! Molto rara!"

Rare. Very rare.

"Da dove vieni?" Where are you from?

"De… dalla España. Er… Spagna." I gestured wildly. "Albacete."

From Spain. From Albacete. My Italian was a wild mixture of Spanish and what I thought was Italian.

His eyes widened. "Con quella?" With that?

I smiled. "Sì."

He shook his head slowly, incredulously. "Sei pazzo!" You're crazy!

"Lo sé." I know.

Wait a minute. Was that Spanish or Italian? Never mind. He understood me.

He laughed loudly and heartily and patted me on the shoulder. "Bravo! Bravo!"

The room was small but clean, with a bed that looked soft and a window overlooking the lake, and I paid forty-five euros, took a long, hot shower, and the water ran brown, dust and road and Italy, and when I was done, I felt almost human.

But I had a problem.

Tomorrow: the Alps. And I had no warm clothes. Just a T-shirt, a shirt, thin leather gloves. No thick jumper. No rain gear. Nothing to protect me from the cold that awaited me up there.

I had to go shopping.

I found a supermarket, "Conad", an Italian chain that looked like any supermarket anywhere, with neon lights and shopping trolleys and people shopping tiredly after work, and on the clothing rack — between underpants and socks — I found a thick woollen jumper, dark blue, twenty-five euros, and a pair of cheap knitted gloves, five euros, and I bought both, put the jumper on immediately, and it felt strange, warm and heavy and scratchy, but good. Just before the checkout, in the bicycle accessories section: a baby blue rain poncho for the occasional shower on Sunday rides.

"Better than nothing!" and at least within the €7.99 budget. "That will be necessary," I thought and went back to the hotel.

In the evening, I sat on a bench on the shore of Lake Garda with a glass of red wine from the supermarket, cheap but okay, and the sun was setting, orange and red and gold, and the lake reflected everything, the colours, the mountains, the sky, and the mountains to the north were dark silhouettes, shadows against the last light, and I looked at the peaks and whispered, "Tomorrow. Tomorrow we'll go up there."

Lake Garda looked like a well-intentioned Windows wallpaper: postcard-blue water, premium subscription mountains, and in between so many ice cream parlours that diabetes should actually be a UNESCO World Heritage Site here.

Lola stood crookedly on the gravel, wedged between two shiny, heavy SUV fortresses.

> **[Notification]** Google Calendar: "In 15 minutes: Team building workshop (online). Topic: Optimising work-life balance."

Then came the sound.

Not a nervous two-stroke croak, but that deep, self-satisfied hum that motorcycles make when they know their owner was addressed with "adventure" in the brochure and responded with "lease payment".

The BMW GS rolled up next to Lola like a spaceship in a model car car park.

Aluminium cases, auxiliary headlights, crash bars – the full "When the apocalypse comes, I'll be riding ahead" programme.

On top of that: neon yellow safety vest, Gore-Tex suit, helmet with more technology on it than my entire life.

The guy flips up his visor and looks Lola up and down.

That look that says, "Nice. For classic car meets. Not for real touring or real men."

"Clean," he says. "You really came all the way here on that thing?"

"From Spain," I reply. "With detours."

He whistles softly. "Brave," he says. The word sounds as if it would have liked to have been "stupid," but then changed its mind out of politeness.

He dismounts and puts the GS on its centre stand. His suit crackles expensively. Well, his entire outfit cost more than Lola and everything strapped to her. The motorbike cost about half a year's salary, has more electronics than my smart home and is roughly three times as heavy as Lola. He pats the tank affectionately. "Minga in the morning, Lake Garda in the evening. Four hours plus coffee breaks. Monday I'm back in the office, credit committee. Gotta go."

I nod. "Sure. Adventure with a right of return."

He laughs. Loudly, smugly. "Well, you can allow yourself a little comfort. Seat heating, handle heating, airbag in your suit. If you ride over the Brenner Pass in that tattered shirt, you might as well make an appointment with the dermatologist."

I look at my faded T-shirt, my crusty forearms, on which the sun from somewhere between Castile and the coast still glows red.

"Too late," I say. "The appointment has already been made internally."

He walks around Lola like a TÜV inspector on rehab. "How many horsepower?" he asks.

"Seven. With a tailwind."

He grins. "My GS has 136. If I feel like it, I'll be back home in four hours."

"If I feel like it," I say, "in four hours I'll be somewhere I've never been before."

There is a brief silence.

From the back of the hotel, I hear the clinking of cutlery, the sounds of a buffet, the kind of laughter that only comes when the drinks are included.

"I always say," he begins, "you have to be able to afford freedom. A decent motorbike, a decent hotel, a decent menu. Otherwise, it's just stress."

I look at Lola, who, with her dusty patina, looks like a walking reason for termination.

"Or you could just call it life," I say.

He shrugs. "To each his own. I've got my kilometres. Minga–Garda–Minga, neatly planned out. That's enough for me. The rest is just stories."

"That's exactly why I set off," I reply. "For the stories."

He looks at me as if I've just said I set off to find my spiritual inner carpet beater. Then he looks at his watch.

"Right," he says. "Spa waiting. Infinity pool, lake view, then a five-course meal. You only live once, right?"

"Yes," I say. "That's why I'm going to the mountains tomorrow. And not the whirlpool."

He laughs again, a little uncertainly this time. "Take care. And if you break down on the Brenner Pass – call the ADAC. But don't block the ideal line."

The BMW starts up, humming richly, revving briefly as if to prove to the car park who's the alpha nightmare here.

Then it rolls away, cleanly, controlled, back towards the hotel lights and dessert buffet.

When the sound fades away, all that remains is the soft lapping of the waves.

I put on my new jumper and watch the spot where the auxiliary headlights have disappeared, and I notice something shifting inside me.

Both are journeys.

His in a weekend.

Mine in a lifetime.

I get up and pat Lola on the saddle. "All right," I murmur. "The wannabe adventurer has his programme. We have ours tomorrow."

She says nothing.

But she smells of petrol, warm metal and exactly the kind of trouble that cannot be summed up later as "wellness".

"What do you think? Can we do it?"

Silence.

But I knew the answer. We had already achieved so much. The Camargue, where the engine almost overheated. The Côte d'Azur and the Formule 1 horror hotel. The park bench in San Remo, where I learned that you could survive even without control. We would make it through the Alps too.

"For Miguel," I said quietly. "For me. For you."

I drank the last sip of wine, and the cold crept through my new jumper, but I remained seated because this was my last peaceful evening before the storm came, before everything became difficult, before the mountains tested me.

Back at the hotel, I called Isabel. My mobile phone had reception again, and I stood at the window, looking out at the dark lake, and it rang three times, then I heard her voice.

"Hola?"

"Isabel? It's me, Kai."

"Hijo!" Son. Her voice was warm, concerned, the voice of a mother who was worried. "Where are you?"

"At Lake Garda. In Italy. Tomorrow I'm crossing the Alps."

Silence.

Then, more quietly: "The Alps? In October? On a Vespa?"

"Yes."

"Kai…" She sighed, and I heard her sit down, thinking about what to say. "Take care of yourself! Please."

Be careful. Please.

"I promise."

Pause. Then, even more quietly: "Miguel is with you. I know it."

My throat tightened and I had to swallow before I could answer. "Yes. I can feel it too."

"He would be so proud." Her voice broke. "So proud of you."

I wiped my eyes, glad she couldn't see me. "Thank you, Isabel. That… that means a lot to me."

"Call me. When you arrive. In Kempten."

"I will."

"Cuídate, hijo." Take care, son.

"Tú también." You too.

I hung up, stood at the window, looked out at the dark lake, at the lights of the city reflected in the water, and I thought: Miguel was with me. I knew it.

And tomorrow I would complete the last part of his journey for him.

The next morning. Seven o'clock.

I woke up early, nervous and restless, and outside it was still dusk, the sun not quite over the mountains yet, and I put on everything I had: T-shirt, shirt, the new jumper, gloves, and I looked in the mirror and looked like an onion, layer upon layer, but better warm than frozen.

At breakfast in the hotel, I sat alone, drank espresso and ate a cornetto, simple but good, and the receptionist came by and saw me in my onion outfit.

"Oggi le Alpi?" The Alps today?

I nodded. "Sì. Brenner Pass."

He shook his head. "Freddo! Molto freddo!" Cold! Very cold!

"Lo so."

"Ma… sei coraggioso." But you're brave.

I smiled weakly. "O stupido." Or stupid.

He laughed. "Forse entrambi!" Maybe both!

I went to Lola, started her up, and she rattled cheekily, calmly and reliably, as if she had thought about it all night and decided she was ready.

"Ready?"

Silence.

I drove off. North. Towards Trento. Towards Brenner. Towards the Alps.

The first fifty kilometres were flat, the A22 towards Trento, but I left it at Rovereto and took the SS12 because I didn't like motorways and because the SS12 was nicer, more winding, closer to the mountains.

The landscape changed, vineyards became apple trees, apple trees became fir trees, the hills became steeper, the mountains drew closer, and Lola purred at sixty kilometres per hour, steady, and I felt good, relaxed, almost cocky.

"The worst is over," I thought. "The park bench, the horror hotel, the Camargue — those were the endurance tests. The Alps? Just one last hurdle."

I smiled.

That was a mistake.

After Trento, the climb began, the SS12 became the SS47, uphill, constant, and Lola slowed down, sixty kilometres per hour, fifty, forty, and I shifted down, third gear, second gear, and the engine worked harder and harder, and the mountains drew closer, huge and overwhelming, and the temperature dropped, I could feel it through my jumper, and my hands got cold, despite the gloves, and I thought: This is going to be tough.

I pulled on my poncho – a little better. Well, not visually. The poncho fluttered and I probably looked like a baby blue Batman on a Vespa. To a benevolent observer. Everyone else probably thought a homeless Michelin man had stolen a Vespa and was fleeing from a life of security.

But I drove on.

At Sterzing, seventy kilometres before the Brenner Pass, I stopped at a petrol station, refuelled again, just to be on the safe side, and the petrol station attendant, an elderly man with a grey beard and alert eyes, looked at Lola.

"Bella Vespa."

"Grazie."

"To the Brenner Pass?"

I nodded.

He looked up at the sky, grey clouds, dark and low, and said: "Oggi pioggia."

Rain today?

I swallowed. "Today?"

I nodded slowly. "Capito. Grazie."

Understood. Thank you.

I drove on. What a bummer.

"We can do this," I whispered to Lola.

But my hands were trembling slightly on the handlebars, and it wasn't just because of the cold.

The sky grew darker, the mountains closer, the road steeper, and I rode into the twilight, and the switchbacks began, the rock face on the left, the abyss on the right, and Lola spluttered, struggled, slowly but steadily, forty kilometres per hour, thirty, sometimes twenty-five, first gear in the tightest corners, and cars behind me, waiting, impatient, honking, but I ignored them, concentrating on the road, the engine, my hands, nothing else mattered.

Then I saw it.

A sign. White with a blue border.

"Brenner Pass 20 km."

Twenty kilometres.

That was doable.

My fingers were numb from the cold, but: doable.

"Twenty more kilometres, Lola. Then we'll be done. Then we'll be at the top. Then the descent will begin."

She continued to roar. I drove. Into the twilight. Into the cold. Into the mountains. The last stretch. The storm was waiting.

Chapter 25 – The Brenner Pass

[Soundtrack Shuffle: ACDC – Thunderstruck]

20 kilometres to the summit. I stood at the side of the road and looked at the sign. "Brenner Pass 20 km."

Behind me: 2,500 kilometres. Ahead of me: 20.

It had taken me almost four weeks to get here. Weeks full of sunshine, breakdowns and improvisation. And now, 20 kilometres from my destination, the weather decided to show me what it thought of my adventure.

The temperature had dropped. Perhaps to 6 degrees. The air smelled of rain, damp stone, thunderstorms. The sky: dark grey. Clouds hung so low that they swallowed the peaks. Like a blanket, heavy and wet.

Wind came up. Gusts that grabbed me and Lola, shook us. I kept riding.

After five kilometres, the rain began. Not light. Not gentle. Hard. Brutal. Like being poured from buckets. Drops hit my helmet so loudly that I could hardly hear the engine. The water ran down my visor. I wiped it away. Two seconds later: blurred again.

I opened the visor. The drops hit my face hard. Cold. Sharp. But: I could see. Better than with the visor closed. A small victory of logic over comfort.

The road transformed. From grey to black. Shiny. Like polished metal. The white road markings – normally grippy – became slippery. My front wheel pulled over them and I felt it: a brief tug, a loss of control. I braked. Slowly. Carefully. 50 km/h. 40 km/h.

Lola fought back. She wanted to go faster. But I wouldn't let her. The temperature continued to drop. 5 degrees. 4 degrees. Maybe less.

My hands went numb. The cheap knitted gloves from the supermarket – soaked, useless. The water had seeped through, ice cold. My jumper stuck to my chest. My trousers: soaked to the skin. Water ran down my back because the poncho wasn't made for this.

I was shaking. Uncontrollably. And I thought: If Miguel could see me now – soaking wet, shivering, on a Vespa built for coastal roads – he would laugh. Or cry. Probably both.

The wind grew stronger. Gusts from the side. Lola swayed, slightly, but enough to cause panic. I clung to the handlebars. Both hands. Tightly. So tightly that my knuckles turned white.

A lorry overtook me. Huge. A semi-trailer with Italian number plates. It pulled past like a ship and splashed a wave of water on me. I couldn't see anything. Completely blind. Three seconds. I instinctively let go of the throttle. Lola rolled to a stop. Then: visibility returned. Blurry, but there. The lorry was gone, disappeared in the rain.

I breathed. Shallowly. Quickly. "That was… okay. Okay."

After ten kilometres, the fog rolled in. First in patches, like smoke over the road. Then more. Thicker. Then: a wall. I drove into it, and the world disappeared. Ten metres of visibility. Five metres. Sometimes less.

I saw the guard rail on the right. Blurred. A grey shadow. On the left: nothing. Only white. The road ahead of me: barely recognisable. I was driving at 30 km/h. Then 25. That wasn't enough. I braked further. 20 km/h. The engine protested. Too slow for second gear. I shifted down. First gear. 15 km/h.

Walking pace. On the Brenner Pass. With a 1967 Vespa.

If that wasn't proof that I had lost my mind, then I didn't know what was.

Behind me: headlights. Yellow, diffuse in the fog. A car, close behind me. It honked. Briefly. Impatiently.

"Pass me if you can. I'm staying here."

The car overtook. Too fast. Disappeared into the fog. Red tail lights. Then gone.

I felt my way through the white wall. Lonely. In the rain. In the cold.

A sign appeared, ghostly. White on white. "Brenner Pass 5 km."

Five kilometres. I could do it. I had to do it.

But my hands. They were barely obeying me. Numb. Stiff. Like wood. I tried to turn the throttle. My fingers slipped. Panic rose.

The incline was gentle. Almost flat. The road ran parallel to the A13 – the Brenner motorway. No tight bends. Just: a steady climb. Kilometre after kilometre. That didn't make it any easier. It made it slower. More gruelling.

Then, three kilometres before the summit, the engine stuttered. Just briefly. A misfire. Like a hiccup.

My heart skipped a beat. "No. Please not. Not now."

I accelerated. The engine recovered. Kept running. But then: again. A stutter. Irregular. Weak.

I drove on, slowly, carefully, praying that it would get better. It didn't. The engine coughed, struggled, lost power.

A sign in the fog. "Brenner Pass 1 km."

"Just one more kilometre. Please, please."

Then the engine died. Just like that. In the middle of the road. One last cough. A rattle. Then: silence. Nothing but fog. Wind. The patter of rain.

I let Lola coast. 50 metres. 30 metres. 10 metres. Standstill.

I stood in the middle of the road. Got off. Pushed Lola to the side, onto the narrow strip next to the road. Put her on the centre stand.

My hands were shaking. Not just from the cold. From panic.

I tried to start her. Kick starter. Once. Twice. Three times. Nothing. The engine turned, but didn't ignite.

I opened the tool compartment under the seat with trembling hands. The lock was stuck. I tugged at it. It opened. Inside: wrench, socket wrench, pliers, spare spark plug. Pedro had given them to me. "For emergencies."

This was an emergency.

I knelt down next to the engine. The rain pelted down on my back. My gloves: completely soaked, drenched. Water poured out when I moved my fingers. I took them off. Threw them aside.

My hands: white. Wrinkled. Like waterlogged corpses. My fingers: numb, stiff, barely responsive.

I tried to grab the spark plug connector. My fingers slipped. Three times.

I rubbed my hands together, trying to generate heat. It hardly helped.

Three weeks in Spain. Two thousand five hundred kilometres. And now I'm stranded at the Brenner Pass because of a damn spark plug that costs five euros. Life definitely had a strange sense of irony.

On the fourth attempt, the plug came loose. Unscrew the old spark plug. 21 mm socket wrench. My fingers were shaking so badly that the wrench slipped away. Fell to the ground. I picked it up.

The spark plug was stuck. I pushed. Pulled. With all my strength. But my fingers were powerless. The cold had sucked the strength out of them. Every movement was difficult and laborious.

The spark plug came loose. Finally. I unscrewed it. Held it up. Black. Wet. Oily.

The new spark plug. I took it out of the plastic bag and tried to screw it in. My fingers slipped. Twice. Three times. I forced myself to concentrate. On the fourth attempt, it caught. I screwed it in. Slowly. Carefully.

Plugged it in. Click. I stood up. Kicked the kick starter.

The engine turned. Ignited. Ran!

"Thank you. Thank you, thank you, thank you."

I drove 200 metres. Then: again. Stuttering. Coughing. The engine died again.

I pushed Lola back to the side. Turned her off. Stood there. Rain. Cold. Despair.

[Notification] Email: "Subject: WARNING for unexcused absence. Dear Mr Ritter, as you have failed to respond to multiple requests..."

Dear Mr Schneider, thank you very much for your warning letter. Unfortunately, I am unable to respond in person at the moment, as I am currently standing in the rain at an altitude of 1,300 metres, trying not to freeze to death. I will respond to your message as soon as I can feel my fingers again. Kind regards, Kai Ritter.

I thought about it. Forced myself to think. The spark plug was new. So that wasn't the problem. Petrol? I opened the fuel cap. The tank was half full.

Carburettor. The carburettor. Of course. In this cold, this rain, at this altitude – water had condensed. In the tank. In the fuel hose. In the carburettor. And the main jet – the small opening through which the petrol flowed. Clogged.

Actually, I had no idea. But I gave myself this explanation. Sometimes self-confidence was more important than expertise.

I fetched the spanner. The pliers. My hands were shaking so badly that I could hardly hold the tools. The cold was in my bones. Deep inside. It pulled at me, sucked the strength out of me. Every movement: as if through water.

I opened the carburettor bowl. Removed the air filter. Found the jets. My fingers slipped. Three times. Four times. I gritted my teeth.

Then: the main jet. A tiny screw. Brass-coloured. With a hole in the middle. 1 mm in diameter.

I reached for it with my thumb and index finger. It slipped away. My fingers: too numb, too stiff. I tried again. And again.

On the fifth attempt: I held it. Unscrewed it. Slowly. Laboriously.

It came loose. I held it up. My hand was shaking so badly that I could hardly see it.

Clogged. A tiny lump of dirt.

I blew on it. Once. My lips: numb, ice cold. The dirt flew out. I held the nozzle up to the light. Looked through it. Clear.

Screwed it back in with trembling fingers.

Locked the carburettor again. Stood up. My legs wobbled. I had to hold on to Lola. Otherwise I would have fallen over. The exhaustion was overwhelming. Not just tired. Exhausted.

Kicked the kick starter. The engine started. Ran. Smoothly. Evenly. Strongly.

"Yessir! We did it, girl. We did it, damn it."

I drove the last 200 metres to the pass. Slowly. Carefully. The engine was running, but I didn't trust it anymore. Not completely.

Then: there. A big sign. "Austria. Österreich. Brennero. 1,370 m."

I stopped. Got off. Stood there.

The rain had eased off. Just drizzle now, fine as mist. The wind: still there, but weaker. The clouds: still low, but with gaps. Shreds of blue.

I looked at the sign. Then back at the road I had come from. Italy lay there, somewhere in the mist. Spain was far away. 2,500 kilometres.

I had made it. From Albacete to here. Alone. On a Vespa that was older than most of my colleagues.

Tears welled up. I tried to hold them back. I couldn't. They ran down my cheeks. Warm on my cold skin. I wiped them away. But more came.

"I did it." My voice broke. Quietly. Trembling. "I did it, damn it."

A few tourists stood by their cars. They looked over at me. Questioningly. A soaked man on an antique Vespa, crying and laughing. Probably not what was in the travel guide.

I didn't care. I stood there. Cried. Laughed. Lived.

I went to Lola. Stroked the tank. The handlebars. "You did it, girl. We did it."

I pulled the photo out of my bag. Miguel. With Lola. In Barcelona. "Mi libertad empieza aquí." My freedom begins here.

"You were right, amigo."

I kissed the photo. Put it back. Then I looked to the other side. Austria. The descent. Serpentines. Steep. Wet.

My stomach tightened. "Oh no."

I went briefly into a restaurant at the pass. My shoes made squelching noises as I entered – the sound of a man who had just crossed an Alpine pass in the rain. My poncho fluttered. The guests stared at me.

I dried myself as best I could with the hairdryer in the toilet. I stood barefoot in front of the hairdryer, my socks pulled over it. It smelled like the neighbour's dog after a long swim in a pond. A man left the cubicle, shaking his head.

I nodded to him. "Brenner. In the rain."

He nodded back. Understanding. As if that explained everything.

Then I drank a hot chocolate and ate a Kaiserschmarrn. I hung my wet gloves on a radiator and my jumper on the back of a chair in front of it. A modern art installation: "The failed mountaineer". Warm up. Dry off. Gather strength for the other side.

The descent. I looked down. The road wound its way downhill. Serpentines. Narrow. Steep. Wet. Everything wet.

My stomach cramped up. The ascent had been gentle. Barely any incline. Easy. The descent was the opposite. Steep. 8% gradient. Maybe more. Curve after curve.

I started Lola. Set off.

After 100 metres, I knew: this is going to be tough. The road was slippery. Slick. Like soft soap. I braked carefully. Both brakes. The front wheel locked briefly. Slipped. I released immediately.

My heart was racing. "Don't brake too hard. Slowly. Gently."

The brakes responded sluggishly. Not immediately. With a delay. I had to press harder. The front wheel: okay, it held. The rear wheel: slipped. Slightly. But enough to cause panic.

A bend. Tight. Right. I braked. Too late. Not enough. I was going too fast. 40 km/h. The bend came. I steered. The rear wheel broke out. Slipped sideways.

I released the brake. Steered against it. Caught it. Just in time.

For a moment I thought, "That's it. I'm falling."

My heart exploded. Adrenaline shot through my body like liquid fire. Suddenly: warmth. Everywhere. In my arms. In my chest. In my face. The cold: gone. Replaced for a moment by heat. Pulsating. Burning.

I was sweating. Despite the rain. Despite the 4 degrees. My hands: suddenly mobile. My fingers: responsive. The adrenaline gave me back my strength.

"Slower. Much slower."

I braked constantly. Both brakes. Gently. Evenly. The brakes got warm. The smell: hot, metallic, burnt. Pedro had said: "Brake drums get hot. Especially downhill. Be careful."

I kept going. Curve after curve. Braking. Steering. Braking. Steering. A rhythm. Monotonous. Exhausting. My hands cramped up. My forearms: burning.

After five kilometres: a straight stretch. Short. 200 metres, maybe. I eased off the throttle. Let Lola roll. Gave the brakes a break.

Looked down. The Inn Valley. Wide. Green. Far below. Maybe another 15 kilometres. To Innsbruck. 15 kilometres of switchbacks.

The next bend. Left. Tight. I braked. Hard. Too hard. The front wheel locked up. Completely. I skidded. Straight ahead. Towards the crash barrier.

Panic.

I released the front brake. Tugged on the handlebars. To the left. The front wheel gripped again. Turned. I steered into the bend. Just in time.

The crash barrier: 20 centimetres away.

I exhaled. Shaking. "That was… that was too close."

Further downhill. The brakes got hotter. I could smell it clearly now. A sharp smell. Metallic. Burnt. The braking performance: spongier. I had to press harder. Much harder.

After ten kilometres, the valley came closer. The hairpin bends: flatter. Less tight. The road: still wet, but a little wider.

Then: Innsbruck. The city spread out. Buildings. Streets. Flat land. I drove the last two kilometres slowly, carefully. Then: city limits. A sign. "Innsbruck."

I stopped. At the side of the road. Under a tree. Got off. Knelt down next to Lola.

Carefully touched the front brake drum. It was hot. Too hot. I pulled my hand back. Then: the rear brake drum. Even hotter. Too hot to touch.

"We made it, girl. We crossed the Alps. Breakdowns. Everything."

My legs were shaking. I sat down on the ground. Leaned against a tree. Closed my eyes. Exhaustion washed over me like a wave.

I sat there. Ten minutes. Maybe longer. Let the brakes cool down. Let myself cool down. Let the adrenaline subside.

Somewhere in Germany, my boss was waiting for an explanation. My flat was waiting for me. Normal life was waiting.

But right now, I was sitting under a tree in Innsbruck, soaked, exhausted, and feeling more alive than I had in the last ten years.

Then I got up. "Let's go!"

I started Lola. She woke up with a motivated rattle. Ready. Reliable. That was enough for today. First, find a place to sleep.

Chapter 26 – Germany Smells Different

[Soundtrack Shuffle: Sting – Englishman in New York]

7 p.m. I stood in front of the Innsbruck Youth Hostel. My left leg was wet and would probably remain so forever. The air smelled of wet asphalt and a day that had been too long.

The youth hostel looked like a waiting room for people who hadn't given up on life yet, but had temporarily put it on hold. Glass. Concrete. Modern. Functional. My soul, shaped by southern European chaos and Vespa noise, wanted to become invisible at the sight of this building.

Lola stood next to me. Dusty, wet, exhausted. She looked like me – only with a better silhouette and an engine that twitched less than my eyelids. We were welded together by oil, rain and the Alpine passes. We both smelled of adventure and much-needed coffee.

I went inside.

The lobby: bright, clean, minimalist. Wooden floors. White walls. A few glossy posters of Tyrolean peaks smiling friendlily at you in the picture, after they almost froze you to death yesterday. It was so tidy that I wondered if my rucksack with its damp socks, oily gloves and squashed tuna sandwich was even allowed on the floor.

At the reception desk: Lucia. Early 30s, dark hair tied back in a ponytail. Big eyes. And a smile that immediately signalled: "I work here, but I have an escape plan."

She looked up. "Good evening! Check-in?"

Her accent was German. Clear, friendly, but there was a melody that didn't sound like the Alps.

"Yes." My voice was hoarse. "A bed for one night. But… how much is a single room?"

After the Brenner Pass, I deserved a night where I didn't have to lie in a room with three snoring strangers.

She typed into the computer. "One moment… the single room with breakfast costs 55 euros."

55 euros. A fortune when you've been living on a street musician's budget for weeks. But it was a luxury. A night where I could throw my underwear on the floor without being judged for it. I would need every free spot to dry. Even my rucksack was soaked. A reward after the Brenner Pass.

"I'll take it. 55 euros. I'll take it. I've slept in Formule 1, I deserve a single room."

She smiled. "No problem."

I gave her my credit card. She took it, looked over my shoulder directly at Lola. The world seemed to stand still for a moment.

"That's your Vespa?"

"Yes."

"Motovespa? Spanish?"

My eyebrows shot up. No one in this part of the world knew Motovespa. It was like a secret handshake that worked across borders.

"You know it?" My voice was almost incredulous.

She smiled. "My grandfather had one. In Seville. I'm half Spanish."

Ah. Now I heard it. A trace of Spanish beneath the German precision. A trace of chaos and warmth.

"Where are you from?"

"From Spain. Albacete."

Her eyes widened. "With THAT? The whole way?"

I nodded. "Today over the Brenner Pass. In the rain."

I left out the detail that the engine had died for half an hour and I had briefly contemplated my own mortality. Unnecessary information.

She whistled softly. The sound was not Alpine. It was deep south and completely out of place in this lobby.

"That's… brave. Or completely ballaballa. In any case, not sensible planning."

I laughed, and the laughter felt like throwing off a wet poncho. "Both, I think. The perfect mix of a thirst for adventure and the realisation that life in an office isn't enough. And planning is the death of adventure."

"My name is Lucia."

"Kai."

She handed me the key chip. Room 312. Third floor.

I turned around. The longing for a dry, warm place was almost painful.

"Kai?"

I turned back. She hesitated. The smile was gone, replaced by a slight tension.

"Have you had dinner yet?"

"No. Just an energy bar that turned into a brown mass in my bag. I wonder if it's still edible."

"I finish work at eight. There's a pizzeria around the corner. 'Da Antonio.' The best pizza in Innsbruck. Honestly. If you… if you feel like it?"

Human warmth. The chance to talk to someone who knew Lola and not just my booking name. The pizza would definitely be better than the brown mass in my bag.

She smiled shyly, hopefully.

"Yes. I'd love to. I need a decent pizza to celebrate the single room."

Her smile widened. "Perfect! I'll come to your room at eight. 312."

Room 312. A single room. A sanctuary.

The room was small, but it was mine. A bed, a desk, a chair, a tiny bathroom. It smelled of cleanliness and the absence of others.

I threw my rucksack on the bed. Took off my wet clothes. The soaked jumper. The damp T-shirt. I hung them over the radiator. The 55 euros were worth it. German functionality might not defeat Spanish humidity, but I had hope.

Within ten minutes, the room looked like a battlefield.

Then: shower.

I stood under the hot water for twenty minutes. The water ran over my head, my back. The cold that had settled in my bones, the cold of the Brenner, slowly melted away. The Brenner, the repair, the descent, the battle against the storm. Everything: over. Washed away.

I felt the tension leave my shoulders. I took a deep breath. Eyes closed. Steam all around me.

200 kilometres to Kempten. That was nothing. Compared to what I had been through, it was a Sunday outing.

At eight o'clock, there was a knock. Short but determined.

I opened it. Lucia was standing there. Jeans, white jumper, leather jacket. She looked like someone who had just made the decision not to spend her life in a youth hostel.

"Ready for carbohydrates and southern flair? I'm hungry for something that doesn't smell like convenience food."

"I'm ready. I can't wait to forget everything that smells like a motorway service station."

We left.

The pizzeria "Da Antonio" was the complete opposite of the youth hostel. Small. Ten tables. Red and white checkered tablecloths. Candles in wine bottles. Kitschy. But cosy. It was loud, a pleasant level of noise that would have immediately resulted in a call for order in Germany, but here it just meant life. An island of the south in the Tyrolean Alps.

Antonio, the owner, hugged Lucia as if he hadn't seen her in years.

"Lucia! Bellissima! E chi è questo?"

Lucia laughed. "A friend. Kai. From Germany."

Antonio shook my hand. Firmly. Warmly. "Benvenuto! Welcome!"

We sat down. Antonio brought water, bread, olive oil. He recommended the Margherita. "The best in Tyrol. Guaranteed."

Lucia leaned back, the tension of the working day seeming to fall away from her. She looked at me with alert curiosity.

"So. Tell me. Why is a German riding a Spanish Vespa across the Alps? That sounds like a rather complicated metaphor for the search for meaning."

I told her while the pizza dough bubbled in Antonio's oven. Lucia listened. Attentively. She didn't comment on the logistics, but on the decision.

"That's incredible." She looked at me. "The courage to just leave when life no longer fits. When you realise that you are successful, but unhappy."

"I felt like I just didn't fit in anymore. In this life."

Lucia nodded. Again, that instant understanding.

"I came here from Munich. Bank job. Good pay. Secure. A life so boring that it felt like an assault on my own happiness. The highlight of the week was the meeting to decide on the new coffee machine."

"And then?"

"I went to Seville. To my grandfather. Worked in a bar for six months. I felt. For the first time in years. When I came back, I couldn't go back to my old life. Not to the bank. Not to the Munich chic scene."

She shrugged. "Now youth hostel. Less money. But I'm happy. Unfortunately, that's an underrated currency in our world."

The pizza arrived. Large. Thin. Crispy. We ate. Talked. Laughed. It was easy. Natural. At half past ten, we went back. The streets of Innsbruck were quiet.

Lola was standing in front of the youth hostel. Lucia went over to her. Stroked the seat. A gentle, almost tender gesture.

"She's beautiful. Despite all the oil and dirt. She's honest."

"We brought each other here."

She looked at me. "I believe that."

Pause.

"Thanks for tonight, Kai. It was nice. A reminder that life exists outside of the plan."

The pause stretched out.

"Are you continuing tomorrow?"

"Yes. To Füssen. Then Kempten."

"Then: good luck. For whatever comes. I hope Kempten is ready for a man who smells of oil and Spanish freedom."

She hugged me. Briefly. Warmly. I stood there. Smiled.

7 o'clock.

I woke up. Bright light. I hadn't actually had to share the single room with snorers. A victory.

I went to the window.

BLUE. Blue sky. Not a cloud. The peaks glowed white and majestic. The day that had almost ended my existence yesterday was showing its chocolate side today.

I laughed out loud. "OF COURSE!"

One day too late. But fate was rarely punctual. It always gave you beauty only when you no longer urgently needed it, but could appreciate it all the more.

I got dressed. The clothes weren't dry, but they were less wet. Progress.

I had breakfast. The breakfast was functional, clean, German. No frills. But edible.

I checked out. Lucia wasn't there. An elderly lady stood at the reception desk, her stern expression perfectly complementing the functional cube. She looked at me as if I were the reason the world didn't work.

I went to Lola. Started her up. She ran. Reliably. As if she knew that today was the day.

I drove off. The sun was shining so warmly that you almost forgot you were in the Alps.

The Fern Pass.

Not the Brenner. Thank God, not the Brenner.

The road rose gently. Wide. Well constructed. No panic. No fear of death. Just asphalt winding its way through the landscape in elegant curves. I drove with my visor open. The air was clear and cool, but no longer the biting cold of yesterday. It was the kind of cold that woke you up, not the kind that wanted to kill you.

Lola purred. Really purred. Third gear. The curves came, but they were friendly. Almost inviting. I leaned into the first right-hand curve. The asphalt was dry. Grippy. The sun cast long shadows across the road.

On the left: a turquoise lake. Fernsteinsee. The water so clear you could see the bottom. On the right: fir trees. Dense. Dark green. And behind them: the mountains. Huge. Majestic. But not threatening today. Today they were just there. Beautiful.

I drove on. Second gear in the tighter bends. Lola took them as if she had never done anything else. As if yesterday the engine and rider had not almost died. I felt every metre beneath me. The slight vibration of the handlebars. The twitching of the machine in the bends. It wasn't perfect. It was never perfect with Lola. But it was real.

The road continued to climb. Not a gradient like on the Brenner Pass, where every metre was a matter of survival. This was gentle. Almost playful. I overtook a motorhome. The driver waved. I waved back. Yesterday, I wouldn't have been able to greet anyone. Yesterday, I was too busy trying not to die.

A sign: "Fern Pass 1209 m."

I stopped. Got off.

I stood there. Looked back at the route I had travelled. The curves. The lakes. The mountains. And further back, somewhere beyond the peaks: the Brenner Pass. Yesterday. Another world.

I had crossed the Alps. Alone. On an old Vespa that smelled more of oil than I did after a week without a shower.

A few tourists were taking photos. A family. Father, mother, two children. The father looked over at me. At Lola. Smiled. Gave me the thumbs up.

I smiled back.

Then I looked ahead. To the north. The road winding its way down into the valleys. Germany. Somewhere up ahead.

I took a deep breath. The air was thin up here, but it felt good. Clean. Clear.

I laughed. Loudly. Freely.

"I DID IT! I REALLY DID IT!"

The family turned around. The children giggled. I didn't care.

The Zugspitze was visible through the trees. The highest mountain in Germany. I wouldn't be going up there. But I would be passing by. That was enough.

> **[Notification]** Kempten City Library: "Return reminder: The book '101 Ways to Slow Down' is 14 days overdue. Current late fee: €3.50. Please return the item promptly."

I got on Lola. Started her up. She started right away.

Then: downhill. To Germany.

The descent was like flying. The road wound its way down into the valley in gentle curves. I let Lola roll. Only braking in the sharper bends. The wind whistled around my helmet. I felt light. Free. Invincible.

Then: a sign. "Federal Republic of Germany."

I stopped. No checkpoint, no customs. Just a sign.

I crossed the border.

The road: wider. Smoother. More perfect. So perfect that it seemed sterile again. The road surface was immaculate, as if freshly polished. German road construction was impressive, but soulless.

The landscape: neat. Well-kept. Clean. The hedges: trimmed. The fields: mowed. Everything in its place. Aggressively in its place. Nature had been put in a straitjacket here.

This was Germany.

And it smelled different. Of cold air. Of organisation. Of the absence of improvisation.

An immediate cultural jet lag.

Around noon, I reached Füssen.

I parked Lola at the market square. "Café am Markt." I went inside. Ordered a cappuccino.

"3.80 euros."

The price was the first indication that I was back in Germany.

The coffee arrived. Perfectly served. I drank it. It tasted of absolutely nothing. Neutral. Bland. German. Not necessarily bad. But not good either. Coffee that did its job without any passion.

Outside: people. Neatly dressed. Lots of down jackets and hiking boots. Punctual. Determined. They looked as if they had already finished planning their day at six in the morning.

No one was just sitting there. No one was drinking wine at three in the afternoon. No one was gesticulating. No one was laughing loudly.

Everything: controlled. Polite. Restrained.

I sat there, with my tanned face and the Vespa outside that smelled of adventure, and felt like I was wearing the wrong uniform. I was too loud, too messy.

"This is my home?"

I whispered it. It felt wrong.

I paid. Went outside. Stroked Lola's handlebars.

"We're almost there, girl. Another 50 kilometres."

Tomorrow I would be in Kempten. At the end of the last stage. But today I couldn't and didn't want to go back yet. I looked for a small guesthouse. And then? Then I would decide. Whatever home meant.

Chapter 27 – Kempten is No Longer Kempten

[Soundtrack Shuffle: Britney Spears – Oops I Did It Again]

Nine o'clock.

I stood in front of the hotel in Füssen, and the sun was shining as if it had a guilty conscience and wanted to make amends – bright and warm and far too friendly for what awaited me. Lola stood next to me, dusty, slightly dented and scratched, as if she had just escaped from several years of captivity in Dakar. But ready. Always ready. That damn Vespa was ready for anything.

I wasn't.

Today: the last fifty kilometres. To Kempten. Home. Or what used to be "home". Now it was more like: the place where my moving boxes had been leading a sad existence as dust collectors for months.

I stroked the seat. "That's it, girl. The last leg."

Lola was silent. She was smarter than me.

I started her up and drove off. The B16. And the Allgäu lay before me – green and neat and so German that it physically hurt. Meadows. Cows. Farms. Everything familiar, everything known, and yet it felt strange.

It was as if someone had bought Germany at IKEA and assembled it according to instructions that consisted only of prohibitions and midday rest times: functional, but soulless.

These meadows were suspiciously perfect. No blade of grass was allowed to be longer than the next. Presumably, there was a Federal Office for Meadow Aesthetics somewhere that carried out regular inspections. "Attention, Mr Müller, your blade of grass number 247 has an impermissible inclination of three degrees. That will be a warning fine and three hours of community service at the shooting club."

The fences: white and straight, without the slightest flaw. The roads: immaculate. With every metre of perfect asphalt, my anxiety level rose. The order felt like a friendly stranglehold.

And then the smell of home – in the Allgäu, that always means a hint of cow dung. It was like a scent brand. Whether you came from the north or the south, as soon as you wrinkled your nose, you knew: you were home.

I drove slowly, sixty kilometres per hour, and thought: Spain had potholes. Italy had chaos. France had character. Germany had precision.

And that was the saddest thing.

Somewhere between Valencia and here, I had learned that potholes had personality. That chaos was honest. That character was more important than perfection. And now I was driving through a country that prided itself on offering no surprises.

A twinge in my stomach. Not hunger. Panic. What would I say to my boss? "Good"? "Interesting"? Or the truth: "I learned on a park bench in Italy that your Q3 reports are as useful as a solar panel in a coal mine"?

That probably wouldn't go down well.

A sign: "Kempten 10 km."

Ten kilometres to home. Or to surrender. To what, exactly? Hard to tell.

I drove on, past places whose names I knew by heart – Oy-Mittelberg, Durach, Waltenhofen. It felt like I was driving through a museum of my own past. "On the left, you can see the place where Kai Ritter fell off his bike in 1987. On the right, the supermarket where he once stole toilet paper. Thank you for your attention."

Then: Kempten. The town sign. "University town of Kempten (Allgäu). 68,000 inhabitants."

I stopped, got off, waited for the feeling. Joy? Relief? The epic Hollywood moment of coming home? Women throwing their bras at me and shouting, "Kai, I want to have your baby!"

It didn't come.

> **[Notification]** HP Smart App: "Warning: Your printer is reporting a critical ink level. Due to prolonged inactivity, the print head is at risk of drying out. Start cleaning programme now to avoid streaking?"

Instead: the feeling you get when you open the fridge door after a long holiday and remember why you should have taken out the rubbish.

I drove into town. Bahnhofstraße. Hildegardplatz. Everything was just as I had left it. The baker's. The café. The kiosk. Nothing had changed. Only me.

And that was the problem. Or the solution. Or both.

I stopped briefly at Residenzplatz and took a photo of Lola in front of the basilica. As a "finale"? I didn't know.

I drove slowly down Bahnhofstraße. The supermarket on the left. Müller's bakery on the right. I stopped. Not because I was hungry. But because I knew: there was nothing at home. Four weeks away. An empty fridge. The ketchup had probably developed a mind of its own by now and the expired milk had moved out.

I needed bread. Milk. Coffee. The basics of German survival.

I parked Lola in front of Müller's bakery. The same bakery where I had bought bread rolls every Saturday morning for eight years. With Sabine. Always at ten o'clock. Always the same: four pretzel rolls, two grain rolls, one pretzel.

Like a ritual. Or a punishment. Depending on how you looked at it.

That was over.

I got off, took my helmet under my arm and walked to the door. She came out as I went in.

Sabine.

Red hair tied back in a ponytail. Jeans. White jumper. In her hand: a paper bag from the bakery. Probably four pretzel rolls, two grain rolls, one pretzel.

Some things never change.

We stood there. Looked at each other. Three seconds of silence. The longest three seconds of my life. Including the time on the Brenner Pass.

Then her face: confusion. Shock. As if she had just recognised a homeless man who used to be her boyfriend.

"Kai?"

"Sabine."

Her eyes scanned me. From top to bottom. Slowly. Like a customs officer inspecting a suspicious shipment.

My tousled hair – uncut for four weeks, flattened by my helmet. My knitted jumper – grey, worn. The Hawaiian shirt underneath, peeking out from the collar, turquoise and pink. My jeans – oily, dirty, with stains that told stories. Not good stories. More like: "This man has hygiene issues."

And behind me: Lola. Black, old, beautiful – a baby blue poncho hung from the handlebars.

"What… what IS that?" She wasn't pointing at the Vespa. She was pointing at me. At my entire appearance. "An outfit?"

"A… a WHAT?" She came closer. Stared. "Kai, what the hell happened? You look like… like a homeless person with bad taste."

"Fair." I looked down at myself. The Hawaiian shirt flashed. "Magnum, P.I. You know him."

"Kai, you were gone for four weeks. Just gone. No message. Nothing. And now you come back looking like a failed Magnum cosplayer who got lost at a Vespa rally?"

"Spain. France. Italy, Austria. With Lola. Across the Alps. Over two thousand five hundred kilometres."

Silence. She stared at me. Then at the Vespa. Then back at me.

"Have you gone mad?"

"Maybe. Or finally sane. The line between the two is surprisingly thin."

"That's not funny, Kai."

"I know. But it's true. And that somehow makes it funnier."

She was looking for something in my face. The old Kai. The man who went to get bread rolls on Saturdays. Who wore neat shirts. Who never wore Hawaiian shirts because "it's silly".

I looked at her and realised: she was looking for someone who no longer existed. And the strange thing was – it didn't hurt. It felt like looking at an old photo. Familiar, but strange. Important, but over.

"You look… different," she whispered.

"I am different. I've been living. For the first time in years."

She laughed briefly. In disbelief. "Lived. With a Vespa and a Hawaiian shirt. Kai, this is a midlife crisis. A cry for help on two wheels. You're an insurance broker. You're structured. Sensible. You plan for risks."

"I was. Now I'm more: improvised, chaotic, and my risk assessment is broken."

Silence. She looked at the bakery bag. "I met someone. Thomas. A nurse. Very… down-to-earth. Reliable."

"I'm happy for you. Really."

And it was true. Thomas sounded like someone who would pick up bread rolls on time. Perfect for Sabine.

She searched for irony. For pain. Found nothing.

"You've really changed."

"Yes."

"And now what? Back to the office? Back to normality?"

I thought of Schneider. Of the 712 emails. Of the flat full of moving boxes.

"No. Not back. Forward. Somewhere. Probably towards unemployment. But hey, at least that's a direction."

She laughed again. Shaking her head. "That won't work, Kai. Life isn't a Vespa tour. It's responsibility. Security. A plan."

"For you. For me, it's apparently a chaotic improvisational theatre without a script. And I play the leading role. Amateurishly."

I turned around. Went to Lola.

"Kai!"

I stopped.

"Good luck." And this time it sounded almost sincere.

"Thanks, Sabine. You too. And say hi to Thomas. He sounds nice. And down-to-earth. Very down-to-earth."

I swung myself onto Lola. The engine roared – that singing two-stroke sound that sounded like freedom. Or a broken exhaust.

Sabine stood there and watched me drive away. In the rear-view mirror, I saw her shaking her head.

I smiled. She would never understand. Some people were made for bread rolls at ten o'clock. Not me anymore.

Around eleven o'clock, I reached Mozartstraße. Quiet. Middle-class. Boring.

I parked Lola in front of number seventeen. She stood there between an Opel, a VW and a BMW like a punk at a CDU party conference.

I took my rucksack. It smelled of adventure and cheap hostel soap, of freedom and everything that probably violated the house rules here.

Horror greeted me on the ground floor. Post spilled out of the letterboxes – an uncontrolled paper explosion of bills and advertising leaflets that looked as if the letterbox had thrown up.

But that was just the prelude.

In the hallway, right next to the stairs, a bizarre still life of modern consumer terror had formed. There they stood: a tower of Amazon packages containing coffee machine descaler, copy paper and 24 rolls of toilet paper, right next to a slightly rotten package from Hello Fresh, emitting a smell that would probably be classified as a chemical weapon in Geneva. And on top of it all, like a rotten cherry on a pile of cream of neglect, sat the lasagne.

My mother had left it there on the very day I arrived in Barcelona. "So you'll have something decent to eat when you come home from work, Kai," she had written at the time.

Four weeks later, the lasagne was no longer food, but a biological experiment with a fluffy layer of mould that glowed almost eerily in the pale hallway light.

Stuck in the middle of this pile was a bright yellow note from the property management company. In the finest bureaucratic German, I was informed that "leaving rubbish and perishable goods in the communal property" constituted a serious violation of fire safety and hygiene regulations. I was to remedy the situation "immediately".

Germany had officially got me back.

I ignored the note, grabbed the pack of toilet paper and unlocked my flat door. I took a step into the dark, stuffy hallway – and almost fell flat on my face. I had tripped over something.

I looked down.

There they were. Sabine's damn Birkenstocks.

They looked at me like two flat, leathery reproaches. They lay there as if they had been waiting four weeks to trip me up on my return. A fitting welcome.

I stepped inside. Dusty. Stuffy. The air smelled of stale Germany.

I threw open the window. Cold but fresh air streamed in. I looked around. Moving boxes everywhere. For eight months. A memorial to my procrastination. "The abandoned man and his boxes." Very emotional.

In the kitchen: two dirty plates. The fridge empty except for a bottle of ketchup. Expired in August 2024. My culinary pet. Soon it would deserve a name.

I stood there and thought: four weeks ago, I had stood in this flat and sensed that something was wrong. Now, after two thousand five hundred kilometres, I was standing here again – and the feeling was stronger. Clearer. More inescapable.

This was no longer my life. It was just the backdrop to it.

As I stood there, it suddenly dawned on me: my car.

It was still at the airport in Memmingen. In the long-term car park. "Long-term" was about to take on a whole new, damn expensive meaning. There had been severe storms in the Allgäu region in recent weeks. I could picture my car standing there – probably with hail damage that had turned the bodywork into the surface of a golf ball.

I had to get it out of there. Fast. It was probably costing me a fortune by now – probably more than the dented car was worth.

I sat down on the sofa. Hard. Uncomfortable. IKEA. A bargain at the time. Today, a punishment.

My mobile rang. Display: "Boss." The drill. Perfect timing.

"Ritter."

"Kai! You're back?" His voice was controlled. Too controlled.

"Yes. Just arrived."

"Good. When are you coming into the office? We have seventeen open contracts. The customers are asking. Every day."

I heard Lola cooling down outside. Little clicking noises. She sounded satisfied.

"I… I don't know. I need a few more days."

"A few days? Kai, we have deadlines! We'll talk on Monday. Nine o'clock. My office."

"Okay." I hung up. Quickly. Before he used words like "responsibility" and "professionalism".

I sat there and thought: I can't stay here. Not in this life that looked like an IKEA ad for loneliness.

In the evening, I tried to sleep. I lay in my bed. The bed I had slept in with Sabine for eight years. It was too soft. Much too soft. As if I were sinking into clouds. Or into self-pity.

My back rebelled. It had become accustomed to park benches and hostel beds. To hardness. To reality. To everything except German premium mattresses.

I had slept on a park bench in San Remo. With the sound of the sea. With the stars. With fear in my stomach and peace in my heart.

Here I had: a premium mattress and an existential crisis.

I stared at the ceiling. White. Smooth. Boring. In Genoa, the ceiling had had cracks. Here there was nothing. Just perfect, sterile white. Like in a hospital. Or an institution.

The silence was the problem. This German silence, which was not silence, but an absence of life. As if someone had muted life. No sound of waves. Just the ticking of a clock. The hum of the refrigerator. The creaking of the heating. The soundtrack of a dying life.

I got up. Went to the window. Mozartstraße. The parked cars, neatly lined up like coffins. Everything bathed in orange light. Artificial. Cold. Absolutely German.

I thought: I don't belong here anymore.

That wasn't a realisation. It was a fact. As clear as the fact that Lola had 7 horsepower or that Miguel was dead.

This street. This house. This flat. Backdrops for a play I no longer wanted to be part of.

But where to go then?

Good question. No answer. But at least a good question.

After three hours of sleep.

The Sunday light fell through the blinds. Those German blinds that could be adjusted precisely. Just the right angle. Suffocating.

I took a shower. The water was hot. The pressure was strong. Everything worked perfectly. And somehow that was the problem. I missed the rickety showers in the hostels. Where nothing was perfect, but everything was real.

I got dressed. Jeans. T-shirt. The Hawaiian shirt from Barcelona. Faded. Dusty. My badge of honour.

Sunday morning in Kempten. The streets were empty. Too empty. The silence of people sitting behind closed doors, waiting for Monday like prisoners awaiting execution.

Lola stood there. A thin film of dew on the tank. Glittering like a thousand tiny diamonds.

"What do we do now?"

She was silent. Wise.

Tomorrow. Monday. Nine o'clock. Office.

The question was not what I would do. The question was what I wanted to do.

I went to the baker's on the corner. Sunday morning. The Germans were buying their bread rolls. Neatly in line. All polite. Quiet. Dead.

"Two pretzels. And a coffee. Black."

The coffee tasted like disappointment. Every sip a reminder of real espresso in Italy. The pretzels were crispy. Salty. I had to admit that. Some things worked in Germany.

But not everything. And definitely not my life.

I had to make a decision. Carry on as before – back to the office, to the life that worked but wasn't lived? Like a clock? Or: something else. Something new.

I went back, sat down on the sofa. Picked up my mobile phone. Scrolled through my contacts.

Isabel.

"Hola?"

"Isabel. It's me. Kai."

"Hijo! You've arrived! How does it feel?"

I looked around. The moving boxes. Sabine's Birkenstocks. The dusty flat. The life that was waiting for me here like an unpaid bill.

"Strange. It feels strange."

"That's normal." Her voice was gentle. "You've changed. But Kempten hasn't."

"I don't know what to do."

"What do you want to do?"

I closed my eyes. I saw images: the coast near Valencia. Pedro's workshop. The Brenner Pass. Everything more real than the flat I was sitting in.

"I don't want to go back." My voice was quiet. "Not to my old life. I… I can't."

"Then don't."

"But then what? I have no job, no money, no plan."

"You have a Vespa." I heard the smile in her voice. "And you have courage. That's more than most people have."

I laughed bitterly. "Courage? I'm scared, Isabel. I'm really scared."

"Good. Fear means you're alive. That's better than being safe and dead. Decide for yourself. Not for your boss. For you."

I hung up. Sat there. Looked at Lola outside. The black Vespa between the German cars.

Tomorrow. Tomorrow I would decide. Today I would just think. And hope that I found the courage to do the right thing.

Whatever the right thing was.

Probably there was no such thing as "the right thing".

But hey – at least I had a Hawaiian shirt.

Chapter 28 – At the Grave

[Soundtrack Shuffle: Pink Floyd – Wish You Were Here]

Nine o'clock in the morning.

I stood in front of the bathroom mirror and saw a stranger. Three weeks of sun had darkened my face by two shades, with white lines where my helmet had sat – a map of my journey engraved on my face. My hands looked like a mechanic's: dirt under my fingernails, small cuts on my knuckles, engine oil in the lines of my hands.

Behind me in the mirror: the moving boxes, the pile of laundry, the brown plant. Everything as usual. Everything strange.

I grabbed my rucksack. Time to unpack. The zip opened. The smell hit me like a slap in the face from the past. La Mancha. Albacete. Nacho's workshop. Kebab from Valencia – the stain was still there. Pedro's engine oil. San Remo park bench. Every T-shirt a memory. Every sock a chapter. And everything smelled as if it had been left to mature in a rubbish bin.

Washing machine. Now.

I went to the washing machine. Opened the door. Then I remembered the message. Three weeks ago.

"Bosch SmartHome: WARNING – Your washing machine has been on a gentle cycle for 8 days. Water is standing."

I had ignored it. Because I had other problems. Because a washing machine that sends messages was an error of evolution.

I opened the door carefully. The smell. Four weeks old, wet laundry. In standing water. This was no longer mould. It was an ecosystem. A new life form. Maybe even intelligent life.

I closed the door again. Quickly.

"Okay. You win. Unconditional surrender."

I got a bin bag. Opened the door again. Held my breath. With outstretched arms, I pulled out the laundry. Wet. Green. Alive.

"You had a good life. But now it's over."

Everything in the bag. Tie it up. Tightly. Then I grabbed the dead houseplant – brown, dried up, a silent memorial to my neglect.

"You're coming too. Together you're stronger."

I stood there with a bin bag full of mouldy laundry and a dead plant. The perfect symbol of my old life. Everything I had ignored for four weeks was now coming back – only more foul-smelling. Today I would do three things: dispose of these biological hazards. Buy washing machine cleaner. Drive to the cemetery.

In that order.

The rubbish bin was behind the house. I went down the stairs, rubbish bag in one hand, dead plant in the other. At the bin, I said goodbye to the plant.

"Rest in peace. You lasted longer than expected."

I said nothing to the rubbish bag. Some things don't need words. The lid closed. Both gone. Done. I parked Lola in front of the chemist's.

Inside, I grabbed a shopping basket. Three packs of tabs. Two bottles of vinegar cleaner. An air freshener called "Alpine Meadow Magic". At the checkout, the saleswoman looked me over briefly – sun-tanned face, engine oil under my fingernails, the smell of petrol and adventure.

"Spring cleaning?"

"Chemical warfare."

She nodded. "Good luck."

The cemetery was on the outskirts of town, on the slope of a hill, overlooking the city and the mountains beyond. The gate squeaked as I pushed it open – a high-pitched, plaintive sound that sounded like a complaint about too little oil.

I walked up the gravel path, past graves with fresh flowers and faded names. A child who had only lived to be three years old. A woman who had lived to be 102. A man who had lived to be 38 – too young.

"At least they have peace here. No meetings. No emails. No boss calling on Saturdays."

Death as the ultimate out-of-office. I had definitely been travelling alone for too long.

Miguel's grave was in the upper part, under an old lime tree. The gravestone: black polished granite, golden lettering.

"Miguel Sánchez García. 1952–2024. Life is a journey. Y nunca termina." And it never ends.

I took the spark plug out of my pocket. The spark plug from the Brenner Pass. I placed it in front of the gravestone.

"Okay, Miguel. I know you're supposed to bring flowers. But you were never normal. So: a spark plug. From the Vespa. The one that died on the Brenner Pass and almost killed me."

The wind rustled through the leaves.

"I wanted to let you know: I did it. Two thousand five hundred kilometres. With your damn Vespa. It's called Lola now. After Isabel's daughter. Long story."

I sat down on the bench next to the grave. Someone had screwed a sign onto it: "In memory of Anna Müller, who liked to sit here."

"Anna, no offence. But I need the seat for a moment."

I looked at the gravestone. At the spark plug in front of it. At the city below. It was strange to be sitting here. Four weeks ago, I had stood at this grave and felt lost. Now I was sitting here – exhausted, broke, unemployed in three days – and felt found for the first time in years.

"You know what's funniest?" My voice sounded hoarse. "Your rules. They worked. All of them. But man, they got me into the shit."

I counted on my fingers.

"'Work less. Live more.' – Check. I've been playing hooky for four weeks. My boss is going to fire me. Or I'll quit. Let's see who's faster."

"'Never say no to an adventure.' – Check. Almost died on the Brenner Pass. Had heatstroke in Valencia. Slept on a park bench. It was fantastic. And stupid."

"'If you're afraid, do it anyway.' – Dude. EVERY. SINGLE. DAY. Afraid. But I did it. And now I'm sitting here talking to a gravestone."

The wind picked up. A leaf fell on the spark plug.

"The problem is, I can't go back now. I can't sit in that office for eight hours pretending that Q3 reporting is important. I can't sleep in that flat anymore, where everything smells like… like nothing. Like waiting. Like procrastination."

I leaned back and closed my eyes.

"You changed me, you bastard." My voice broke. "And now I don't know what to do. I have exactly 53 1/2 days of money left. Then I'll be broke. Just like you were with the bar."

"The difference is: you had Isabel. I have… I have moving boxes and expired ketchup."

Silence.

Just the wind. The birds. The ticking of my watch.

Then, quietly: "But you know what? I don't regret it. Not a single kilometre. Not the breakdown. Not the park bench. Not the rain. Nothing." I opened my eyes and looked at the gravestone.

"You were right. All along. Life is a journey."

I stood up. Touched the cold granite with my fingers.

"Thank you," I whispered. "For the Vespa. For the rules. For… everything."

"And sorry it took me so long. But hey – better late than never, right? Is that what you say when you visit a cemetery? I don't know. I'm new to this sort of thing."

I turned around and walked down the path. With every step, I felt lighter. The grief remained. But the paralysis was gone. At the gate, I turned around again. I looked up at the lime tree. At the bench. At the gravestone.

"Hasta luego, amigo!" See you later.

Not goodbye. But: see you later. Because Miguel was right.

Life never ends. Only its form changes.

When I parked in front of my house, Mr Zimmermann was already waiting. He stood against the wall of the house like a submarine on patrol, arms crossed, his face as tense as if he had just discovered an unpleasant truth about homeowners' associations.

Mr Zimmermann was the self-appointed sheriff of Mozartstraße 17. Admin of the house group on WhatsApp. Author of notices about proper waste separation. Owner of a font called "outraged capital letters German".

"Mr Ritter!" He approached me like a prosecutor who had just found evidence.

"Mr Zimmermann." I took off my helmet.

"We need to talk!"

"Do we?"

"The lasagne!"

"Ah. That."

"Three weeks! In the hallway! That's a hygiene issue! Section three, paragraph two: no perishable goods in the stairwell!"

"I disposed of it yesterday. When I arrived."

He blinked. "Oh."

"Yes."

"Well. Fine. But still—"

"Mr Zimmermann." I interrupted him politely. "I spent three weeks in Spain, France, Italy and Austria. Crossed the Alps. On a 1967 Vespa. I slept on park benches. I almost died. Twice."

He stared at me.

"And you know what the craziest thing is?"

"What?"

"No one there was interested in lasagne."

I picked up my rucksack.

"Have a nice day."

I left him standing there. I heard him say behind me: "Across the Alps… on a Vespa…"

Back at the flat, I took out my mobile phone. The WhatsApp group "Vespa Brotherhood" had 47 unread messages. I scrolled up. The last few days:

Nacho: Alemán is still alive?

Nacho: Or did he sell the Vespa and take the train home ●

Pedro: Impossible. Kai is too proud.

Ricardo: I bet €20 he can do it

Ricardo: Who's against it?

Nacho: I'll take the bet

I grinned. Typed:

Me: I'm home. Lola is at the door. All parts still attached.

Three points immediately. Then:

Ricardo: SEE! €20 please, Nacho!

Pedro: Photos or it didn't happen

Nacho: ¡Increíble! You really did it

Nacho: Maria would have liked that

I went down to Lola, took a photo in front of my house, with the number plate visible and Kempten in the background. Sent it to the group.

Pedro: MY repairs held up

Pedro: Of course. Who do you think I am? A German?

Ricardo: When are you coming back?

Ricardo: Next tour of Portugal?

Nacho: Or are you staying there and getting boring?

Nacho: Punctual. Neat. Dead at heart

Me: Never.

Me: I promise.

Pedro: Good. See you soon, hermano 🛵

Nacho: Take good care of Lola! She's part of the family now

Ricardo: And if you have any problems… just ride your Vespa ●

I put my mobile phone away. Smiled. Tomorrow I would quit.

I had done enough for today.

Chapter 29 – Office 365

[Soundtrack Shuffle: Queen – I Want to Break Free]

Eight o'clock in the morning.

The laptop came to life with that unnecessarily cheerful Windows sound, "Bimbam-bling", which sounds like a system promising you that your soul is about to be reformatted and converted to be office-compliant. The screen flickered, loaded, and showed me the reality I had been ignoring for four weeks.

The number of unread messages: 712.

Seven hundred and twelve pieces of evidence that the universe hated me – or at least my old job. The subject lines looked like they had been written with the Caps Lock key stuck to the keyboard of a choleric department head: "URGENT: Return required", "Final warning: Deadline 24 hours", "IMPORTANT: Missed customer appointments" and so on. An endless list of urgent matters, all equally urgent, which meant that none of them were really urgent.

I read the first few lines and waited for the panic, for the trembling in my stomach, for the fear that would have previously overwhelmed me like a predator. But it didn't come. My stomach remained calm. The only sensation was the slight warmth of the coffee cup in my hand, this cheap German supermarket coffee that tasted of nothing but was hot – and that was enough.

That was new.

I closed the laptop. The screen went blank with a dull, final click, and I sat there in my flat, between the moving boxes and the expired ketchup and the life I no longer wanted to live, and whispered, "It's over."

Helmet on. Jacket closed. Lola started on the first kick, as if she could sense it, as if she knew that today was the day when everything would change.

The company building was made of grey concrete, with a mirrored façade that looked like the façade of a bank or a prison – hard to tell the difference. In front of it stood a German middle-class court of black and silver limousines: BMWs, Audis, Mercedes, all neatly parked, all polished to the point of soullessness.

I steered Lola over the kerb, right in front of the main entrance, where the wheelchair symbol was, and parked her there – not because I had to, but because I finally didn't care, because the rules that applied here were no longer my rules.

The automatic door hissed and cold, air-conditioned air hit me, that artificial wind that smelled of floor wax and fear and the years people had spent here without living.

Mrs Meier sat at the reception desk, a person so efficient that she probably archived her own emotions. She looked up and her eyes widened. She stared at my jeans, my worn T-shirt, my tanned forearms. I smelled of petrol, not aftershave; of the street, not the office.

"Mr… Mr Ritter?"

"Good morning, Mrs Meier."

I walked past the counter and she remained seated, rigid, an automatic door opener that had just lost its operating system.

The lift spat me out on the third floor, right in front of Mr Schneider, my department head, the Gant shirt incarnate. A coffee cup trembled in his hand and his face went through three colours:

red with anger, white with shock, purple with the effort not to explode.

"Ritter! Where the hell have you been?!"

"Road trip, Mr Schneider. Spain, France, Italy. Very educational."

The coffee cup twitched. A drop landed on his shirt. He didn't notice.

"That's inexcusable! That's not acceptable! You can't –"

"Yes, I can."

"We'll… we'll discuss this in my office. Now."

His office smelled of closed windows and suppressed years of life, of file dust and despair. Schneider sat down behind his desk and folded his hands as if he were about to condemn an enemy continent.

"Mr Ritter." His voice was now controlled, cold, professional. "Do you understand that we cannot continue to employ you if you behave like this?"

I pulled the envelope out of my jacket's inside pocket, the envelope I had written last night with trembling hands, with a pen that was almost empty. I placed it on the table, between his folded hands, and it was as white and neat as my Vespa was dirty.

"My resignation."

Schneider stared at the envelope as if it were a bomb – something dangerous, something that didn't belong here.

"What?"

"I'm resigning. With notice. Four weeks. But I'll take that as remaining holiday. Starting today."

He opened the envelope slowly, as if it might contain something poisonous, and read it. His face turned white again, then grey, then expressionless.

"You… you can't do that. We have projects. Clients. Commitments."

"You'll find someone else."

"But—"

"Mr Schneider." My voice was firmer than I thought, clearer. "I've been away for four weeks. And nothing has collapsed. The office is still standing. The clients are still alive and haven't missed me for a single day. They didn't need me. Not really."

He was silent, and I could see something working inside him, as he considered what to say, how he could convince me to stay. But then he laughed briefly and bitterly, a laugh that sounded like an office door slamming shut.

"I'll give you three months. Then you'll regret it. You could have had a future here. Something solid."

"We'll see." Solid as a prison, I thought. Solid as concrete.

"Four weeks of remaining holiday. Approved. You don't need to come back."

"Thank you, Mr Schneider."

I left.

It happened in the corridor on the way to the door. Stefanie.

She was standing by the photocopier, which was whining because it had run out of paper – that special sound office equipment makes when it knows no one is going to fix it. She was in her mid-twenties, blonde hair forced into a bun, blazer two sizes too big, as if she were trying to fit into a role that wasn't made for her.

I knew her. The new girl. The one who always came in first and left last. The one who still believed that hard work pays off.

She looked up. Saw me. Saw my jeans, my T-shirt, the leather jacket over my arm.

"Mr Ritter?"

"Stefanie."

"Are you… leaving?"

"Yes."

She stared at me. In her eyes I saw something I recognised. Hunger. Not for food. For a way out.

"Forever?"

"Forever."

"How… how do you do that?"

I hesitated. Then I saw the notepad on the photocopier – one of those yellow Post-it pads that were scattered around the office like little reminders of things to forget. I tore off a sheet and looked for a pen.

"May I?" I took her pen.

I wrote. Slowly. Five lines.

Work less. Live more.

Never say no to an adventure.

If you're afraid, do it anyway.

The best stories start with "screw it".

Never regret what you've done, but what you haven't done.

I gave her the note.

"A friend taught me that. Miguel. He's dead. But he was right."

She took the piece of paper. Read it. Her eyes welled up.

"Thank you," she whispered.

I nodded. Walked on. Behind me, I heard the photocopier whining away. But I didn't turn around.

I drove to "El Corazón Rojo", Miguel's bar. When I arrived, Isabel was standing in front of the door with a broom in her hand, sweeping the steps. The sign above the door was still hanging crookedly, as it had been for months since Miguel died. She looked up when she heard me and smiled.

"Hijo! You're free!"

"I am free."

She dropped the broom and hugged me. I smelled garlic and olive oil and home. When she let go of me, she said, "Come in. I'll show you something."

The bar was empty, quiet, and the smell was still there, that mix of old red wine, forgotten olives, garlic and old wood. But it no longer smelled of death, but of possibility, of the future.

"I thought Luisa was going to turn it into a nail salon or a hairdresser's?" I asked in surprise.

"Oh, don't get me started – she just mocked it because of the smell and called off the deal. She wanted me to gut and renovate everything. That's not something you can just do."

"I see. So what are you going to do with the shop now?"

"To be honest, I have no idea!"

She went to the coffee machine, made two espressos and we drank them at the bar, standing up, just like Miguel always did.

"And what are you going to do with your new-found freedom?" She looked at me questioningly.

"First of all, I'm going to write down my story. There's a lot to process! After that, I have no idea – something new, something different! My money will last about 53½ days, haha." I said it with a laugh that was somewhere between courage and panic.

"Miguel would be proud of you," she said quietly. "He would have said: Finally."

I nodded. I couldn't say anything. Sometimes the most important things are those for which there are no words.

In the evening, I sat in my flat and opened my laptop again – but not to read emails or check sales figures, but to write.

I opened a blank document, stared at the white screen and the blinking cursor, which looked like a heartbeat on a monitor. Wait. Wait. Write.

The first words came with difficulty. I typed. Deleted. Typed again.

"I had firmly resolved..."

Delete.

"I had firmly decided..."

Delete.

"I had..."

And then, suddenly, it flowed:

"I had firmly resolved not to cry today. Or laugh. Or get emotional..."

Miguel's bar. The beginning of the story. My story.

I wrote and the words came easily now, flowing like water. I wrote about Nacho and Carmen and Pedro and Ricardo and Signora Bellini and the park bench and the Brenner Pass and everything that had happened in between. As I wrote, I felt something open up inside me, something that had been closed for a long time.

My phone vibrated. A message.

> **[Notification]** Microsoft Office 365: "Your access has been disabled. You no longer have access to company data."

I stared at the message. Then I laughed. Briefly. Dryly.

"Bye," I muttered to the phone.

A second later: pop-up ad.

"TODAY ONLY: Flights to Barcelona from €49! Book now!"

I looked at the screen. Barcelona. Where it all began. Where Ricardo was. Where Pedro was.

I clicked the pop-up away. Not yet. But maybe soon.

I wrote until midnight, until my fingers ached and my eyes burned. When I stopped, I had twenty pages. They were the first twenty pages of something that might become a book, might become nothing, but it was real, it was mine, it was important.

I got up, went to the window and looked out onto Mozartstraße, at Lola standing under the street lamp, black and shiny and ready – always ready. I smiled.

My freedom had never begun. It had always been there.

I had just forgotten to look.

Outside, Lola stood under the lamppost. Black. Patient. Ready.

Like me.

And that was all that mattered.

www.ingramcontent.com/pod-product-compliance
Lightning Source LLC
LaVergne TN
LVHW041109080826
845145LV00007B/1747
* 9 7 8 3 9 8 2 7 9 2 1 2 5 *